CH00431969

Ragnekai
Winds

Book One of The Old Wounds Trilogy

An Urami World Novel

To Suzy!
Thank you for your
interest in
my book!

Really hope
you enjoy it!

May the Winds
blow kindly
for you.

Peter Buckmaster

Peter
Buckmaster

Ragnekai Winds
This paperback edition 2017
Peter Buckmaster asserts the moral right to be identified as the
author of this work.
ISBN-13: 978-1981153367
ISBN-10: 1981153365

This novel is entirely a work of fiction.
The names, characters and incidents in it are the work of the
author's imagination. Any resemblance to actual persons, living
or dead, events or localities is entirely coincidental.

Copyright © 2017 by Peter Buckmaster
(www.buckmasterbooks.com)
Printed by CreateSpace
First Printing, 2017

For Mum
I finally wrote a book!
Wish you were here to see it.
You are so dearly missed.

Ragnekai Winds

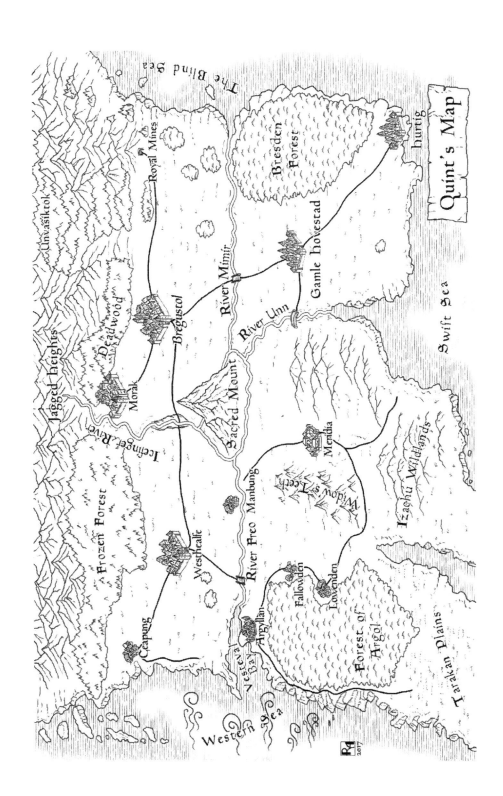

Quint's Map

Prologue

From beneath her cowl, her face in shadow, the Grey Sister peered out. Her pale green eyes looked upon an old man lying on a large but simple bed, under a maroon blanket and recently changed cotton sheets. The blanket slowly rose and fell where his chest was. This was accompanied by a wheezing that sounded more like an ancient wind seeping through underground cracks. A thin sliver of saliva drooled from the corner of the man's mouth. His eyes were closed to the world. She stood motionlessly nearby, as was her duty.

"It won't be long now" whispered someone to her left. She turned ever so slightly towards the speaker, the setting sun's light coming in the windows behind him creating a rotund silhouette. The portly man wore pristine white robes, with gold and silver cuffs and collar. A similarly designed biretta with a single ruby attached at the peak adorned his balding head. Her simple, grey hooded woollen gown was a stark contrast to the richness of his attire.

"Till what?" croaked the man abed, eyes flicking open.

So you were listening thought the Grey Sister.

A fit of coughing followed the old man's words. Shrouded in the drab colour of her order, she quickly put a cup of water to his lips. He let the water drip into his mouth, and then pushed the cup away irritably. His eyes turned to the man who had spoken too soon.

"Till I die, Brother Eswic?"

More coughing erupted from this now frail man. His voice was hoarse but still held a strength, albeit one waning in its power.

"If so, will I meet the Ever-Father, eh? Or am I to be cast into the Abyss to be tormented for eternity by Oblivion?" He paused. The holy man said nothing in response. "Or will I just cease to be? One for the philosophers, eh? Not much room for discussion with your lot!" he finished icily.

The Grey Sister could feel the tension that was creeping into the chamber. So much hung in the air here. Not just the sickly-sweet scent that accompanied illness but also the whiff of ambition and perhaps deceit. She again adjusted her field of vision a small fraction to bring others in the room into view.

Her movement was so subtle that an observer could be forgiven for thinking she was a statue, until they noticed that statue had moved since last they looked. She was as seemingly motionless as the four pillars that stood in the corners of the room, brooding sentries that kept watch over this dying man. Carvings of ivy were etched into their stone, circling each in spirals until the pillar sprouted a square head that met the ceiling. The two pillars beyond the bed were untouched by sunlight and were lit solely by the torches lining the walls. To the Grey Sister, the ivy seemed alive with the flickering flames, slithering serpents ascending into the darkness above. Unlike these pillars and the huge tapestries that clung to two of the walls, there was no design on her cloth, making her look more a shadow of a past age that lingered.

Another man stepped forward. He was tall and spindly, wearing a long, black coat that buttoned right up to his throat. His equally jet-black hair was swept back and tied in place at the back of his angular head. His lips were pursed, waiting for the right moment to speak. The Grey Sister knew that this man was well aware when to speak and when to hold his tongue.

The poorly man in the bed turned his head to him, the effort clearly causing pain. His words came out in a rasp.

"Any words of counsel, Chamberlain Worsteth? Anything I am neglecting?"

The Grey Sister knew the question was goading in nature and waited to see how it would be answered. She marvelled that the old man could still fence verbally even as the sickness ravaged his body. Chamberlain Worsteth did not take the bait though, and stood there silently.

"Or perhaps some advice on how I can rid myself of this

cursed ailment" the frail man muttered, a resignation now in his voice that would never have been heard before the sickness took hold.

Perhaps the fight is finally leaving him.

Worsteth clasped his hands before himself, almost wringing them in a show of helplessness. The Grey Sister was impressed by the act. The chamberlain spoke in his clipped tones, each word precisely delivered.

"The work of the High King is never done, Your Grace. There is much that needs your steady hand in guidance, but it can wait until Your Grace is in good health again. I beg your forgiveness that I know not what has brought on this malady so suddenly. To be sure, it is a most evil sickness that ails you, but I feel sure Your Grace will recover soon."

High King Sedmund's laugh caught in his throat and erupted more like a cat coughing up a fur ball. It seemed he did not share his chamberlain's optimism.

"Good health?" he croaked, "I was in good health not two months ago. And now I feel as if I am sliding into an early grave." There was a pause as the old man stared at the ceiling above, his jaw tightening. "To perhaps make peace with my father" he murmured.

Worsteth looked away, seemingly at a loss for anything to say. The administrative matters of a kingdom were where his skills lay, thought the Grey Sister, not words of comfort. She watched him bow his head and take a step back, perhaps inviting another in the room to say something. Or perhaps just wanting to be away from this room altogether. The chamberlain was likely unused to the oppressive air that came with sickness, something with which she was all too familiar.

"Speak not of such things, Your Majesty."

The strong, commanding voice had come from slightly farther back in the room. The Grey Sister knew the voice well and had a feeling close to sadness for this man, knowing what would follow. She breathed deeply but barely audibly. Her order had always kept to the shadows. *Be unseen but be ready*

7

when called upon. The words etched deep into her consciousness.

The High King Sedmund inhaled and spoke. "Come forward, Torbal. I cannot see you. I cannot see your eyes. I would look into your heart now, General."

Sedmund gasped sharply as some pain stabbed at him from within. The Grey Sister could feel all those in the room tense suddenly. But the High King regained his composure and the tension dissipated somewhat.

The general marched five steps forward, coming smartly to a halt. He wore a wine-red cloak clasped over a pale grey tunic, a bronze hawk skilfully stitched into the chest area. A white mane of hair sat proudly atop his strong features that looked to have been chiselled from the mountains. Craggy but crafted. His beard was not trimmed carefully like Worsteth's but grew gracefully and gave the man a regal quality. The general was at least fifty years of age but was still clearly in robust health, certainly capable of handling himself.

The Grey Sister knew this was not a man to be underestimated. If the High King was indeed destined to succumb to this sickness, General Torbal would subsequently play a major role in the governance of the Rihtgellen Kingdom and the wider realm it ruled. Torbal had the loyalty of the military and that was no small thing in a power vacuum. Beneath her cowl, she mused on how this unarguable fact would rile the others present.

The general spoke softly. "You know my heart, old friend. And I know yours. Your heart beats throughout all the lands. Without your will to bind us, we risk rupturing this kingdom and falling prey to forces of ill intent."

Torbal locked eyes with Brother Eswic as he said this. *A warning? A subtle threat?* The Grey Sister was surprised this had been directed at Eswic and not another. Torbal spoke again, this time to Sedmund and in a tone that suggested the general loved his liege in a genuine fashion.

"This malady will not defeat you. This is just another battle where you will gain victory, as we have done so many times in the past."

A shadow of a smile crept onto Sedmund's face. The Grey Sister could see Torbal had touched him, reminded him of a path they had ridden together.

Sedmund turned his eyes to the ceiling, perhaps remembering better days. The small woman in grey lifted her eyes also. She studied the faces of those in the room, her movement slight as she shifted her gaze from one to the next. The head of the church, Brother Eswic; the Royal Chamberlain, Chancellor Worsteth; the High King's Shield, General Torbal; and one other who had yet to speak. The sun had disappeared in the west now and only torch-light touched those present. The new moon meant darkness would swallow the realm this night.

A silence was now upon the room, perhaps waiting for Sedmund to say something. High King Sedmund. The most powerful man in Ragnekai, or Marrh, as the realm used to be known. Ruler of the Rihtgellen Kingdom and the realm of Ragnekai. The kingdom had existed in some form for almost two hundred years, and enjoyed regional superiority for the last seventy. This man had continued the reign over the lands that his grandfather had won by both diplomacy and the sword.

Finally Sedmund answered Torbal.

"I do not intend to falter now, Torbal. The Ever-Father must wait a while longer for me. There is much that needs to be done. Much that must be guarded."

His eyes wandered to the far side of the chamber, where nobody stood. Sedmund then closed his eyes. The silence that had been briefly broken now returned, save for the hoarse breathing of the ruler of the Rihtgellen Kingdom. Brother Eswic looked to Worsteth, the chamberlain holding a shared look with the leader of the church momentarily before turning to focus on the general. Torbal stared at the floor, seemingly unwilling to meet the other two in any kind of non-verbal exchange. A slight shuffle of a slipper on the stone floor behind caught the attention of all three men. A strikingly handsome lady emerged from the shadow and looked upon the dying man.

"Perhaps we should let His Grace rest now" whispered the lady, the fingers of her felt-gloved hands knitting together as her hands rose to her chin.

"Such kind words, Lady Ulla" hissed Brother Eswic. "And are you keeping your brother Orben abreast of His Grace's health? Will you be returning to your home in Helliga with *glad* tidings?" He stared at her with barely concealed hatred. "I wonder if our dear ruler's sickness is the will of the Ever-Father or by a more mortal design."

Ulla took a measured step towards the supposed authority of the Ever-Father in this mortal realm. Her ashen-blonde hair was tied in two braids falling beside her face, reaching down to her mid-riff and perfectly accentuating her beauty. Her icy blue eyes seemed like deep pools of secrets, seeing all but revealing nothing. She wore a deep violet cloak about her, its hood hanging loose at the back.

"Careful what you say, *most* devout of the Ever-Father's servants" she said softly.

Brother Eswic may have been at the pinnacle of his holy hierarchy but he withered in front of the lady. The Grey Sister could feel the authority and menace exuding from Ulla. Being the sister of the second most powerful man in the realm did have its merits, she thought. And if the seemingly inevitable happened, her brother Lord Orben would arguably take Sedmund's mantle.

But will they call him High King *Orben? And how long will his reign last?*

Brother Eswic turned away now, muttering to himself, perhaps saying a prayer. The Grey Sister, with movement as imperceptible as a shadow creeping up a wall at sunset, shifted her gaze to Torbal. The general looked genuinely sad that Sedmund was so ill and weak. The Grey Sister found this curious that a veteran of battle would let his emotions be so visible to all around him. Perhaps this was to his credit. Torbal was relatively free of the tedious scheming that was an everyday part of court life. The sturdy general coughed and

10

moved a few paces back, perhaps wanting to avoid this new tension that had reared its ugly head.

Ulla spoke again, her voice gentle.

"High King Sedmund, you and my brother may not be friends or even allies, but there is peace between our peoples. I would urge you to appoint someone to manage the affairs of the realm until you are restored to health. Like gardens, realms have a habit of running wild if they are not tended. Weeds can spring up."

Lady Ulla emphasized the word *weeds* as if in warning. A warning to Sedmund? Perhaps Torbal. She had not directed the comment at anyone or turned her eyes away from Sedmund, but the Grey Sister speculated on whom the weeds might be.

"Name someone you can trust to uphold the peace and not let it disintegrate into petty squabbles that could spark a greater conflict."

"You have someone in mind, I take it?" asked Worsteth pointedly. The Grey Sister again moved her head a tiny degree so that the chamberlain was in her field of vision. The man had a slight smile on his lips.

Does he really believe Ulla means him?

"Yes. I do, as it happens" she almost purred. The chamberlain visibly puffed out his chest.

"General Torbal." The feline delivery had disappeared and the words were a dagger to Worsteth.

The slender man spluttered as he choked down whatever he was going to say. He looked at Ulla with disbelief, then turned his eyes to Torbal, a certain venom contained within them. The Grey Sister knew he had just seen his chance for greater things crumble before him. She did not miss the subsequent look shared between Worsteth and Eswic.

Torbal looked at Ulla and the Grey Sister could see he was taken by her beauty. This was a man who could stand tall on a battlefield and inspire his troops to victory. And yet he seemed almost nervous when confronted by a strong lady with allure. The Grey Sister saw he was about to speak but his mouth closed again before any word came out. In her plain garb and silent role, the little lady did not experience the interactions between men and women that revolved around lust and desire, but she had seen it bring many a man down.

"Come now, Torbal" Ulla said in a voice that was once again demure and silvery, so gentle to the ears. "Do not be so humble. We all know the people would support you if you were steward of the throne until the High King recovers. You are well respected and a known leader. And you have the backing of the military…which is always an advantage in these precarious situations."

The Grey Sister could not help but again admire Ulla's oratory skills. So soft and generous when talking directly to Torbal, yet steady when bringing in the wider audience. And then sly when making a point intended for certain people in the room. Weight given to certain words, slight alterations in tone, subtle movements of her eyes and hands. This lady was a true master of speaking and persuasion.

The Grey Sister's attention returned to the man abed as the others continued to talk. She peered closer. The tiniest of gasps escaped her mouth. She moved closer to him, her cloth slippers whispering across the stone floor. Her hand extended from her robe and she placed her fingers against his throat, trying to find a pulse. There was nothing. The man was dead.

Her grey cloak hiding all her features, she quietly turned and walked the few paces towards the people still conversing. Brother Eswic visibly jumped as he noticed her at his side. Now she had all their attention, she gestured to the man lying abed, and then hung her head as low as she could. She did not see their reactions, only heard their gasps and a moan that sounded like Torbal's.

The Grey Sister retreated to the shadows, her work done for the moment. She would now become unseen again. But ready to serve when called upon.

Part One

Ch 1

Anton

26th Day of Aprus, The Day After Sedmund's Death

The bark was rough under Anton's hands, yet he pressed his palms harder as if he were trying to sink into the tree. He was breathing as shallowly as possible, desperately trying not to make any sound. He stood motionlessly against the trunk of this thick tree that had seen many winters. What tree it was he had no idea. She would know. She knew everything about the Forest of Argol.

The sun at high noon could penetrate the forest's leafy canopy with powerful lances of light but the now setting orb brought only a glimmer to the murky undergrowth. The gathering gloom helped Anton conceal himself in the shadows. His charcoal-grey tunic and trousers, and jet-black hair that grew in unruly waves, also aided him in this endeavour. He did not look up to the dwindling light but instead stared straight ahead at her. The girl was crouching and peering at something in the undergrowth, her back turned, seemingly unaware of Anton in his hiding spot. She had taught him a thing or two about moving stealthily through the forest, how to blend with the wood and leaves, and now she would regret it he mused. Anton drew a breath slowly through his nostrils, tension building within him. Almost.

The girl abruptly straightened. Anton froze in place, willing every muscle in his body to remain utterly still. He was aware how well she knew the sounds of the forest, even the scuttling of wood mice — if he made even the slightest unnatural noise, he would fail in his objective. The girl brushed her hands on her long, hunter-green coat and sighed, but then continued to search for whatever it was she was looking for. Anton let out the breath he had been holding and stepping out from his concealment, gradually crept forward, treading carefully to avoid any twigs that were waiting to snap and give him away. So close now. He almost had her. Then his foot caught against a root. He looked down to navigate his boot out of the snare, stepped clear of it and looked back.

She was gone.

"How in…?" he blurted before clamping his hand over his mouth.

"Shades!" he cursed under his breath, scanning the wooden sentinels around him.

How did she do that?

Anton yelped as a face suddenly appeared in the air before his eyes, upside-down and grinning. The young man stumbled backwards and fell, landing hard on his rump. He looked up at the girl he had been trying to catch unawares, hanging as she was by her legs from an overhead branch.

"Emiren! You scared the Spirits out of me!" Anton moaned, feeling more foolish than anything.

"Which is what you were trying to do to me!" retorted the girl, her auburn hair and weather-worn coat trailing down towards the forest floor. She then swung herself, grabbed another branch and landed with a light thud before him, her smile now accompanied by raised eye-brows. Emiren had passed her seventeenth summer last year and her pale face had an almost ethereal beauty to it. Where her hair was the colour of autumn, her eyes were a deep ever-green. Anton would often tease her that she was found growing from the ground by the Old Stream. He made jokes about her hair and eyes in the hope she would realise he paid attention to how she looked and would find something in his words. Alas, Emiren's head was buried so deep within the Forest of Argol, Anton wondered if any man would be able to reach her.

The two had known each other all their lives. And Anton wanted to know Emiren the rest of his life. He sighed inwardly as he looked into those beautiful eyes, almost losing himself in the moment. He caught himself and huffed.

"Thought I was being quiet" he mumbled to her.

Emiren screwed up her face. "The thunderstorm two moons ago was quieter than you."

Anton adopted an expression of mock outrage. "A bad teacher always blames their pupils" he replied, sticking his chin out.

Emiren laughed and punched him lightly on the arm. Then suddenly she drew close, her face moving to his neck, sniffing. Anton felt his heart race and his stomach flutter as thoughts sped through his mind.

Could this be it?

He turned slightly to move into the kiss.

Emiren drew back. "I smell Lorth Weed on you. Where have you been?"

Anton felt as if his heart had dropped into the pit of his stomach, a long fall after it had seemed set to burst from his chest. For a moment he had actually believed his wish had come true. Was he really that foolish? *Apparently so.* He recovered swiftly and gestured back to where he had been hiding.

"Over there, I guess" he muttered.

The girl pushed past him and set about rummaging through the undergrowth. Anton looked up through the trees to the twilit sky and gulped in the cool, evening air. He exhaled out of the corner of his mouth, his head slowly returning to look at what the flame-haired girl was doing. Still searching. Cursing silently, he walked over to where Emiren was.

"Got it!" she exclaimed, removing a small knife from a sheath in her belt and cutting some of the weed she had smelt upon him. Anton couldn't even remember the name of it now. His world had suddenly seemed on the brink of a long-sought desire, only for that to crumble and fade into the deep green depths of Argol Forest. He looked around himself at the trees, some three-people high, others stretching up into the gathering shadows. Anton suddenly felt they were all leaning down and giving him looks of pity. He shook off the notion and turned back to see if Emiren had finished.

The girl rose before him, holding a handful of something out to him. Her smile told him this weed was something important but he had no idea what. Emiren knew the forest like he knew the cellar of The Oak & Hammer, his father's inn. And she was as clueless about the barrels and bottles there as he was about these trees and plants, despite Emiren's many efforts to teach him.

"Lorth Weed" she breathed, her eyes alight with excitement. Anton smiled, waiting for her to say more. "This will help Janwarin's passing."

Anton's smile slipped away as he realised why Emiren was glad to find this plant. It must be one of those weeds that could numb pain or make a person sleep more. Janwarin was a village elder who had fallen sick three lunar cycles past and the word was he was near to his end, near to meeting the Spirits in the Evercold.

Anton held Emiren's gaze and shrugged, "So my attempt to frighten you wasn't all wasted?"

Emiren flashed her teeth again in a quiet laugh. "No" she said kindly, her eyes wide. Anton's breath caught in his chest. *So beautiful.*

"Come, we must get back" said Emiren. "Try and keep up!" she cried as she leapt off in the direction of home.

Anton laughed despite himself and set off after the spirited girl. He ran in the wake of her long coat, now flapping behind her as she hurtled through the forest. He marvelled at the way she dipped and swerved along hidden paths that only she seemed to know. Anton caught up with her and the two of them hurried on, leaping over fearsome roots that threatened to trip the unwary. They broke onto one of the well-worn paths and Anton pulled ahead, extending his stride. Emiren's laugh disappeared between her breaths as she raced to deny him a win.

Anton emerged from the forest border, the open space so fresh after the earthy scents within the trees. He quickly leaned against a battered old sign-post, feigning boredom with an exaggerated yawn.

"My father runs faster than you and he has a life-time's worth of ale in here" mocked Anton, slapping his mid-riff as Emiren emerged from the forest.

The young lady rolled her eyes as she walked past him. "I think I can hear Argol whispering about a clumsy giant that just crashed through its depths!" she teased, and then pointed to his head. Anton put his hand up and found more than one leaf in his dark mop of hair. He brushed them away and fell in beside Emiren as they approached their village, Fallowden.

The two of them walked in a comfortable silence to the village gate, which was beginning to close. It was as tall as two villagers, thick logs held together with rope and iron rings. Both the gate and the palisade served as more of a marker to the village's boundaries than an actual defence of all who lived within. Anton's parents and grandparents had lived in the village all their lives and only his grandfather had experienced an attack—from Throskaur raiders, arriving down the River Freo from the Western Sea many, many years ago. The wooden wall and watch-towers had been built after this attack but had not been needed thereafter as the port city of Argyllan had grown and created a bulwark of sorts at the mouth of the River Freo, protecting the settlements farther inland.

Some said that it was the rise of the Rihtgellen Kingdom that had scared off the raiders. It was indeed possible that the Throskaur had stopped coming after realising they were kicking a larger beast with their raids, and deciding they didn't to want to provoke a retaliatory assault upon their home. The general word now was that they rarely left the Barren Isles to the far west.

A few of the wiser folk in Anton's village said it was more likely the storms that churned the Western Sea were responsible for the lack of long boats coming this way. Such speculation was often accompanied by grumblings that the possibly unnecessary *protection* provided by High King Sedmund had

19

come with a price measured in taxes. Anton's father Nicolas would talk about this topic endlessly to anyone who would listen. Whatever the reasons behind the disappearance of the long-boats though, the reality was that the majority of Fallowden's people had known no conflict in their lives and this was no small thing in Anton's humble opinion.

Anton only understood half of what his father talked about though. The realm was a big place and he had only seen a small corner of it. He had been to Argyllan and seen the port city for himself. He had been overwhelmed by the sheer size of the place compared to Fallowden. Rows upon rows of houses and shops and other buildings. Anton reckoned there were about two hundred folk who dwelt in Fallowden and a further sixty or so who lived nearby in homesteads. His father had told him there were ten times that in Argyllan and Anton could well believe it. He had been amazed at the bustle and constant movement of people on the streets.

But what had really taken his breath away was when he had gazed out at the Western Sea. Argyllan sat comfortably at the south of the Bay of Vestevel, the River Freo snaking off to the east. The bay was sheltered by the White Sisters, cliffs that jutted out from the north-west, broke for a stretch, and then continued on down the entire south-west coast. They created a cove that didn't suffer the battering from the storms. Anton had looked out upon the towering walls of chalk, lined with streaks of flint, and been suitably impressed. But when he and his brother had joined a fisherman friend of his father's, on a little jaunt out of the bay, Anton had beheld the Western Sea in all its majesty. There had seemed no end to it, just a vast blue expanse with the white crest of waves rolling over the surface in chaotic tumbles.

And Anton had witnessed first-hand one of the storms his father had told him so much about. All the fishing boats had returned swiftly to dock as their captains felt the change in the air and saw the tell-tale sign of gulls and cormorants heading to shore. The sky had turned from a misty blue to a thunderous, heavy grey in moments. The lightning had flashed behind the clouds, with deafening crashes and ominous rumbles, and the sea had become a cauldron of tempestuous water. It was the first time Anton had truly respected the awesome power of nature.

Anton and Emiren hurried to the closing gates. The two guards on watch gave each other a look and one raised an eyebrow.

"One of these days you two will have to jump the wall" said Loranna, a tall lady with shoulder-length onyx hair and a face that was home to watchful eyes. She held a long staff loosely at her right side, her left hand resting gently on her hip. The staff was beautifully carved, and Anton would have thought it a simple ornament had he not seen Loranna going through the Sixty-Four Forms. When she spun the staff, it was akin to watching a whirlwind that could make a crack like thunder when striking the practice post. Her skills were testament to how much practice she undertook, despite never having had to use the weapon in combat. At least, Anton didn't think she'd ever been in a real battle.

"Reckon *she* does climb the walls occasionally" chuckled Banseth, Loranna's partner on watch, pointing at Emiren. Two short staffs poked up over his shoulder-line. Anton had seen him go through the moves also and had winced more than once when the two sticks connected. Banseth's hair was longer than Loranna's and would have been as dark if not for the pepper grey streaks threading through. Where Loranna's eyes were always alert, Banseth's were almost lazy. But his ears were what made him a capable look-out. It was said he could hear a squirrel climbing the palisade on a quiet night. And quiet nights were all Fallowden heard these days; not even squirrels disturbed the peace.

The two guards posted at the front gate were more a formality, a greeting to merchants and travellers that came to Fallowden. The night-time closing of the gates also helped create a community where people stuck together and soon noticed if someone had not returned by nightfall.

Anton smiled, touched his left palm to his chest in respect and Emiren did likewise. Loranna and Banseth returned the gesture. The two of them walked along the main street that ran through the village, their boots kicking up tiny dirt clouds. They passed the village Council Hall, the largest building in Fallowden. Anton noticed Emiren looking up at the roof where a twirling spire of smoke was drifting into the dusk sky. The girl sniffed the air and whispered to him, "Gallinap. Which means Master Aine is seeking guidance from the Spirits. I would use Banelok in this season but…" She trailed off as Anton offered her an expression he knew she could read only too well. Anton placed a hand on her shoulder and smiled.

"Your ability to hold your tongue on matters of herb-craft rivals my father's ability to resist a glass of wine *before* lunch."

Emiren shoved him and hissed "Cheeky bog-dweller!"

Anton grinned.

They passed between cabins, village shops and a few larger halls, all built with the timber from Argol. The villagers would cut wood from fallen trees or chop down entire trees to provide lumber for themselves and to sell to Argyllan. In areas that had been harvested years ago, seeds were planted and saplings began to grow. Fallowden rotated the lumber collecting over a wide area. It had been this way for over two hundred years and Argol never suffered unduly. It was the foundation of the villagers' lives and they cared for it as such.

Anton and Emiren came to the fork where they had to part ways to reach their own homes. "Sleep well, Anton" said Emiren in a quiet voice. Anton almost lost his voice, again so enraptured by his friend's beauty and warm spirit.

"I will" he managed. He took a step closer, suddenly envisioning a farewell hug. Emiren started and slapped her head.

"I forgot to pass on the Lorth-Weed!"

Anton let himself fall into his self-made pit of despair again, inwardly berating himself for continually entertaining such fantasies. Emiren was already hurrying off back the way they had come, no doubt to deliver the root or whatever it was to Sister Jessa at the hospice. He watched her go. She twirled as she moved, waving to him and grinning in that maddeningly infectious way of hers, and then faded into the gathering night. Anton sighed.

Anton trotted the last few hundred yards to the inn that was his home. His father Nicolas was outside emptying a bucket into the drain. "Welcome back, wandering son of mine. Any chance you can lend a hand to Cale? We had several thirsty souls come in with the setting of the sun." Anton nodded and hurried inside.

The sights, sounds, and smells of the inn were as precious to him as doubtless Argol was to Emiren. Old Beo was perched on his usual stool by the bar, quaffing from a mug of ale. There was a sudden eruption of laughter and Anton looked to see Kall holding court with his fellow hunters. Kall had a gift for turning everyday stories into a veritable theatre of comedy. Then Anton caught the whiff of tobacco and located its source in Master Lukas, one of the village tutors. The teacher was standing at the bar, puffing on a pipe. He hailed Anton as the young lad walked over.

"Best be giving your brother a hand, Anton. That table over there has worked hard today, I'm thinking." he said, nodding to a group of half a dozen villagers who were crashing their cups together with a noisy toast. Anton grinned and slid behind the bar where his brother was washing out some tin tankards.

"Ah, good, getting swamped here. Draw three pints of Oak Foot for the table by the fire and then fetch their meals from the kitchen, if you don't mind. Megan is too busy cooking to bring food out."

Cale stood up and looked at Anton.

"Been running through Argol with Emiren again?" his older brother asked. Anton felt himself blush so turned quickly to the sink to scrub his hands.

"Three Oak Feet then" he said, hoping to distract Cale.

23

"Oak Foots, badger brains!" his brother laughed. Anton set to pulling the ale and saw his brother was still watching him.

"Yes." He sighed. "And no."

Cale slapped him on the back. "One day, little brother" he whispered. "Good things come to those who wait."

Cale turned away before Anton could mumble thanks. He appreciated his brother's optimism but wasn't sure being patient was the best course of action. Emiren burned so brightly that Anton felt he could soon be lost in a crowd of star-gazing young men.

Ch 2

Rencarro

The cool winds of the lingering spring glided over the battlement walls and gently buffeted the lone figure standing there. Grey eyes set within sharp features above a clean-shaven jaw, an almost silver length of braided hair that ran down his spine, and a poise that projected control.

Lord Rencarro, ruler of Meridia, looked out over his lands from high up on the north wall of the city. Lands that reached out east to the clearly defined border of the Helligan nation, where the River Unn flowed into the Swift Sea to the south, separating Meridia from its eastern neighbour. Lord Rencarro was glad to have this natural barrier between his land and the Helligan nation; it meant their shared border could not be argued.

Rencarro turned his gaze west to the somewhat less clear border that marked the Argol Forest region. The Widow's Teeth, a stretch of sharp shale that seemed to have been pushed into a line of peaks by giant hands, were a grey blur in the distance. The rocks cut the land and only a fool would try to go over them, so sharp were they. But the Widow's Teeth didn't stretch the entire length of the land between the River Freo and the Izachu Wildlands, where only animals and wild beasts roamed. The Teeth were not a complete barrier; just a feature of the landscape that forced roads to curl around their tips.

Rencarro looked out north to the Sacred Mount. It was impressive even from such a distance. A lone mountain that towered over the centre of the realm of Ragnekai. Its summit was still white with snow but the warmer weather meant this would soon disappear almost entirely. The Sacred Mount was perhaps the only place in the realm that did not belong to anyone, although those in the north might say otherwise.

Inhaling deeply of the crisp morning air the lord nodded to himself. He reigned over a large expanse of land with a reasonably large population that looked to the city of Meridia and its lord for security, stability, trade and the rule of law. The Meridian lord surveyed all that was visible to the naked eye, his mouth set firmly within his aging but handsome face as he took in all that was his.

It was not much past dawn but already there were farmers working their lands and carts moving from their homesteads up the main road into the city proper. Rencarro laid a hand on the cool surface of the fifty-foot wall that encircled the city. It was good stone, brought from the quarries just south of Meridia over a hundred years ago. It did not bear the scars of battle like Bregustol in the north, but it had protected his people nonetheless. Of that Rencarro was certain. The city of Meridia was a place of safety that exuded power. Power was control. Thus, peace reigned in his lands.

He clenched his teeth, his pale grey eyes filling with anger. He knew it was all only half true. Meridia certainly was a city with status and influence but it was beholden to Bregustol, capital of the Rihtgellen Kingdom, seat of the so-called High King Sedmund.

High King Sedmund. Rencarro sneered inwardly. In all seriousness, he wondered how they could lay claim to ruling the entire realm of Ragnekai. In the sphere of statesmanship, he knew they must acknowledge Bregustol's place at the top of the ladder, but he doubted the small folk gave it that much thought.

Rencarro conceded that the Rihtgellen ruler did reign over a large area of this realm, in particular the region of Westhealfe and the north that was home to Bregustol. The Helligan nation though, to the east of Meridia, was merely biding its time Rencarro believed. And the far north-eastern lands of Unvasiktok, only kept away because that barbarian chieftain Vorga led them and was said to honour an old pact. And what about the lands beyond the northern forests where the Jagged

Heights loomed large? Sedmund claimed these to be part of the *Kingdom* also. Rencarro wasn't even sure anybody lived there, considering how cold and harsh the climate was that far north. Some said in those mountains there dwelt a people who lived underground and seldom ventured into the daylight, and it was whispered, were not entirely human. Rencarro fancied that was an old man's tale, concocted after one too many ales.

Despite the early hour of the morning, he was already clothed in leather trousers, sturdy riding boots, a fading purple doublet and a long grey over-coat with silver embroidery. The silver stitching was sparse however. Rencarro was not interested in finery. He knew his authority came not from trinkets and adornments but his voice, his wit and his birth right.

Winds continued to swirl around him. He enjoyed their freshness and the way they made him feel alive.

I resist the wind and stand firm, then I push back. Just as I must do with Sedmund and the court in Bregustol.

The ruler of Meridia felt an abrupt chill in the wind as it gently pummelled him. It was an unusual cold for spring. An ill wind he thought, and it gave him a slight unease. Rencarro turned on his heel, meaning to begin his daily inspections.

His long legs and stride were about to take him away from the battlements when something caught his eye. A lone rider galloping fast down the main road between the villages. The horse was soon charging up the paved road that led to the city gates. Rencarro squinted in the morning sun and saw that the rider's colours were grey with an orange sash that trailed behind. One of Rencarro's Velox Riders. The Velox were an elite regiment within the Meridian military, with very specific skills that allowed Rencarro to quickly learn about events in the realm. This rider would not be stopped at the city gate but waved right through. The Custodia city guard knew not to impede the riders in grey when they displayed their orange sash that flickered like fire about them. The Velox Rider would have important news with him.

Rencarro's long legs took him quickly to steps that led him

down into the Second Tower. From there he hurried across a walkway, then down another flight of stairs, taking them three at a time. He arrived in his solar moments before the messenger did. Rencarro was breathing evenly, despite his exertion. The Velox Rider was clearly fatigued. The Lord of Meridia ushered in the man and nodded to signal he was ready to hear the news.

"My lord!" the messenger spoke, the excitement in his voice contained but perceptible. "He's dead. Sedmund is dead."

The words hung in the air. Rencarro felt he could see them rise to the ceiling, and beyond them formed an image of proud High King Sedmund crumbling like an old stone wall. Sedmund was dead. A myriad of thoughts raced through the lord's mind but he quickly regained his composure.

The Velox Rider was panting slightly behind a tight veil that hid all his features save his eyes, which Rencarro recognised. This one was Tacet. These messengers did not use their names openly, keeping to a legacy of anonymity. It had no huge significance in a time of peace but Rencarro had a feeling that, with the coming of this news, this secrecy would be put to good use in the days ahead.

"How?" he demanded.

"The sickness took him" replied the messenger.

Rencarro hid his surprise and instead grunted his acknowledgement.

You couldn't beat your own frailty, old man.

"How has Bregustol reacted?"

As the messenger started to answer, a man walked into the room. Marcus, the eldest son of Rencarro. As tall as his father, a touch broader, with shorter hair that held a deep chestnut colour but the same grey eyes. There was a swagger to his walk and a slight arrogance in the half-smile that seemed a permanent fixture on his face. Rencarro's son succumbed to finery more than his father and wore well-oiled leather boots with shining gold buckles, leather trousers that had a thin silver line running up the sides, and a cotton shirt unbuttoned slightly to show off a gold chain with a ruby set in its centre link.

Rencarro had given up trying to tell Marcus that such fancies were pointless and only gave noble families like theirs a haughty air.

"Marcus. Listen well. Sedmund is dead" Rencarro told his son.

Marcus cocked his head, his lips pursed, the half-smile gone and eyes wide, genuine astonishment on his face that quickly disappeared.

"The old man falls into the Void, huh? May his soul suffer eternal misery." His son's voice was laced with bitterness. Rencarro turned back to the Velox Rider and nodded for him to continue.

"There is unrest and confusion, my lord" Tacet said. "As you know, Sedmund sired no children but it also seems he named no heir, so the rule is currently being shared by Worsteth and Torbal."

"Named no heir?!" cackled Marcus, his voice loud and intrusive to Rencarro's thoughts. The father looked at his son, knowing how simply the young man would view this turn of events. Rencarro did not doubt Marcus would push for Meridia to move on the capital Bregustol immediately and claim leadership over the lands. His son had a passion for the old legends where heroes rode into battle and emerged largely unscathed, their enemies laid waste around their feet. Rencarro had tried to impress upon his son the brutal reality of battle and how nobody ever emerged unharmed, even if their physical body bore no wounds. Yet Marcus saw glory in the tales and was eager to join the ranks of these mythical heroes.

But to march on Bregustol with Helliga practically barring the way would be suicide. Lord Orben, ruler of the Helligan nation, would likely move on the capital himself. Marcus had sadly not inherited much of the wit of his father, nor had he been blessed with the quiet intelligence of Rencarro's beloved wife, dead four years now. The intellect seemed to have slipped past Marcus and gone onto Eligius, the younger brother. Who, in turn, sadly lacked the physical presence and skills with a blade of his elder sibling. Rencarro wished his wife were still at his side. Shansu had always had a way with Marcus and while she had lived Rencarro had seen a chance for Marcus to develop into the kind of leader Meridia needed. That hope now seemed lost to the winds.

Ignoring Marcus' comment and laughter, Rencarro instead pressed for more information.

"What of the church? Do they support those two? And Ulla? Is she still in Bregustol?"

Marcus was visibly riled by his father's lack of response to his presence in the room. Rencarro hoped his son would at least listen to what the messenger had to say but could see Marcus already fiddling with an ornamental dagger on a shelf near the hearth.

"Brother Eswic has withdrawn to the Holy Sepulchre to pray for four nights and five days, it is said."

Rencarro snorted. *Holy men and their numbers,* he thought sardonically. Would the brother come out sooner if he had any revelations or stay in a bit longer if nothing came to him?

The messenger took a breath to signal the next piece of information was to come. Rencarro looked up.

"Ulla has returned to Gamle Hovestad."

Even Marcus paid attention to this.

"The witch flies back. Most likely wanted to escape execution for the crime of poisoning Sedmund" Marcus mocked.

The look in the Velox Rider's eyes suggested to Rencarro that this wasn't as stupid a comment as it seemed.

Could it be true? *Did Helliga murder the High King?*

If Ulla had gone back, guilty or otherwise, then it might indicate Helliga was looking to take advantage of the power vacuum. Rencarro locked the thought away for later and again questioned his subject.

"The people. The masses. What sense do you get of their feeling?"

Rencarro knew there would not be an accurate answer to this but he needed every morsel of information he could get to help him in his decision as to how to proceed. He knew he must act. The Helligan nation would move, of that he was certain. Bregustol's grip on the realm would weaken. The north-west would probably stay loyal but would they seek more autonomy? Would Vorga and the northern tribes decide Sedmund's death effectively tore up any truce or bargain? Rencarro knew he could not just sit behind his walls and wait to see how things would unfold. He must be decisive and perhaps aggressive. Meridia was the weaker faction in the realm but now was an opportunity to alter the balance of power and climb a rung up the ladder. Meridia could rise to an equal footing with Helliga, if he played this well.

The Velox Rider spoke from behind his veil. "The small folk see Torbal as the natural successor or so rumour goes. Worsteth is seen as weak without the authority of Sedmund. If Torbal should summon the legions from Westhealfe and Morak, he would certainly wield far greater power than the church."

Rencarro smiled inwardly at the perceptive nature of Tacet; one reason why Rencarro had elevated him to the ranks of the Velox Riders. General Torbal was a native of Westhealfe and enjoyed an almost fanatical loyalty from the soldiers there, a fact Tacet had obviously considered. Rencarro knew that his Velox Riders would not just carry communications but would observe, investigate and act on their own initiative. The entirety of their skill set was known only to Rencarro and his Second, Sylvanus. One day he would have to tell Marcus the full extent of their training, but he was loathe to do it anytime soon. His son would be tempted to abuse their talents.

As if summoned by his lord's thoughts, Sylvanus appeared at the doorway. His lithe frame stood to attention, his balding head bowed slightly in respect, his weathered face showing no emotion as he walked in. Sylvanus acknowledged the Rider and Marcus. The latter's face barely concealed his misguided enmity towards Rencarro's Second. Rencarro knew Marcus resented the fact that Sylvanus was above him in terms of rank and had his father's ear in a way the young man never would.

Rencarro sighed inwardly. Was there any way he could steer Marcus onto a better path towards leadership? Eligius, his second son, simply did not have the physical prowess or charisma to succeed him as ruler. Marcus could bring a room of soldiers to laughter and bawdy cheer; Eligius achieved the exact opposite, his presence somehow dampening any lively spirit. And yet Eligius had the keen mind Marcus clearly lacked. If Marcus could just learn from both Sylvanus and Eligius, then the future might be secure. Rencarro didn't plan on leaving the mortal world for many years yet but knew that as things stood, he would have to name Sylvanus to succeed him. Sadly, Rencarro could not imagine Marcus lying down quietly and accepting Sylvanus becoming lord of their lands. *Even more reason to act swiftly and create a different future* thought the current ruler of Meridia.

"Sylvanus" hailed Rencarro. "The Rihtgellen Kingdom is in mourning it would seem."

Sylvanus raised an eye-brow. "How tragic" he said softly but in a voice devoid of any feeling.

Rencarro allowed himself a slight smile at Sylvanus' sarcasm. This was a man of subtlety, a man who would think before rash action and act with purpose. Rencarro needed his Second, now more than ever.

He quickly relayed to Sylvanus what Tacet had told them so far, and then both of them proceeded to question their man, exchanging looks as they did so. There was an unspoken communication between the two men, one forged over twenty years of comradeship. This closeness clearly burned Marcus but Rencarro would not push aside his most valued advisor for the sake of his son's pride.

"What do you think, Sylvanus?" enquired Rencarro, as he motioned for the Velox Rider to drink water from a pitcher standing on a small table. Tacet bowed his head and withdrew a few paces.

Sylvanus was about to speak when Marcus interrupted.

"Father, now is our chance to seize power! Mobilise our

forces. Muster our people. Let us sail up the Unn, round the Sacred Mount and land as close as we can to Bregustol. Strike at the heart of Sedmund's kingdom while the people mourn and confusion holds. Take Bregustol before Helliga does and buy the northern tribes' loyalty with loot seized. We fortify the capital and control the trade and the Ruby Road."

It was clear Marcus could see his father was not excited by this train of thought.

"Father! You cannot be thinking to just sit back and let Orben become ruler of half the realm! He will move, have no doubt about it."

Rencarro waited for Marcus to calm himself. Sylvanus patiently stood by, head lowered tactfully. Marcus bit back whatever he'd been about to say next and breathed deeply.

"Good" said Rencarro, "Marcus, your courage serves you well and I do not doubt your desire to swiftly take the serpent's lair. But we must look at the longer game here. We simply do not have the strength to take on the combined might of Bregustol and the Helligan nation. We may be able to take a capital in chaos as you say but defend it to the west and south? The northern legions would rally under Torbal, even if he doesn't become the de facto ruler anyway. Orben may well join such a battle and we would be annihilated. Or worse, Helliga would come this way and destroy our home if they see us taking up residence in Bregustol."

Rencarro paused. He could have also pointed out that trying to invade the north-east by river would be over before it really began. Catapults, scorpions and bowmen would rain down death upon boats coming up the river. Rencarro didn't want to humiliate Marcus though. Now was not the time for a harsh lesson.

Marcus threw up his hands in exasperation and turned away. Sylvanus raised his head and looked to Rencarro, who nodded to his second.

Sylvanus began, his voice slow and measured. "As my lord has just reasoned, we do not have the numbers to hold

Bregustol and defend our home here in Meridia." Sylvanus avoided looking at Marcus. Rencarro appreciated the man's tact. His Second continued.

"We want to avoid any conflict with the Helligan nation. Their military may not be as large as it was in yesteryear but it is highly trained and well-equipped, and I also believe Orben hides his real strength from outside eyes. They could take the capital and hold it even if the legions march east from Westhealfe. So let them. What Vorga would do in the north is difficult to predict. It is unlikely he will risk all-out war with Helliga and the Rihtgellen Kingdom. He doesn't have the numbers. Nor the discipline for that matter. More likely he will join the side that looks to have the upper-hand or stay put in those cold wastes he calls home."

Sylvanus paused and awaited a signal from his lord. Rencarro gestured for him to continue.

"Argyllan."

One word but it spoke a thousand. Marcus looked at Sylvanus with incredulity.

"Argyllan?! Why in the name of the Widow would we want to invade that little piss-hole?"

Rencarro sighed. He had an idea what Sylvanus was thinking.

"I did not say anything about invading, Marcus. We would occupy the region, under the pretext of protecting the people there now that the influence of Bregustol is no longer certain. People will fear raiders from the Barren Isles if they learn there is civil unrest in the north, despite the likelihood that the Throskaur are a spent people."

Sylvanus held up his hands, palms outwards. He continued.

"There need be no blood spilt by our own blades. We simply move a large number of troops into the port of Argyllan itself, marching the north route past the Widow's Teeth. Another force would go south of the Teeth and take control of the town of Lowenden. We come in from the north and south and take hold of the entire region. We are there to help, of course."

Sylvanus smiled slyly. Rencarro now saw the brilliance in his Second's plan. Marcus obviously didn't.

"To what end? We spread our forces thinly just so we can boast about having more land in our name, although we couldn't do that openly, or the ruse would fail. And then, at some point in the future when the fighting ceases, we withdraw? Is that your grand plan, Sylvanus?" Marcus clearly believed he had out-thought the older man. Rencarro stepped in.

"Marcus, for the love of your mother, listen till the end of what Sylvanus has to say. I believe you will see the merit in his plan." His son snorted quietly and shrugged his broad shoulders.

"Marcus," said Sylvanus, directly addressing his lord's son, "think about what will be happening while we do this. Orben marches his forces north, crossing the Mimir, to seize the capital. Torbal summons the legions from Westhealfe and Morak in response. Then we have a very long and bloody conflict in the north-east. All the while we are fortifying ourselves in Argyllan, recruiting from the local population. If we are seen as saviours, we should be able to entice a lot of young men into our ranks. Meridia will be safe with the Helligan nation engaged far away. When those two powers are war-weary, maybe two years down the road, then we make our move. We cross the River Freo and take Westhealfe itself. The north-west will be weak and we will be strong, having not lost untold numbers of soldiers to conflict. The south-west will support us because they believe we are lessening the chance of bloodshed anywhere near them. And," Sylvanus raised a finger to emphasise his point, "with many of their young men in our ranks, we will have something of a *local* thirst for conquest. The result? Your father rules half of Ragnekai, while the other powers still fight. The balance of power will have shifted well and truly."

Even Marcus could not disguise his interest now. Rencarro himself felt an excitement building within him. It was probably not as simple as Sylvanus had just outlined, with so many unknown quantities. But this was a viable course of action. Promising even. Quietly secure a solid hold over the entire south-west while Torbal and Orben bled each other, and then move on to the north-west. Avoiding the shinier prize of Bregustol was the better move initially. In five years' time, Meridia could be riding high in the realm. Not only strong but also popular with the common folk as Rencarro's area of influence would see little conflict.

Marcus grunted, which Rencarro took as a sign his son could see the worth of Sylvanus' plan. Rencarro nodded slowly, gathering his thoughts.

"We must move with haste, as the Helligan nation will be readying itself already. If Ulla did have anything to do with Sedmund's death, then Orben will have begun planning months ago." Rencarro pondered on something. He looked at Sylvanus, who instantly knew what his lord was thinking.

"Spread some *news*?"

"Yes. Let people hear that Ulla is likely behind the High King's death and she is now back with her brother, plotting to take the capital. Also, we need to instil some fear in Argyllan and its people. Perhaps a few reports of Throskaur raiding ships seen off the coast. Or Helligan agents caught within our borders." Rencarro paused, nodding to the Velox Rider Tacet, who had been standing quietly to the side after refreshing himself. Tacet bowed his head, knowing an order had just been given, and left the solar. Rencarro turned back to his son and Sylvanus.

"We need for them to *want* us to be there. To feel safer with our soldiers in their lands."

Sylvanus stood up straighter.

"It will be done."

No more needed to be said on this front. Rencarro knew Sylvanus would begin organising a mustering of men from the Meridian lands as soon as this meeting was over. And he knew that he and his Second shared a vision here, one that could change the course of history as it unfolded in this realm.

Rencarro turned to his son and allowed a small smile to form on his lips.

"Marcus, I would speak with both you and Eligius. I think it is time your brother joined you and I in holding the reigns of leadership."

Marcus visibly gained something in stature at the words. Rencarro knew Sylvanus could see what he was doing and sadly, but gladly, knew Marcus would not realise. He continued, gripping Marcus's muscular shoulders.

"I have roles for both of you in this course of action. And both of you will be tested. Hold onto your desire to lead our men into battle, nurture it within you and then unleash it when the time is right." Rencarro held his son's eyes, seeing the fire within, hoping he could control those flames. Marcus nodded grimly.

Rencarro clapped his eldest on the back.

"Tell your brother I expect the two of you here at noon for lunch. We have much to discuss."

The Meridian ruler's mind was alive with the promise of a greater future for his people, and the hope that the following months and maybe years would mould Marcus into a leader of which his mother would have been proud. Marcus' eyes glistened as emotion rose from within. He quickly turned to go, shared a look of perhaps temporary mutual respect with Sylvanus, then left the solar.

Sylvanus raised his eye-brows and dipped his head in acknowledgement of his lord's skilful handling of a risky factor in this grand design.

"Wine?" he said, proffering a glass of deep red.

Ch 3

Emiren

28th Day of Aprus, Three Days After Sedmund's Death

Emiren had spent the morning in Argol gathering more Lorth Weed, this time by herself, and the afternoon helping Sister Jessa in the hospice. She had meant to stop by the inn to have lunch with Anton but time had slipped away. Emiren felt sure Anton would understand, kind hearted as he was. She had no siblings of her own but Anton was like a brother to her, always there for her and always able to make her smile.

The sun was low in the sky when Emiren arrived home, having said her farewells to Sister Jessa and Janwarin. She promised the sickly man she would stop by again tomorrow so he could tell her another story. Janwarin seemed to brighten up when Emiren sat there listening to his tales. Sister Jessa had noticed and whispered to her another visit would be appreciated. Emiren didn't mind at all. She listened to all manner of stories from Janwarin and learnt herb-lore from Sister Jessa, although her teacher would often comment that she was the student and Emiren the wiser one in this area. Emiren could admit she was more familiar with the wilder side of herb-lore, roaming Argol while Sister Jessa spent her days in the hospice.

Emiren's father was sitting outside their humble dwelling, stirring a long, wooden spoon in an iron pot that hung over an open fire. Their home was a simple building but sturdy and well-kept. It was a large enough cottage for the three of them, and sheltered them from the harsher weather and winter cold. Lumber from Argol had provided for the wooden frame and the walls were made from wattle and daub. Emiren had helped her parents carve Words into the horizontal logs.

Emiren would often close her eyes and run her fingers over the Words, reading them without sight. Her mother Megari had told her when she was younger that the Words held power and had been passed down through the generations. Her mother was vague about what the powers were and Emiren felt it was more something that helped the villagers in hard times; hope to hold onto. But she was drawn to them nonetheless. She could read all the Words that adorned her home and had heard more from the older folk in the village. She sometimes asked her mother if they would ever need to use them. Her mother always replied, "Just remember them."

The broth her father was tending was bubbling away now and sent an irresistible aroma of thyme wafting through the air. Emiren quickened her pace, eager to join her family and that wonderful scent. Quint looked up.

"I knew you'd come if I started cooking." He winked.

A shaggy, grey bundle of fur burst from around the side of the home and nearly knocked Emiren over as it leapt at her.

"Tarak!" She laughed, pushing the wolf away. "Let me breathe, you big lunk."

Tarak immediately sat and raised his left paw. Emiren raised her left hand to her chest and smiled at the wolf.

"It smells delicious, Da" Emiren said, returning her attention to what her father was doing. She breathed in deeply. Tarak walked over to Quint and slumped down, resting his weight on the man's left foot.

"Ow! You're far too big to be doing that now, old boy!" Quint grumbled as he pulled his foot from under Tarak. The wolf just let out a deep sigh and rested his head on his paws. Long gone were the days when he could curl up on Quint's lap and both would doze off in the afternoon sun.

Tarak was a Tarakan wolf. They were seldom seen anywhere other than the Tarakan Plains it was said so Emiren had felt Tarak was a good name, in that it informed people what he was, not just who he was. Many of the villagers had taken it as another sign that Emiren was connected to nature somehow when the ten-year-old girl walked home one day with the small cub in her arms. Her mother and father had been vehemently opposed to Emiren keeping the beast at first. They had taken the creature away and left it just inside the borders of Argol. But Emiren had snuck off after darkness fell and somehow found the little fellow. It was more likely he had found her but the result was the same. Her mother, Megari, found the two of them curled on the floor of Emiren's room in the morning, sleeping soundly. Quint had agreed with Megari that it would be more trouble to keep them apart and so Tarak became a part of the home. And also a famous addition to the village of Fallowden.

Megari came out of the front door and smiled at Emiren.

"Hunger brings my daughter back to me as always."

Emiren's mother's hair was a similar colour to hers but now losing its fire as age crept up on her. Emiren had always thought her mother the most beautiful lady in Fallowden and would often tell her she only became moreso with age. Her mother would just smile her gentle smile.

Megari joined her husband at the pot, sitting on a tree stump that had been smoothed down by the elements and human labour. She inhaled the aroma, cocked her head and shrugged.

"I might let your father cook for our neighbours one day" she teased, smiling at Emiren.

Quint rolled his eyes and Emiren laughed.

"Mum, Da is the best cook in our family. Out of the men, that is." Quint's head shot up.

"Oi! Reckon I might just enjoy my stew with Tarak here. What do you say, my furry friend?"

Tarak let out another deep sigh, as if to say *You humans and your quaint banter.*

Emiren sat down on the same bench as her father and squeezed his arm. "Hurry up and serve it. The smell is driving my stomach wild."

Quint grinned and ladled generous helpings of the stew, which was packed with carrots and turnips, into three wooden bowls. Megari passed out three spoons.

The sun had almost set now and the darkness was only kept at bay by two flickering torches set in iron sconces a few yards from the lodge, two lanterns hanging from the porch that fronted their home and the fire by which they all sat. Other flickering glows could be seen a slight way off as their neighbours also ate their evening meal. Before they began eating, Quint looked to Emiren and said, "How about you say a few words tonight?"

Emiren thought for a moment and then began a low chant. Megari and Quint hummed along with her. Tarak's ears twitched and he let out a low sound that Emiren always took to be a wolf's hum.

"Soil that keeps, rains that weep.
Sun that shines, trees that climb.
Rivers that flow, winds that know.
We remember the Words all, and will heed the Spirits' call."

The three of them dug into their meal, with various sounds of appreciation from Emiren and her mother. They each tore off chunks of a loaf Megari had baked that afternoon, the crust crispy but the bread within light and still slightly warm. It was a good stew, as it always was. Quint seemed to find a new flavour every day, yet somehow the taste was always familiar to Emiren, always her father's.

After some time had passed with solely eating, Quint put his bowl down and stood up. He stepped inside their home and soon came out holding a shank of meat. He tossed it to where Tarak was and the animal immediately sat up. Tarak looked at Quint and bowed his head.

"You're welcome, boy. I swear to the Old Stream though that Waddet leaves the choicest cuts for you." Quint chuckled. "Guess he appreciates the lack of jackals round here, which is in no small part thanks to you." He stroked the wolf's head as Tarak set to devouring the red meat that clung to the bone.

"The traders didn't arrive this morning," commented Megari, "I wonder what is keeping them. The weather can't be causing any strife on the roads. Been clear skies for almost a week now."

Quint inhaled through his teeth. "It is a bit odd, I'll agree. Those traders have such tight schedules. Never known them to miss more than half a day and that is only when the Wind Spirits are blowing something fierce."

Emiren nodded. They all knew how the traders came when expected and left as soon as they had bought and sold various wares, hurrying on to the next settlement, or even one of the big cities. The children of Fallowden would always await the wagons with barely contained excitement, as most of the traders were friendly sorts who would throw the little ones sugar-drops or fruits foreign to the village. Emiren was recently becoming aware though that the traders had purpose in this show of generosity. With the boys and girls in such high spirits, their parents were in more indulgent moods and would often buy trinkets that were supposedly from far-off lands. Emiren wondered how far away *far-off* really was.

To the auburn-haired young lady, the town of Argyllan was far away, being a day's wagon-ride from Fallowden. The Forest of Argol on the other hand seemed at once vast and yet also felt like part of their village. Her family had camped out near the western edge of the forest a few times, near the edges of the Tarakan Plains. It had taken two days to get there but time in the forest tended to melt away. Time was something that Emiren was sure the traders would never cease to notice. She looked up.

"Where would the traders be coming from, Da?"

Quint paused to quaff from a mug of ale he had quietly acquired.

"Meridia. They come north of the Widow's Teeth and make their first stop in Argyllan, where they off-load the bulk of their wares. They buy supplies there and bring them down to our village, then onto Lowenden and its markets, before trundling back to Meridia again, this time travelling south of the Teeth, past the Izachu Wildlands. I think they used to have a trade route the opposite direction, going to the Helligan nation, but word has it that it has dried up a bit. Too long a journey east maybe."

Quint leaned back in his chair and smiled wistfully.

"Wish they stayed a bit when they came though. Would be nice to share an ale or two with those fellows at Nicolas' inn. Bet they have some tales to tell! I reckon some of them have been as far as the capital. Imagine, all the way over the other side of the Sacred Mount. Part of me envies them" he finished with a far-away look in his eyes.

Megari chuckled softly, laying a hand on her husband's arm.

"The Sacred Mount" murmured Emiren. The first time she had seen it from the bank of the River Freo was when she was only waist-high to her father and could not believe such a gargantuan thing could exist. On a clear day one could see the summit of the Sacred Mount, far up in the sky. Mostly though, clouds would gently nestle around the top of the mountain, looking like some mystical land forbidden to the people far below.

Her father had told her that a few had reached the summit but many more had died trying. Pilgrims and adventurers generally climbed to about half-way, as from there on the Sacred Mount became much steeper.

Emiren always felt that the rivers circling the Sacred Mount were created by the Spirits to cleanse it, so clear and strong was their flow. She remembered asking as a child if the water rushing past in the Freo was from the Western Sea. Quint had told her to watch the water and then think once more. Emiren had felt silly as she saw the river was flowing in the direction of the sea so the water must come from elsewhere. Quint had made his way down to the edge of the river and scooped up the water, drinking as much as he could before it leaked out from his cupped hands. Emiren had done the same. It had tasted so pure and fresh.

"One day we'll taste the sea and you might be a little

surprised" her father had said. The young Emiren hadn't understood then but now of course knew the water in the sea had salt within it. She had not tasted it yet though. She looked forward to the day when her family would travel to some distant shore and put the deepest of waters to their lips.

The three of them talked into the night until Quint's yawns became so frequent he couldn't finish a sentence without his mouth opening wide. Tarak got up and padded into the cabin. They all laughed quietly and followed him in.

Emiren bid her parents good-night and made her way into the bathroom. A copper tub stood in the middle of a red tiled floor, half-full of water. A brazier kept an urn of water steaming away to its side. Emiren took a thick cloth so as not to scald her hands and poured the hot water into the tub. She replaced the empty urn with a full one from the floor and put another log into the brazier.

The tired girl removed her clothes and tossed them onto a wooden shelf on the wall. Then she took a bowl, filled it with water from the tub, retrieved the soap and brush and proceeded to scrub away the smells and sweat accumulated in Argol. When her skin was pink from all her efforts, she washed off the soap with more water from the tub and replenished the bath with hot water from the second urn that had now heated up to a decent temperature. She lowered herself into the steaming tub and let her body's aches drift out into the water. Her red hair splayed out like shafts of sunlight as she submerged her head. She rose again and took a breath, her mind focusing on nothing at all, the waters gently drowning all worry and thought. The Forest of Argol and its paths swirled around in her consciousness, but it was if she had no control over the images flooding her mind. After a while, she sighed and decided it was time to leave this watery haven.

After drying herself and putting on a light cotton chemise, she slipped inside her room where Tarak was already curled up beneath the window. Her body felt ready for a deep sleep after the bath. She leant down to kiss Tarak on the head, his fur warm and full of the scents of Argol. She climbed into her bed, her eyes heavy and she soon began drifting into the realm of sleep.

Emiren fell into a very lucid dream that night. She saw her home from above as if she was floating. The Words carved into the beams glowed a pale orange. She found herself rising higher into a darkening sky. As she did so, the vaporous shapes of the Spirits flew past her, whispering the Words as they went. Emiren felt dizzy. She turned and turned, suddenly finding herself looking out over the Forest of Argol. The entire forest seemed to be swaying in a steady rhythm, side to side. A voice sounded from afar but she couldn't make out what it said. Then she looked up and saw the moon, full and milky white in an ever-blackening sky. The moon was shrinking. No, that wasn't what was happening. The sky was swallowing the moon. Only it wasn't the sky—it was a deep shadow enveloping the night sky's guardian. A chill filled Emiren's bones, then something tugged at her arms and legs.

She gasped, jolting upright. She was in her bed, drenched in sweat. Tarak had raised his head to see what was wrong. *It was just a dream*, she told herself. Emiren lay back again and breathed slowly and surely. The young girl fell back to sleep and this time her dreams were just wisps of cloud.

*

The next morning Emiren came into the living area, yawning and shuffling. She sat down at the table with a whispered good morning to her parents who were already there. It took her a few moments to realise something was amiss. Neither Quint nor Megari had said a word and both sat with hands clasped together resting on the table.

"What?" asked Emiren, "what is it?"

Quint looked at his wife, then to Emiren. His eyes were full of worry. Something had happened. Emiren was wide-awake now and leaned forward as if trying to instantly draw forth the whole story from her parents.

"Please tell me."

Megari found her voice. "A rider came in the night. A messenger from Argyllan. It seems High King Sedmund has died." She stopped, perhaps waiting for that to sink in.

Emiren sat back in her chair. She knew who Sedmund was but was not sure why this should be of such concern to them. The ruler of the lands had been old anyway. Would his death make much difference? Wouldn't his son or daughter take his place? Emiren looked up with a questioning look.

"Who will succeed him?" she asked softly. Emiren felt a tension in the air now and it seemed somehow, they should speak quietly.

"That is the problem." replied Quint. "Nobody knows."

Emiren frowned. "But…how can that be? Didn't he have any heirs?"

"No" whispered Megari. "And the manner of his death is uncertain. A sickness that came about suddenly."

Emiren looked at her mother, then her father, waiting for them to say more. She often felt she should understand more from what her parents said and now was such a time. What was strange about a sudden sickness? People always felt fine till they were sick.

Quint spoke up.

"We have a power struggle in the halls of the mighty. It might be short and life will go on as normal. But it might not be over so quickly. If so, I fear the realm will slide into conflict of some sort or another. History can be difficult to forget if you were on the losing side of it."

Again, Emiren knew she should pick up on what was unsaid here. She couldn't though so patiently waited for her father to say more, knowing he would realise she was lost when it came to history and the politics of the realm.

Quint gave her a gentle smile. "Your books probably have a layer of dust on them a finger thick."

Emiren grinned sheepishly. "Why do I need books when I

have you, Da?"

"Cunningly spoken, daughter of mine. Well, where shall I begin? Firstly, get some breakfast to eat while I enlighten you."

Megari sliced some wheat bread and put it on a plate for Emiren. This was followed by goat's cheese and some swiftly torn lettuce leaves. Her mother then filled a clay cup with milk from a jug.

Quint had been rummaging through a chest in the corner. He returned to the table with an old map. He unrolled it out on the table and weighted down the corners with his own cup and plate from breakfast and his wife's. Quint motioned for his daughter to break her fast.

"Right, let's go back to Sedmund's grandfather Grindan, who was the one who brought the realm under one rule. A long time before even your old Da was born, the maps of Ragnekai looked a bit different to this one. The Helligan nation was dominant in almost the entire eastern half of Ragnekai and enjoyed the lucrative precious stones trade that came from the mines in the north-east. What we now know as Bregustol was the capital of this state. Grindan and his people were farther north in Morak, which is more a fortress than a city from what I have heard."

Quint paused to let Emiren take it in and also to make sure she was listening properly. Emiren rolled her eyes as if to answer Quint's unspoken question, her mouth full of what was a delicious cheese and fresh bread. She hoped her father hadn't noticed her surprise at this last piece of information. Emiren had until now assumed Bregustol had always belonged to the Rihtgellen Kingdom. Megari smiled faintly at Emiren.

My mother knows me too well.

"Alright, Emi", continued Quint, "Sedmund's grandpa, Grindan, wanted that trade and much more besides. He was a cunning man, so they say. He married the sister of the Westhealfe ruler, which effectively united the north-west. Doubtless there were some words spoken behind closed doors that helped to seal this marriage and union. Grindan then made a bargain with a warlord from the Unvasiktok Tribelands, far to

47

the north, east of the Jagged Heights. It is believed he aided this chieftain in a civil war that had been brewing for a generation. Some say Grindan lit the spark to this conflict. That warlord, Tonrar, then launched relentless raids on the caravans bringing stones from the mines. Helliga responded with all its might, as Grindan knew they would. Bregustol, or Nortrone as it was known then, was left severely undermanned. Grindan then struck."

Quint gave her a look that said she should be reacting more to this story.

"Told you he was cunning" he said.

Emiren frowned, unsure if her father was admiring what she deemed as treachery. She nodded to show she had understood, eager to hear more and took a big gulp of milk. Her body received the nourishment gratefully and Emiren felt her mind finally waking up. Quint pointed to the region to the east of Fallowden.

"Our neighbours in Meridia then amassed their army on the western banks of the River Unn, even venturing over the Unnbro Bridge into Helligan territory. Grindan had been busy with his rather dishonourable diplomacy, ensuring Meridia was on his side too. Nortrone, the capital, was besieged by two powerful factions and was facing a vicious and unpredictable enemy to the north-east. Word came of Meridia threatening its western borders to the south. The Helligan nation resisted for a time but their king was smart enough to see the balance was not in his favour."

Emiren started to wish she really had listened more to the teachings of Marin and Lukas, the two Fallowden Masters. In fact, she wished she had attended more classes, as all too often she had missed them whilst roaming the depths of Argol. She could have at least dusted off those books.

Megari cut Emiren more bread and cheese, obviously noticing her daughter had an appetite this morning. Her husband continued, moving his hands south from Bregustol as if he were dragging something.

"The Helligan people retreated to the south-east, war-weary and defeated."

Emiren nodded. She started to feel that they were blessed to live in a time of peace. She couldn't imagine so much bloodshed.

"Grindan settled into his new home, renamed Bregustol. Morak and Westhealfe were secure and undamaged from the conflict. Meridia hadn't fought at all, so just returned home knowing they had been on the winning side but also slightly wary that their still powerful eastern neighbour would not forget what had passed. The Helligan nation for its part, licked its wounds in the south-east and fortified Gamle Hovestad."

Quint finished quickly as he noticed Emiren yawning.

"I'm fine" she said, sitting up straight and taking a deep breath.

Quint leaned forward, resting his forearms on the table. "Grindan then declared himself to be High King of the entire realm, which was the beginning of the Rihtgellen rule. Helliga was beaten, the Unvasik tribes were satisfied with the plunder from this dark episode and the north-west was of course revelling in the glory their countryman had procured for them. And our neck of the woods just sat quietly, counting our blessings that the conflict had not cursed these lands and hoping peace would prevail. So, to sum up, Grindan brought the realm to its knees by means fair and foul."

"What an evil man" muttered Emiren.

Megari sighed. "Emi, it is not so clear whether or not this was a good course of events. The realm has had no civil conflict now for two generations. We live here in Fallowden and know nothing of war. If Grindan had not done what he did, who knows what would have happened? We might still be waking up every day to a darker, more violent world. We cannot praise Sedmund's line but I am not so sure we should condemn them either."

Emiren frowned, but she knew her mother was right. She looked up at her father expectantly, waiting for more. He nodded and spoke again.

"Grindan died and his son Stenric took over the rule. He secured what his father had achieved, setting up various trade agreements and laws that lessened the possibility of the other peoples rebelling against Rihtgellen rule."

Quint clucked his tongue. Emiren could see her father held some measure of respect or even mild awe towards these men. Her father went on.

"Very little blood was spilled under his rule and the folk of the realm came to accept the way things were with some contentment. Of course, there was some disgruntlement that many laws and treaties favoured Stenric's people and especially the capital Bregustol, but life was good enough that they stayed at just that, grumblings. Also, Bregustol had people from all corners of the realm passing through it and a great deal of silver changing hands, so there was a feeling that everyone was sharing in Bregustol's status as the capital. Stenric was very astute at giving the common folk enough to be content with but not so much that he ever ran out of his own silver, so to speak. He sweetened the honey pot for the north-west and Meridia, making sure they would support him in the event of a Helligan uprising. The realm was very secure."

Quint leaned back in his chair and took a gulp of barley tea. Emiren made a mental promise that she would seek out the village Masters and beg their forgiveness for being absent so much. She realised though that it might be a bit late for her to restart her education, being seventeen. She looked over the map again as her father continued the history lesson.

"Then came Sedmund the Slow...as he is known in some circles" Quint said with a wry smile. "We know little here about what goes on in Bregustol, but I have heard rumours that Sedmund has not, or should I say, *did not* do enough to hold tight what his forebears gained. Some say he spent a great deal of time delving into the past. And not just the recent past but the time before these lands were settled. I have no idea why but he maybe neglected the present with this fascination of ages

50

gone by. I have heard it said that those within Gamle Hovestad no longer grumble and that silence is a real concern."

Megari spoke up. "And now the High King has left this mortal realm. It seems he dithered in matters closer to home as well, not leaving a son or daughter to take his place."

Emiren thought about all the people beyond the Argol region. The Tarakans to the south were such peaceful people. She had heard tales of Meridian art and Helligan music, magnificent architecture in Bregustol and delicious foods that came from the Westhealfe region. So much good couldn't just collapse. Surely the realm wouldn't break apart just because one man had died. All the people in these far-off lands that she had never visited surely didn't want war. She voiced this thought to her parents.

Megari sighed. "That may be so, Emi. But it is not the common folk who set the course that will become the future. It is those in power. And many of them care little for those beneath them. The Helligan nation…"

Quint picked up her thought. "Orben, the ruler of the Helligan nation, may see this as an opportunity to take back their home of long ago. If he does, and they succeed, who knows what will happen? Will we lose order in the lands? Will young men leave their farms and families to go and fight in someone else's war?"

Megari shook her head. "There is so much we don't know. We must just hope for good to flow through the lands and peace to endure."

Emiren felt her mother was bringing the conversation to an end, so she just reached out and took her mother and father's hands. They sat like that for a while until Tarak padded in. His appearance brought them all into the present world and they stirred into their daily routines. Quint went out to his workshop to light the furnace. Megari started clearing the table while Emiren sat there with the Tarakan wolf beside her. She finished her breakfast in silence.

Her thoughts swirled around, trying to imagine an old man dying in Bregustol, armies on the move and terrible barbarian

51

men from the frozen north stalking the lands. Tarak nuzzled her arm.

"I know. You'll protect me, my friend." She smiled and ruffled his fur. The wolf rubbed his head against her leg, seemingly content she had understood his intention.

Ch 4

Torbal

General Torbal, the High King's Shield, stood on a balcony of the Royal Palace, situated in the centre of Bregustol, capital of the Rihtgellen Kingdom. A kingdom now without a king, a realm without a ruler. Sadness clutched at Torbal within; the loss of his friend felt as keenly today as it had the moment that the Grey Sister had indicated he had passed from this mortal realm.

The wind blew Torbal's snowy mane of hair, bringing with it a light chill from the ice-capped Jagged Heights to the far north, clearly visible in the distance, their lower climbs obscured by the murky green of the Deadwood. An apt name if ever there was one.

Torbal breathed deeply, a whole host of thoughts tumbling over in his mind. He knew he lacked the cunning and perception that Sedmund had possessed. He had been the rock on which his king had stood to make his proclamations and then the hammer that carried out the royal will. Torbal had verbalized this image to Ulla as they lay in bed one night together, likening himself to a blunt instrument. She had scolded him, telling him his heart beat powerfully with more honour than any man she had known. And now his lover was gone too, back to her homeland in Helliga.

Torbal was reasonably certain Sedmund had not known of this affair. An affair with the sister of the High King's main rival, in terms of the rule of the realm. Torbal felt guilty for hiding this from his old friend but both he and Ulla had agreed the time was not right to reveal their secret. This also applied to telling her brother Orben of their relationship. Now it was too late for Torbal to tell Sedmund. He wished he could have shared his happiness with his friend. He coughed, releasing the emotion that had been building in his throat.

Torbal looked north over the city. Bregustol stretched out beneath the palace in all directions. There were no buildings this side of the palace that could compare in sheer size. If one looked out from a south-facing balcony, they could not miss the Holy Sepulchre, an incredible feat of construction but an eyesore to Torbal's mind. He remembered how this had been perhaps the spark that had ignited a cautious flame between Ulla and himself.

At a banquet one evening, he had found himself to one side, a mug of ale in hand, enjoying the sound of the harp's strings. He had seen Ulla approaching him and had tried to politely escape but she had caught him. They had talked of the differences between the religion here in the north and what was practiced in her homeland to the south-west. He had been impressed with her keen intelligence and had picked up on a hint of this lady not entirely believing in a higher power. Much like himself. The conversation had turned to how one saving grace of religion was that it inspired great works of architecture. Torbal had made his feelings known about the Holy Sepulchre and Ulla had laughed. It was the first time he had heard her laugh so freely and he had been utterly enchanted. Torbal mused that he should thank the Holy Sepulchre for something.

His thoughts soured though as picturing that towering monstrosity reminded him of Brother Eswic. Torbal loathed the man but had tolerated him as Sedmund had always argued that religion was necessary for control of the masses. Torbal found this notion distasteful but couldn't deny the reality. But he despised how Eswic abused his authority, always pushing for more *adoration* of the Ever-Father in the form of more churches and expeditions in search of holy relics. *Fool* thought Torbal. The man was trying to rewrite history, bringing new *evidence* of the Ever-Father's hand in shaping the realm of Ragnekai. Trying to create a history that would give some sort of divine right to the Rihtgellen rule over the lands.

Torbal also suspected Eswic was not as holy as he professed to be. There were rumours of unsavoury behaviour by the church's highest voice. Hypocrisy was something else Torbal loathed.

Inevitably Torbal then thought about Worsteth, the Royal Chamberlain. Torbal could see the King's Ministry from his vantage point. There was nothing spectacular about these buildings but they did occupy almost an entire district. Torbal placed his hands on the smooth stone wall that was between him and a fall to the lower levels of the palace. Of course, administering a city of over twenty thousand people must take a great deal of work, he conceded. Torbal didn't dislike Worsteth to the same degree he did Eswic, but neither did he trust him. The man was too ambitious. And too entrenched in all the workings of the realm.

So, there were three factions as it were, that existed in the absence of a High King. Eswic had the Church and all its influence, Worsteth effectively ran the kingdom, and Torbal himself had the loyalty of the military. He shook his head, wishing Ulla were here to listen to his concerns. The potential power he commanded was something Ulla had none too subtly made clear at Sedmund's death-bed. He knew this was likely to push Eswic and Worsteth closer together and so had felt frustrated with Ulla. There had not been time to air his feelings though as rumours had suddenly run rampant that Ulla had poisoned Sedmund. Torbal had ensured her safe exit from the city and had received word from some of his most trusted men that she had crossed into the Helligan nation without incident. He wanted her by his side, needed her even. But she would have been in danger if she stayed. Of course, her flight had only succeeded in confirming what some believed. He cursed.

To the Abyss with all this!

Torbal then berated himself for having unwittingly sunk into the religion here in Bregustol, its various beliefs and notions entering his lexicon. The Westhealfe native did not believe in the Abyss or the Ever-Father. He felt far from home in more ways than one.

Torbal knew he was not equipped to deal with the unseen enemies of whisper and rumour, and had no idea how to talk with his two peers. The Ministry and the Church were likely now discussing how to take him out the equation. They needed an ally to command the army, someone to support them in taking up the reins of power, and not someone who was a symbol of the previous ruler. He didn't fear assassination, even though he knew Eswic at least would be happy to have it happen. But his own death would bring utter chaos, coming so soon after the death of Sedmund. Westhealfe was a loyal part of the kingdom but if the people there suspected Torbal had been murdered, there would be an uprising that would be a gift to Orben.

What will be their next move?

The patter of footsteps behind him made him turn. A fatigue rushed over him but he stood smartly as Worsteth approached, bowing his head in respect, something Eswic had never done. Torbal returned the gesture. Worsteth came up to the balcony and looked out, saying nothing. Torbal looked at him, and then turned his gaze across the city.

Finally, the Royal Chamberlain spoke. "These are difficult times, General."

"Agreed" replied Torbal, perhaps a bit too gruffly. "The city mourns Sedmund's passing."

"It is a terrible loss" said Worsteth softly.

And then lapsed into silence again. Torbal knew Worsteth had something to say and furthermore believed it would be something unfavourable to himself. But he also wished the thin, spidery man would just spit it out.

"You came with tidings?" proposed the general.

"Hm? Ah yes, yes, there is a matter I wish to discuss with you." Worsteth leaned closer and said in a low voice, "Away from the sound of church bells, as it were."

The smile was well executed but Torbal had looked into too many men's eyes not to see where the truth lay. He suspected

Eswic knew exactly what Worsteth was about to say and had probably agreed upon the words with the chamberlain this very morning.

"Well, speak freely here, Chamberlain. I believe the walls do not have ears, despite what some say."

Torbal tried to put on an air of levity but he was not suited to deception. Something Ulla had said was to his credit. Torbal suddenly had an uneasy feeling that perhaps his belief about the walls was incorrect.

Worsteth breathed in deeply. "I feel somewhat embarrassed to speak of this with you, but I feel it is best I do so before looser tongues start to wag."

Torbal could see where this was leading and the fatigue began to feel like a shadow made solid and heavy, which hung upon his shoulders and sought to drag him down.

"The Lady Ulla is back in Gamle Hovestad by now, would you say?" Worsteth continued. Torbal's jaw tightened.

The chamberlain did not wait for an answer, which Torbal took as evidence this was all a show and the desired outcome had been decided already.

"I am one who personally despises rumour and idle talk."

Worsteth swept away at some dust or grit that may or may not have been present upon the wall, in what Torbal presumed was an effort to reinforce the notion that the chamberlain found gossip distasteful. The general let him continue with this charade.

"But with the realm in such a precarious position, I cannot ignore all that comes to my attention."

Worsteth turned to face Torbal. They were of a similar height but of very different stature. The general was broad where the chamberlain was lean; a solid frame opposite a wiry, angular one. But this was not a physical battle and Torbal knew Worsteth held the powerful weapon of information.

"Forgive me for asking but were you and the Lady Ulla engaged in a relationship?"

A straight-forward question, albeit one with a fair amount of preamble. Torbal suddenly felt tired beyond reason. He knew he could not win this battle. He was a man who needed his sword, shield and battle-cry to claim victory. Ulla could have sent Worsteth whimpering away into the shadows with her controlled eloquence and wit. Torbal envisioned the elegant contours of her face in his mind and sighed.

"Yes" he replied simply.

Worsteth's reaction was pure theatre. He inhaled sharply, shook his head and acted as if he were at a loss for words. "General, this is…" he spluttered.

"Shocking?" Torbal offered.

"Why yes. Indeed, I had thought the rumour to be some scandalous gossip. Torbal, if I may be familiar, what were you thinking? Ulla is Orben's sister and was not trusted at all by our late king. Was it wise to become so close to her?"

He's enjoying this thought Torbal. *I had thought him to be a better man than Eswic.* Torbal held the other man's eyes.

"Unwise? Perhaps. You misjudge her though. The realm's peace is her only priority."

As soon as he said it, he knew it sounded weak. Worsteth's raised eyebrows confirmed as much. Torbal knew Ulla. But to everyone else here, she was an outsider and one who happened to be the sister of Orben, ruler of the Rihtgellen Kingdom's enemy of old. Torbal wondered if he was perhaps naïve to believe the enmity was all in the past.

The Royal Chamberlain lowered his head and spoke in a hushed tone. "I must confess I do not know how best to proceed here. If word gets out that the rumours are true, we will have a certain amount of civil unrest."

Torbal read the implicit threat in Worsteth's words but also couldn't deny the truth of his statement. The facts did not put him in a positive light. Bregustol was not Westhealfe. People here were fickle and seemed to revel in wild rumour and scandal. Torbal knew the only course of action open to him. And he was certain Worsteth knew it too. And Eswic.

He placed a hand on Worsteth's shoulder, the thin man

flinching, which brought Torbal a small measure of satisfaction.

"I think I am needed in Westhealfe" the general said.

Worsteth nodded and smiled thinly.

Ch 5

Rencarro

As with every sunrise, Lord Rencarro stood atop the battlements on his city's walls, looking out across his lands. Today though the view from the south wall was different. Ranks of Meridian soldiers were stood to attention below him. He had mustered over a thousand men for this campaign to complement the regular army, which stood at around two thousand spears. He had pulled in hardy men from the small villages that peppered the surrounding countryside. Some were hunters, a handful had seen combat in lands farther north as mercenaries, and some had even fought against the Xerinthians in their attempted invasion of Ragnekai almost two decades ago. But mostly they were farmers and craftsmen, leaving their homesteads and shops in the hands of wives, sons and daughters.

The general lack of experience did not bother Rencarro greatly. If things proceeded as he and Sylvanus foresaw, the realm would slide into conflict but these men below him would see nothing of battle. He would initiate training nonetheless and the production of better weapons and armour. All below wore the colours of Meridia, green and white, and carried a spear from the Meridian armoury, but few of those mustered possessed anything more than boiled leather and an iron cap.

This is just the beginning though.

The beginning of a new chapter in Meridia's history. Orben would send the Helligan forces north to strike at the heart of the Rihtgellen Kingdom. Blood would flow and both sides would weaken. Rencarro cared little for who actually won between the two factions. As long as they were reduced in power, while he built his strength, he was content for either side to emerge victorious.

Rencarro had not touched his Custodia city guard, which would remain in Meridia, roughly a thousand strong. They would keep order here and guard against any raiding, which was unlikely in any event.

Below him was a strong force he deemed, enough to occupy Argyllan and the surrounding area under the guise of protecting the people. Rencarro would take the main host, around two and a half thousand, north of the Widow's Teeth. This force was a mix of regular soldiers and those mustered. Marcus would take the southern route with five hundred men, make camp outside the town of Lowenden and then make a show of patrolling the area around Argol Forest. The number of men was enough to secure the lands but not so many that they would be perceived as a threat. Sylvanus would have the last couple of hundred, mostly cavalry, and hold in a position just south of the Teeth. Sylvanus would be ready to act if needed.

His Second would also be leading a team of engineers and builders. Rencarro had a mind to construct a fort against the Widow's Teeth, using the jagged shale as a natural defence to one side. It would serve as a look-out and provide a focal point for training grounds to season all the new recruits he hoped to gain in the coming months. If all went well, he would have barracks there within a year. Rencarro also wanted Sylvanus to be ready to assume control if Marcus proved himself unworthy of the task his father had set. He was certain Marcus did not suspect Sylvanus had this secondary mission.

Rencarro knew this was all a gamble but he felt the odds were in his favour. He doubted there were any trained soldiers anywhere near the Forest of Argol. Argyllan had a decent number in their city guard, but there was certainly no fighting force of merit in existence south of the River Freo and west of Meridia. The small folk should be concerned about the unrest in the realm and should hopefully fear external aggression. Raiding was not in the too distant past, so it was quite feasibly still a worry for the people.

Rencarro wondered if Ulla had indeed poisoned Sedmund. The motivation was there but had Orben really been foolish enough to commit an act that, if guilt was proven or even generally accepted, would rally the entire north against him? Rencarro had met Orben a few times at the annual council Sedmund had imposed upon the realm's leaders. He had never spoken with him in any depth but the man had never struck Rencarro as one to take such risks. Ambitious yes, but not foolhardy. Orben had not attended these last five years though, with his sister attending Sedmund's court in her brother's place. Perhaps distance from the High King had emboldened him.

No matter, thought the Meridian ruler, *our forces will be welcomed in the south-west, rather than shunned.*

Gradually they would pull the reins away from those currently leading the people, always in the guise of aiding the small folk. Then, in the not too distant future, he would be in control over a truly vast stretch of territory, which meant resources, including an endless supply of lumber, trade routes and manpower. Rencarro knew if he just sat behind his walls, the trouble would come to him eventually and he would be in a weak position. This was the best course of action with which to secure the strength necessary to push back against whichever faction won the northern battle.

A possible fallibility in this plan was Marcus. Could he trust his arrogant son to fulfil the task given to him? Marcus had not wanted to take on the somewhat less exciting task of securing the lesser populated area. He felt he was the natural choice to take Argyllan, arguing his father should stay in Meridia to be a beacon of power. Rencarro disagreed of course. With a much greater population in Argyllan and so many troops at his command, Marcus would no doubt be tempted to move in strongly and with a certain brutality. The risk that they would be seen as invaders rather than saviours, was too great. And after all, Rencarro was the ruler of Meridia and must show himself to be in command of a large military force. The people of Argyllan must see him as their only shelter against the storm that was brewing; only then would they follow him after it had passed. Argyllan required diplomacy as well as authority supported by strength. Rencarro hoped his younger son Eligius and Marcus would make a capable ruling partnership after he was gone. They must. One could not rule without the other.

Eligius would administer the daily workings of Meridia till his return. With his father's authority behind him, Eligius should have no trouble keeping the city running in Rencarro's absence. The ruler of Meridia wondered just how long they would be away as he looked out again over the gathered troops.

Sunlight glinted on spear-heads below as banners snapped in the spring winds. Rencarro felt a surge of pride as he surveyed the men gathered. Perhaps dark times were ahead but there was a certain thrill in being able to put out such an army with himself at its head. This was the first time he had done so and he suddenly felt giddy with the rush of power. Rencarro chided himself. He must remain calm and above all, patient. He was playing the longer game here and could not afford to leap hastily at a quick victory.

He envisioned a future where all went according to plan. He would return to Meridia and rule from there. Eligius would rule in Argyllan, a place suitable for his particular character and skills. And Marcus would get his wish to lead the men into battle. With Sylvanus to guide him of course. Perhaps if the city of Westhealfe were taken, Marcus would make his seat of power there and would find the wit and cunning to rule. Meridian power would stretch far and wide. Rencarro had even spoken with Sylvanus about the Tarakan Plains. Tarakan Mares were famous throughout the realm for their speed and agility, and rumour was that the Tarakan people were masters of the bow on horseback. They were a nomadic people and had historically shunned conflict of any kind. But if the tales were true and Rencarro could work some diplomacy, a missile cavalry would be an excellent addition to his army. Sylvanus had chuckled at this, resting a hand on his lord's shoulder, saying "One thing at a time, my friend. First we make our home a little more spacious."

Footsteps behind brought him out of his reverie and he turned as his Second approached. "We are ready, Lord Rencarro" said Sylvanus, a hint of pride in his voice.

Rencarro allowed himself a smile. "This is it, old friend" he said clasping Sylvanus' fore-arm in a strong grip. "Today we set out to claim our future. Your plan is sound and I believe the winds favour us this day." He paused. "Well, we shall see."

Rencarro stepped to the edge of the battlements and signalled to a waiting trumpeter, who proceeded to blow three sharp notes. The general clamour and murmur amongst the soldiers faded quickly as they all looked up to their liege, standing fifty feet above them. Rencarro took a deep breath and began.

"Fellow Meridians" he boomed. It was unlikely those farther back could hear him that clearly but as was always the case with a crowd, word would filter back. This was why Rencarro knew to keep it simple. Short sentences with regular pauses to allow the whole body of troops to at least come together in one spirit.

"A glorious day!"

A cheer erupted. Spears clashed against shields. Rencarro waited a few moments, then raised his hands to signal calm. The soldiers obliged.

"And the first of many!"

Rencarro punched one fist in the air. The desired effect came swiftly. The roar rushed to him like a wave, and a myriad of shining points shot up a few feet higher.

Raising his hands for quiet again, Rencarro kept them up, palms outward but slightly downward.

"Sedmund is dead." He paused very briefly.

"The Rihtgellen grip on the realm is crumbling." Another pause.

The men understood the manner of his delivery and waited in silence for this part of the speech to finish.

"Orben will be greedy. And suffer."

He then slowly turned his head from one side to the other, his gaze taking in all his men. He hoped they would feel each of them had been noticed. The tension was palpable. Rencarro gave it another moment, then cried out as loud as he could.

"Meridia will rise!"

He threw his arms in the air and looked to the sky above as the army erupted in a cacophony of shouts and cheers.

Sylvanus leaned in close behind him, raising his voice to be heard above the din.

"Nicely done. They seem ready to thrust their spears up Orben's arse right now."

Rencarro turned from the battlements and with his Second in tow, proceeded to his solar to meet his sons and captains.

"They may lose that enthusiasm when they are told their less than glorious mission."

"Aye, that may be true" remarked Sylvanus. "But many will return to their farms and homes in due time. Those who stay on will be the ones who have a hunger for a more adventurous life. And I suspect the majority of them will be glad to be far from the bloodbath that will inevitably beset the north east."

Rencarro nodded in agreement.

"All except my son perhaps" he muttered.

Ch 6

Anton

It was the first day of the month of Maia and Anton could not contain his excitement. Today Fallowden would celebrate the Bealtaine Festival. Anton hoped he could share a drink with Emiren, leap over the fire with her and maybe hold her close in a dance. Bealtaine was a time to flirt and find a mate after all. He suppressed his smile as he hurried down the stairs to the inn proper, knowing his brother Cale would make a few *witty* comments. Anton knew he'd be teased but was determined not to make it too easy for his elder brother.

The previous day, the villagers of Fallowden had helped the livestock farmers lead their cattle into summer pastures. The weather was warming and spring would soon make way for summer. When the beasts were settled, thanks had been said but as tradition held on the eve of Bealtaine, there were no farewells. All had returned to their homes, thirsty for an ale but also seeking a good night's sleep so they could make an early start on the day of the festival.

The village of Fallowden would today receive all those who lived outside its wooden walls; farmers and homestead families, and even a few travellers coming through. There would be much merriment, aided by good food and even better beer. Anton's father, Nicolas and his brother Cale would be busy this day.

Anton paused, suddenly realizing he would be busy too. He slapped his forehead, chastising himself for being a forgetful fool. His thoughts of Emiren had chased away the reality of this festival. Those thoughts now melted away as he imagined the inn bustling with inebriated customers. How could he have forgotten this was perhaps the inn's busiest day of the year?

"The Spirits don't like a melancholy man on Bealtaine" came his father's voice from behind the counter. Anton snapped out of his slump in mood and put on a cheery smile.

"Where shall I start, Da?"

"He probably just realised he is on duty today and can't go off climbing trees."

His brother's voice came from where his father stood but was disembodied. Cale's sandy hair then rose above the counter with two bottles emerging in his hands.

Shades, he knows me better than I know myself.

Cale stood up straight, placed the wine on the counter and grinned at his younger brother. Nicolas chuckled and then grunted, "To work!"

The three of them bustled around in a graceful dance of toil and labour. Tables were cleaned a second time, glasses checked for the smallest of dirty smudges and barrels brought up from the cellar. The inn's cook, Megan, came in halfway through this whirlwind of activity and moved straight to the kitchens, singing as she went. Anton called out a greeting as she breezed through and noticed Cale's gaze linger on Megan's back a moment more than was necessary. Anton stopped what he was doing and stood there, hands on his hips. Cale noticed he was being watched and blushed a colour Anton hadn't thought possible in his big lunk of a brother.

"What?" he asked in a show of innocence.

"Been drinking Da's vintage already? It's just that you're a bit red in the face" Anton said in a matter-of-fact way. He ducked as a damp cloth suddenly sped towards his head.

"Shut your trap, badger-boy!"

Cale was laughing though as he realised the game was up for him too.

At that moment, Nicolas came up from the cellar.

"What's this? Not enough jobs for you two work-shy lay-abouts? I'm sure there are a couple of particularly nasty errands I can find if that's the case."

The two brothers quickly got back to work, attacking their chores with a renewed fervour. Nicolas nodded and went to the kitchens. Anton and Cale exchanged a grin and got on with their jobs.

By mid-morning the inn was ready to open. The brothers had done a fine job cleaning up, Nicolas had made sure there was plenty of the best wine and ale to quench thirsts, and already subtle aromas were drifting in from the kitchen where Megan was busy. Nicolas poured himself a small glass of Argol Ruby, a fine red bottled in the vineyards just south of the town of Lowenden.

"Well done, lads. Your mother would be proud of the way you help your old Dad."

He raised the glass to his lips to hide the emotion that always came when he mentioned their mother, who had passed away two years ago. Anton felt her absence keenly in that moment. His mother had brightened the inn and their lives with her frequent laughter and gentle singing; her death had left a quietness that would settle upon the inn every night after the customers had left.

The bell above the front door tinkled as the first patron came in and all three pushed down the sad memories and drew forth smiles to present to their customer.

"Master Aine!" hailed Nicolas. "Blessings of Bealtaine be with you! Might you be needing a splash of red to set you up for this busy day?"

The village elder exhaled and mopped his brow with a cotton handkerchief. "Blessings of Bealtaine be with you too, Nicolas, and your two fine sons."

He nodded at Anton and Cale in turn. "A half of Green Wisp, if you please. I fear wine won't quench my dry throat" he said as he approached the counter.

Master Aine was dressed like all of them with his tunic and bracae but differed in that he wore a cloak, striped with purple and green and fastened by a richly coloured wooden brooch. The torc around his neck signalled he was a village Master. It was a carefully crafted piece of silver but had tarnished, losing its shine.

Nicolas pulled the ale for Master Aine and set the wooden cup before the elder, who moved to place a copper by it. Nicolas held out a hand. "Please, Master, permit me to show a small kindness this day." The Master put his copper away, thanked Nicolas and took a deep quaff.

"Ah, I swear the Green Wisp tastes better here than in Argyllan."

Cale spoke up.

"It's the taste of home, Master."

Aine nodded, taking another swig. "Won't dispute that, young Cale. Fallowden is a good home and home to good people. Cheers!" Master Aine downed the last of the ale, wiped his mouth with his handkerchief and sighed.

"Nicolas, what do you hear about the wider realm?"

Nicolas placed his hands on the counter and shook his head. Master Aine spoke again.

"Forgive me, perhaps this is a topic best left for another day."

Nicolas shook his head again but this time it was in a friendly manner.

"No, no, Master Aine, we are worried for sure. A minstrel was in last night, passing through from Meridia on his way back to Argyllan and he spoke of a large force gathering there. Is Rencarro going to war, so I asked him. The fellow didn't think Rencarro would make an aggressive move. So I pressed, *why the mustering?* The man looked at me and he seemed a bit afraid, which of course sent a chill or two through me. Then he says, I just hope nothing comes down the River Freo from the Western Sea." Nicolas let that hang in the air.

Anton felt the festival spirit suddenly drain from the room. He saw Cale staring at the floor and Master Aine frowning in obvious consternation. Nicolas sucked in through his teeth.

"Freo" muttered Master Aine.

Anton looked to his father. "Father, we'll be alright, won't we?"

Master Aine responded to Anton's question.

"Anton, I fear there are worrying times ahead, but I also know that the people round here, and down in Lowenden, and then all the folks in Argyllan, we are a strong bunch and can band together in times of need. If some rum folk do come down the Freo, looking to steal some wares and cause trouble, we'll make sure we send them packing." He spoke bravely but it didn't ease Anton's worries entirely. He knew the people in this region were not fighters.

Nicolas added to the Master's words. "And nobody would be foolish enough to start anything here, what with Lord Rencarro being our neighbour."

"And what if Rencarro is leading all those men off to a war in the east?" asked Cale, destroying the feeling of safety Nicolas had given them with his comment.

Anton wanted to say something, something that would give them all hope and more than that, something to lend support to his father. But he had nothing. He wished he had talked to that minstrel though. He could have learned something and gained a story to tell Emiren.

Silence settled in the tap-room of the inn, each man lost in his thoughts. Master Aine coughed and stood to leave.

"Let us enjoy Bealtaine, my friends. Today is a day of joy. Leave our worries for the morrow" he said cheerily but his voice was lacking in conviction. He waved a farewell and moved to the door, where he was almost bowled over by the storm of auburn hair and hunter green coat that suddenly flew into the inn.

"Hey there now, Mistress Emiren" the Master cried, finding his balance. "You nearly finished my day of merry-making before it had begun."

Emiren stopped dead, composed herself and apologised.

"Forgive me, Master Aine. I feel like the Spirits are swirling inside me today. Blessings of Bealtaine be with you!" she cried and gave the old man a big hug. He laughed with the moment.

"A thousand blessings be with you, young lady. You bring

light wherever you go."

He waved farewell a second time and this time made it out the door, all the while chuckling to himself.

Anton marvelled at Emiren's ability to dispel all the fear and anxiety that had been hanging in their midst not three moments ago. Her natural energy and boundless enthusiasm for life was infectious. And greatly alluring.

"Mr Giestarn, Cale, blessings to you."

Emiren had become suddenly shy. Anton wondered if she'd perhaps expected he would be alone in here. Anton knew that Emiren sometimes didn't think much before acting.

Nicolas smiled and poured a half of a half of Green Wisp.

"Here Emiren, wash the dust out."

Emiren grinned sheepishly, accepting the cup. She downed the small measure in one and let out a huge gasp of pleasure. Her eyes were so alive and almost shining as she cried, "Ah, Mr. Giestarn, your inn has the finest ale in Fallowden."

"Only inn in Fallowden" quipped Cale.

Nicolas adopted a mock frown and Emiren giggled. Anton felt a pang of jealousy that his brother had made Emiren laugh so easily.

"The finest ale in all Ragnekai then!" she said, raising the cup in the air.

"You must have been on one almighty pilgrimage of ale to know that."

Cale again. Emiren laughed louder than before and punched Anton's brother on the arm. Cale also laughed until he looked at Anton. He excused himself and wandered out to the kitchen. Anton relaxed his jaw, suddenly aware he was clenching it. He felt guilty. He felt foolish.

"Anton, come with me to see the Bealtaine bonfire being lit!"

"I'm sorry, Emi, there's so much to…"

"Be off with you, lad" interrupted Nicolas, a gentle smile upon his face. "Just be back before the midday bell as that's when things will erupt here. Go on, enjoy yourselves."

Anton wanted to hug his father and tell him he had just made him the happiest lad in the entire realm. He worried his emotions would spill if he did though so whispered a thank you and turned to Emiren.

"Come on!" she said, grabbing his hand and pulling him out the door. Anton felt as if he was caught up in a wind that would never stop but would roar through mountain passes and over oceans alike. Emiren truly was a force of nature.

Emiren let his hand go when they were outside the inn, much to Anton's disappointment, and they walked on towards the village square. They passed villagers bustling here and there, everyone crying greetings to each other and wishing blessings. Emiren seemed to absorb the cheer of those they passed, becoming more beautiful with each step. Anton sucked in a deep breath, telling himself to keep his feet on the ground.

The village square was crowded but the two of them weaved through the press until the fire-pit lay before them. Carefully cut branches filled the pit, kindling peeking out. A drumbeat suddenly began and Anton's excitement started building. Chatter faded away as the drums put out a steady rhythm. The beat seemed to infuse the villagers with a burst of emotion and many grabbed each other's hands. Anton gradually moved his left-hand outwards, searching for Emiren's. Only to find she wasn't there.

Emiren had disappeared from his side. Anton wondered if he was destined to be forever losing her. He searched the crowd of villagers, trying to find where she had dashed off to. He was still peering around when the villagers parted on the opposite side of the fire-pit. Through the divide came Emiren, Sister Jessa, Loranna and Banseth. They were carrying a litter upon which lay Janwarin. Anton felt a lump in his throat as he saw how weak and frail the old man had become. And he felt a surge of feeling for Emiren, seeing her care for this man with the compassion she possessed in abundance. Anton stared at her and knew he loved her. Emiren was a sun that rose on his day and a moon that he could gaze upon every night.

The young man from Fallowden watched as the four carriers

set the litter down and helped Janwarin to a sitting position. Loranna then produced a flint and tinder, and proceeded to light a torch Banseth had ready. The spark caught and the torch eased into a gentle flame. Janwarin said something to Sister Jessa, who motioned to Emiren and they helped the sickly man stand.

Janwarin then whispered into Emiren's ear. The crowd was now hushed, waiting upon the words of this most respected of their people.

Emiren called out in a voice as clear as spring. "Master Janwarin apologises but he says you've taken his breath away."

The crowd laughed good-naturedly.

"So he says I should speak for him. He says he didn't want to ask Banseth because…" Emiren leaned in more closely to Janwarin and Anton appreciated the little show they were creating here.

"He's as deaf as an oak tree!?" cried Emiren in mock surprise.

Banseth cupped his free hand to his ear. "Is someone speaking?"

The villagers roared with laughter, the guffaws becoming harder as Loranna pretended to clean out Banseth's ears with her fingers.

Emiren called out again. "Friends!"

Janwarin smiled and whispered in her ear again.

"Blessings be upon you all on this special day!"

The crowd clapped and nodded with enthusiasm, sharing comments with each other and gripping shoulders of those next to them.

"Strange winds are blowing through the realm."

The murmuring quieted down and smiles fell from the faces of the people of Fallowden. Anton spotted Quint and Megari, Emiren's parents, over to the left. Quint had his arm round his wife and she was leaning into him. Anton hoped that could one day be himself and Emiren.

"I may not be with you in the days to come…" Emiren's voice cracked with emotion as she repeated Janwarin's words.

"But I know the Spirits will guide you all and whatever storm approaches, Fallowden will see the sun pierce the dark clouds." Tears were running down Emiren's cheeks.

Janwarin gestured for Banseth to hand him the torch. Then he murmured some more words to his Voice on this day.

Emiren took a deep breath and cried out, "Let the Bealtaine fire be lit!"

Janwarin tossed the torch with what little strength he still possessed and it twirled into the pit, instantly catching the kindling. A crackling sound erupted and flames began to dance. The bonfire was soon snapping and sending cinders up into the air. The villagers clapped and cheered. A fiddler started a jig and a piper joined her.

Anton stared into the flames, thoughts about his future swirling.

"What did you think?"

Anton jumped. Emiren was at his side. "Shades, Emiren, how do you do it? You appear and disappear like a forest sprite from the old stories."

"Maybe I am" she giggled. "But you are forever day-dreaming, Anton."

Her face became serious. "What did you think though? I didn't want to tell you Janwarin would light the fire. We wanted it to be a surprise for everyone and to give Janwarin what might be his last chance to see all his friends together." She seemed almost bashful to Anton.

"You were...it was beautiful, Emiren."

Anton almost stumbled backwards as she hugged him. "Thank you" she whispered in his ear. "You are such a good friend."

His heart pounded in his chest as she pulled back. He felt dizzy with the atmosphere of the festival and the incredible nature of this young lady standing before him.

"Come on, let's get in the line so we can jump the fire!" she cried with excitement.

And Anton was once again swept up in the tempest whirling

around her. He laughed despite himself.

"I'll never meet another like you, Emiren" he shouted out as she pulled him through the crowd. He wasn't sure if she had heard him or not, but he didn't dwell on it. He sensed something had shifted in the world and he was about to take his first steps upon a new path.

Ch 7

Rencarro

The march around the north tip of the Widow's Teeth had been a pleasant one, with clear skies and spring winds taking away some of the heat from the bright sun. The thought of conflict was far from the minds of the soldiers. Or that was how it seemed to Rencarro as he shared light banter with his men while they marched and he trotted up and down the lines on his mare.

There had been some initial grumblings when the soldiers had been informed they were heading to Argyllan to protect the people there from raiding. This obviously didn't conjure up as much excitement as the idea of striking out east and then north to conquer Bregustol. Rencarro felt sure though that, as they marched farther away from the capital and of course away from the Helligan nation, the men were counting themselves lucky. He was positive that when the blood started flowing between the Rihtgellen Kingdom and the Helligan nation, there would be a huge collective sigh of relief.

They were in sight of Argyllan's eastern gate now and Rencarro was surprised to see quite a crowd gathered before the city walls. He knew word would have reached them of the Meridian force's imminent arrival but he hadn't been expecting any kind of warm welcome. Rencarro had been prepared for a bit of delicate diplomacy but here he was looking upon the people of Argyllan waving and cheering. *This will boost the men's morale,* he thought.

Rencarro felt a sudden urge to rear his steed and brandish his spear in the air. It would have probably received a cheer, but he needed to set a certain mood from the onset. He needed to act with a particular humbleness hereon and not give the people of

Argyllan any reason to think the Meridians had any ambitions for the city. So he cantered on, his jaw set and no smile upon his lips. Coming smartly to a halt, he raised his fist, praying that his men would immediately see the signal and obey the order. He heard the forward lines halt with a near-perfect stamp and then orders shouted back.

Impressive. There is potential here.

A man dressed in a pale blue overcoat with a gold-chain around his neck and grey hair receding with age, stepped forward from the others. Rencarro recognised the mayor of Argyllan, Michel Morel. The man was no fool but Rencarro had sensed no strength of character in him when they had met the previous year.

Rencarro edged his horse on a few more yards, then dismounted and without stopping strode over to Morel. He could see worry on the man's face and felt confident the plan had a good foundation in this.

"Mr. Mayor" said Rencarro, offering his hand.

Morel took it and Rencarro was satisfied with the lack of grip.

"Lord Rencarro, welcome to Argyllan."

There was a bit of murmuring behind him but the soldiers made no move otherwise, standing smartly to attention. Rencarro had made it clear to his captains that the first impression was important and to make sure all soldiers under their commands took pride in the colours they wore today. This was the sort of careful tact of which he knew his son Marcus was simply incapable. He hoped things would go smoothly to the south.

"I apologise for the arrival of so many soldiers to your fair city, Mayor Morel. It must be unsettling seeing so much steel approaching Argyllan. These are worrying times however."

The Argyllan mayor shook his head. "Lord Rencarro, your presence here will calm the nerves of our people. Rumours are abound. Some saying Throskaur long-boats have been sighted, prowling along the coast" Morel said anxiously.

Rencarro smiled inwardly. Tacet and his fellow Velox Riders

had done their work well indeed.

The mayor continued. "Even more worrying are whispers that the realm is cracking and stronger cities will look to move on their smaller neighbours. A question that seems to have spread like the plague here is what will Westhealfe do now that Sedmund is dead and nobody seems to know who rules the realm."

Rencarro wanted to laugh at the irony but kept his face a mask of concern. He set a hand on Morel's shoulder. "I pray the talk is idle and the threat just a shadow in all our minds." He paused for effect. "Yet we would be foolish to dismiss these rumours completely. There is a history of conflict in this realm. It may be many years in the past, but some do not forget" he said grimly. Fear flickered in the man's eyes and the lord knew he could push this farther.

"The city of Meridia gives us strong walls to the east, hopefully warning the Helligan nation from engaging in any foolhardy ideas of expanding their borders. But you will forgive me if I say the port of Argyllan will make neither raiders nor Westhealfe tremble."

Morel nodded and Rencarro continued, sowing the seeds.

"And yet Argyllan is a prize in the eyes of many. To Argyllan comes trade from the Western Sea and the River Freo, and also commerce from the north west. We cannot just *hope* nobody is tempted."

Rencarro could see he had the man now, well and truly. Morel was not a man to think in terms of a city's strategic value, nor was he one to even consider taking anything by force. The man looked as if he were imagining every terrible possibility coming to pass.

Rencarro looked back at the waiting Meridians. "Mayor Morel, I don't like the idea of heavy boots trampling in your city, but we must remove any notion of Argyllan being an easy target. Therefore, I would ask your permission for my men to initially camp here outside your walls but if quarters could be found for as many as possible within the city itself…" He let the sentence hang for a moment, then continued. "I feel we should make our presence known."

Rencarro knew the man was scared but was surprised at how swiftly he responded.

"Yes, yes, Lord Rencarro" he practically spluttered, a shade of relief coming to his slightly portly face. "You are welcome here and we cannot tell you how much we appreciate your strength in these dark times."

Dark times, mused Rencarro. *That's a quick step up from worrying times.* A thought suddenly crossed his mind that Morel might not be the man he needed to organise the settling of his troops.

As if in answer to this, Morel gestured for another man to come forward. "This is Camran. He is the city's quartermaster. He will see to all your needs."

Rencarro quickly took in the measure of the man. Not as tall as Rencarro but of a tough build, unlike the mayor. His black hair, streaked with grey was tied back, and his dark green eyes were set under heavy eye-brows on a face that was no stranger to the sun and wind. His nose was bent, possibly from a brawl, although he did not strike Rencarro as a violent man in the slightest. He was dressed in a brown leather jerkin and faded hosen. The man offered his hand and Rencarro was satisfied this time that there was a strong grip.

"An honour to finally meet you, Lord Rencarro."

The man called Camran spoke with a confidence but no hint of arrogance. Rencarro was pleased. This was a man he could work with. Mayor Morel had already withdrawn and was talking in a low voice to who Rencarro presumed to be councillors.

"Well met, Camran. I can see Mayor Morel has the utmost confidence in you so you are the man I would look to this day. I have a lot of foot-sore troops to placate."

Camran smiled gently and Rencarro realised he had to be careful. This quartermaster was not one to be lulled with flattery. Rencarro hoped he wasn't *too* perceptive.

79

"Let's get started" said the Argyllan good-naturedly, motioning for some of his own men to come forward.

Rencarro nodded and turned to the waiting Meridians. "Set up camp!" he shouted, "And have a care how you clumsy oafs go about your business! You wear the uniform of a Meridian soldier so act like one! No rations for any fool who thinks this is a day of rest."

Rencarro turned back to Camran and offered a slight smile and raised eye-brow. Camran hid his grin behind a hand and started barking out orders himself.

The grassy area before the city walls became a hive of activity with sergeants liaising with Camran's men and then directing soldiers here and there. People flowed in and out of the city's gates, and the skeleton of a Meridian camp soon became visible. The bustle was slightly chaotic to the eyes but there was an order to it, and no time was being wasted.

When everything seemed to be in hand, Camran approached Rencarro and coughed politely.

"Perhaps my lord could spare time for a quick word in my office before Mayor Morel invites you to the City Hall for some formalities."

"Of course. Lead the way." Rencarro beckoned to a Meridian officer. "Atticus, keep an eye on things here. Tell Julius to go on ahead with the mayor. I will be along soon. And have someone take Amacum to be stabled."

Atticus saluted smartly and moved off to carry out his orders.

Camran gestured to the gate and the two walked through, with many an Argyllan looking their way. Rencarro was pleased to notice that Camran wasn't milking his association with the Lord of Meridia. He seemed eager to just get on with the task in hand and didn't stop to introduce Rencarro to his fellow residents.

Camran's office was just inside the gate, not ten yards from the eastern wall. It was two stories and well built. Timber beams crisscrossed walls that once might have been white but were now a dull colour difficult to describe. Camran opened the door and motioned for Rencarro to enter. Inside was simple but tidy. Rencarro could see Camran was a practical man with no need for aesthetics, much like himself.

"Please take a seat, my lord."

"Please dispense with the formalities when it is just the two of us, Camran." Rencarro smiled. "I think I am a man much like yourself, in that I want to get a job done and have little time for pomp and ceremony."

Camran chuckled. "I was thinking the same thing."

The quartermaster took out a bottle from behind his desk and two glasses, so clean they were almost sparkling Rencarro noted.

"A drop of rum…" Camran looked up. "Rencarro?" He grimaced, then laughed. Rencarro laughed with him.

Camran spoke again. "I have to admit though that a bit of formality helps sometimes. Feels just a tad strange saying your name…my lord."

"Ha! True indeed." Rencarro accepted the rum and raised his glass. "Well, if the winds favour us, all this doom and gloom will just fade away and this will be the first rum of many you and I share."

Camran raised his glass too and then they knocked the rum back. It was a fine rum, although Rencarro knew he was no expert. There was a deep taste of vanilla but it wasn't overly sweet. And gave a good burning sensation in the throat. Camran poured another shot.

"Sun's Flame, they call it. Comes from the Radiant Isles far to the south west. We get the odd trader coming up from there in the autumn. Most of the year though they simply can't sail the Western Sea due to those ungodly storms."

"Damn those storms" remarked Rencarro as he downed the second shot.

"So, I must ask, my lord," began Camran, "what is really happening out there in the realm?"

Rencarro knew this conversation would be a more crucial one than any to come with the mayor. If he could set a small fire of fear within Camran but also induce the feeling that the quartermaster was in control and not fanning the flames, as Morel was bound to do, he would lay some important groundwork for the coming months. An unsuspecting ally in the Meridian plan to effectively annex the south west region.

"The realm does indeed stand on thin ice at present."

Camran nodded grimly, as if his own appraisal of the situation had been confirmed.

"But we are certainly not in a state of open war" remarked Rencarro. He sighed. "I won't lie to you. The politics of kings and lords frustrate me. There is a great deal of ambition mixed with deceit behind the closed doors of the High King's palace in Bregustol. I believe Sedmund was a steady hand and calmed the various factions within court."

Rencarro paused to take a sip of rum, peering at Camran as he did so. The quartermaster seemed greatly interested in this insight into a world he obviously thought about but had never experienced.

"General Torbal is a good man."

"You have met the King's Shield?!" Camran was clearly in awe of Torbal.

"A number of times. And yes, his reputation is well-deserved."

Camran's eyes were wide. Something bit deep within Rencarro. The quartermaster had been polite to him outside when they met but he obviously did not see the Meridian ruler in the same league as Torbal. Rencarro moved on with the conversation.

"When I visited Bregustol at the turn of the year to attend an annual council, Sedmund was in rude health. His relatively swift demise from illness is cause for concern. And questions. Though the rumour that he was poisoned by Ulla is likely malicious, and dangerous, gossip."

He sucked in air between his teeth, making a thin, whistling sound.

"But we have no way to know for sure. Is Orben about to lead the Helligan nation in a mad grab for the capital and in so doing, plunge the realm into an era of blood-shed?"

Camran was silent. The glory seen in a general like Torbal was perhaps tempered by the realisation that battles were soaked in the blood of men. Rencarro was well aware how the songs and stories of war tended to leave out the unpleasant details. He only had to look to his own son, Marcus, to see the unfortunate consequences of this.

"And while I have not heard first-hand of these sightings of Throskaur longboats, I do know that pirates see opportunity in a realm that is cracking." Rencarro placed his cup on the desk and asked if he might have a last drop before heading off to meet the mayor.

"Of course, my lord." Camran looked troubled as he poured. Rencarro was pleased. The quartermaster voiced his thoughts.

"The folk here, myself included, know nothing of war. The realm seemed so secure with the king being…" Camran looked up. "I mean, the *High* King."

Rencarro smiled conspiratorially. "Be at ease. Outside of diplomacy, few use the full title." He hoped Camran would take this morsel of information as a sign of trust.

Camran gazed out the window. "This city would not do well if raiders were to come calling. That is, if your men weren't here." Camran turned to look at the Meridian ruler. "Praise the Spirits, Lord Rencarro, I think Argyllan will sleep sound at night under your protection."

"That is my hope."

"Another shot?"

"Thank you, but I must keep a clear head. A lot to do if my men are to integrate themselves here without too much disturbance to the good folk."

Rencarro stood and offered his hand.

"My thanks, Camran. For the rum and the knowledge that you are a man I can rely on in whatever lies ahead."

The quartermaster took the outstretched hand and they shook firmly. Rencarro sensed he had lit a spark of pride in the man, and perhaps some courage. But more importantly, he'd given Camran much reason to want the Meridians here in Argyllan. Rencarro said farewell and left the quartermaster's office, a faint smile on his lips.

Ch 8

Anton

3rd Day of Maia, Eight Days After Sedmund's Death

As he navigated his way through Argol Forest, Anton still felt a thrill from his time with Emiren at the Bealtaine Festival two days ago. It had been like a dream for him, dancing with this girl whose soul seemed to be bursting with the Spirits' light. Yesterday he had been cleaning up the inn with his father and brother, but his mind had been whirring away, reliving those precious moments. He knew Cale had noticed but his brother hadn't teased him at all. Maybe Cale saw that something was growing between himself and Emiren.

Last night, as Anton lay in bed unable to sleep, he'd let his imagination run wild with possibility. And then he had endeavoured to think up some ruse to make it all a reality. He needed to make Emiren see him in a different light, more than just Anton the Friend. He wanted her to take him seriously, look upon him as a man, rather than a lad.

The tidings of Meridian soldiers arriving at Lowenden had been of great interest in the day, but he had suddenly latched upon this news and viewed it from a different angle last night, seeing an opportunity. He had literally jumped out of bed and started pacing the room. Cale had woken up and told him to get to sleep or he would throw the bucket of dregs over him in the morning. Anton had grinned and climbed back into bed.

And now here he was, moving stealthily through Argol, on his way to Lowenden. He was embarking on a little adventure that would be a bit of fun in itself and could serve as a sign Anton was more than just an innkeeper's son. A little conversation with some Meridian soldiers, hopefully some banter, and an exciting story to take back to Emiren. If he could find out something about what was going on in the realm, if he could learn about the wider world beyond their village, if he could present himself as more than just an innkeeper's son, then maybe he might light a spark within Emiren. Part of him thought the notion was stupid but the promise of what could be flooded him and he ignored the doubts.

As he weaved his way through the trees, trying to use relatively untrodden paths, he recalled the conversation he had with his father yesterday afternoon after the news had arrived of the Meridian soldiers coming to Lowenden.

His father had told Anton and Cale that the troops were a reassurance but also a sign that the realm was teetering on the brink. His father had desperately hoped a new ruler would step forward in Bregustol and things would settle. But he'd also voiced his fear that the Helligan nation would deem the time right to embark upon a path of vengeance.

Anton said nothing at the time but part of him felt any kind of conflict would be well away up in the north-east. If the Meridians were here, then the Argol region was surely safe from the pirates that supposedly dwelt on the Barren Isles. Anton had talked with Cale later that evening, voicing his thoughts but Cale had not shared his optimistic outlook.

"Conflict has a habit of spilling over edges" his brother had remarked. Anton was aware his brother had read far more history than he had himself but simply refused to believe this gloomy perspective. He knew this was because he didn't want anything to ruin his newfound hopes of becoming more than friends with Emiren.

As Anton neared Lowenden, he stopped to consider how best to approach the town and the reported Meridian camp. He was still thinking when he heard voices ahead. Two male voices he reckoned. In the forest, not too far ahead.

A tingle rose within him. This was it. A bit of careful spying on Meridian soldiers. He hoped it wasn't just two woodsmen about their work. That would be embarrassing, going back to Emiren and telling her what a couple of fellows from Lowenden were going to drink that evening in their local inn.

Anton moved deeper into the forest, with the intent of circling round the voices and coming at them from an area of more cover. He now appreciated all the little things Emiren had taught him about woodcraft and moving with stealth through Argol. He kept the voices, barely audible, to his left and picked his way through undergrowth, carefully holding branches up instead of just barging through.

He was closer now and could hear the men more clearly. The language being spoken certainly wasn't the common tongue. It was the Meridian language he realised with excitement. Surely he had stumbled across a couple of soldiers. He could speak some Meridian, although he doubted his accent was up to much. With traders drinking at their inn, his father had insisted both he and Cale try to learn the language of their neighbour. Nicolas had also tried to teach them basic greetings in the Helligan language and even some Tarakan words but neither Anton nor Cale showed much aptitude for languages. Emiren was fairly fluent in the Meridian language and it was probably down to her efforts that Anton understood as much as he did.

Anton focused again on the voices and where they were. If he could ingratiate himself to these Meridians by making his greeting in their language, maybe they would spare him some of their time.

He caught a glimpse of movement and ducked down, suddenly feeling his confidence drain. He peered through the trees and could make out two men standing facing each other. It was difficult to be sure but it looked like they were both wearing the colours of Meridia. He felt a surge of excitement as he spotted what could only be a sword at one man's waist. Definitely Meridian soldiers but why were they out here by themselves?

For a moment Anton wished Emiren were here to share this little adventure with him but then reminded himself that would defeat the whole purpose of his escapade. He strained his ears to hear what they were saying but found his linguistic skills were not so good.

Something villagers something something don't know something maybe a name.

A cackling laugh from the second man.

Something your father something Argyllan.

The first speaker.

The plan something good, definitely a name, something like Silvans.

The second man, the one who had laughed.

Anton was taken aback by the curse word he heard next, one he remembered all too well. Cale had taught it to him and they had sniggered about it for hours, like all boys do when they learn a naughty word.

Stupid arse-eater something Meridia something.

Were they talking about the people of the Argol region, Anton wondered with resentment. He was surprised to hear what sounded like arrogance. Anton supposed Lowenden must seem quaint and full of country bumpkins to the city folk of Meridia. This adventure was not turning out to be much fun. The laughing man spoke again.

Argyllan something my father something, Lowenden stinks something shit.

Now anger was truly rising in Anton. Who did they think they were to speak crudely about his homeland? The likelihood of him sharing any good-natured banter with these soldiers seemed pretty much non-existent. He sighed, disappointed that his grand plan for winning Emiren's affections was now dust in the wind.

Not much of a plan to begin with really.

The crunching of twigs startled him. The men were moving and coming this way. Anton panicked and rose from where he had concealed himself. He turned to head back but caught his foot in a root and tripped, and the crunch and grunt of him falling into brush shattered the relative silence of the forest.

"Ho there!" came a voice, speaking in the common tongue.

"Who goes there?" came the other.

"Draw your sword Marcus!" hissed the first voice.

Ch 9

Emiren

Emiren could not understand why Anton had headed off into Argol without her. She had spotted her friend plunging into the forest as she was returning from collecting more herbs for the hospice. She knew she had her head in the tree-tops at times but was well aware Anton didn't love the forest the way she did. He came more because she asked him to and that was something she appreciated. Anton was a true friend and she had felt that so deeply at the Bealtaine Festival. So, as she entered Argol at the exact spot he had a short time earlier, she wondered what he was up to.

The likeliest explanation was that Anton was intrigued by the news of Meridian soldiers arriving to the south and was going down to Lowenden for a closer look, judging by the direction he had taken. But then why had he come through Argol and not taken the open road skirting the forest? She returned her attention to following his tracks through Argol, which was not difficult. Anton had learned a thing or two about moving through the forest with care but was still a drunken ox compared to her. She smiled despite herself, seeing where he had taken an overgrown side-path missing the larger, more navigable path just a few yards away. She stopped. Emiren suddenly considered the possibility he was trying to move in secret.

Is he meeting someone?

This made her feel cold inside. She felt silly for what she presumed might be jealousy. If Anton had a lover, it was none of her business. But then again, she felt it was. They were such close friends, it would be wrong of him to keep something so important from her. She pressed on, emotions swirling inside.

She would find him and tell him he didn't have to hide anything from her. But her first thought spurred another one.

What if he's making love with this girl in the forest?

She blushed hard at that yet continued her tracking. It was easy to follow his path. But her pace had faltered, now the thought of catching him in a girl's arms had swamped her mind. It was clear he had been heading towards Lowenden so that meant the theory he was going to have a look at these Meridians soldiers still held. Of course, his lover might be a girl from the town, which would explain why Emiren knew nothing about it. She pressed on, an anxious feeling growing in the pit of her stomach. If Anton did indeed have a lover and she found out about it, would it change their relationship? It saddened her to imagine a world where Anton was not around for her to tease and walk with.

She had been walking a while and was lost in thoughts when she suddenly realised she was close to Lowenden now, but had still seen no sign of Anton.

Then Emiren heard the voice. It was a man's voice but not Anton's. A sense of unease gripped her as she moved quietly towards whoever was there. Emiren saw an area of light ahead which she knew to be a clearing. She saw movement and slowed her approach even more.

The sight that greeted her eyes as she peered round the trunk of a maple tree made her gasp. Anton was there in the clearing. A man in light armour, a sword in a scabbard strapped to his waist, was with Anton. And then there was the body. Another man lay on the forest floor, unmoving, a mess of blood leaking from somewhere and colouring the grass a sickly reddish-brown. Emiren's whole body tensed. Her stomach lurched and it was all she could to do to stop herself vomiting. She pressed herself against the trunk and breathed slowly. The auburn-haired girl tried to understand what she was seeing but couldn't fathom what had happened here. The man had one arm round Anton's shoulder as if he were comforting him.

"Rest easy, my lad. Seeing a dead body can shock even the

hardiest of men."

The man was speaking to Anton in a soothing tone. Anton himself seemed to be shaking and terrified. Emiren felt the same fear and it paralysed her.

"It is unfortunate" the man went on, "that you killed this brave soldier."

Anton shook himself from the man's arm, turning to face him. In doing so, the young man's own body obscured Emiren's view of the older man. She heard Anton's voice but it wasn't clear. His voice was carrying in the opposite direction to Emiren and he trembled as he spoke.

"What?! I never… It was…"

"An accident?" The man cut him off. "Yes, an accident. Something unintended." The man reached out an arm and placed it on Anton's shoulder again. Emiren felt a chill. She couldn't believe Anton had killed the fallen soldier. Her mind swirled as she tried to understand what could have possibly occurred. The men were obviously Meridian soldiers but what had they been doing within the forest and why was Anton with them?

The man continued, his voice hardening. "And only you and I know."

What happened next were moments seared together in one horrific passage of time. Emiren saw the flash of a blade in the man's other hand. He brought the dagger around, changing his grip so the weapon pointed down. He pulled Anton closer. She didn't move. She couldn't. Even as he plunged the blade into Anton's neck just above the collarbone.

Only then did she scream.

The man spun round to where she was, letting Anton collapse to the forest floor to join the other dead soul. He held up a hand, palm outwards. He carefully and slowly slid the dagger back into a sheath at his waist, still bloodied with the life of her friend. Then both hands were up in a gesture that would have spoken peace were it not for what Emiren had just witnessed.

"No…" she croaked, her voice lost in disbelief and grief. She stepped into the clearing on legs that were close to folding, stopping only a few yards now from the Meridian soldier and her fallen friend. "No…" she whispered, the reality of where she was blurring with hideous images crashing through her mind.

"Peace, girl. You are safe now. The assassin is dead. There is no danger." As he spoke, the man edged closer to Emiren. Emiren looked to where Anton lay, tears spilling from her eyes.

"Anton…" she choked.

The Meridian looked at her, glanced back at Anton's body, and then his eyes fixed upon her. His hands dropped to his side and his posture changed.

"Shit" he muttered. "A friend no doubt."

He seemed to be about to turn away and leave the clearing but he suddenly reversed his stance and sprang at her.

Instinct had kicked in the moment he gave up the pretence, and Emiren had tensed her own body to move. As he leapt towards her, she bolted back through the trees. She sped past the maple, ducked a low-hanging branch from another, weaved past a thick oak, and leapt a fungi-infested stump. She could hear him behind her, crashing through the forest.

Death had never felt so close before. She had never felt its cold breath on her neck. Emiren had never had to run for her life.

She knew she was pulling away from him, such was her skill in navigating the Forest of Argol. But she couldn't keep running forever. She tried to think but the only thing in her mind was, *Don't stop.*

Then she saw it. An old hiding place of hers. Brother Beech she had named him. She increased her stride, then leapt up and grabbed a branch. Swinging herself up, she climbed swiftly another few feet, then tucked herself into a hollow area of the tree. She was surprised she could still fit in the space as it must have been a few years since last she hid here. Curling up, she ceased all movement of her body. Only her breathing, ragged and short. She tried to calm herself. The memory of Anton's unmoving body in her mind's eye made her clench her eyes against hot tears.

"Girl!"

The shout was loud; close by. Emiren froze, trying to will all sound from around her to fade into nothingness.

Please don't find me. Please Spirits protect me.

She realised she was sobbing quietly and a blabbering of low noise was coming from her mouth. She clamped her hands to her mouth and gritted her teeth, trying to end all sound. Her eyes burned from the tears that flooded out.

"You would be wise to come out" the man said. "There need not be any more blood spilt today."

Emiren didn't believe a word. She felt an insidious, creeping fear as she heard him approaching her tree. Suddenly there was a whooshing sound and a crash of dry wood splintering. Then a curse muttered. Was he probing the woodland with his deadly blade? Emiren prayed to the Spirits again that the man's sword or bloody dagger would not suddenly pierce the bark around her. She was up high though and she doubted the man could so easily climb to where she was, even if he knew which tree she had ensconced herself within.

New sounds filtered through the forest from the direction Emiren had fled. More than one person was approaching. Then shouts and calls in the Meridian language. Emiren was fairly fluent but her current state of anguish suppressed her comprehension to some degree. She could only make out some of what was said.

"General! Where are you?"

"Lord Sylvanus. Are you safe?"

"We heard a scream."

"Lord Marcus has been killed. General!"

Emiren heard her pursuer, this general, curse again. And then a strange sound. A grunt and a gasp, and then something landing in the undergrowth beyond Emiren. She didn't dare peek out but was confused what had happened to the man.

Then she jumped as his voice rang out.

"Here! I am here." The man's voice was almost gasping, as if he were in pain.

The clumsy breaking of undergrowth grew louder and voices rang out.

"General! What has happened?"

There was more crashing of heavy boots and bodies through Argol. Emiren started to pray to the Spirits, overwhelmed by a terror and a deep sadness that she would never see her parents again.

"Yes, yes. Here. I am here."

Emiren heard the newcomers reach where she presumed the man, Anton's killer, to be.

The man who had chased her said more but it was too quick for her to understand. Another voice said something about death, presumably repeating their discovery of two dead bodies.

Anton.

It bit deep within her, a horrible agony as the image of seeing her friend being murdered coursed through her mind.

"Be careful, men" the general cautioned down below, "There is another assassin close."

Assassin?!

The Meridian word was too close to the common word for Emiren to have been mistaken. This general was telling his men she was an assassin. Emiren felt anger rise and mingle with her fear. The cold-hearted cunning and sheer falsity of the Meridian general was stoking a blaze of rage within her.

"General Sylvanus, you are wounded!" cried a voice.

"It is nothing. Marcus was not so lucky."

Emiren tried to focus on what was being said but had trouble keeping up, one reason being that this General Sylvanus was relating events that had not occurred.

Emiren heard something about a simple village boy and his girl, not being careful, assassins attacked, something about Marcus, who was presumably the dead man Emiren had seen first. Emiren couldn't take it all in. Lies upon lies and poor Anton now with the Spirits.

My sweet Anton.

The general continued below, now seemingly giving out orders. He was telling his men to search for the second assassin and he was describing Emiren's hair colour and the coat she wore. He told them she knew the forest well. She began to tremble, knowing she was now being hunted by many. The words spoken were a hideous, twisted tale, bearing no resemblance to the truth. She clenched her fists so tightly they went numb.

Spirits, make them see his falseness.

"Yes, my lord" said one, and Emiren heard someone move off, shouting commands to presumably other soldiers farther away. The next thing she heard quelled the fire of anger in her and gave cold, icy breath to her fear. The general called out after the soldiers. The words were spoken clearly and with no room for argument.

"These assassins are deadly. Sent by Orben I believe. Kill her."

All Emiren could do was hold herself and beg the Spirits to conceal her in this hiding place. She heard him speak again to more soldiers, reckoning he was standing not more than five yards away and the same distance going down. Her ears took in the words, but her mind just let them dissolve before they were understood. She was in a void now, her whole sense of reality fading. She felt as if her death was upon her and all she could do was wait for its unforgiving touch.

Acknowledging responses from the other men followed the general's commands and then Emiren heard them hurrying away. Emiren was sure *he* was still there though. Something inside her wanted to leap from the tree and rake his eyes out, but it was as if she had given in to the merciless events that had erupted this day. She curled herself tighter and waited. Waiting for the end. Finally she heard him move off but also heard other voices nearby. Soldiers searching. She waited.

It was dark when Emiren awoke. She couldn't believe she had fallen asleep in this tree. Then it came flooding back. She moaned and cried, this time making no effort to hide her sobs. Anton was dead. The truth of it made her stomach ache and her head pound. Emiren tried to breathe more deeply and slow her racing heartbeat. She focused on the sounds of Argol, listening to the tiny rustles of nocturnal wildlife. It managed to calm her and she was able to think. She needed to get home and tell her parents what had happened, and warn Fallowden that these Meridians were not so noble. Why would they come to protect the Argol region and then murder poor Anton? It didn't make sense.

The man's face returned to her mind. And his name. Sylvanus. She felt a surge of unbridled hatred for the murderer of her friend. She must get word to her parents so that this man could be brought to justice. Yet what power would the people of her village have against trained soldiers?

Her spiralling thoughts were interrupted by a sound that was definitely not a badger or a fox. It was something bigger. A soldier? Emiren stiffened and tried to sink into the tree itself. Something or someone was coming closer.

She hugged herself, the terror once again threatening to overwhelm her. Whatever it was stopped at the point Emiren knew must be almost directly below her. There was a sniffing. Then a low growl. Emiren sat up and looked out and down. "Tarak!"

She could see the wolf's eyes and a rough outline of his body. She scrambled out of her nook and almost fell to the forest floor, so relieved was she that Tarak had found her.

She wrapped her arms round his neck and cried, her body shuddering with sobs. Tarak nuzzled at her neck but otherwise didn't move. He just let her pour out the tidal wave of emotion. Finally, Emiren pulled back.

"Tarak, oh Tarak. Thank the Spirits. I should have known you would find me. Mum and Da sent you to look for me? They must be so worried. Tarak, Anton…" The words caught in her throat. She couldn't say it. She hugged him again and said, "Let's go home."

The two of them set off at a very slow pace. The moon was waxing, perhaps less than a week from being full. Here and there pale white filtered through the branches, illuminating the forest floor. Even so, Emiren relied on Tarak's sure-footing and sense to lead her. She recognized the paths as they trod them but would have surely got lost without him.

Progress was slow and Emiren worried the sun would be up before they made it back to Fallowden. She wanted to get home in the dark so those soldiers wouldn't see her. If she was found before she reached Fallowden, she knew she would never look into her mother's eyes again. She shivered despite it being a mild night, feeling as if she were in a nightmare to which there was no end. Only the presence of Tarak gave her some hope that she could reach her parents and safety.

They had been moving for what seemed a long time, but she judged they had only covered two miles or so in distance. Emiren was fairly sure they were nearing the forest's borders though, which meant they could maybe move out onto easier terrain. Then she saw the shimmering wisps of orange ahead. Torches. She stopped. Tarak also stopped and turned to her. Emiren tried to quell the panic rising. The soldiers were obviously patrolling the forest borders, looking for her. How could she get past them?

She fell quietly to her knees and Tarak padded over, leaning his head on her shoulder. "What do I do?" she whispered to the wolf. "Tarak, they will kill me if they find me."

She knew he couldn't understand complex human speech but she felt he could sense some of what her words meant. Stroking his ruff, she clenched her jaw, trying to decide what to do.

It didn't take her long but she was scared to go through with it. This path would give her the best chance to avoid death at the hands of these soldiers and it would also give her the opportunity to fight back. She held Tarak's head and looked into his eyes.

"Tarak, I must go to Argyllan. Argyllan. I will find Uncle Camran. Camran." she repeated. She thought that if she could reach Argyllan before day-break, it was possible she could stay ahead of any messages sent by the Meridians. If she could reach her uncle's home, she could hide there while he got word to her parents. Then the truth would be made known to everyone.

"I need you to go home, Tarak. Home. If you go back, Mum and Da will know you found me and I am well. Please go back home, Tarak. To Mum and Da. I will go to Uncle Camran. Do you understand?"

Part of her felt this was futile but something within her gave off a glimmer of hope that somehow her parents would realise she was alive, if Tarak returned and did not howl for her.

Tarak didn't move though, staring at her with wide, amber eyes. She gently pushed him, urging him to go.

"Go, Tarak, go home. Home. Go to Mum and Da. I am going to Argyllan. Go."

Tarak seemed to understand and slowly turned. He began to move off in the general direction of the bobbing orange glows, which helped Emiren get her bearing somewhat. She quickly realised though that moving through the forest at night without Tarak would be very slow and her taking a wrong path was now a possibility. Emiren couldn't see or even hear Tarak now. She prayed to the Spirits to guide him home and further prayed her parents would understand her message.

Then she headed in what she believed to be a northerly direction, taking her away from the soldiers and their torches. She trod carefully, wary of twisting an ankle on a wicked root. Emiren kept moving but couldn't hide from the fact that without Tarak guiding her, she would never reach Argyllan before the break of dawn.

Ch 10

Torbal

A sight for tired eyes, General" said Nerian, Torbal's Battle Sergeant, as they rode their mounts over the ridge and saw Westhealfe in the distance. Their party of about a hundred men and women on horse-back had made good time from Bregustol, crossing the Icefinger River at the Black Stone Ford early this morning. The spring air was fresh and Torbal agreed whole-heartedly with Nerian's sentiment.

Torbal turned to his Battle Sergeant.

"That it is, Nerian. Seeing this city takes away the fears I have about tomorrow. Something about Westhealfe calls to me and says that one should face each day as it comes. And enjoy an ale while doing so."

Nerian laughed loudly, causing his horse to whinny. They continued up the Vesten Causeway, the clip-clop of hooves a gentle sound to accompany the swaying motion of being in the saddle. Torbal gazed upon the city ahead.

Where Bregustol was big and bustling, Westhealfe was inviting and somehow intimate. Or so Torbal thought. Westhealfe had walls like any other city but somehow gave off the air of a warm inn on a cold and stormy night. Wherever you hailed from, you would be welcome in this city. The capital Bregustol was completely different; an unruly mix of the various peoples from around the realm, seemingly forever colliding into each other but never stopping to share a word. Westhealfe felt more like a melting pot where the colours swirled and crossed, mixing here and there, and then devolving into their primary state again.

"What'll be the first ale to quench your thirst, General?" asked Nerian.

Torbal considered the many ales Westhealfe had to offer. Broken Fist? An amber ale that went down perhaps a little too easily. Torbal had heard the name was to remind patrons not to drink too much, lest they start a brawl.

Night Song? A dark brew that was too bitter for some. Torbal enjoyed it though with salted pork. He didn't torture others with his own dulcet tones though, as some did who took the ale's name to heart.

A more expensive brew that originated from Helliga was Stormadei. It took some beating, Torbal had to admit.

"General?" Nerian prodded.

Torbal laughed. "Apologies, Nerian, my mind was at the bottom of a barrel. How about yourself? Is there an ale you always have after a few days on horse-back?"

"Maiden's Whisper" the battle sergeant replied without hesitation.

Torbal shifted in his saddle, turning his upper body to Nerian, surprised he would choose a very light ale favoured by young men and women who flirted while they drank in the city parks.

Nerian nodded, a wistful smile upon his face.

"Yes, not what you'd expect from a grizzled old soldier like myself, General, I'll grant you that. I move on to hardier stuff afterwards but my first is always Maiden's Whisper. A little tradition of mine. It was the ale that brought my beloved wife Annis to me."

Nerian stroked his horse's mane.

"I quaff a mug of that before leaving Westhealfe and again on my return. I'm not one for superstitions but this one sits well with me" he explained, shrugging his shoulders.

Torbal nodded.

"And may you enjoy many more Maiden's Whispers."

Nerian talking about his wife brought Ulla's face to Torbal's mind. He imagined her giving him one of her knowing smiles as she introduced him to another wine. The King's Shield had grown up with beer being his primary thirst quencher so had not been so familiar with the pleasures of the grape. Ulla had educated him in the subtle differences between wines, and they had shared many an evening slowly sipping from glasses that made a satisfying chime when tapped together in toast. Torbal suddenly wondered if those nights were gone forever.

"Are you remembering the High King, General?" Nerian's voice broke his thoughts.

"Yes" he lied. "I wish he were still here to guide us. I have little faith in Eswic and Worsteth. Things will crack and crumble somewhat before we restore a sense of normalcy to the realm, I fear."

As he said this, Torbal looked past Westhealfe and saw the same mountain range that could be seen from Bregustol; the Jagged Heights were like great, hulking behemoths on the horizon, always there if you looked north. On this side of the Icefinger river, the Frozen Forest brooded at the feet of the mountains, like some inky green fog. As uninviting a place as the Deadwood. Torbal doubted anyone lived in those forbidding places anymore. Sedmund would have disagreed.

Nerian coughed.

"It's not my place to speculate, General, but do you think the Helligan nation had anything to do with the High King's death?"

The question angered Torbal. Not just because the implication was that Ulla had done the deed, but also because Torbal didn't have a clear answer. He was positive Ulla had not poisoned his friend, but he couldn't be sure her brother Orben was innocent. The rumour that Sedmund had been poisoned had become a *truth* very quickly in Bregustol, with even Torbal himself contemplating who the assassin might be.

Were you just struck down by illness, old friend?

"I do not believe Orben would have ordered something so treacherous." Torbal intentionally avoided mentioning Ulla.

He snapped his fingers.

"Wolf's Howl."

Nerian was confused. "Pardon, sir?"

"Wolf's Howl will be the first ale I shall drink in Westhealfe" said Torbal with a wink.

Nerian laughed and Torbal smiled, pleased he had changed the subject. Torbal motioned to a captain who had been riding just behind Nerian and himself. The three then proceeded to talk about ale and pies, as their horses took them ever closer to home.

It did feel so good to be away from Bregustol and the detestable Brother Eswic and the scheming Worsteth and all the damn people who yearned for what Torbal would term chaos. If it were not for Sedmund and the legacy Torbal wished to protect, he would have been happy for the Abyss to take them all. But the general knew there was work ahead. Diplomacy, negotiation, persuasion, deception perhaps and no end of talking with those he wished to be far away from.

Once more he wished Ulla were at his side. He felt there was nothing he couldn't do if she were with him to handle the more intricate aspects of a kingdom. *We could rule together* he thought, then immediately worried he was becoming too ambitious. But that wasn't it. It wasn't the power he sought. He wanted the realm to settle and life to go on, and he knew he couldn't achieve this alone. There was much to consider.

The Royal Mines to the east of Bregustol were one issue. Incredible wealth travelled down the Ruby Road and Torbal knew this was one of the more urgent matters he needed to consider. He would have to leave Orben and his ambitions to Ulla. He hoped she could dissuade him from any rash course of action.

Torbal then considered the Argol Forest region, south of the River Freo. At least he could expect no trouble from there. They were a simple folk, much like the people of Westhealfe but without the raucous and tempestuous nature of this city. And without any kind of military force Torbal noted.

Beyond the forest of Argol were the Tarakan Plains, of which Torbal knew little save that the folk there lived a nomadic life. And to the east of Argol lay Meridia.

Torbal recalled the Meridian ruler, Rencarro. He was a strong leader, albeit the ruler of the weakest of the four main city states. Torbal raised his eyes to the sky and tried to put himself in Rencarro's position. What would the man do? Torbal felt reasonably confident he could predict the actions, or at least the designs of, Worsteth, Eswic and Orben. But Rencarro was more of a mystery. A possible ally? The thought came to Torbal and yet again he yearned for Ulla's insight and diplomatic skills.

The general let out a huff, exasperated with the tangled and fraying threads of a realm without a single ruler.

Nerian pointed ahead and commented cheerfully that they must be expected. Torbal kicked his horse into a canter as he saw about a dozen riders waiting patiently before the city gates. Their leader hailed them as they approached.

"General Torbal, welcome home!"

Torbal's concerns and worries lifted noticeably at the words. Home indeed. He smiled and raised a hand in greeting to the Captain of the Home Guard, Beornoth. Then Torbal spotted a youthful woman atop a grey mare, her almost silver hair tied in a braid that hung afore her left shoulder. Eyes the colour of jade shone and Torbal's heart soared.

"Lucetta!" he cried, overjoyed at seeing his niece again.

"Uncle!"

The young lady kicked her horse into motion and trotted up to Torbal and his own steed. Both dismounted and embraced. For a moment, as he hugged his niece, Torbal felt he could almost forget about the rest of the realm and just leave others to work it out.

"It is so good to see you, Lucetta. How fare your parents and my nephew?"

Lucetta squeezed his thick arms and chuckled. "All is as ever was."

"The city walls shake then!" he remarked and they both laughed.

Torbal turned to his riding party.

"Come, let us renew our acquaintance with our home!"

Everyone cheered and Torbal remounted his horse. Lucetta

was back on her mare with one fluid motion. The combined parties then entered the city.

As their horses' hooves plodded along the main thoroughfare that led through to Saxnot Keep, people stopped what they were doing and waved to the group. Some called out to the general.

"Welcome back, General! It's been too long!" called out a rosey-faced lady who was busily cleaning the window of her candle shop.

"General Torbal, we share your sadness" came a voice from somewhere above street level.

"The general is back. All is well again!" cried an elderly woman holding the hands of what were presumably her grandchildren.

"Thank the Winds, General Torbal has returned. Finally someone who can keep Lady Lucetta out of mischief!"

Torbal and Lucetta spotted the innkeeper who had shouted to them, leaning out his establishment's ground floor window and waving.

Torbal recognised him and the inn, The Pale Moon.

"Not even I am up to that task, Galan!" the general roared in reply. Lucetta grinned and made an obscene gesture in Galan's direction, who adopted a shocked expression.

"Careful. They won't call you Lady if you keep up with that sort of vulgarity" chided Torbal, a smile upon his face.

"Father gave up on me long ago, Uncle."

Torbal chuckled.

The general was genuinely touched by the sentiments called out and the palpable affection he felt here from his people, but subsequently felt the heavy responsibility he now bore upon his shoulders more acutely. He could not just rest easy here, enjoying the many comforts of what was his home. The realm needed him now.

Beornoth guided his horse to Torbal's side and coughed politely.

"General, if I might relate tidings we received this morning."

Torbal knew these tidings would do nothing to assuage his concerns.

"I take it this is something that cannot wait till we are all rested and fed?" asked Torbal, keeping the annoyance from his voice. The expression on Beornoth's face was answer enough. Torbal sighed.

"Very well. Enlighten me."

Beornoth cleared his throat. "It seems the Meridians have made some movements since the High King's death."

Torbal was surprised. "The Meridians? Surely they are not massing on the Helligan border."

"The other way, sir. Lord Rencarro has moved troops to the Argol region" explained Beornoth. "A large number are in Argyllan and a smaller force is down near Lowenden. There have been no reports of violence. Quite the opposite. The people of Argyllan seem very happy to have them there."

Torbal frowned. *What is Rencarro up to?*

He looked to Beornoth, indicating for the captain to continue.

"The word is they are there to protect the citizens."

"From who?" demanded Torbal. "We have made no aggressive move."

Beornoth nodded. "The First Lord had the same reaction to this news. Nobody is sure why the Meridians would station troops in Argyllan of all places. If anything, the danger is to the east."

"Agreed" said Torbal gruffly. A thought occurred to him. "Are they planning to invade the Veste region?" He was fairly sure Rencarro was not fool enough to contemplate such a move, but he could not think of any other reason for their presence on the other side of the River Freo.

"Again, the First Lord voiced this possibility but our scouts patrolling the banks of Freo and also agents within Argyllan say the number of soldiers is too small to be an invasion force. It doesn't make much sense." Beornoth shook his head, frowning in defeat.

Torbal shared his feeling. He thanked the captain, who let his horse fall back and allowed the general to ride with his niece again. The two of them rode in silence for a time, Torbal brooding over this latest turn of events. He had a clear picture of Ulla in his mind, holding up her forefinger and indicating she had seen through the fog and understood a matter still confounding Torbal. A brilliant mind and an exquisite lady, he mused.

"Uncle?"

Lucetta's pure voice brought him back to the moment.

"You are troubled?" his niece asked.

Torbal sighed and turned to his niece as the horses continued on their way.

"Very much so, I am afraid to say. There is much I must discuss with your father and mother. Bregustol, and thus the entire realm, is not in the best of hands with Worsteth and Eswic. My dear friend Sedmund may have seemed a cold and distant ruler to some but he truly strove to preserve the peace of the realm. He was well aware that a ruler must look backwards as much as forwards if he is to protect his people."

Torbal turned his eyes back to the street ahead and saw Saxnot Keep coming into view.

"Sedmund was one man, and his rule was respected as *the* High King. Worsteth is an administrator, Eswic a holy crusader and I am a soldier. The three of us cannot rule the realm with any sense of harmony and there would be no single vision."

Torbal turned to his niece and smiled sadly.

"It would be better if one were to step forward and take the role of High King in duty if not name. However, Worsteth is more ambitious than I feared, and I sense he is somewhat detached from the notion of the lives of the common folk being of the same worth as our own."

Torbal leaned forward to stroke his steed's mane, trying to calm himself.

"Eswic would be an unholy disaster at the helm. We would see religious persecution on a level that would bring about bloodshed all over the realm."

They rode on some yards in silence and Lucetta eventually prodded her uncle. "And then there is you. Uncle?"

Torbal didn't answer immediately. He looked ahead to the ever-growing walls and tower of the keep, trying to find words that would satisfy his niece but he simply felt weary again. Was the only way to save the realm from those two fools to proclaim himself ruler until a worthy successor to Sedmund could be decided upon? He knew he could take power as he had the loyalty of the military. This thought took him back to Ulla's words at Sedmund's deathbed. Had she been warning the other two and perhaps pushing him to take this course of action?

Torbal was certain though that pushing Worsteth and Eswic aside with the implicit threat of force would at the least set a dangerous precedent, and at worst, ignite a power struggle that would divide the north and practically hand the realm to Orben on a bloodied platter.

"Uncle?"

Torbal took a deep breath and shook his head.

"No, Lucetta, I am not the one who should rule Ragnekai."

He dearly wanted to say more, to reassure this young lady who was so full of hope and dreams for the future. She would understand in time. He needed to speak to Lucetta's father Kenric, his brother-in-law and the First Lord of Westhealfe. Rencarro's movements would be the first thing to discuss. Torbal reluctantly acknowledged he should then tell Kenric and his sister about his relationship with Ulla. He almost winced as he envisioned the reaction from his sister, who was a fearsome lady when angered.

"Let the city walls shake, eh?" he said aloud to Lucetta and winked.

His niece looked at him quizzically and then smiled.

"Good to have you back with us, Uncle. Let the realm tremble! I am ready."

Torbal laughed loudly and hastened his mount, the others following suit.

Ch 11

Rencarro

5th Day of Maia, Ten Days After Sedmund's Death

H as word been sent to Eligius?"
"Yes, my lord, General Sylvanus sent a swift rider.
The general ordered that Eligius be guarded at all times."

Rencarro nodded. "Good." He turned away from Atticus. "Leave me."

Atticus left the room, leaving Rencarro alone with the silence that seemed to have ridden in upon this ill news, coming to him and wrapping the Lord of Meridia up in its chilling embrace.

"The Widow is cruel" he muttered.

Rencarro could not take in what had happened. Assassins had struck and taken the life of his eldest and injured his Second. It didn't seem real. Had the realm fallen into war already, with clandestine murder taking them all unawares? Had Orben sent the killers? Was he looking to knock out the leadership of Meridia while he pushed north to take the capital? Did he seek to sow seeds of chaos in the south to ensure there was no opportunistic attempt to create a new border between Meridia and the Helligan nation?

Rencarro breathed deeply, trying to focus on what lay ahead, whilst struggling to contain the grief he felt for Marcus' death. *My son.* Those two words brought a rush of memory. Marcus' birth, teaching him to use a bow, sparring with him, hunting with both his boys. So much. And suddenly it was no more. Rencarro choked on emotion and sobbed, his head in his hands.

"Forgive me, Shansu" he whispered. He had promised his dying wife he would watch over Marcus and Eligius, guide them to becoming men their mother would be proud to see. And now Marcus was gone. A sense of failure mingled with the sadness, a bitter mix to endure.

The Lord of Meridia poured himself a cup of wine and knocked it back, a dribble of red dripping onto his tunic. He moved to pour himself another cup but his hand stopped and he held the bottle as it was, standing there on the table. Getting drunk might ease the pain but would do little else, save fog his mind. He reached for a pitcher of water and refilled his cup with this instead. He drank and then stood up.

The windows were letting in the morning sunlight and warming the room. Rencarro felt neither warm nor cold, just numb to his core. Death in battle was a terrible thing but not unexpected. This had swept in upon dark wings. He wondered if his son had realised he would die. Did Marcus have a few moments before his life slipped away? Time to look upon the Widow's face and hopefully snarl defiance.

Rencarro looked at a tapestry on the wall and studied it. It depicted the sun as a deity frowning down upon a sailing ship, whilst the moon, also a deity presumably, had an expression of mischievous glee. The captain of the ship was drinking from an urn while his sailors lay around him on the deck, seemingly asleep. Rencarro did not know the story behind this. Possibly some Tarakan tale with their belief in the sun and moon being gods.

There was a quiet but firm knock at the door.

Rencarro didn't want company at this time but knew he must do what was needed now. He must shut his grief away and then let it out in small ebbs when he was alone. As he had done with the death of Shansu.

"Enter."

The door opened slowly and Camran the quartermaster looked in. Rencarro felt a sense of relief. Camran was perhaps the one person whose company he could tolerate right now. In fact, he almost welcomed it.

"My lord. Please say immediately if you would rather be alone."

"Come in, Camran. It is perhaps not a time for me to be

alone."

The quartermaster stepped in and closed the door behind him. He produced a bottle that Rencarro recognised as the rum they had shared the day the Meridians arrived in Argyllan.

"A drink cannot take the pain away but perhaps a drink shared can dull it."

Rencarro wanted to refuse, having only just stopped himself consuming more wine, but he felt Camran could bring him some succour on this day. He motioned for the Argyllan to take a seat and did the same.

"I am truly sorry to hear of your son's death, Rencarro. When our children are taken before us, it is an evil world."

Camran poured a small measure into two small glasses he had brought with him. The glasses were square and Rencarro was impressed with their craftsmanship.

Camran noticed him studying them. "My brother's work. A gift to me last time he visited." Camran raised his glass and Rencarro did likewise.

"Let justice be done" said Rencarro.

Camran nodded solemnly. "And may your son rest in eternal peace."

They drank the rum, the sweetness somehow lifting Rencarro's spirits. They sat there for some moments in silence.

Finally Rencarro looked up and sighed.

"My wife died four years ago. The physicians said it was the Shadow Within that took her, slowly spreading throughout her entire body. Marcus couldn't bear to look at her in her final days. My younger son Eligius hardly left her side. Two very different men."

Rencarro paused, then touched his glass on the bottle. Camran poured another small measure and waited patiently. Rencarro did not drink immediately this time, instead looking at the amber liquid and wondering what the Radiant Isles were like. He felt part of him wishing to find a boat this day and sail there, leaving all the pain behind.

But Rencarro knew that grief had no boundaries and no

concept of distance. It followed you wherever you went and was relentless in its pursuit.

"I had hopes that whatever turmoil engulfed the realm now, events would make Marcus into a better man and make Eligius stronger."

"The worst of times can bring out the best in us" offered Camran.

Rencarro nodded. He felt an inner-calm returning with Camran's presence. The lord was a man who felt he needed no one to hold him up and always sought to be a pillar of support to those around him, and a symbol of strength to the people he ruled. With Shansu's death he had needed to hide his grief and absorb that of his sons. But in this moment, he accepted the fact that he would not be able to suffer Marcus' murder in silence.

"The Void take those murderers!" he spat, his voice croaking as emotion threatened to overcome him.

Camran reached out and placed his hand on Rencarro's fore-arm. He said nothing but held his hand there. In another time the Lord of Meridia would have rejected the gesture and reacted with disdain. Now though, pride and stubborn notions of masculinity meant little to him. His son was gone.

"How do I go on, Camran? Marcus would be alive now if I had not..." Rencarro checked himself, realising he was saying too much.

"There is no blame here, Rencarro. That lies solely with those who committed the act and whoever ordered it. You set out on a noble course and fate has been cruel beyond belief." Camran's words were full of compassion and Rencarro felt a twinge of guilt hearing the quartermaster speak.

Where has my ambition brought me?

Camran removed his hand and shook his head. "I have no children of my own. Not even married. Married to Argyllan is what the folk round here say of me. Perhaps." He shrugged. "But I have a niece and can imagine the pain her parents would feel were she taken from them. You have been treated so harshly by the Shades."

111

Rencarro raised an eye-brow.

"Forgive me. I am from a little farther south so have faith in the Spirits. You speak of the Void. We say the after-life is the Evercold. Not a cheery thought at face value but we will say of those who have passed on that they will warm the Evercold and the Spirits will be drawn to this warmth. The Shades shy away from both that warmth and the Spirits."

Camran looked at Rencarro and said with conviction, "From what I know of your son, I believe he is setting a fire in the Evercold now and daring any Shade to put out the flames."

There was something in the image that made Rencarro smile. He nodded. "Yes, Marcus was a brave soul and ready for a challenge. I will keep in mind your belief of what comes after this world. When I go there, I plan to find Marcus and start a blaze with him that will burn so brightly, the Shades will be forced to find a new name for their world."

Camran slapped the table and laughed. "If I get there before you, I will find Marcus and tell him to prepare for your coming. If I arrive later, then I shall enjoy the warmth."

Rencarro chuckled and was surprised at how laughing in the face of death could push away the sorrow. He held out his glass, again admiring the perfect symmetry in its shape. Camran poured another shot of rum.

"Let the fires burn brightly in the Evercold" declared Rencarro.

"And the Shades beware!" added Camran as they clinked glasses.

Ch 12

Emiren

5th Day of Maia, Ten Days After Sedmund's Death

Night had fallen. Emiren crouched within the trees of Argol forest, looking out to the city of Argyllan. She had made it this far, navigating her way through the forest, and avoiding the Meridian soldiers who were hunting her. In hindsight that had been the easier task, such was her skill in woodcraft. Getting to her uncle's house from here was a much shorter distance but full of risk.

She could see the Coastal Road winding away to the left, a pale serpent disappearing around Argol on its way to the Tarakan Plains. That same road led in this direction to a triangle of paths over to her right, connecting to the Forest Road that led down to Fallowden and Lowenden. Beyond the road was the southern section of the Argyllan city walls. Flickering orange glows illuminated the top of the wall and Emiren could see Meridian soldiers patrolling, the white of their uniforms contrasting with the darker green of the fabric it accompanied. There was also the odd bobbing ball of flame, its bearer padding his way slowly along, stopping here and there to share a word with his fellows.

Emiren looked to her right and saw a whole host of camp-fires and torches igniting the darkness of the night with their crackling light. Her uncle Camran lived over on the east side of the city but with all those soldiers camped there, entering the city that way would be impossible. Emiren would have to climb over the wall on this, the west side, and then make her way through the city, hoping there were few soldiers patrolling the inner streets at night.

The young lady from Fallowden had accepted that news must have reached the Meridians in Argyllan of a red-haired, young female assassin, considering the length of time it had taken her to get to the port city. She had been forced to hide in the trees in the daylight hours, when soldiers were roaming far and wide, and then move carefully at night. She was tired and foot-sore, and her body ached from sleeping in hollows or up in trees. At least she wasn't hungry or thirsty though, being adept at living rough in Argol. Yet Emiren still couldn't take it all in, all this madness. She couldn't even be sure that her parents had understood Tarak and the meaning of his calm return without her.

Finding sanctuary with her uncle was her only hope now. She focused on the corner where the southern wall joined the western one in a small turret. There was a torch burning away there but Emiren could see no movement. This was where she would have the best chance of scaling the wall unnoticed. It was over a hundred yards to the wall though, crossing open space and cutting across the road. She would have to make a dash but was prepared to throw herself flat onto the grass and lay still if she saw soldiers walking this way along the wall. Her long coat was a dark green and she believed — hoped — she would appear as nothing more than a dark patch of grass.

She scanned the movement upon the wall. One soldier was walking to the eastern side, his torch becoming a small point of light rather than the visible flames of those on this end. Laughter rose up and she saw another of the patrolling soldiers had stopped and was sharing a joke with a stationary man. She took a deep breath and broke from her cover. She crouched low as she hurried through the darkness to the corner of the southern wall. Clouds had drifted across the moon and the darkness deepened. Emiren thanked the Spirits for small mercies.

She made it to the wall without hearing any shouts of warning or any clanging of bells. Despite there being a great many soldiers here, it appeared as though nobody was expecting any kind of attack this night as the walls were sparsely manned. Emiren pressed herself into the shadows of the wall and listened. There were more voices out there, but they were much farther away, nearer to the eastern gate. She closed her eyes and tried to slow her breathing. Then she heard a new sound. The gentle crashing of waves on the sea. Emiren felt a strange kind of comfort hearing this, though she had no idea why. Maybe the voice of the sea signified freedom to her, rolling and tumbling its waters in the vastness, prisoner to no-one.

Calmness settled within her and she knew she was ready to move again. She turned and ran her hands over the wall, searching for a handhold. The stone barrier was not in a particularly good state of repair and there were various pieces of rock jutting out, along with nooks and crevices to aid her. She scaled the wall easily enough and slid over the top onto a wooden walk-way. Crouching down, she looked around. There was nobody there. She breathed a sigh of relief and eased herself off the walkway, landing lightly on the ground. She then scanned the houses nearby until she saw one that suited her next, slightly crazed, idea.

Emiren climbed the iron ladder that was bolted to the side of the two-storey house, ascending as quietly as she could for fear of waking the inhabitants. Emiren knew she would be spotted if she scampered through the streets of Argyllan so had decided the roof-tops were the best way to stay undetected. It would also help her keep her bearing in a place ten times larger than Fallowden.

She managed to pull herself onto the roof and warily stood up. If she followed a straight line from where she was, she would be too close to the city wall and was sure to be spotted. Her eastwards path to Uncle Camran's house would have to start from a point farther into the city. She looked north. She could see a cluster of orange spots in the distance and decided that was the harbour area. Taking this as a marker, she studied the dark roof tops ahead of her. When she was satisfied she had her bearings, she began her perilous journey across the tiled roof-tops.

Her footing was sure and she was soon advancing at quite a pace. The buildings in Argyllan were fortunately either part of one haphazard whole that created a length of roof with no gaps, or they were crammed close together with the leap between two roofs three strides at most. Emiren found herself hoping that there were no thieves who roamed the Argyllan roofs at night.

After having traversed many houses, Emiren stopped to catch her breath and lowered herself just in case there were any eyes peering out of windows. She estimated she was almost midway across the city now so could change direction and start heading eastwards. She rose and began once more this rather unorthodox method of navigating Argyllan.

After a time, she came to the end of a street. There was no chance she could leap to the house on the other side. Squatting down, she examined her surroundings. There was nothing for it. She would have to go down to the street, cross over and then climb up again.

Getting down was relatively easy. Emiren had been climbing the trees of Argol since she was a little girl so gripping a timber corner post and descending was no great feat. But she felt extremely vulnerable on the cobbled street as soon as her feet touched down. The moon was peeking out from the clouds now and the candles in the street lamps glowed faintly. Although it was the middle of the night, Emiren felt as though she were in the midday sun. She hurried across the street and quickly moved towards a house whose ground floor was far wider than its second floor, giving Emiren an easy path to the roof tops once again.

This next part of her passage across the city was more fraught with danger. Twice she had to flatten herself against the cold tiles to hide herself from eyes below. The first time, it was a pair of soldiers quietly conversing as they made their way below her. The other time she found herself in plain sight of an inn from which a couple of bawdy revellers were exiting. She thanked the Spirits the ale was keeping them focused on not tripping over their own feet as they stumbled past where she perched.

The clouds were all but gone when she came upon what looked to be the market square. She berated herself for not having given a little more thought to her route. Emiren should have remembered the large open square in the heart of the city and so could have avoided this yawning chasm between her and her uncle's house.

Furtively glancing around, she saw no movement nor heard any human sound. It was a risk but she judged she could sprint across the plaza and cut into one of the smaller alleyways on the opposite side, thus avoiding the main street. She took a deep breath and made her way down to the ground once again. Then sprinted.

She was halfway across when she heard the clip-clop of a horse. She increased her pace, not daring to look back. The clip-clop became a canter as she neared the far side of the square. There was a building ahead with a stair-well going up to a second story and she made for it. The sound of the horse's hooves on the cobblestone was definitely closer.

I've been seen!

She took the stairs two at a time and upon reaching the top, leapt up to grab a ledge of a window that was set in the roof. She swung herself up. Once on the roof she ran, no longer treading carefully, no longer caring if she made any noise. All she knew was that she had to get out of sight from whoever had been on that horse.

Eventually, Emiren slowed her mad race across the roof-tops and listened. She could still hear the horse but it was fainter. She stopped and carefully crouched behind a chimney stack. Her breathing was ragged but she managed to take in small gasps of air.

Emiren wished the clouds would return to hide the moon, which seemed to shine brighter than ever. She wondered if the rider had seen her climb onto the roof. If they hadn't, there was a good chance she could remain hidden as people tended not to look up. She was about to start looking around for where to go next when she heard the soft clip-clop of horseshoes again. She pressed herself flat against the chimney, peering out so she could get a view of the street below.

A lone figure on horseback entered her field of vision. Emiren watched as he trotted his mount below the roof where she was perched and then down the cobbled street. A long braid of hair hanging down his back was swishing in time with the motion of his ride. The braid ran over a spear that was hung diagonally across the rider's back, moonlight glinting off a wickedly sharp blade. Emiren guessed he was a Meridian soldier and not one of the city guard. She couldn't see the colours of Argyllan's neighbour to the east but the rider just seemed too erect in his saddle, too certain of himself not to be a trained soldier. Suddenly the man jerked the reins and his mount stopped. With his back still turned, he called out.

"Will you not come down? So as we may speak like civilised people."

Emiren froze. How could he have known she was there? It seemed she was not as well hidden as she had thought. Was he certain where she actually was or was he just trying to lure her from her hiding place? As if to answer this question, the man pulled the animal around and stared up directly to where she was perched. The stone chimney against her body suddenly felt like a tomb, cold and remorseless.

"Spirits save me" she whispered. Fear gripped her that this was to be her end. She breathed deeply through her nose, trying to locate a calmness within herself. Emiren whispered the Words quietly. She felt the wind hasten up her legs and then arms. Was death approaching? Was that the Shades of the Evercold caressing her? She clenched her teeth and looked straight at the man. Then she replied in a clear voice, "I can hear you from here. I don't think I'll come down."

A pause.

"So be it. I am just wondering what you are doing running across the roof tops. Are you a street urchin?"

Emiren replied she wasn't before she realised that a street urchin would have been a good guise to adopt.

"I see" the soldier said, his voice level and calm, his face hidden in the night's shadow. "I am at a loss for your choice of nocturnal activity then. Pray enlighten me, girl."

"Are you from Meridia?"

"A query answered with a question. Curious. I am from Meridia and I am beginning to suspect you may be a thief."

The man looked up to where she was, partly concealed by the chimney. Emiren wanted to try and slide down the far side of the house but she knew this would only make her appear guilty of some crime.

"I am no thief," she said, her voice trembling, "just a traveller from a village to the south."

As soon as the words were left her lips, she regretted them. She should have made up something but her thinking was a jumbled panic.

The soldier did not reply immediately, which Emiren took to be a sign he did not believe her. However, his next words were gentle and caught the young girl off guard.

"I may be a bluff old soldier but I have family too, young one. Am I wrong to think you are running away from home?"

Emiren remained silent.

"Be at ease. I too ran away when I was around your age, if you are fifteen years or thereabouts. There was an argument between my brother and I, and things got heated." The rider stroked his horse's mane, seemingly caught up in the memory.

"My father was quick to anger and I..., well, I can barely remember now exactly why I felt the need to run but it turned out to be a little adventure. A painful one too, when I finally came back and got a good thrashing."

The man chuckled.

Emiren relaxed slightly. Maybe this soldier could help her find her uncle. He didn't seem to be aware of *assassins* roaming the land. She eased herself out from behind the chimney, stood on the sloping roof and looked down.

"Can you help me?" she said, fighting back tears.

The soldier peered up at her from where he sat on his mount.

He seemed to be studying her in the moonlight.

"You can't be that much younger than my second born. Come down and let us find you food and warmth."

Emiren found this offer difficult to resist. She wanted to let this man help her but hesitated.

"Your hair is catching the moonlight. I might be mistaken but it looks a deep chestnut brown, the same as my wife's."

"No, it's auburn actually. My mo…"

Emiren gasped and stared at him. He stared back.

"It is you, isn't it?"

His voice had lost all its warmth and was now as sharp as a knife.

"The red-headed girl who murdered my son."

Emiren froze.

"No, I'm… No, I didn't see. That soldier killed my friend."

Tears came to her eyes and Emiren felt her world collapsing once more.

"Who sent you? Orben? Are you from the north?" he demanded, edging his horse closer to the building upon which she was perched.

"Please. Please listen to me. One of them was already dead when I first saw them. Then the other soldier murdered Anton."

"Liar! You and the boy were sent to take the life of my son. Tell me who gave the order and I will let you live. And stop the sobbing. You will not fool me with your theatrics, which is no doubt how you took my son unawares."

Emiren couldn't understand anything. She tried to remember what was said in the forest that day but her mind was a mess. She tried desperately to remember a name. It came to her.

"Sylvanus!" she blurted.

"Yes, Sylvanus survived the assassination attempt. But you took my son from me, you little witch!"

"No" moaned Emiren. "Sylvanus lied. I don't even know how to kill."

She wanted to run but her legs felt like lead. They weakened beneath her and she felt herself sway. She placed a hand against the chimney stack to steady herself. Bile was rising in her throat. This nightmare was endless.

"Come down and I will give you leniency if you tell me who was behind the murder."

"By the Spirits" she wept. "Anton was an innkeeper's son and my father is a glass-blower. We are no assassins. Please believe me, soldier of Meridia."

"I am Lord Rencarro, the *ruler* of Meridia" he replied, teeth gritting as he spoke. "And Marcus was my son."

Emiren moaned as he slid off his horse to the cobbled stone. He unslung his spear in a fluid motion but without haste. He let the spear slip in his grip until the shaft hit the ground with a sound like a smart knock on a crypt door.

"Now tell me, girl. Who are you?"

Emiren wept uncontrollably.

"I am no-one. I did not kill your son. I am no-one. Please, please."

Emiren began to move back. She would receive no mercy from this enraged father of a murdered son. She had to run again. Emiren turned to flee but as her weight shifted, a tile came loose beneath her foot. She lost her footing and slid to the edge of the roof. She gasped and grabbed wildly as she felt herself slipping over the edge. The girl from Fallowden could have easily righted herself within the Forest of Argol but those trees were far away now. Her feet swung in mid-air as she continued her slow but inevitable slide off the roof. Her nails raked down the roof tiles, scraping the skin from her finger tips. Then she fell.

A lucky lunge gave her one hand on a window ledge and she thought for an instant she would be able to climb back to safety. But the fatigue within her was too great and she lost her grip. She dropped the six or so feet to the street and cried in pain as her ankle twisted, leaving her collapsed in a heap upon the cold cobbles.

Emiren looked up and saw this Rencarro had remained as motionless as a statue. His eyes met hers and she saw a smile slowly spread across his face, the moonlight giving his features a skeletal appearance.

The Meridian rapped the spear shaft on the stone underfoot again, the sound far more terrifying than before. Emiren was in despair. Back in Argol she had been hidden from the horrible spectre of death that Sylvanus represented. Now she lay prostrate before sharp steel and a man burning for vengeance. She closed her eyes and sobbed silently.

Rencarro spoke again but his voice was calm.

"Why did you flee to Argyllan?"

Emiren wanted to answer but her voice was lost in her terror. She wanted to tell him her uncle was here and he could confirm the truth in what she had said. She wanted to tell this man everything about herself in the hope he would believe she had nothing to do with his son's death. But she was helpless in the face of this terrible reality that had crashed down upon her. Pain was swirling in her left ankle, tears were rolling down her cheeks and no words came.

Rencarro's head lowered and he seemed in thought. He moved closer, bringing himself to tower above her. She moaned, her eyes fixed upon the spear's deadly point. His voice was low as he continued to draw out Emiren's agony.

"You know how it feels to take a life, don't you?" It was said as more a statement than a question. "You know how it feels when you draw out the blood of another. The knowledge that you have sent some poor soul to the Void."

He paused and turned his head to look at his weapon, twisting the shaft so the blade rotated in the pale moonlight. He spoke once more, his voice trembling.

"It really is quite something to kill a man. You take away all he strived for, all he was at that moment and all he would ever have been. You steal his very *essence*." The last word came out as more of a hiss.

Emiren prayed to the Spirits to end this torture. She prayed inwardly for them to take her to the Evercold now. She wanted it to end.

122

"Murderer!" he suddenly cried and twirled his spear so the blade was now pointing downwards, directly at Emiren. Both his hands gripped the shaft and he raised the weapon high.

"Mother" she croaked.

Part Two

Ch 1

Lorken

Lorken was gradually coming out of his slumber when he became aware of a small hand on his cheek. He opened his eyes, blinked away the sleepiness and gazed at his youngest child. Eira was just shy of five years, her birthday on the first day of Maia. She raised her eyes to see her father waking and gave him one of her gentle smiles. Lorken felt a quiet calm settling within. He doubted watching the sun rise would give him the same sense of peace. Whatever his city of Gamle Hovestad or his Lord Orben asked of him today, Lorken was content now to just let it all happen.

"Good morning, little one. Are you up early or have I slept too long?"

Eira tilted her head and puffed out her cheeks. No words came from her mouth. None ever had. Lorken and his wife Jenna had no idea why their daughter was mute but still held out hope that it was just something she would overcome. The local physician, one of the better ones in Gamle Hovestad it had to be said, had stated there was nothing wrong with her tongue or throat, and had suggested starting with other forms of communication. Lorken's two sons Darl and Torg, who were much older than little Eira, seemed more adept than him at understanding Eira's various methods of *talking*. She would use hands, body movement and eyes to speak to her brothers. Jenna just hugged her daughter a lot.

Lorken pulled Eira closer and held her tight. "You'll talk one day" he sighed. He had such things to tell her when she came of age and hoped she would be able to tell him a thing or two by then.

Lorken could hear Darl and Torg were already out in the yard chopping wood. They were in a rhythm, one swinging his axe down as the other raised his. It amounted to a continuous stream of *thunks* that you could march to, so regular were the chops. Darl was sixteen, already built like his father and Torg was catching up despite being three years younger. Lorken grinned, musing their family trade of carpentry was a good one; they were always in demand and it made his boys stronger than the average lad.

Lorken thought about what the lads were like in the other cities of Ragnekai. Tall? Proud? Reckless? He wondered what version of history they were told. Lorken doubted the Helligan nation was given its fair due in their tales of times gone by. Maybe that would change one day. Gamle Hovestad was a much prouder city since their Lord Orben had come to power. A better place. A stronger place. A place that didn't bow too low to those in Bregustol. Lorken always felt a sour taste creep into his mouth when he thought about Bregustol and the Rihtgellen High King who lorded over the realm.

It wasn't Sedmund who stopped Ragnekai being invaded all those years ago, he thought sourly.

Eira scampered out of the bedroom and Lorken reluctantly got up. He half-heartedly stretched and took a few deep breaths. It cleared his head. Momentarily. He trudged out of the room, his hand sweeping back his long, sandy hair from his face. He grabbed a small iron ring from a shelf and threaded his hair through so it hung down his back, between his broad shoulders.

"Svard and you working hard last night then?" enquired Jenna as he entered the eating area. Her voice carried a note of humour.

"You know Svard. He had some tales to tell, no mistake. Reckon Ruben the inn-keep did well by us last night!" He smiled ruefully.

"Just don't go and drink away all our money. I want Eira to go to the school and learn her letters" scolded Jenna gently, her eyes moving down to their daughter who had sidled up to her father and was now clinging to his leg. Lorken walked to the round, oak table that sat in the centre of the room, Eira with her arms wrapped round his leg, half sitting on his foot. He moved like a man with a peg leg, almost stumbling as he tried to sit down. "You're getting heavier, Eira." He chuckled.

He sat down, running his hands over the table surface. *Good workmanship* he thought to himself. His boys had made the table as a gift to their mother. Jenna had practically collapsed with emotion when she saw the new table appear one morning, her two sons sitting at it enjoying the breakfast Lorken had made for them. That was a rarity in itself. Lorken looked down to the rim of the table where there was an etching of their family glyph and the two boys' glyphs. Darl and Torg couldn't read so well, the same as Lorken, but he had made sure they could write their names. One day those glyphs would be in their District Hall. Or so Lorken hoped. Just like Svard's name would be in the Great Hall, up in the Hellag district where Lord Orben's keep was situated. He doubted his own name would be anywhere, but he would be proud nonetheless if his sons proved themselves in some way to be counted amongst the Worthy.

Jenna put down a wooden platter before him. Black bread, some of the strong cheese he liked and a slice of ham upon it. She then set down a flagon. When Lorken went to drink from it, he frowned.

"No ale to break my fast?"

Jenna playfully cuffed him round the head.

"You had more than enough last night. Have some barley tea to wash out the brew."

Lorken made an exaggerated grimace and held his nose as he drank deep. It was refreshing.

His wife too tied her hair back with a ring, although her ring was silver and her hair a midnight black.

"So what exotic borderland has Svard come back from this time?" she enquired with a sigh. Svard was First Ranger in Lord Orben's army, roaming far and wide, patrolling the borders of his liege's lands, bringing justice to brigands and always returning with stories that made Lorken envious at times. The two had been friends since childhood, everyday hurtling through Bresden Forest, which crept right up to the city walls of Gamle Hovestad. They would climb trees and flee from wild animals which were real and terrifying monsters, which were of course imagined.

Lorken snorted with laughter as he tried to recount some of the things Svard had told him the night before. Jenna's eye-brows lifted and she shook her head. Lorken finally finished telling Svard's tale, albeit an abridged and clean version. Jenna could do without hearing about the two ladies Svard had *encountered* in the bawdy tavern that sat at a crossroads on the Seventh High Road.

"Svard certainly sees some sights. Just be sure he doesn't tempt you to join the Rangers or the Sentinels. You're needed here, my husband."

There was a hint of anxiety in her voice that Lorken didn't miss. He looked at her, holding her gaze with his light brown eyes. Ever since Lorken had joined the Free Guard, Jenna had worried he would come to like it too much. The Free Guard was a collection of units technically in Orben's standing army but made up of volunteers who only trained twice a week. They numbered in excess of a thousand and enjoyed some perks, like eating two hearty meals a week and having some good meat to take home to their families. But it was pride that encouraged many men and women to join. Being in the Free Guard they could feel part of Orben's armed forces and thus closer to the heroism of the warriors of old. The stories of yesteryear were the ones where the Helligan people stood proud in the realm.

"Never worry about that, my love" he replied. "My home is here, my work is here and my family is here. Most of all, my heart is here."

Jenna teared up slightly. She clearly did harbour a worry that he would be enticed by the adventures his friend had and get itchy feet.

"That's good," she managed to whisper. Jenna cleared her throat and went to washing crockery. Lorken watched her and not for the first time, considered himself lucky to have landed such a fine lady. He gazed at her curves that perfectly lined the cotton dress she wore. He felt himself becoming aroused and was thankful when Jenna left to fetch more water from the well outside.

"Banish thoughts of the flesh from the mind!" he muttered to himself as he began eating.

Lorken slowly munched on his food. Eira was now under the table, playing with some wooden blocks Darl had made for her. Lorken leaned back and peered down to where she was. He was surprised to see she had somehow managed to balance the blocks into a topsy-turvy structure.

"How did you do that, little one?" asked Lorken.

He stared hard at it, unable to see how the blocks didn't just tumble to the floor. Eira grinned and placed another block on top of the creation. It still stood. Lorken swallowed his mouthful and pushed his chair back. He got down on his knees and crawled under the table. He lowered his head to the floor to get a look at the base of the structure. It just didn't make sense. The blocks should tip over.

Dust from the floor swirled as he moved, making its way up his nose. He sneezed and banged his head on the underside of the table. His resulting reaction to the pain was a clumsy motion of the hands which scattered the blocks. Lorken's heart sank. He wiped his nose and glanced at Eira's face, afraid of how upset she would be. Eira smiled and laughed a silent laugh. Just breath escaping. She gathered the fallen blocks and start playing some sort of game with them. Lorken returned to his seat and shook his head. The child was a wonder. And so dear to him. Jenna had no need to worry about him yearning to join the Rangers. His home life was just too perfect.

When he had eaten his fill, seen to his ablutions and his stomach had settled, Lorken went out to help his lads. Darl and Torg had finished chopping wood and were now sawing it

131

down into planks. The springs in eastern Ragnekai were cool but the boys had worked up a sweat, their bare backs shining in the sun.

"Pick up the pace, you lazy lads!" called out Lorken as he approached. Both boys stopped, exchanged a look and then turned to their father, who was grinning broadly.

"Sorry Far" said Darl, "we'll try harder to match your incredible work-rate this morning."

"Very drole, young man. But very true."

Lorken joined them in the work and the three of them quickly slipped into a rhythm with saw and plane. The muzziness in his head from the ale last night soon faded and he enjoyed the toil with his boys. He was sure Svard would still be asleep, if he had slept at all. When they had parted, his friend had been debating on whether to take the long way home, via a certain drinking hole where the Rangers spent their coin and some of the more free-spirited ladies of the city frequented.

Crafty bugger.

Ch 2

Svard

Svard heard the banging on the door but ignored it. His head was still clouded from the night's drinking with Lorken and he was loathe to leave the warm confines of his bed. The banging continued, this time accompanied by a loud voice.

"Open up, you lazy oaf! Orben, ruler of our beloved Helligan nation, doesn't like to be kept waiting."

Hearing the name of his liege lord, Svard found the will to move. He rushed out of bed, tripping on his furs as they tumbled around his feet and letting out a few choice curse words.

"Bit early for that kind of language, don't you think Svard?" said the voice, now at a lower volume. Svard recognized that voice, and sighed, knowing he was in for some cutting remarks. The tall Helligan warrior picked himself up, covered the short distance to the door, unlocked it and threw it open to find the unforgiving face of Kailen, Lord Orben's personal messenger. Svard coughed politely and motioned for her to come in. Kailen did so but made a show of holding her nose, her hazel eyes twinkling with mischief.

"Smells like a brewery in here. A brewery where some fool's shat on the floor. Do you share your lodgings with wild animals, First Ranger?"

"Enough of the rapier wit, Kailen" said Svard wearily, "What does the Old Man want? Thought today was my day of rest."

"No time for rest now, old chap. Orben has need of you, Rorthal and Brax."

Svard's eyes flicked up at this. Summoning the Battle Sergeant, the First Sentinel and himself, the First Ranger, told

Svard a great deal. This was something major and also of a military nature, unlikely to be mere scouting. Svard looked questioningly at Kailen but her handsome features gave nothing away, save a certain humour in the eyes. Svard rolled his own.

"Never one to tell more than is necessary, eh Kailen?"

Kailen raised her eye-brows and sauntered out the door, calling over her shoulder.

"Be in Orben's solar before the next hour begins. I am sure all will be revealed."

Svard watched her lithe form depart, her long pony-tail of bronze-tinged hair swishing across her back. He would find her attractive, indeed most men did, were it not for how annoying she was. She fulfilled her role as Orben's personal messenger perfectly, which meant others were drip-fed information. Kailen also carried out her work with a certain style, not just keeping back details but hinting at them maddeningly. Svard couldn't imagine her ever getting married. For that matter, he couldn't imagine himself getting married either.

Svard hurried to dress. He took off his cotton short-trousers he had worn to bed and realised he had been standing in front of Kailen bare-chested. *And she didn't even acknowledge this fine body* he thought to himself, with a touch of hurt pride. Svard was muscular and his body had been through various scrapes. Many women would pay real attention to him when he took off his shirt. But not Kailen. She was clearly very much in control of her emotions. *Or not interested,* he thought with resignation.

Svard was soon on his way to Orben's keep, which sat almost dead centre of the city of Gamle Hovestad, the capital of the Helligan nation, in the Hellag district. He glanced at the sundial in the market place and realised he needed to pick up his pace. He started to trot along, waving to the innkeeper of one of his favourite haunts, The First Hammer.

"Heard you spent good coin at The Black Stone last night, First Ranger" the man called, hands on hips in a show of indignation. "Be sure to save some of your wages for my fine brew" the innkeeper finished with a grin.

Svard replied without stopping, jogging backwards and calling out. "Might be I can gather a few coppers for Stormadei!"

"A few coppers?! You'll not get Mad Badger Ale for that, you old rogue!"

Svard grinned and carried on, waving his hand. The various inns in Gamle Hovestad did well by Svard and his fellow Rangers, and possibly even better with the Sentinels. Many were unmarried and had no children, so their pay often went into the bottom of a beer barrel. Svard needed good ale with his comrades and friends after a scouting excursion. He was proud of what kind of soldiers the Rangers were and what they had achieved. Svard hoped they would rival the Rangers of Helligan legend one day and now as the First Ranger, it was his chance to make it happen.

As he hurried along, his thoughts turned to the night before with Lorken. While he would never give up what he had now, he had a certain envy for Lorken and how his friend since childhood had a beautiful wife, three wonderful children and a good, stable home. He often thought it was in Lorken that he saw what the Rangers strove for. The peace and safety within which families like Lorken's could prosper. The Helligan borders were secure, banditry in the lands was practically non-existent and the coasts were well watched for signs of raiders. Not that anything would come out of the mists of the Blind Sea to the east, nothing ever had, but the southern ports carried out a fairly busy trade. And of course, only eighteen years had passed since the attempted invasion of Ragnekai.

When Lorken would raise a mug of ale to salute his friend for keeping the Helligan nation secure, Svard would return it saying something like, "You keep the heart of our lands beating and I'll make sure nobody sticks a knife in it!"

As Svard approached Lord Orben's keep, he started speculating what this was about. Was the Rihtgellen Kingdom disputing trade routes again? Had the Lady Ulla given Sedmund a bloody nose? That last thought had him grinning.

The tall Ranger skipped up the steps to the keep. The guards on duty knew him on sight and waved him through with a smart salute. Svard saw Rorthal, Helliga's Battle Sergeant ahead and hailed him. Rorthal turned and grinned. They clasped hands, both grips firm.

"You look a little bleary-eyed, old friend" commented Rorthal, his shaven head a contrast to the forked beard which reached almost to his stomach.

"Ales and tales with friends, Rorthal. Thought I would be able to sleep it off today though. What's this about by your reckoning?"

Rorthal shrugged his massive shoulders.

"No idea. But since it is you, me and that old dog Brax, it won't be the weather we're discussing."

Svard's face cracked a smile. It was always good to share some time with the burly battle-sergeant. The two walked on and ascended well-hewn stone stairs, their boots rasping as they climbed. Both knew the way well, coming to Orben's solar at least once a week individually. They passed sentry guards, nodding to them as they went. The sentries returned the nods with even smarter salutes than the guards outside, showing their respect to the two soldiers. Svard and Rorthal had certainly earned that respect.

"Ha! Late as ever!" boomed a loud voice as they came out of the stair-well onto a wide corridor. Brax, the First Sentinel, stood a few yards from the door to Orben's solar. If Svard was tall and lithe, and Rorthal broad and built like an ox, Brax was somewhere in between. He had height and width accompanied by muscle, but had a certain lethargic air to him. Svard knew this belied his friend's true abilities and further knew Brax was more than happy for people to underestimate him. In fact, Svard reckoned the whole idle movement he projected was something the man had perfected over the years.

"Didn't want to die of boredom talking to you, you old dung heap" retorted Rorthal.

"Well, I guess it is boring for you to talk to me as your tiny brain cannot comprehend the subtleties of my fine mind."

A roar came from a room just beyond, clearly audible despite the door being shut.

"If you three are not in here in the space of two breaths, I will have you all castrated and your balls made into ornaments that I will hang over my hearth!"

The three hurried on, the door opening as they did, Kailen smiling smugly as they stumbled through. Orben stood at his map, which was a huge table that had been carved expertly into a likeness of the realm as it was known. He leaned on the edge with his fists, his piercing blue eyes shining out from his craggy face, various shades of grey hair framing it and a neatly trimmed beard surrounding a sternly set mouth.

"You can waste time with your banter when I'm finished" he growled.

"Yes, my lord" said all three in almost perfect unison.

It was then that Svard noticed the striking lady standing to the side. A lady whose beauty seemed to grow each time Svard laid eyes upon her. Golden hair fell to either side of her face in long braids, like two finely crafted pillars that were the gateway to that precious face with its high cheekbones, full lips and eyes as blue as the River Mimir.

"Lady Ulla" Svard managed in an almost whispered voice, wondering why she was here and not in Bregustol. Orben's sister moved towards her brother and smiled at the three men. But said nothing.

"Sedmund is dead."

Initially Svard thought he had misheard his lord. Then he noticed the silence and the look on the faces of Brax and Rorthal.

"Yes. A surprise to myself also" said Orben. "My sister had been keeping me abreast of his condition, but it wasn't known he was that sick. It seems whatever malady ailed him ran through his body much more quickly than anyone foresaw, including of course his physicians and those female monks he keeps."

Orben was standing up straight now, hands behind his back, eyes locking on each man in turn.

"Kailen, tell them the situation in Bregustol."

Kailen stepped forward, no playful smile on her lips now. She told them about Sedmund's passing and Lady Ulla returning to Gamle Hovestad immediately as rumours had already begun to circulate of her having poisoned the High King. Orben's aide also told them how the capital was in disarray now with the people unsure who was in command of anything. It seemed General Torbal was sharing the rule with the chamberlain but Ulla did not expect that to last. Something about the church having a hand to play.

Rorthal blew out a breath when she was finished.

"Things are about to change then, my lord."

"Quite so. But we must be careful how we proceed" said Orben.

The ruler of the Helligan nation motioned for them all to stand around the map-table. Svard admired the impressive work. It was not just a painting or an etching; there was relief carved into it. Svard had seen the table many times before but had never actually bothered to examine the detail. He noticed that the area that comprised the Helligan nation was not entirely accurate. He frowned but then the probable reason dawned on him. If Gamle Hovestad ever fell to an enemy, this map would mislead whoever had taken the city. Svard marvelled at Orben's cunning. It seemed his lord had considered all eventualities.

The First Ranger saw Orben look at his sister, who seemed troubled. The corners of her mouth twitched and then she gave an almost imperceptible nod. The lord of the Helligan nation turned to Kailen and the three soldiers.

"This is an opportunity. A chance to redress past wrongs and alter the rather uneven balance of power in the realm. Sedmund did not plan his passing well or perhaps did not care. Neither my sister nor I can fathom why he did not simply name Torbal to rule after he was gone. He may not have been the best man in the long-term, but he would have ensured stability until a new ruler was chosen by popular vote or some such method."

Orben paused, gazing down at the map.

Svard agreed with what his liege had said. If the Dark Raven was beckoning Sedmund into the Great Hall beyond, why hadn't the man passed power to Torbal, who was respected even in the Helligan nation? Svard glanced again at the Lady Ulla. She seemed distant.

Orben's voice grabbed his attention once more.

"There are many unknowns before us. The Veste region, the south-west, the northlands of Unvasiktok and of course Meridia. How will they move now? We cannot know for sure but I believe we can make a few assumptions and then act upon them. Which is why I have called you here now. Not just to relay the news, which I am sure I don't have to remind you, is for the ears of those in this room alone. For the moment anyway."

He huffed and looked to his sister, then back at the three soldiers.

"No, I want to decide upon a course of action for the Helligan nation within this day."

The three men exchanged glances, a sudden heaviness to the air. Lady Ulla seemed to feel it too and stepped lightly over to the windows, throwing them open. A fresh breeze entered and cleared Svard's head. Orben turned to his messenger.

"Kailen, be so good as to pour some wine for all of us, yourself included. We have much to discuss."

Kailen smiled warmly and did as she was asked.

When each of them had a goblet of dark red wine and Orben had signalled for all to take a sip, he began.

"Brax, what is the current strength of the Sentinels?"

Orben questioned each of them in turn and gave only nods to their answers, with the occasional look shared with his sister. Svard noticed Kailen writing notes in a small, leather-bound book she had pulled from a pouch at her waist. More wine was poured after a time and then the questioning resumed.

Finally Orben fell silent. He looked at his sister but this time there was an almost unspoken conversation between them, conveyed only by their eyes. Svard assumed they had already discussed what they would do. Yet he detected a hint of disagreement between his lord and the lady. It was as if Orben was seeking approval from her but she wasn't ready to give it. The ruler of the Helligan nation seemed frustrated while his sister looked sad, which surprised Svard. Nobody here had any love for Sedmund so why would the Lady Ulla be affected by his passing? Svard decided it was none of his business and probably involved intricacies that were too complex for him to bother with.

Though as Svard gazed at his lord's sister, he couldn't help but be near enchanted by her beauty. She was regal but not haughty, with a manner that spoke of great intelligence and the utmost perceptiveness. The perfect balance to her brother's ambition and cunning. But Orben ruled here and Svard knew he was a stubborn ox when all was said and done. He had a feeling that even if the Lady Ulla had misgivings, Orben would carry out his plan regardless. The possibility that his lord's sister did have concerns though, said quite a lot. It told Svard that Lord Orben was about to set into motion something rather ambitious. Probably a reckless move. Svard hoped he was wrong.

Orben spoke again. The decision had been made.

"Listen well. The Helligan nation will rise again. Sedmund's death is not just an opportunity but a calling I believe. A calling for our people to reclaim what is rightfully ours."

Orben paused. He held each of their eyes in turn and nodded grimly.

"Remember gentlemen, no plan is as likely to succeed as the one which is unknown to the enemy until the sword is drawn. Utmost secrecy is essential as we position our pieces on this board" he said, gesturing to the table-map.

Svard was unprepared for what he said next.

Ch 3

Lunyai

27th Day of Aprus, Two Days After Sedmund's Death

Lunyai was far from her home on the Tarakan Plains. She was away to the north east, having travelled to the centre of Ragnekai and climbed about halfway up the Sacred Mount. The camp that she shared with her fellow pilgrims was nestled within a natural hollow of rock that sheltered them from the cold winds. There were fifteen of them in the group, all except one of them on their first pilgrimage. The Elder who'd come with them was resting near the camp fire with her eyes closed, but Lunyai knew that Imala was awake and alert to any sound that had no place upon the Sacred Mount. She felt safe knowing the older lady was with them on this most special of journeys.

Lunyai stared up into the darkening sky. The sea blue following Yaai the Sun's voyage west was ebbing away as Her brother Tlenaii the Moon took his place high above. Lunyai raised her arms, stretching her fingers towards Tlenaii. Her almond skin, so coloured by Yaai, would be illuminated by Tlenaii when he proudly showed His full form. But not this night. This night Tlenaii was but a thin crescent that gave off little light in the deepening shadows of the night sky. She shook her midnight black hair, ran her fingers through it and breathed deeply of the crisp evening air.

"One day I will reach you, Tlenaii, our Brother. If you do not come back to your Mother, then I will grow wings and come to You!" she said with a conviction that was always felt when she looked upon Tlenaii.

Lunyai had been born under the full form of the Son of the All-Mother, a story her own mother never tired of telling her. When she came into the world, Tlenaii had shone a most brilliant white. As her father had held the baby Lunyai up to that beacon of the night, her mother Chenoa, had seen Tlenaii's spirit shoot forth and envelop the new-born baby. She was blessed, or so her mother had told her.

Lunyai did feel blessed. She felt blessed for the love of her parents and much more besides. She felt blessed to live with her people on the Tarakan Plains, to ride upon the endless grasslands, and to be able to see Tlenaii many nights each cycle. Tlenaii would change His shape but she could always see His true form in her mind's eye. Some nights she truly felt her people's Brother was looking down upon her, His gaze piercing the night sky and finding her wherever she was. And she felt blessed now to be on the Peregrika, the Tarakan pilgrimage to the Sacred Mount.

Lunyai's thoughts drifted back to her home now, far away past the Forest of Argol and beyond. The Tarakan Plains were where her people lived a nomadic existence, settling in a place for two cycles of the seasons, then moving on. Even though the pilgrimage to this most revered of mountains had taken her and her friends far, she felt as long as Tlenaii held the night over them, all her people were together. And with the daughter of the All-Mother, Yaai, slowly gliding across the skies in the day, the Tarakan people were ever watched and guided.

Lunyai closed her eyes and imagined the smoke spires that would be rising from her tribe's settlement. She could almost smell the meat roasting and inhaled deeply through her nose. Mehdi hare for sure and the thought of it made her stomach grumble faintly, despite the fact the pilgrims had already eaten their evening meal. Lunyai pictured Old Ramma the Yiyaka adding the final herbs and spices to his cauldron of broth, tasting it and no doubt grimacing because he felt the flavour was not there yet. Anyone else would have been satisfied three songs ago but not Old Ramma. Lunyai often wondered if the Yiyaka just made everyone wait so long to make sure all were ravenous and breathing in the delicious smells. She smiled and stood up.

"Our Brother, tonight is a night for tales I believe. I know my people are there on the Plains under Your watch, sitting round the fire and awaiting a story. What tale will I hear tonight, with so little of Your light out there?" Lunyai grinned and swept her arms through the air, twirling as she did.

She inhaled the cool air again, letting it fill her lungs and send new life throughout her body. She knew it would be warmer on the Tarakan Plains now, as they lay farther south and not so high above the level of the seas, but the air around the Sacred Mount was fresh and bracing, and she felt like her soul was being washed clean. This was not just any mountain; it was the Sacred Mount that sat encircled by the All-Mother's Ring, a joining of four rivers, where waters eddied and flowed.

The Sacred Mount was huge for a lone mountain and was the Watcher of the Realm, gazing over it in all directions. It was the place from where the All-Mother had sent forth her daughter Yaai and son Tlenaii, to guide the people. Lunyai felt such happiness to have come to the birth-place of her people's guardians. Guardians who had given the Tarakan people the peace they held so dear. Other lands had squabbles and had even seen conflict in ages past, but the Tarakan knew nothing of borders and petty power struggles. They roamed the vast plains in the south-west of Kayah, which those in the north called Ragnekai, giving and taking from the land as the All-Mother deemed right. Never in one place for more than two full turns of the seasons, caring for the land so that the next tribe could settle there after they had left.

Lunyai could not understand the tales of wars between the people who inhabited the lands circling the Sacred Mount. She knew some king was ruler over the large cities and his people had not always been the most powerful. But Lunyai found it difficult to understand peoples that warred against each other and built towers of stone upon the All-Mother, covering her beauty and stopping the growth of the world around them. Her people were wise to have drifted south all those years ago, and to now avoid contact with those folks as much as possible. Her

143

father, Songaa, certainly thought so and her father was usually right about the wider world.

Lunyai looked up again to see that Tlenaii was being hidden by The Grey Ones. She smiled, knowing that The Grey Ones had no real power over Yaai and Tlenaii. They only wanted to bask in Their glories or play mischievously. Even the mighty Thunder Rider, one of the All-Mother's many brothers, could not stay too long under Yaai's radiance.

Lunyai began to sing The Song of the Tarakan, the Tarakalo. Her voice was soft and even, the words drifting into the night sky. She felt sure Tlenaii was listening.

"All-Mother forever with us on the plains.
Bathe us with Your purest of rains.
Trust in us to care for Your lands
As we trust in You to guide our hands.
In the day Your daughter shines so bright
As Your son protects us in the night.
All-Mother, we take all You give.
All-Mother, with You we all live."

A voice crept through the night from behind her. "I do believe we can have a story this night" said Imala, now sitting up straight.

She beckoned her young charges over to her. Lunyai scampered over and sat cross-legged with the other young pilgrims near the fire, which was low but still crackling enough to give off some warmth and light.

Imala sprang to her feet. She was surprisingly agile and quick for one her age. The young pilgrims' attention was now fixed upon the Elder. Eight young men and six young women, who'd all reached their sixteenth year this cycle. Lunyai glanced up again at Tlenaii the Moon. The Grey Ones had drifted away and His crescent was clear. The Tarakan girl smiled.

Oh Brother, did You send The Grey Ones away yourself? You would listen to Imala-Shi's tale too?

144

Lunyai knew Imala would choose her tale accordingly.

"*A Lost One Returns*" she announced.

Lunyai was right. This tale needed Tlenaii to be seen but not to shine too brightly. There was a tale for whatever form Tlenaii took and however the Grey Ones chose to behave. Tales passed from generation to generation, some too fantastical to be entirely true but all born in a truth of yesteryear. Lunyai waited patiently.

Imala began the story of a young boy who ran away from his tribe after misunderstanding something his father had said. Lunyai knew the tale well but she listened intently anyway. Her father often told her to pay even greater attention to stories she had heard many times before. This was when one could see a new truth, he would say.

"You know the path the story will take so focus on what you see as you walk that path."

Lunyai could hear his quiet voice in her head. She smiled and leaned in closer so she wouldn't miss a word Imala uttered.

Not long after the story began, the characters in the tale sang the Tarakalo. At this point Imala motioned for everyone to join her in singing. Lunyai and her people sang together in the same measured rhythm and pace that bound her people's sense of time. The song was sung to a child the moment they came into the world as a new-born baby, and then sung countless times in the early years. The Tarakalo was a part of their very being, etched onto their souls. Yaai and Tlenaii governed the passing of days, nights and months, while the All-Mother controlled the seasons. The Tarakalo bound the Tarakan people in all the day-to-day concerns that fell into these cycles.

When the pilgrims had finished the song, Imala continued with the story. "And so it was that Lunki crept away from his tribe's settlement and stole out onto the wider plains…"

Lunyai thought back to the last time she'd heard this tale. Her mother had been standing at her side, her arm through Lunyai's. She was now a head taller than her mother. The glow of the fire illuminating her mother's face now mingled in her mind with

145

the flickering flames dancing before her on this night. Imala continued to wrap them up in her telling of A Lost One Returns, just as Lunyai had felt her mother's love surround her that night.

"Tlenaii gave no white path for Lunki to follow…"

Lunyai knew her father would not be scouting this night under the thin form of Tlenaii and the darkness this meant. Before she had left for the Peregrika, her pilgrimage, she had begged her father to let her go scouting with him. Songaa had softly chided her for being too eager. He had reminded her she would spend enough time travelling as she made her way north to the hallowed Mount where they now camped. Songaa told his daughter to stay at the settlement the last few nights before her pilgrimage.

"See what you will be leaving and you will understand why you are going" he had said to her. Lunyai had felt she understood what he had meant then, but it had only truly become clear after she had arrived at their destination. She missed her parents.

Imala was nearing the end of the story and Lunyai realised she hadn't listened quite as intently as she should have. Imala caught her eye and raised both eyebrows. The young Tarakan girl grinned sheepishly and raised her eyes to the sky where Tlenaii rode high. A Grey One slid in front of the moon again but the golden points of Tlenaii's crescent reached out. Lunyai tilted her head sideways and looked upon her Brother. She saw an animal there, with horns. *A tatanka*, thought the girl. Lunyai took a deep breath and made a deep, grunting noise. She laughed as Imala and the other pilgrims looked at her with startled eyes.

"Forgive me, but Tlenaii showed me a tatanka" she told them, trying hard not to laugh.

"And He shows me a restless Imp!" commented Imala.

Their guardian raised her hands to either side and touched fingers with the two pilgrims sitting at her sides. The circle then repeated this gesture, until it became one ring.

"Let us try to calm the wild animal in Lunyai here."

"But Imala-Shi, Tlenaii is always trying to tell me something."

"Perhaps He is" sighed the older lady, raising her fingers and so lifting the circle they had made. "Just be patient. He will tell you when you are ready."

Imala held the circle high for a moment, and then let it slowly drop, until fingers parted and arms fell loosely at their sides. The Elder talked to the young men and women about how to interpret Yaai and Her brother Tlenaii. Imala cautioned them against reading what they wanted in the skies and not seeing what was really there.

"Just as Lunki misunderstood his father because he had set his heart on a particular path, we too can so very easily see our desire as it hides the truth. We often think we know what is in the dark of Tlenaii but can we be so sure? Ask yourselves if what you see is what is truly there or what you *want* to be there."

Imala cast her eyes around the group, settling her gaze on Lunyai a moment more than the others. Lunyai thought she understood and inwardly accepted she was guilty of a lack of patience.

Soon Imala told them to prepare their blankets and be ready for sleep. There would be much to do in the morning when Yaai rose again. "We must not waste Her kindness with too much slumber" she said sternly.

Lunyai lay down upon her blanket, her fellow pilgrims doing likewise, some shifting as they tried to find a comfortable position. Lunyai lay still, knowing she would fall asleep even if there were a great root in her back. Tlenaii brought her peace and her slumber was always restful. She closed her eyes and breathed deeply and slowly. The shadow of sleep crept upon her and started to swallow her. Her mind started to drift upon the sea that lay between the waking world and the world of dreams.

She felt herself floating, sliding across an expanse smooth as glass, Tlenaii's crescent above her and also reflected upon the surface an arm's length from her. She stretched her arms and looked to her right. A tatanka stood on the sea of glass. It snorted and then struck the ground with its hoof. The glass shattered and Lunyai fell through into darkness, careening down, down, down —

With a gasp, she jolted back to the waking world. It was dark. The Grey Ones were hiding Tlenaii. Hiding her Brother's sight of the world as if they didn't want Tlenaii to see something. She felt an uneasiness and turned onto her side.

She sang the Tarakalo softly to herself. How many songs it took for her to finally fall asleep she didn't know. She had another dream but the images were confusing, lacking in shape and colour. A sickly grey blurred everything. She slept that night but did not feel rested come morning when Yaai rose in Her majesty.

Ch 4

Lorken

29th Day of Aprus, Four Days After Sedmund's Death

No. No, you can't. It's not right. You're not a soldier, you're a…" Jenna's voice broke down into sobs. Lorken's heart ached for her and the pain he was causing.

"I cannot deny our lord" he said softly. "If I refuse, I'll be charged with disobeying Orben's command."

Lorken put his hand under her chin and raised her eyes to meet his.

"And it will make me a coward" he whispered.

Jenna fell into his arms and they hugged fiercely, as if to part from this embrace would be to let go forever.

After some time, Jenna eventually drew back and wiped her eyes. She looked up and held his gaze.

"Yesterday everything was perfect. Today our world has fallen apart. Will the pieces come back together? Or is this the beginning of conflict and turmoil that will last generations?"

Her voice was steady as she asked these questions. Lorken didn't have the answers but perhaps Jenna was speaking not to him but to the world and the Helligan deity, the First Warrior.

Lorken shook his head sadly. "I don't know" he replied. "All I know is that we have no control over certain things and can only decide how we face all that the First Warrior places before us and all the Dark Raven throws at us."

He kissed her forehead and held her close again.

"I will come back. Svard will make sure of it."

"I'll hold him to that" she whispered into his ear, and slowly slipped away from his arms.

Lorken went out to help his sons with the day's work after Jenna had started to make lunch. He found them both seated at a worktable, whittling away at small pieces of wood.

"What are you up to, lads?" he called.

Darl and Torg looked up as one. "Finishing the bed-posts for Maxan" said Torg.

Lorken sat down across from them and viewed their work. "You two certainly have skilled hands. Your grandfather would be impressed and he was a grumpy old sod."

Lorken smiled but immediately saw the cloud hovering in his sons' thoughts.

"Look lads, I don't like this any more than you but we are Helligan, our Lord is Orben and he has given the order. I am a member of the Free Guard and so must march with our brothers and sisters. Would you have me hide away and let others fight for us?"

"Of course not, Far" spoke up Darl, "but we just don't understand why Helliga will march in the first place. Nobody has attacked us. Who are we fighting?"

Lorken found a certain gratification in his son's questioning of the whole situation. Lorken too was unsure why Orben had given the orders to march. The general rumour circulating was that with Sedmund dead, Bregustol was now ruled by their religious leader and the chamberlain, and the military was gathering. Orben's intelligence network suspected the new rulers wanted to send out a clear warning to the realm that the Rihtgellen Kingdom was in good health and its dominion over the realm far from finished after Sedmund's passing.

But Lorken had doubts. Even if all this were true, why did it need the mobilisation of the Free Guard? Gamle Hovestad's defences along the River Mimir were solid according to Svard, with the Bridge of Helligad heavily fortified on both sides, Rihtgellen and Helligan towers facing each other across the strong currents of the River Mimir. Did the Free Guard's mobilisation signify that Orben needed numbers for something more ambitious? Did he mean to march on the capital and retake the throne for the Helligan nation?

"Far" came Darl's voice again, bringing him back to the

150

moment, "the people in Bregustol haven't done anything to us. Going to war with them doesn't seem right."

"I know, I know" Lorken sighed, feeling a slight despair and anger himself. "But there is history here, as you well know. Lord Orben may be looking to set right an injustice inflicted upon our people."

He wasn't convinced of what he was saying though; pride was not a good reason to get hundreds of good men and women killed. He shrugged.

"If Bregustol is pulling its forces together, we need to make sure those spears and arrows don't come anywhere near our homes. Agreed?"

This argument made more sense.

Both boys looked at him and he felt their eyes searching his for answers. He knew there were no good ones.

"I suppose so" muttered Torg.

His younger son suddenly put his work down and placed his palms on the work-surface, covered as it was in saw-dust.

"We can come with you, Far. We can help. Darl and I know how to use a bow and are stronger than boys older than us. We can—"

Lorken raised a hand to stop him.

"Don't let your mother hear you say that, young man. She's suffering enough with me having to leave."

He reached out and took a hand of each son as Darl also set down his work. He looked at them hard, his jaw set and squeezed their hands.

"I have to go but you two have to stay. Your mother needs you here, your sister needs you here and most of all, *I* need you here. I can't go off with spear in hand worrying about home. With you two here, I can march easily. Or as easily as can be sweating under a heavy helmet and carrying a bloody shield!"

His joke brought slight smiles to their faces. The two boys exchanged looks and both nodded.

"We'll make sure all is well here for when you get back, Far" Darl told him. Lorken fought back the tears he could feel rising.

"Now get back to work. Maxan probably wants to sleep in that bed tonight so pick up those tools. I'll be back in a while to help you, not that you need it these days." He smiled. "Just going to talk to Eira. Not sure she understands what is going on."

Lorken slapped them both on the shoulder and headed over to Eira's playhouse, built by her brothers.

Lorken spied through the window. Eira was inside, taking her blocks out of a sack and putting them on a tiny table that was the perfect size for her. He knocked on the door. Eira opened it and smiled at her father. She beckoned him to come in. Lorken scoffed.

"Don't know I can fit in there but will give it a try."

He squeezed through the door and found he could sit down in the half of the play-house without the table. Eira sat at the table on a small stool, stacking the blocks.

"Eira, your Far has something to…"

He stopped and stared at what she was doing. Just as before, Eira had created a seemingly impossible top-heavy tower with the blocks. A tower that should've already collapsed.

"How do you do that?" he whispered.

Eira smiled and clapped her hands. The sound startled Lorken; he was so used to total silence from her. The girl then rearranged a few blocks and the construction became truly absurd in its breaking of the laws of nature. Lorken's eyes widened with disbelief. He looked at his daughter, who seemed to have no awareness that what she was doing was anything out of the ordinary. Lorken reached out a hand gingerly, afraid he would topple the creation. Something tingled in his fingers as his hand got close. He withdrew his arm and gazed again at his daughter.

"Eira, are you doing that?"

He didn't mean his voice to be harsh but something in it must have unsettled Eira as her smile disappeared. The blocks fell to the table and then a few farther onto the floor.

"I'm sorry, little one" said Lorken, feeling guilty but also slightly afraid. How was his little child holding the blocks in a way that defied nature?

Eira clapped, once again making Lorken jump. She pushed past him and out the door. Lorken tried to follow but found himself getting stuck. "Damn it" he cursed. "Eira, wait there!" he called after her.

Lorken followed his daughter into their home. He found her underneath the table again. He sighed and got down on his hands and knees for the second time in less than a few moments.

Eira sat cross-legged and was looking at her father intensely. Lorken felt slightly unnerved, both from this staring and by what he had just witnessed inside the playhouse.

"Eira, you seem to have some tricks under your hat."

The girl looked puzzled and patted her head to indicate she wasn't wearing a hat.

"Figure of speech, young one. Now, will you take care of Mormi while I am away? Can you do that for me? I'll be marching off to the north with your Uncle Svard."

Eira shook her head.

"I know he's not your real uncle but he's a brother to me, so that makes him your uncle" Lorken said gently.

Eira made a face and Lorken guessed he had misunderstood her. Or maybe Eira just didn't understand what was going on. He smiled at her.

"Oh Eira, you are why I joined the Free Guard. Can't leave it all up to Uncle Svard to protect our lands. I am going to help that rascal keep Gamle Hovestad safe."

So as not to bump his head again, he carefully reached out to hug her. She surprised him by grabbing his face with both hands and staring into his eyes. He looked back, seeing an intelligence in his daughter's eyes that belied her years.

Her hands dropped from his face and he leant in to hug her. She returned the hug, gripping her father fiercely.

"We'll talk one day, Eira."

Ch 5

Lunyai

3rd Day of Maia, Eight Days After Sedmund's Death

Lunyai and the other pilgrims hiked cheerfully up the road to the port-city of Argyllan, their journey to the Sacred Mount now on its return leg. The eager Tarakan girl had enjoyed the ferry boat around the Mother's Ring, the rivers taking them along with their currents. Yaai the Sun had watched over their passage, shining brightly but not too fiercely. Lunyai had rested her fore-arms on the gunwale and gazed somewhat dreamily at the rushing water their boat was gently slicing through. As they had approached a jetty of the River Freo, a Kingfisher had settled three arm's lengths from Lunyai. She had watched the little bird, marvelling in the turquoise blue of its feathers. Her mother had often told her how Yaai gave colour to the world around them, giving beauty to everything the All-Mother had created.

They had disembarked at the jetty, which was a mile or so from Argyllan. They could have taken the ferry all the way down the Freo and docked within the city port itself, but Imala insisted they needed to stretch their limbs. Lunyai was tired but the walk worked out the stiffness in her legs after the ferry ride. She looked ahead to see Imala speaking with Enyeto, a lad who had grown much in the last year. He towered over the elderly Imala but was now leaning in to hear her words, nodding as Imala explained something with effusive gestures. The Tarakan Elder was ever the teacher, thought Lunyai. Enyeto, Lunyai and the others had learnt so much on this pilgrimage. And gained a new understanding perhaps of their people and why they lived the way they did.

Lunyai heard the sounds and commotion of many people before they came into view of a large camp that sprawled before the walls of Argyllan. Lines of green and white tents were formed in neat rows, with all manner of weapons and tools resting on racks between them. Soldiers moved smartly through the avenues in this little military village, going about their business as if there was nothing unusual about their being there just outside Argyllan.

Lunyai looked at Imala for some kind of explanation but the Elder seemed as puzzled as she was. Not just puzzled but very worried.

"What has happened in the world since we last passed through?" the Tarakan Elder wondered aloud.

Lunyai nor the other pilgrims had an answer and a certain disquiet fell upon the group as they continued on towards the city gates, albeit now at a more cautious pace.

A line of farmers and traders with their wagons and carts stretched back from the city gates. The Tarakan pilgrims joined the queue, Lunyai searching all around for some clue as to why armed soldiers were here in abundance.

Lunyai moved closer to Imala.

"Is there war in the realm?" she asked nervously.

Imala took her time in answering, her neck craning around as her eyes took in the scene around them.

"Not war now, I think, but I sense a storm is coming. These soldiers wear the colours of Meridia, which is Argyllan's neighbour to the east. They are clearly not here to attack the city, nor have they done so judging by what my eyes can see now."

Lunyai looked at some soldiers passing in their green and white uniforms. One of them caught the Tarakan girl's eye and smiled. She smiled back but frowned inside. Imala was right; this certainly wasn't the scene of a battle.

"I don't understand" she whispered to Imala.

The Elder turned to her charge and smiled warmly. "Neither do I, young one. So we must be patient and see what we can discover from the guards ahead. Keep your eyes and ears open!"

"I will keep my eyes on your face and my ears will hang on

your words, Imala-Shi" replied Lunyai with a determined smile.

Imala chuckled.

"You are wise to look to older eyes and ears, Lunyai. I feel you will be a strong leader one day."

Lunyai was taken aback by the sudden praise and just stood there, mouth agape. She didn't see herself as a leader at all.

Imala laughed again. "Tame the wild horse within you. Help the lonely wolf in its plight. Seek to learn about differences rather than speak loudly and without thought about what you perceive them to be. And love the All-Mother with all your heart, as She is not as eternal as Her two children."

Imala finished speaking and looked into Lunyai's eyes. The Tarakan girl saw kindness mixed with sadness in the Elder's.

She tried to take in all that Imala had told her but too many thoughts swirled within her mind. Voices ahead brought her attention back to the world and she saw that their group was almost at the city gates now.

Soldiers were processing the flow of traffic entering and leaving Argyllan. The group shuffled forward, now behind a trader and his wagon. A large dog was nudging his master's legs, an Argollat mastiff by the looks of it. If the dog was big, its owner was huge. Even tall Enyeto would have looked small had they stood together. The giant turned, as if he could feel Lunyai's eyes upon him. The shock of reddish hair upon his head was matched by a beard that was tied into a single braid. He grinned at Lunyai, rolling his eyes, presumably to say this was taking a long time. Lunyai tried to smile back but found herself suddenly feeling tiny, not just in stature. The man turned back and the Tarakan released a breath.

Lunyai had felt as safe on the Sacred Mount as she did on the Tarakan Plains that were home. Imala had been there with them, while Yaai and Tlenaii had guarded them from above. Now they were among the people of the world and conflict seemed on the horizon, Lunyai felt uneasy. She breathed in, reminding herself the pilgrimage was not just about seeing the magnificent world the All-Mother had created but interacting with the folk who lived upon Her lands.

Imala greeted the soldier in charge at the gate when their turn came.

"Yaai shines on you, good captain. We are pilgrims seeking entrance to Argyllan. We have lodging with the Cromlech Brotherhood in the south-east quarter."

The soldier looked at each member of the group with an attentive eye. Lunyai could see no ill-will in the man but there was a caution mixed with mistrust.

"Tarakans, eh? Well, Argyllan has ever welcomed your people. You may enter. Rest yourselves well with the brotherhood but do not linger too long here. Ill winds are blowing."

Imala began to ask what he meant but a horse farther up the line began to whinny and buck around, sending travellers scurrying to a clear distance as the horse's owner tried to calm the beast.

The captain waved them through as he called to a couple of his men to help the man with the restless animal.

"The Meridians are here to protect us from the north so aid them by staying out of their way!" he called to the pilgrims as they passed through the gate. Lunyai thought she had misheard but one look at Imala assured her those had been the words.

The north? Has the wider realm fallen into war?

Imala led Lunyai and the other young Tarakans to the monastery of the Cromlech Brotherhood. They would stay here three nights, study with the brothers and then take the coastal road back to the Tarakan Plains. They would be met at Yaai's Stone by members of their tribe with horses, which they would ride the rest of the way. The Tarakans were reluctant to have their horses travel beyond the Plains and rarely ventured themselves out into the wider realm.

It was maybe three songs walk to the monastery and Lunyai was glad to see the simple design of the building and the way the walls had been built round the few trees that grew there. It was clear the Brotherhood cared for the All-Mother's work in a similar fashion to the Tarakans. The Cromlech brothers themselves were welcoming, dressed in very plain brown robes with shaven heads and no facial hair.

The pilgrims were led to a dormitory where white cotton undershirts lay upon humble cots alongside pale blue woollen robes. Lunyai felt herself relaxing after the tension at the gate and was more than relieved when a brother quietly told them there was a bath-house through a door on the far wall, where they could wash away the dust and fatigue of their travels.

When the pilgrims were alone they started chattering like excited birds, putting down their belongings and then making eagerly for the bath. Lunyai wondered where Imala was. She presumed the Tarakan Elder must be getting news from the Cromlech Abbot, perhaps learning what had led to the heightened presence of soldiers, of whom Lunyai had seen many more as they walked to the monastery. She noticed her friends had already left the room and hurried to catch up.

The baths were like the caring hands of the All-Mother on her weary limbs. Her skin was glowing from where she had scrubbed the dirt off before entering the surprisingly hot waters and now was turning an even deeper shade. She had seen Enyeto step into the waters and thought to herself he would make a good mate when her time came. He was physically powerful and seemed fertile. And Lunyai knew he was respectful and listened to the Elders. Tlenaii had blessed her with His blood some five years ago so she believed she could bear children. Yet something inside Lunyai was not ready for the change becoming mates with another would bring.

Maybe she was a *restless imp*, as Imala had said. She longed to be back on the Plains, riding on her horse, Ahote, feeling the wind buffet her as she gathered speed. Galloping across the Plains was a feeling like none other for Lunyai. She looked forward to the day when she would venture farther afield with her father and explore areas her tribe had never dwelt in her life-time. The Plains were vast, stretching away to the south-west. And yet there was a part of Lunyai that was curious about the realm beyond her homeland. Although the Tarakans shunned contact with others in general, they did not stop people journeying upon the Plains. However, the number of travellers was not great. As Lunyai's mother Chenoa had commented more than once, "The Plains don't go anywhere."

It was true. The Plains reached higher towards the skies than the Argol Forest region, looking out over the Western Sea. The Coastal Road winding round the north tip of Argol became a steep climb up onto the Plains that fell off to the west and south in brilliant white cliffs. Beautiful it was said if one were at sea, and Lunyai knew they reflected Tlenaii the Moon's brightness, which helped guide many sailors who were upon the Western Sea at night.

These cliffs and the Plains resting high beyond them did result in the Tarakan homeland being the end of the realm in a sense. One could not travel over the Plains and reach a city. Anyone entering the Plains would have to leave them at some point by going back up along the Coastal Road or around the Forest of Argol, heading north-east to Meridia. The latter route afforded a view of the Izachu Wildlands, a region uninhabited by people. The terrain was too uneven to build upon and the vast numbers of wild animals there deterred even hunters. The Tarakans felt a kinship with the beasts there though, both having migrated south hundreds of years ago after the Coming.

But traders and journeymen did come on occasion to the Plains, seeking to acquire Tarakan bows, ointments and also fruit that grew in abundance on the Plains. The Tarakans showed them hospitality and made sure nobody lost their way in the immense sea of grass. Even the number of traders was dropping these days though, many finding the journey to the nomadic Tarakans too long and thus of lower profit than other areas of the realm.

Lunyai mused that this was possibly why she felt an urge to see the wider world. She was happy that the Tarakan people lived their lives as the All-Mother taught them and suffered no external interference but something inside her worried that the Tarakan people would be forgotten. She wanted the numerous folk of the realm to know about her own people and the way they cared for everything the All-Mother gave them.

But we don't want outsiders to disrupt our ways.

The young Tarakan lady found it difficult to reconcile her desires. It just didn't seem possible to spread Tarakan teachings and yet have their homeland untouched.

"You cannot dip your arm into the river and expect it to be dry when you pull it out."

Her mother's words and although seemingly obvious, there was wisdom to be found there. Maybe Lunyai had a bit of a wandering spirit within her. The thought of thrusting both arms into the river, drawing them out swiftly and splashing her face with the cool water, was exciting.

Maybe I am not yet ready to settle upon the Plains with a mate.

Ch 6

Lorken

Lorken gazed upon what lay before the Helligan soldiers. The city of Meridia. Not Bregustol. Lorken reflected that the rank-and-file of the Helligan army had not been told before they departed Gamle Hovestad that they were heading to Bregustol, but all had assumed that was where their fates lay. Then, camped at Raven's Point, senior officers had apparently been briefed. After this the word had spread like wildfire, with sergeants struggling to maintain an orderly fashion by which the revelation was relayed to the men and women.

Lorken had thought it must've been a jape at first, something to stoke up morale. But it quickly became clear it was no joke and the Helligan army would strike out west, march on Meridia and take the city. The revelation left Lorken slightly bewildered. Meridia was no true friend of Helliga, especially when one considered the part the former played in his nation's defeat and withdrawal from the north all those years ago. But open war with them seemed a strange path to take. The two city-states had even fought side-by-side against invading forces less than twenty years ago. The Helligan nation's real enemies lay to the north as did their capital of old. Why was Lord Orben about to open a battle upon two fronts?

The next morning, they had set off in a westerly direction, heading towards the River Unn instead of crossing the Mimir. The Helligan soldiers had marched a good fifteen miles each day, setting their last camp a couple of miles from the city of Meridia. By this time of course, it was well known they were coming. Villagers stayed in their homes and the fields were bereft of labouring hands.

Lorken had enjoyed the boisterous camaraderie of the first two nights, with camp-fires, ale and songs that sang of the Helligan nation of old. He was swept up with it and laughed with newfound comrades. On the third night though, the reality started to seep in and it was noticeable that those from the Free Guard, like Lorken, did not laugh or sing as much. Nobody in the Free Guard had ever seen any kind of combat outside training, and harsh as training had been, Lorken knew the coming battle would be of a starkly different colour. Instead of blue bruises on the skin, there would be a crimson colour to the clothing. Where in training one had lost their footing, soon they may lose a limb. Or their life.

Now the Helligan forces stood in formation facing the city of Meridia. Green and white flags danced in the wind atop the walls as red and white flags snapped back below on the fields before the walls; fields now trampled under thousands of boots.

"Those walls will take some beating" commented Lorken to the figure standing to his right.

"Hm?"

"The walls" repeated Lorken to the soldier, "they'll take some beating."

The morning sun fell upon their surface, showing neither age nor damage, just a dapple grey of hard rock. The walls were maybe ten soldiers high and would require both the siege towers and a great deal of courage to conquer. *With a huge loss of life* thought Lorken grimly.

"The Meridians will take a beating, more like!" laughed the man. He winked at Lorken, and slapped him on the back. "Ready for this little scuffle today?"

Lorken shivered despite himself and shook his head.

"Geir, you have seen battle so I hear."

"Aye, was part of Orben's campaign to bring the Belfri Isle under his rule. Those islanders were tough little shits. Got three scars to prove it." He grinned.

Lorken felt even more ill at ease. It didn't make much sense but part of him wished there were another green boy like himself beside him. At least they would speak the same language.

Geir nodded backwards. "Got some decent lads here and the best captains in Ragnekai. Don't worry, Lorken, this night we'll be quaffing some Meridian ale in their own kitchens." He laughed and elbowed Lorken.

Lorken suffered the not-so-gentle dig and decided not to tell Geir it was more likely they'd be sipping wine as the Meridians weren't great lovers of beer.

Lorken craned his neck to survey the Helligan soldiers amassed around him. Most of the Free Guard had been mixed into the Spear Infantry, whose initial function would be to protect the missile troops from any sorties the Meridians might make.

The missile contingent was quite significant. Svard had given Lorken a quick tour of the camp the second night on the road and introduced his friend to the various elements of the Helligan war machine. The ballistae had impressed Lorken the most. Exceptional wood-work and a great feat of engineering. Svard had told him he'd be even more impressed when he saw them in action.

Lorken had felt unsure about that, as that moment would likely be when the spark was lit and the chaos of battle took hold. He was certain it wasn't like the songs and he'd be lucky to come of out this unscathed. *If I make it out at all* he thought and had an instant where he felt the black shadow of the Dark Raven's wings encroaching upon his soul.

There were a large number of longbow archers, a smaller number of crossbow soldiers with huge shields strapped on their backs and even a squad of slingers, all complimenting the mighty firepower of the ballistae. Lorken hoped this part of Orben's force would win the battle without the need for close-combat. He wasn't a coward but he didn't share Geir's apparent lust to charge in and engage the enemy face-to-face.

Enemy.

The word sounded strange at that moment. *It wasn't long ago*

163

we were neighbours with these people reflected Lorken. He tasted bile in the back of his throat. He hawked and spat it out at his feet.

The infantry had numbers but the experience and skill lay with Orben's elite soldiers, the legendary Sentinels with their pole-axes. Svard had told Lorken that the Sentinels would likely be the ones going over the walls via the siege towers. Fearless they were said to be, and supremely skilled with their deadly weapon.

Svard was not amongst the main host. With his Rangers he was off somewhere, presumably leading an assault on another area of the wall. Lorken hadn't been able to find Svard the night before to have a last word. They had exchanged glances yesterday morning as Svard had ridden past on a magnificent midnight-black destrier. The look had spoken many words. It was enough to give Lorken the courage he needed to stand firm with his comrades now but was unlikely to steel his nerves when the horns rang and battle commenced.

He shifted his helm and looked at Geir. His shield brother looked confident, cocky even. Geir was physically imposing and Lorken felt small standing next to him, despite the fact he was a decent size himself. Lorken wore a knee-length chain-mail shirt over a boiled leather jerkin and woollen kilt. On his head was an iron helmet, felt cushioning inside, and a nose-guard reaching down between his eyes. He clutched a spear made of ash with a leaf-shaped, steel tip and an iron-bossed oaken shield. A short sword hung at his side. Lorken was certainly dressed as a soldier but Geir actually looked like one; eyes burning keen for battle and that grin that spoke of having seen this all before.

Lorken felt so new to this. Six months of training had strengthened him mentally but he hadn't been at it every day and he would always come home to his family. He figured this was why he felt disconnected somehow from all that was happening now. Svard, on the other hand, lived and breathed the life of a soldier. First Ranger no less. Lorken was in awe of him at times but relieved at others that he didn't face the kind of dangers his friend did.

Until now. Until this day when they had finally arrived at the city of Meridia. Today was the day the world would take on a different hue.

The sun was climbing up into a clear, blue sky and Lorken felt as though whatever power drove the weather had not been told that today swords would be unsheathed. It just seemed too perfect a day for men and women to spill each other's blood. Lorken looked up to see birds flitting here and there across the azure expanse. He then saw what looked like carrion birds off to the west and quickly turned his attention back to what was before him.

Lorken could see Meridian soldiers up on the battlements. Faceless and anonymous for the moment being so far away but they bled the same colour as he did.

If I make it back, my lads will see me anew he thought. Perhaps like all fathers, he did feel a certain kind of pressure to be something of a hero for his two sons. He gripped his spear more tightly. If he stayed close to Geir and the men and women around him, he might just see the next sunrise and bring home some glory for his boys.

There was some commotion behind him and Lorken looked back to see soldiers parting to allow other forces through. He glimpsed one of the ballistae moving smoothly through the ranks.

"Looks like we're about to put our best foot forward" he commented to his companion, doing his best to speak in a tone of indifference.

"You are new to this game, aren't you?" chuckled the woman to his left. Freda was her name if Lorken remembered correctly. She was as tall as him, lithe and solid, with blue swirling designs inked into the skin of her bare arms. She too had seen battle before, being part of a Helligan long-boat crew that had protected the trade routes out upon the sea. Freda had shared a few tales about fighting pirates round the camp-fire the night before. She had advised Lorken not to wear heavy armour if he ever joined a crew. Lorken had thanked her for the advice, inwardly thinking he was unlikely to give up the life he had for seasickness, scurvy and a much-increased possibility of drowning.

Geir nudged Lorken and pointed up to the soldiers manning the Meridian walls.

"We'll begin this little jaunt in the countryside by knocking some of those bastards off the walls. Us infantry here won't be moving an inch for quite a while yet, so just relax and enjoy the show."

Lorken allowed the tension within him to dissipate slightly. He could well imagine the damage those siege machines were capable of. The sheer velocity of anything they shot would be devastating. The Meridian walls might be able to stand against their might but he doubted there would be much left of a soldier if hit.

Geir laughed at the unsettled look on Lorken's face.

"Trust me" said the taller man, "those walls will be deserted by the time the siege towers roll up."

Geir looked over his shoulder at the slowly advancing ballistae. Then he turned back to Lorken and said in a growl, "Poor bastards haven't got a chance!"

Freda laughed and bared her teeth in a snarl.

Lorken smiled nervously, feeling a sense of bewilderment mixed with fear. He looked around again and his gaze fell on the massive siege towers, which stood idle within the midst of the ranks. Lorken squinted, trying to see their construction. They had been put erected surprisingly quickly the day before with previously built sections brought from Helliga upon huge carts. Lorken had wanted to help with the work, reasoning his skills could be put to good use and wanting to learn a thing or two. But the siege engineers seemed a proud lot. His offer to lend a hand had been politely but firmly refused. The towers now stood as tall as the Meridian walls, animal hides covering the forward side, ready to be doused with water in case the defenders used fire. The sides at the top of the tower looked unusually bulky to Lorken, slightly out of line with the rest of it.

The Sentinels would be the ones who would assault the walls in them. They were said to be without equal in combat prowess and never hesitated. Certainly, they had led the charge to repel the invasion a generation ago. *Fearless.* Svard had once told Lorken though that all men feel fear at the precipice of battle and what made the difference was how a soldier controlled that rising terror. Svard had then shrugged and said that once the battle had begun, there was only the instinct to survive. Lorken hoped his own instinct to survive was a strong one. After all, it had never been put to the test.

Freda suddenly crashed her spear against her shield.

"HELLIGA!" she screamed. Others took up the call and soon Lorken found himself shouting the name of his homeland too. It felt as though a wave of courage seemed to ripple through the ranks, steeling the blood of veterans and green boys alike.

The instant the chanting stopped though, Lorken's guts churned. He felt gas noisily escaping his back-side and prayed to the First Warrior that neither Geir nor Freda had heard. Without turning his head, Geir said "And here comes Rorthal. Enjoy the entertainment."

Freda whooped and yelled the Battle Sergeant's name as the burly soldier rode forward upon his horse, a look of something bordering on boredom upon his face. He turned to where the call had come from, spotted Freda jumping up and down and grinned.

"Freda, you still alive?" he called out.

"I told the Dark Raven to kiss my arse!" she shouted back.

Rorthal and the soldiers within ear-shot laughed.

"I can see why he gave up on you then. Wouldn't want my nose anywhere near that shit-hole!"

More laughter.

Lorken laughed too. It was a nervous laughter but it helped to keep at bay the fear scuttling around inside him.

The Battle Sergeant kicked his horse into a canter and started riding along in front of the first line of the infantry. The four ballistae were now in position beyond Rorthal. The archers were spilling out from each flank and forming units ten wide and five deep. Lorken could feel the tension building all around him.

Rorthal rode the line up and down one more time, then slowed his mount.

"Men and women of Helliga!" he cried.

A roar went up from the mass of soldiers.

"Today we begin a new chapter in our history. Today we..."

Lorken couldn't hear the rest of this sentence as Rorthal had moved away from his position. But laughter from the other end told him Rorthal had ended that part of his speech with another wry comment.

"...of luck as Lord Rencarro isn't even home!"

A cheer.

"Silly fool is to the west catching fish."

Lorken was surprised to feel something resembling courage taking shape within him. Rorthal was creating an atmosphere one might encounter before a match of *knattleikr* in the autumn.

"So our job today will be that much easier. Anyone who wants to..."

Rorthal's voice was lost again. Lorken waited for the Battle Sergeant to return.

"What say we blow these wine-drinking fops a few kisses?"

The response to this was deafening and Lorken suddenly realised his voice was screaming out as loud as any other. Geir was roaring with laughter and Freda was making a twisted noise that sounded like some unholy beast's mating call.

Rorthal turned to face the Meridian walls and the ballistae in front of him. He signalled for the crews to begin and Lorken heard the bowstrings being ratcheted back. Huge bolts were loaded. Then the crews stood ready.

Rorthal signalled to a trumpeter who blew three sharp notes that rang out clear and cold in the spring air.

Ch 7

Svard

Svard waited a few moments after the third horn had sounded, making sure there was no mistaking the signal. Nothing else came so the First Ranger nodded to his four captains.

"Right lads, here we go. Make a good show of this and we might get up nice and close to the northern wall. If the Dark Raven decides to shit on our little ruse, then fall back and we'll wait for Rorthal's next signal."

Svard's captains, men who had been through many brutal encounters and harsh scrapes with him, nodded and took up their positions with their respective squads.

Then all five groups, Svard's included, emerged from the barn of the homestead they had acquired the night before. Svard had made it clear there was to be no killing; the objective was to scare the families out of the homestead, not just burn it to the ground. The plan was then to make a show to those fleeing that he and his men were moving on to join the main host. Svard was pretty sure none of the fleeing civilians had looked back though so it was perhaps effort wasted.

Now, wearing simple tunics over their light chain-mail shirts, the men hurried towards the city alongside three horse-drawn wagons, each laden with what would appear to be wares. They moved as quickly as possible in a diagonal line that would bring them close to the northern city walls. The hope was they would give the appearance of villagers seeking refuge within the city and making for the western gate. With Rorthal and the main force causing havoc on the eastern walls, there was unlikely to be much of a presence on this wall anyway.

The horses pulled the wagons across the meadow that ran up

to the wall. Svard could see soldiers on the battlements but they were few and most seemed to be looking to the east.

Good old Rorthal. Making some noise over there.

Svard tried not to think about Lorken. He had confidence his friend could fight when the battle began but he knew he wouldn't be close to watch his back. Still, he had done what he could to give Lorken a better chance of surviving what was to come. Svard had made sure an old friend of his, Geir, would be next to Lorken in the ranks. Svard had saved Geir's life some years ago and he knew the burly soldier would do all in his power to stay with Lorken.

They were nearing the walls now but kept their diagonal course. A straight dash would have made it clear they were not harmless villagers fleeing the violence on the eastern wall.

"Steady now lads, keep the pace" cautioned Svard.

The point where the northern wall connected to the western wall came into sight and there were noticeably fewer men here. Svard saw a couple of heads bobbing up and down along the battlements as they moved to the east, presumably ordered to support those already there.

That's it. Don't worry about us, chaps.

One soldier was looking down at them and they were close enough to hear him shouting in the Meridian language. Svard could understand the soldier was telling them to hurry but left it to one of his squad to respond.

"Our thanks! There are so many!" shouted the Helligan Ranger in the Meridian language.

Nicely done, Erland. Impressive accent too.

The Meridian soldier on the wall waved them on and then turned his attention to the east. The Rangers, forty-five of them in total, kept their wagons moving, coming ever closer to the city wall.

"Cuyler" called Svard to one of his captains, "be ready."

Cuyler motioned to his squad and they withdrew bows and quivers that had been concealed under canvas in the backs of one wagon.

"Now!" called Svard and the ruse was discarded as the men sprang into action. Cuyler's men nocked arrows to their bows and held their distance, while Svard and the others pulled forth grapples from the wagons along with their weapons.

There was no warning shout from above so Svard knew they were unnoticed for now, but their luck was unlikely to last. He motioned for his men to make haste.

Svard then heard the whoosh of an arrow being released behind him and a gurgled gasp immediately after from above.

"Solitary guard. Clear!" called Cuyler as five Rangers made ready to hurl their grapples. It was a high throw but Svard had confidence they could make the distance.

They swirled their hooks and as one released them. All five grapples cleared the battlements. Each man then pulled gently but swiftly. Four caught but one came away, falling down.

"Above!" cried Svard and they all cleared the area where the grapple fell.

"Out of luck there, Stian" remarked Svard. "No time for a second throw. Four will do. Up the walls!"

The Rangers holding the grapples tested their strength and then made a run at the wall, leaping up and planting their boots against the stone, bodies now horizontal and parallel with the ground. They began to ascend the wall, gripping onto the knotted rope, all the while Svard praying to the First Warrior to give them a climb unhindered by missiles launched from above.

Svard watched as the four of them made it to the top and slipped over the battlements. Still no word from Cuyler and his archers.

Four more ropes came spiralling down from above, joining the ones already there. Svard grabbed one and was followed by seven more Rangers. The climb was hard but the ropes were knotted and every Ranger had thick, muscular arms used to hauling their own body weight.

A shout came from above, followed by the loud clash of steel upon steel.

The Dark Raven flies past.

171

The Ranger climbing next to Svard suddenly disappeared, his rope twirling down after him. Svard heard a thud and his anguished cry from below.

Curse the black wings! Must be a few up there.

He kept climbing, willing the four up there to stop any more ropes being cut without getting themselves killed in the process. Then there was the rush of arrows as Cuyler and his men found their targets. Screams from above and what Svard deemed to be an undesirable level of noise.

Svard reached the top and hauled himself over the battlements. There were at least twenty Meridian soldiers pushing his men back. The width of the battlements took away some of the numerical advantage but the four Rangers were beset.

Svard reached behind his head and pulled forth his blade. He smiled grimly and charged, shouting a command at his men as he leapt forward, sword held high. They parted smoothly, giving him the space to deal death. His first cut took a Meridian in a downwards arc across the neck. Blood spurted forth and the hapless man fell back, clutching his throat.

Svard already had his blade ramming through the stomach of another. He grabbed the soldier by his collar and pulled him closer, the steel doing irreparable damage to the man's internal organs.

Another Meridian swung a short sword at him but Svard retreated a step, turning and bringing the unfortunate man impaled on his blade round to block the blow. The assailant only succeeded in cutting deep into his comrade's shoulder blade, hastening the man's death.

Svard let go of the collar and pushed the man off his sword with his boot, the soldier falling back lifelessly into his fellows, who were showing the tell-tale signs of fear in the face of a more skilled opponent. Svard's men saw it and as one they pushed forward as a small wedge, Svard at the point felling two more soldiers.

Behind Svard six more Rangers were coming over the wall.

The remaining dozen or so Meridians saw their strength in numbers suddenly obliterated and began to retreat. Svard snarled at them and they fled. He held up a fist to check his men from pursuing.

"Hold our position. Get another rope down and get the others up."

Svard went to the wall and looked over. He saw Cuyler attending the Ranger who had fallen.

"Tarben lives" shouted up Cuyler, "but his day is done."

"Get him on a wagon. Two men take him back to the homestead. Await our return." Svard rang off his commands in quick succession.

Before long the remaining forty-two Rangers all stood upon the battlements. Svard signalled his men to move and he led them farther into the city but well away from the battle at the eastern wall.

Ch 8

Lorken

5th Day of Maia, Ten Days After Sedmund's Death

Lorken gazed up at the battered areas of the Meridian walls. The ballistae bolts had crashed into the walls in explosions of iron, wood and stone. Many soldiers manning the walls had been knocked back from the impacts. Others had simply deserted their posts and a couple of unfortunate ones had found themselves at the end of a speeding bolt, their bodies impaled and thrown into the air. The walls still stood but whether they were now effectively manned was another question.

Lorken had gazed in awe at the awesome power of these siege weapons as they shot their bolts of destruction towards the beleaguered city. He had noticed however that his respect of the ballistae was perhaps not shared by all. A strange atmosphere seemed to have descended upon the infantry. There was a general shuffling as men and women grew tired of standing stationary, and Lorken even heard two soldiers just behind him discussing which inn in Gamle Hovestad had the best ale at the best price. Lorken was amazed they could be thinking about anything other than giant bolts streaking through the air.

Lorken was startled when the Battle Sergeant Rorthal trotted by on his horse and called out the order to cease firing. An eerie silence followed as Rorthal scanned the battlements left to right. He gave an extended grumbling grunt, which Lorken took to mean he wasn't satisfied yet. The burly Battle-Sergeant turned his horse and shouted out.

"Archers forward! Steady rain of arrows just beyond the wall. Think there are still some of those fools hiding up there."

The order was relayed along the lines and the squads of archers moved forward, taking up positions roughly three hundred yards from the wall. As they formed up, the ballistae were rotated and then wheeled back. There were shouts of gratitude from the infantry to the crews and the odd insult.

"You leaving already? Got some lass waiting back home?"

"Yah, your wife."

Lorken chuckled as did Freda and Geir beside him.

"Second act coming up now, Lorken" said Geir cheerfully.

Before Lorken could reply there was a hissing and the sky ahead was suddenly a dark, shuddering blur. Like a swarm of insects buzzing through the air. The swarm seemed to hover momentarily in mid-air and then swooped down past the wall. The erupting screams confirmed Rorthal's suspicions about some Meridians still bravely manning the walls.

Poor souls.

Lorken flinched as he saw the response from the castle walls. Black flecks across the sky. He stepped back a pace instinctively and the soldier behind grunted in annoyance. Geir gripped his arm again. "Hold firm" he growled, "They won't reach us."

Lorken watched in terror as the Meridian arrows streaked towards them. But they fell at least twenty yards short of the Helligan archers. Geir looked at him, head cocked and eyebrows raised. It was a look of *I told you so*. Lorken laughed despite his fear.

"Our longbows have the greatest distance this side of Bregustol" commented Geir, with pride clear in his voice. "Constructed from the same yew that I guess you use for your work."

Lorken nodded. Yew was an excellent wood for bows; the sapwood had good tension and the heartwood compressed well. A thought crossed Lorken's mind. It had been nigh on impossible for him to get any yew this spring. The woodcutter he did most business with had kept shrugging and telling him Lord Orben's carpenters had been snapping up any and all yew-wood.

175

Geir pointed up at more arrows flying from the city. They again landed short of their targets and the Helligan soldiers jeered at the defenders behind the walls.

"We can hit them but they can't hit us. You'll see today the difference between us and them." Geir grinned. "We know how to fight!"

Lorken nodded, feeling almost pity for the Meridians. It really did seem that the two sides were unevenly matched and the Helligan nation would take this city without breaking a sweat. He wondered what would happen then. Hopefully the citizens would just stay inside their homes until there could be a clear transfer of rule.

Geir was still rambling on next to him.

"I don't think this city and its people are very familiar with warfare in general. They've maintained order and defended their lands against raiders and vagabonds, but that has been mostly down to numbers and better equipment. And of course those walls. Don't think they ever imagined a return to the old days of open war within the realm. Poor bastards."

The air was still filled with the hiss and whoosh of arrows but Lorken could see there weren't many coming from Meridia anymore.

Perhaps they've seen the futility in this.

A quick toot-toot sounded and was answered by another. The Helligan long-bows ceased their merciless hail and the archers smartly responded to each unit's commander shouting out orders to shoulder weapons and retreat behind the infantry.

The Helligan Battle-Sergeant rode his steed around to the front, once again surveying the state of the defence. He seemed satisfied the missile contingent of his forces had done enough damage. He raised a hand, and another horse and rider approached.

"Who's that?" enquired Lorken to Geir and Freda.

The shield-maiden answered, a giddy excitement in her eyes.

"Brax, the First Sentinel!"

Geir nodded. "One of only two Helligans worthy enough to

stand with Rorthal and be counted as an equal."

Lorken felt a burst of pride hearing this, knowing for sure Svard was the other. He reasoned that he would be allowed to feast in the Great Hall upon their return, having seen active duty. Raising a mug with Svard and maybe sharing company with the mighty warriors of the Helligan nation.

Quite a story to tell the boys!

Rorthal was pointing at various places along the wall and Brax was nodding. The discussion ended and Brax motioned to someone out of Lorken's view. A roar of many voices erupted, followed by more orders being hurled around, some directed at the infantry and thus Lorken himself.

Our turn now thought Lorken, all excitement draining from the Helligan carpenter.

He managed to execute a neat left-turn along with his fellows and march twenty paces before halting. The unit then made the right-turn to face their shields back toward the city walls. Lorken could hear creaking and the vocal exertion of many men, women and beasts of burden back where he had just been standing. The siege-towers were moving.

Freda crashed her spear against her shield.

"The Sentinels are getting ready to show the realm why Helliga should be feared." The fierce grin she gave Lorken was infectious and he couldn't help but emit a small laugh.

The two huge towers came into Lorken's peripheral vision and he took a sharp breath, marvelling at the sheer size of these siege engines as they trundled along at a slow but steady pace. The tops still struck Lorken as being bulky at the sides, but he had to admit he'd never seen a siege tower before today.

Rorthal's horse neighed and he shouted for attention.

"Right, listen up! Now the archers have given those little rabbits a few pricks here and there, it's time for…"

His voice became inaudible once again, as the Battle-Sergeant rode farther down the line. Soldiers standing where Rorthal was now laughed heartily and Freda joined them, despite the fact she couldn't possibly have heard what was said. Rorthal returned their way.

"…can't let Brax and his Sentinels have all the fun though so let's go and knock on that gate there, see who's at home. I'm just dying to introduce them to my little friend here!" he cried as he unstrapped a vicious looking mace from his saddle.

The Helligan infantry whooped and cheered, clashing their spears against shields and bellowing out oaths and promises of delivering destruction unto the doomed city's defenders. Lorken cheered but could not find the words to anything heroic.

"Rams!" cried Rorthal and soon two rams were following in the tracks of the siege towers, already within two hundred yards of the wall.

"All advance!"

Rorthal was now moving his mount alongside Lorken's unit, keeping time with the marching soldiers. The First Sentinel Brax had slipped away without Lorken noticing. He craned his neck and looked over the front two ranks, searched around and saw him jogging on foot up to the right siege tower, joining the ranks of men pushing the wooden behemoth.

"Rams. Down the centre, take down that damned gate!" shouted Rorthal. "Brax will take his boys either side and storm the walls." The Battle-Sergeant pointed to the left and right of the gate with his mace.

"Dathus, take your cross-bows and support the infantry. Anyone so much as pokes their head out up on those walls, I want a bolt between their eyes. Sten, take your slingers and hold to the rear. Watch for any sallies. Move!"

Lorken heard acknowledgement of these orders, and then more were being shouted out by presumably Dathus and Sten. Running feet pounded and chain-mail clinked somewhere to their left.

"Infantry, form turtles after ten paces, counting down…NOW!"

Lorken counted the ten paces, then raised his shield so it was above his head, the shield in front over-lapping his by half a foot. The air quickly grew heavy beneath this roof of wood and iron, the smell of sweat filling his nose as they advanced slowly towards the walls.

"Geir, you promised you'd wash this time" shouted Freda, "You stink like my man's breaches after a two-week at sea. First Warrior save me!"

"The way you smell, Freda, I can understand why your man spends two weeks away at sea!"

Lorken heard the muffled laughter of soldiers around them. He wondered how much farther there was to go as he felt his arm beginning to ache. All he could see now was the grass beneath his feet and the Helligans around him.

"It might get heavy but keep it raised. Better to have a sore arm tomorrow than a smashed skull today" said Geir, almost as if he'd read Lorken's thoughts.

Rorthal was shouting somewhere beyond this wholly unnatural cocoon. At first Lorken couldn't make out much but it sounded like more bravado and jokes to boost the courage of all under his command. It seemed to work as laughter rippled along underneath the shields.

"...but the only question I have is if we'll be in their Great Hall in time for a spot of lunch!" Rorthal's voice was clear again.

After what seemed an eternity of this slow movement underneath their protective shell, Lorken began to hear the ominous notes of the music of battle ahead. The unmistakable sound of crossbows being fired was joined by voices, but Lorken couldn't tell if they were cries of anger or agony.

He felt a strong nudge from his right. Geir. His comrade-in-arms looked into his eyes and nodded. The levity and bravado were gone. His voice lowered so that perhaps Freda couldn't hear.

"Stay with me brother. This is it now. You will see the worst of men today. You will feel the hot wash of blood on your face. You will see the innards of comrades spilling to the floor. You will feel the resistance of flesh and bone as your spear pierces another man. It will make you sick. It will make you want to

179

run. But you must stay strong and keep going. Keep with me and I promise you will return to Gamle Hovestad."

Lorken was at a loss for a moment. The reality of where he was suddenly slammed back into him like an almighty gust of wind from the Dark Raven's wings. He felt his stomach knot and he inhaled sharply, trying to master his fear. He coughed and tried to laugh.

"You better keep that promise" Lorken croaked, "else my wife will cut your stones off. And she would scare The First Warrior when angry."

Geir laughed heartily. "If that doesn't put a healthy dose of fear in a man, I don't know what will!"

Their jollity disappeared in an instant as something hard and heavy crashed onto the roof of their shell. It wasn't directly on Lorken's shield but his arm felt the impact. This was followed by another crash, and another, becoming a hammering rain of stone. Lorken gasped as a man to Freda's left cried out and fell to the ground, blood and bone peeking out where his shoulder had been. Their shell obviously had a few cracks.

"Hold tight! Let's skewer some of these pebble throwers!" roared Geir. Lorken couldn't help but be in awe at the way Geir and Freda whipped courage and fearlessness into their fellows with their words and strength of spirit. They stoked fire within the ranks. If he stuck close to them, he felt he had a very good chance of making it back to Jenna and his family.

Screams started to flood the arena of battle, peppered with the rattle of stone upon oak as the enemy hurled more rocks. Then a new sound joined the cacophony. The thunk of bolts piercing shields. Lorken realised the sound of crossbow bolts moments earlier had been theirs. And it was now clear that the Meridians also possessed this weapon.

The soldier behind him cried out in pain. Lorken glanced back to see a crossbow bolt protruding from his forearm where it was now pinned to the shield. He was swiftly pulled back and another man took his place. The advance continued. Lorken reasoned they must be almost at the walls now.

A slow but steady crashing boom grew louder as they inched their way forwards. Lorken realised it was the ram battering the gate of Meridia. The rain of stones dried up and Lorken heard fewer crossbow bolts slamming into their wooden shields. Were the defenders abandoning the walls and rushing to the gate? The threat from above would soon be a threat before them.

A splintering crash was followed by cheering. Lorken knew the gate had been breached, at least partly. Screams followed the cheers but Lorken couldn't tell which unfortunate soldiers were making them. *Meridian or Helligan, we all scream the same as death takes us.* The Dark Raven was beating His wings not ten yards in front of Lorken. Death was close.

"Hold firm, here we go" growled Geir as their unit narrowed itself to get through the bottle-neck at the gate. It was clear many Helligans had made it through but Lorken had no idea if they had all been cut down as they entered the city.

Horns suddenly blared behind them and Rorthal's booming voice rose above the din.

"Infantry, halt the advance! About turn and form shield walls! Dathus, cover the gate!"

Lorken's nightmare seemed to take on an absurd twist as he retreated with Geir and Freda back to where they had been only moments ago, the men and women within the turtle carefully back-stepping. Nothing was falling from above now, which Lorken took to mean that the Sentinels had the walls.

The infantry wheeled to face southwards, the turtle becoming a shield-wall. Lorken, now in the second rank, looked out over his shield but couldn't see what the new threat was. A distant rumbling and slight tremor in the ground caused him to gasp as he realised why Rorthal had dragged them back. Mounted soldiers were coming.

"Infantry!" bellowed Rorthal, "Keep that shield wall tight. We have cavalry approaching! Right-wheel, quarter-quarter."

Lorken moved as one with his shield brothers and sisters, each block turning an eighth of a circle in carefully measured steps; those on the inside of the turn practically marking time on the same spot, those on the outside taking long strides. All turning to face the mounted force that could be seen approaching from the south-west. A huge cloud of dust surrounded the approaching riders. They were many and were moving at speed.

"Archers! Twenty yards back and defensive formation. Watch the city walls! Sten, you and your slingers are with me!"

The orders came fast but the Helligan soldiers obeyed swiftly and without fuss. Lorken saw the soldiers with their slings and bags of what he knew to be perfectly chiselled stones, jogging along after Rorthal's horse and stopping in a position to the left of the infantry. Rorthal charged back across the front of the infantry.

"Looks like we've got some uninvited guests approaching our little brawl today!" he yelled. "Shield wall, brace!"

The soldiers in the front row locked shields with a noise like a thunderclap. Lorken moved forward with Geir and Freda on either side of him, and tightened up against them. He peered over his shield. The threat was only about five hundred yards away.

Lorken felt himself being jostled and moved along within the war machine of the Helligan army. All around were tightly pressed and presenting a hard wall for those horses to consider. Lorken hoped the Meridian cavalry would lose heart but the shaking of the ground told him they hadn't yet flinched.

"You might feel a bit of a bump" Freda joked. Lorken didn't know how his shield-sister could keep making japes at a time like this but nodded in response, his trembling hopefully appearing as eagerness to engage the enemy.

The horses' hooves became louder, the sound becoming one with the vibration in the ground beneath their feet. The pace quickened and Lorken saw they were in full charge. "First Warrior protect us!" he whimpered.

"Hold steady!" barked Geir, twisting his head to repeat the call to all around but Lorken felt as if it was directed solely at him. He gritted his teeth and set his shoulder against his shield, right leg back and digging in. Lorken was grateful he wasn't in the front row. If the cavalry didn't break off their charge, some in that row would surely perish.

The ground shook as the horses approached. There were easily over a hundred heavy cavalry bearing down upon the centre, hoping to break the lines and maybe give the soldiers in the city some relief.

Two hundred yards.

"They're not stopping! Brace!" yelled Rorthal from behind them. Lorken dug in harder with his right foot, weight pressing down on his left knee, knuckles white as he gripped spear and shield with all his might.

One hundred yards.

"Hold!" shouted Geir next to him. Lorken squeezed his eyes shut.

The riders must be less than fifty yards now.

"HELLIGA!" screamed Freda.

Then it came. Crunching impact. In the space of a breath, chaos was unleashed. A crash like lightning struck at Lorken's feet. His shield crushed against him and his feet slid in the mud. Screams erupted all around, horrifying sounds of men, women and horses dying. His body was squeezed to the point he couldn't breathe.

Still an oppressive force pushed against him. Lorken's shield angled and the rim came up to his face, starting to dig into his cheek. Shouting and growling surrounded him as the Helligan soldiers regained their footing after the impact and began to push back against men on horseback still trying to break through the wall.

Suddenly the space before Lorken opened up as the Helligan soldier in front of him fell. The man in the front row had been obliterated by the charge. Lorken stared at the fore-legs of a horse flailing in the air and sheer terror overwhelmed him. He couldn't move. The Dark Raven was perched upon his shoulder.

Then a figure pushed past him and thrust a spear into the

horse's belly, withdrawing it just as quickly and darting back two steps. Hot blood sprayed across Lorken's shield, coming over the rim and lashing his face. He raised his shield thinking the horse would collapse upon him. It teetered a moment, then collapsed sideways, trapping its rider beneath it.

Freda stepped forward again and rammed her spear into the rider's neck, the man jerking grotesquely and then laying still. The stench of human entrails and feces from both horse and human filled the air.

"Lorken, with me!" came a shout from his right. Geir shoved Lorken forward, Freda moved to his left and the three of them filled the gap, becoming the front line of the shield wall. Along the formation, others did likewise. Lorken wondered if any of the first line had survived the first impact.

Horses were still before them, their riders swirling round, darting into the few remaining gaps that had been punched in the shield wall but had yet to be filled by the ranks behind. The riders shouted and cursed, hacking down with their blades. Lorken held his shield tightly and raised it instinctively as two riders looked to trample over them with their mounts.

Lorken squeezed his eyes shut and was surprised to feel no impact. He peered over his shield and saw the riders trotting back and reforming. It seemed they would charge again.

Shouting came from behind. It was Rorthal bellowing a new order.

"Front two ranks advance!" Rorthal again. "Clean up! And Sten, stone any of those bastards who get jumpy!"

Lorken again found himself swept up with the singular movement of a hundred men and women. They methodically bore down on riders who had been thrown from their mounts. Some lost heart and started to retreat towards their comrades who were still ahorse. Some were felled by hurtling stones striking their helmets and cracking skulls within. Others drew their swords and stood firm.

Lorken saw a riderless soldier ahead. His leg was clearly injured and he could not escape from the approaching line of spikes. Lorken knew this man was his to kill. He gritted his teeth as the shield wall moved forward in an inevitable advance of death. Already spears were piercing other Meridians down the line, their pleas for mercy falling on deaf ears. Lorken's man turned to face them, knowing he could not escape. He readied his sword and cried something in the Meridian language.

Lorken felt his spear and shield push into the man. His shield was held by the soldier's weight but the spear found little resistance, puncturing its way into the man's mid-riff. The point encountered what was inside the man, what gave him life. Hot blood ran down Lorken's spear, passing through the hole in the shield wall and onto his hand. He gagged but still pushed forward.

"Draw back the spear!" hissed Geir, "Else you'll be carrying that dead man all the way to the Swift Sea."

Lorken hastily pulled back on his spear. The body of the dead man was drawn into his shield, making Lorken's left-shoulder ache with the effort of effectively holding up a corpse. Then the spear slid out, accompanied by a sluice of blood and the body crumpled to the grass. Lorken stepped over the man as the shield wall moved ever on. Dead eyes stared up at him with what Lorken could only perceive as an accusing look.

Shouts came from ahead somewhere. The remaining riders—still at least fifty it seemed, though Lorken couldn't tell for certain—were not ready to flee yet. His eyes kept flitting down to the blackening blood that caked his right arm.

"Today *they* die!" Freda screamed and snarled.

It was as if the senior cavalry officer heard her as he pointed his sword directly at Lorken's position with Geir and Freda.

"Bastards die!" screamed the Meridian in the Helligan language and spurred his horse into a charge.

They were only thirty yards away and the horses were already moving fast. Lorken had no time to think or wonder at what might be. He braced along with Freda and Geir, and all the other Helligan soldiers remaining in their shield wall.

Lorken was knocked down as a horse crashed into his shield.

185

He fell to the floor, his shield on top of him, his spear lost. A crushing weight slumped upon his shield. An explosion of agony in his side. He tasted blood. He couldn't breathe. It was dark. There were only the sounds of steel clashing upon more steel, followed by screams and gurgles. Blackness swirled before his eyes.

Then the weight upon him fell away and his shield was pulled off him, filling his vision with sudden daylight. He took a breath, gasping at the burning in his chest and lungs.

"Lorken!"

A female voice. Freda.

"Shit."

Lorken could only see a white blur now that seemed to be clouding at the edges.

"He's gone!"

Another voice.

"Shut your mouth. He will make it!"

"Freda, look at him! He's a dead man."

A strange sound and a cry of pain.

"Bitch!"

"Get back to the gate, damn you!"

Lorken heard the words but was losing any sense of where he was. He couldn't feel his arms or legs, and it felt like there was a fire burning in his stomach. He would have bellowed in agony but his throat just gurgled.

Then Freda's face appeared in front of him, looking down.

"Stay with me, Lorken. Those riders are dead or running. Victory will soon be ours."

Hands shook him roughly. A foul stench hit his nostrils as the pain seemed to fade in his body. Lorken felt so cold, as if he were suddenly at the summit of the Sacred Mount and covered in frost.

"Lorken, steady now, you'll be fine. Just got to get you some bandages. You've bled a bit but I've had worse."

Lorken looked up into Freda's eyes and saw the truth of his injury there. He coughed, choking on warm blood, the copper taste filling his mouth. And then he felt it. He understood it. He knew. He was going to die. Panic took him and he squirmed. He reached for Freda and grabbed her arm, his grip quickly evaporating.

"Freda. Jenna. I want to see Jenna." He gasped. "First Warrior, please. Please take me home. Jenna. Where is she? My boys. I need to tell them. Eira."

A spasm of coughing hit him and he tasted more blood in his mouth, mixed with something else.

His vision was blurring but he could still see Freda's face looking down on him.

"Forgive me, Jenna. I love you, no…please, you must know how much…I love you Jenna."

His words were sputtering out now, tumbling and losing clarity.

The cold was spreading throughout his body like an icy, chill wind, seeping into his core. There was a hollow feeling in his heart. An overwhelming sadness gripped him as he saw the faces of Jenna, Darl, Torg and Eira. He loved them. He was losing them. He would never hold them again.

"No, no, no!" cried Freda.

A shiver. Then darkness clouded his vision.

Ch 9

Svard

Svard and his men were close to reaching their objective now. They had come down from the walls and were running through the streets. Not wearing Helligan colours and the fact they were already in the city gave them the element of surprise over the one squad of Meridian soldiers they encountered. No Rangers fell but a score of the city's guard felt the crushing weight of the Dark Raven.

Meridia's residents were mostly shut inside their homes now, obviously praying the walls would hold back the force at their gates. Svard and his men did see the odd citizen wandering the streets but those brave few fled at the sight of almost fifty armed men moving swiftly through Meridia.

Salus Keep suddenly came into view as they rounded a corner. It had the appearance of a small castle that had fallen from the sky and landed in the city, such was the difference in architecture to the buildings around it. Dark grey rugged stone in contrast to the white walls and natural clay tiles of Meridian houses. A turret occupied each corner of the three-story structure and a stout wooden door was shut and guarded.

Svard nodded grimly, acknowledging the fact his map had been accurate. He hoped the information was too. Rencarro's son Eligius should be in that stronghold and his capture would hopefully bring about a swifter end to the taking of Meridia.

"Cuyler, sweep left, get into position in front of that single storey house and take out the initial advance" called Svard as they slowed their pace.

"Asger left flank, Gudbrand's squad on the right. Rest of you with me. We breach that door before word gets out Meridia has a rat problem."

The Rangers swept forward into the open space before Salus Keep, the city's guard only now waking up to the fact that there were enemy soldiers advancing upon them. The few outside the door shouted up to their comrades inside as Svard's men bore down on them.

Then something happened that took the Helligan First Ranger and perhaps all his men by surprise. The door opened and more soldiers poured out to join their fellows.

Damn fools! This is going to be easier than I thought.

Arrows from Cuyler's Rangers suddenly sliced through the air above their heads and took down two of the guards. The sudden assault from unseen archers had the desired effect and the Meridians crouched and looked around wildly.

Svard roared an oath in the Helligan language and surged forward, his men quick to keep up with him.

"Stigr, the door! Keep it open!" yelled Svard as he engaged the hapless Meridian soldiers.

Svard easily parried one outstretched blade and used his momentum to barge the bearer to the ground, the First Ranger's boot coming down hard on the fallen guard's ankle with an audible crack.

He punched another guard in the face with his sword's hilt, blood exploding from the man's nose as he fell backwards, then spun round and down to cut deep into a prone leg. A scream accompanied the sound of a weapon clattering to the stone steps.

Stigr and his squad had charged the door, leaving the other Rangers to deal with any guards outside the keep who would try to stop them. Svard's captain pushed through and now the door was well and truly open. The guards outside were now dead, incapacitated or fleeing. Those who ran didn't get far, falling with arrows from Cuyler's men protruding from their backs.

"Hold! Asger, Gudbrand, get Cuyler over here and form a defensive position in front of the keep. No one gets in. Go!"

Svard beckoned to the other Rangers.

"After Stigr. No more killing now. We want the son alive."

Svard entered the keep to find Stigr's men holding the entrance hall. A handful of Meridians formed a defensive semi-circle at the foot of the stairs to the next level. Two more soldiers were crouched upon these stairs but they looked ready to flee upwards when they saw Svard and twenty or so others stream in.

Svard called out to the Meridians in the common tongue.

"There need be no more death this day. Your city will fall very soon. Bring forth Rencarro's son and let words finish this battle."

"Never!" cried one courageous Meridian, who immediately gasped as an axe embedded itself in his chest. Svard looked to Stigr, whose weapon now fell to the fall with the dead man, and nodded. This tactic had been used before, slaying one brave man in grisly fashion to deter others from trying to be the hero of the day.

"You are outnumbered and outclassed here. This is no boast. It is a truth. Lay down your weapons and let us spill no more blood."

Svard could see hesitation in their faces. They were obviously fearful of the possibility that if they lowered their arms, the Helligan Rangers would slaughter them.

Svard stepped forward and carefully placed his blade upon the stone floor, his eyes never leaving the beleaguered Meridians.

"I am Svard, First Ranger of the Helligan nation. I lay down my sword now and ask that you trust my word. A huge force has breached your walls to the east. The sooner Rencarro's son can announce Meridia's surrender, the fewer of your brothers will die. The outcome of this battle is certain. The number of corpses yet to be decided."

Svard's voice was calm and clear. His arms were spread wide, hands with palms facing outwards. As he spoke he looked each of them in the eye but lingered last on the soldier who appeared to be of the highest rank there. The captain was the one on the

190

floor with an axe in him.

Nobody moved. There was no move to fight but also the Meridians made no move to lower their weapons. Svard waited, breathing evenly and hoping the Dark Raven had seen enough blood for one day.

After some moments, the man Svard presumed to be of rank, slowly let his blade fall to his side. He spoke up to all the men in the room. Erland moved closer to Svard and translated in a whispered voice.

"He says he doesn't want to make a final stand here today. They've been betrayed. When our lord returns, there will be… Couldn't catch it. And he will ask Lord Eligius to negotiate an end to this violence."

Svard nodded.

The expressions on the other soldiers' faces ranged from relief to anger, but all lowered their weapons, and then placed them on the floor. Svard motioned for his men to stand down. He told Stigr to tell the Rangers outside to make no aggressive move.

The Meridian soldier who had spoken called up the stairs in his own language. Svard was fairly certain there was nothing suspicious in his words but looked to Erland to be sure. The Ranger gave a quick nod and Svard let himself relax a little. It seemed they would soon have Rencarro's son.

A voice called down in the Helligan language. It was not a commanding voice but clearly well-educated.

"I am coming, Helligan captain. Do I have your word that there will be no more blood-shed this day?"

Svard replied in the same language.

"I am Svard, First Ranger, and you have my word that none of my men here will draw blood. But I cannot speak for the Helligan force currently swarming the eastern city. The sooner we can announce a surrender, the fewer lives will be lost."

The Meridian soldiers on the stairs descended and made way for a young man, slight of build, no more than five and a half feet in height, with a head of scraggly black hair. Svard saw a keen intelligence in the lad's grey eyes. It was clear Eligius' strength lay not in his arms but in his mind. Svard again mentally acknowledged the accuracy of the information he had been given back in Gamle Hovestad.

"It seems you have caught us unprepared for your arrival" Eligius said, still speaking in the Helligan language. Svard was impressed with the fluency and no trace of a Meridian accent.

"I had been told you inherited your father's wit and intelligence. I see that is true and more" commented the First Ranger.

"Did your agents say a similar thing with regards to swordsmanship when they assassinated my brother?"

The question was unexpected and Svard frowned. He hadn't been aware that Rencarro's other son, Marcus, had been killed. Furthermore, he had no knowledge of any command from Orben to carry out clandestine killings.

"You have me at a disadvantage there, my lord" stated Svard, thinking a bit of polite respect might yield greater cooperation. "I had not heard of your brother's death. An assassin's blade is no way for a warrior of his skill to die."

Svard locked eyes with Eligius and he felt the other man studying him, perhaps searching for truth or falsity.

Eligius then laced his fingers and looked down at his hands, his two thumbs rubbing circles in each other. His head snapped up.

"Well then, shall we end this bloodshed? Your Dark Raven will not be so pleased, but I believe your First Warrior may respect us if we all hold back with our blades."

Svard was again impressed with how well acquainted Eligius seemed to be with the Helligan language and culture.

Wouldn't be surprised if he knows more of our history than I do.

Both Helligan and Meridian soldiers carefully exited the keep and filed out into the area before it. The Rangers formed up into a defensive formation and waited.

Eligius issued a string of orders to two soldiers who seemed to be captains and gave a few commands to a man who was clearly some kind of administrator. He then turned to Svard.

"With your permission."

Svard nodded and gave out his own orders.

Soon Svard was walking down the streets he had been running through not long ago, with Eligius and a handful of Meridian soldiers. Svard's own men marched either side of their party. Other Rangers had accompanied Eligius' men to relay the news of surrender to the rest of the city.

The sounds of battle could soon be heard ahead and Svard hoped they could put a stop to the violence quickly. He was all too aware that Lorken was out there in the midst of the fighting.

The first combatants came into view. Two Sentinels cutting through a squad of Meridians with ease. The difference in fighting skill and prowess was horribly apparent.

"Sentinels, hold!" shouted Svard in his own language as Gudbrand waved the red and white flag of the Helligan nation.

The Sentinels instantly fell back into a defensive stance.

Eligius called out to the surviving Meridians and blades were lowered wearily. Those of the city guard still standing looked at their fallen comrades, their faces creasing up in anguish and exhaustion.

"Gudbrand, take your squad and hurry through to the gate relaying the order to stand down. Find Brax if you can. Cuyler and Stigr, you two and your men go with him." Svard turned to Eligius.

"I hope you can persuade your men to stand down too, Lord Eligius."

Eligius did not answer immediately. He was looking at the dead bodies turning the cobbled streets a dirty brown colour. Svard pitied him but knew there never were any bloodless battles, and so every man and woman must learn how to fight. The Meridians had been overwhelmed here far too easily.

As their group moved on towards the gate, the sounds of battle dissipated, the word of a surrender obviously reaching those engaged. Svard saw Sentinels standing in guarded formations, their pole-axes held across their chests. And he also saw the city guards of Meridia looking like a storm had raged through their home and was now suddenly gone, leaving only devastation in its wake. Some were sitting on the ground, others were attending to wounded comrades and some just stared at Svard and his group as they passed.

"Svard!"

The First Sentinel approached them in his almost lethargic manner of walking, his own pole-axe held loosely at his side and showing signs it had dealt death this day. Svard did not greet his friend with a hearty laugh as they had done in previous skirmishes and battles. Something was different about this day. Today had been the first battle in a war that might last generations.

"Brax. Well met, First Sentinel. This is Lord Eligius, the son of Lord Rencarro. He has agreed to the surrender of this city."

Brax nodded and spoke respectfully in the common tongue.

"Lord Eligius. My men have been ordered to stand down and our Battle-Sergeant out beyond the city walls is relaying the command to his troops also. I believe there will be no more blood spilt this day."

Eligius answered in the Helligan language, his voice laced with bitterness.

"I have surrendered my city to avoid further death to my people. Though I see you have made many widows and orphans this day."

Brax's face registered surprise with Eligius' fluency but showed no remorse. He grunted.

"The Widow and the Dark Raven dance together in death."

Eligius narrowed his eyes at the Helligan warrior.

"A pity the Keeper and the First Warrior could not temper Lord Orben's ambitions."

Brax shared a look with Svard, shrugged and then walked away, shouting out orders to his Sentinels.

Svard could see the city gates now and the tops of the siege-towers peeking over the battlements. He noticed Eligius scanning the scene, almost as if he were studying it. The young man suddenly stopped, his eyes squinting up at what could be seen of the towers. Then he let out a deep breath.

"A clever design, First Ranger" he remarked. "The front gangplank is only a hook I take it, and not an exit from the tower. The sides drop down and soldiers exit from an unexpected angle, giving the attackers an element of surprise. Am I missing anything?"

Svard was impressed that Eligius had understood the construction of the Helligan siege towers. They were indeed made with a front draw-bridge with a hooked end that would drop onto the city walls and hold the tower firmly against the wall. But when this drawbridge dropped, the defenders would see a blank wall instead of charging attackers.

"There are small portals in that front panel from which crossbow bolts will be fired" explained Svard flatly.

Eligius nodded.

"It seems the Helligan nation hasn't lost its passion for war."

"Which I imagine your people appreciated when the Xerinthian invasion was thwarted" retorted Svard.

"You speak truly, First Ranger" said Eligius, a tension in his voice. "But today Meridia pays for that passion with blood."

Svard said nothing, wanting to get away from Eligius and find Lorken.

"Lord Orben has been busy preparing for this it seems" said Eligius in a matter-of-fact way. "The rumours of your Lady Ulla having a poisoned hand in the High King's demise gain weight."

Svard ignored the comment. He wanted to punch the smaller man but knew that would be giving in to petty anger. The First Warrior had sheathed his sword this day. But he didn't have to tolerate the young lord's company any longer, he decided. The fighting seemed to have come to a total halt and now they just had to ensure the uneasy peace held.

Svard gave orders to Erland and Asger to accompany Eligius to wherever the Meridian needed to go to ensure it was known throughout the city that the Helligan nation now ruled here, and that no citizen would be hurt on condition they abided by this. He also told Eligius to order all the city guard to gather outside the city walls, leaving their weapons just outside the gates. Eligius was about to say something but Svard turned about and walked off. He'd had enough of Rencarro's son. It was unsettling how much he knew about the Helligan nation.

Svard marched through the city gates, stepping over fallen soldiers, almost all Meridian but the odd red and white uniform of a Helligan soldier could be seen. He looked at faces but there was something in his gut that told him Lorken was not among those fallen. Then he saw the carnage outside the city and froze in his step.

What happened?

It was clear there had been a bloody engagement between the Helligan infantry and what had to be Meridian cavalry. Svard had been told that the Meridian's strength in horses would be at too great a distance to reach the battle. Yet the scene before his eyes told a very different story.

Svard searched through the soldiers that were still standing and those that were part of a sickly mess across the field. His eyes locked upon a female soldier.

"Freda!" he called.

The shield-maiden turned and wearily bowed her head in respect. Or was it something else?

"Where is Geir?" he asked as he approached her.

Her voice was rasping.

"Geir took a wound to the head. He lives, First Ranger."

Svard didn't have to ask his next question. He followed the path of Freda's eyes as they looked over to a row of bodies in Helligan uniform.

No! No, no, please, not him.

Svard sprinted over and looked upon Lorken's body. He fell to his knees and gathered his friend in his arms. Svard shook Lorken but the Dark Raven had already come. The First Ranger screamed in anguish.

Ch 10

Lunyai

5th Day of Maia, Ten Days After Sedmund's Death

The other Tarakan Pilgrims were getting themselves ready for a good night's rest before their long trek tomorrow. There were many miles to travel down the Coastal Road before they reached the Plains and Yaai's Stone. Lunyai was excited at the thought of being back on a Tarakan Mare, feeling the wind buffet her as she galloped across the vast grass expanse.

The Tarakan girl was tired and knew she should join the others in their slumber but couldn't resist the urge she felt to walk under Tlenaii's light once more. Tonight Tlenaii the Moon was showing almost His full form and Lunyai wanted to bask in the soft white glow.

She asked Imala for permission to go for a moon-lit stroll and the Elder gave her consent, although she warned Lunyai to avoid patrolling soldiers and not cause any mischief. Lunyai smiled and touched fingers with Imala, promising she would return in the space of ten songs and slipped out of the monastery into the night, the cool air like a splash of cold water to her weary eyes.

She looked up and saw the Grey Ones sliding across Tlenaii. "There are no tales this night" she whispered. "Let Tlenaii shine down on me with His light and send a riddle if He so desires."

Lunyai thought ahead to what it would be like when they were home again with their families. At their evening meal, Imala had asked them if they felt any different from when they'd left. All had said they did and felt ready to cross into adulthood and take on all the duties that meant. Imala had chuckled and told them they were ready for all the Plains had to send their way, but reminded them to keep their minds ever open as nobody ever had *nothing* left to learn. Lunyai had suspected there were many things on the Plains and in the wider world that they were not ready for yet, but she felt Tlenaii the Moon and Yaai the Sun had smiled upon them on this Pilgrimage.

When they had bathed that morning, Enyeto had hinted he'd like for the two of them to take a walk together that evening. Lunyai had noticed he was aroused and she had perhaps stared. Enyeto had suddenly mumbled something and hurried off to dry himself. Lunyai worried she had embarrassed him and tried to apologise at the evening meal but he had sat away from her. She didn't really comprehend men. Her mother had talked to her about the All-Mother's Ways and how men and women would come together in adulthood, so she was aware of these truths. Yet when they returned to the Plains, all of this might suddenly become real. She was again unsure she was ready to be with a mate.

Lunyai walked on through the night, her soft leather moccasins making no sound at all on the cobbles. She looked up to see Tlenaii peeking out through the Grey Ones.

"You are teasing me, Our Brother! You know I need more than this pilgrimage to understand the world." She laughed to herself and began to twirl as she walked, enjoying the relative quiet of Argyllan when its people were asleep.

Lunyai rounded a corner and abruptly stopped her spinning, slowing to a stroll. Two soldiers were patrolling the streets, although they didn't seem to be paying much attention to anything. One visibly jumped when he saw her.

"Out a bit late aren't you, young one?"

"It is never too late for Tlenaii!" she exclaimed, raising her hands and gesturing to the moon.

The soldier who had asked the question seemed confused but his partner nudged him and said "One of the Tarakan pilgrims, Luca. They worship the moon."

"Oh." The one called Luca was still frowning. "Well, don't catch a chill." They moved on past her.

"Catch a chill?!" said Lunyai indignantly to herself. "I am Tarakan. We live on the Plains where the All-Mother sends Her winds to make us stronger."

Lunyai carried on, reckoning she had been gone almost two songs now. Imala had tried to explain to all of them why the Meridian soldiers had come to Argyllan but again Lunyai couldn't make sense of it all. The Tall King, or whatever his title was, of the lands north of the Tarakan Plains had died and now everyone seemed in a state of mild panic. Lunyai considered how different it was back in her homeland. When one of the Tribal Council's Elders passed into the All-Mother, they would ask another to become an Elder. Then life went on.

These lands where people lived in stone houses bewildered Lunyai. Building houses of stone meant you had to stay rooted to one place, which to Lunyai's mind, created a certain possessiveness in people. Land suddenly belonged to one tribe and not another. All land was part of the All-Mother anyway so it belonged to no-one according to the Tarakan people. One tribe lived in one place for a time, then moved on. The land was shared and there was never any conflict arising from who owned which area. You cared for the All-Mother's land and kept it in good health ready for the next tribe to live there. *These stone-dwellers*, Lunyai thought and was pleased with her new word for them, *are chained to one spot with their walls and gates.* The All-Mother gave them freedom over all her lands and they had just given it up. Lunyai simply couldn't fathom the minds of these *stone-dwellers*.

Movement out of the corner of her eye suddenly caught her attention and she looked up. A shadow had flitted across the top of a building to her left. She peered up and could just make out something moving over the house beyond. *An animal?* She was intrigued. She changed her intended course that would have begun the second side of a square back to the monastery and hurried to try and catch another glimpse of whatever was up there on the roof tops.

It was difficult to keep track of the swiftly moving beast but

Lunyai could hear its scampering feet. She wasn't far behind. She swerved into an alleyway as two men stumbled out of a building on the right of the street. It looked to be an inn and the men had clearly had too many of those ales these stone-dwellers seemed to drink in vast amounts. She pulled back into the shadows, not wishing to be caught in conversation with these two fellows. The Tarakans drank fermented milk but never to the point they lost their balance. The two men passed her by. She wondered if they would make it back to their homes or end up sleeping in a doorway.

Lunyai emerged from the alleyway and scanned up high for the elusive shadow. There was no sign of it.

"Tlenaii, guide me, where did that night-crawler leap to?"

She set off in the direction she judged to be correct and broke into a light run, worried that she would now never find out what animal lurked on the Argyllan roof-tops at night.

The street opened up ahead into the Market Square where they had bought some delicious pears yesterday. As she approached the square, now devoid of market stalls and noisy traders, she caught a new sound. The clip-clop of a horse. And then she saw another shadow. But it wasn't an animal this time. It was a human. And this human was running over to the far-side of the square. Lunyai stopped and silently watched as a rider on a horse emerged from a street to the left and picked up a trot in the direction the runner had taken. Lunyai knew she should get back but was fairly sure Imala would be asleep already so a little longer out wouldn't cause any trouble.

Lunyai broke into a run. As she crossed the square, she looked up and saw Tlenaii had pushed the Grey Ones away and was shining down on her. *Helping me see this little mystery clearly,* she thought to herself and smiled before taking in a deep breath and plunging down the alley into which the rider and the runner had disappeared.

As she entered the side-street, Tlenaii's light lessened and she felt a sudden sense of unease wash over her. The Tarakan girl slowed her pace and began moving forward more cautiously.

She heard voices. One was female, the other male. The female voice seemed in anguish. Lunyai listened, trying to make out what was being said. She strained her ears, but it was like listening to her parents talking outside their *wam* while she was supposed to be sleeping. Cautiously she moved forward, her footsteps light on the grubby, grey stone beneath her moccasins.

The alley bent round and she saw the rider. She kept to the shadows and inched her way towards the man until she could see clearly. The second person was up on a roof-top. Lunyai decided there hadn't been two shadows but just one that had come down from on high and had now climbed up again. Lunyai couldn't imagine why. The girl or woman, Lunyai wasn't sure which, was crouched behind a chimney stack. She could hear the voices clearly now.

"I can barely remember now exactly why I felt the need to run but it turned out to be a little adventure. A painful one too, when I finally came back and got a good thrashing."

The rider let out a small laugh. It appeared to Lunyai he was trying to coax the person on the roof down. And it was working. The girl emerged from behind the chimney and moved into view of both the soldier and Lunyai. The Tarakan girl reckoned she was not much older than herself.

"Can you help me?" came a voice, cracking with emotion. The girl was obviously in distress. Perhaps there had been some trouble at her home, Lunyai speculated.

"You can't be that much younger than my second born. Come down and let us find you food and warmth." The soldier seemed to be a kindly man and Lunyai thought she might also step forwards and offer her help to the girl.

"Your hair is catching the moonlight. I might be mistaken but it looks a deep chestnut brown, the same as my wife's."

"No, it's auburn actually. My mo…"

The scene before Lunyai's eyes abruptly changed. The girl's distress shifted to terror and the soldier lost his kindly manner — anger coloured his voice.

"It is you, isn't it? The red-headed girl who murdered my

son."

Lunyai gasped. Who were these people and what had passed? *Murder?* The word was like Banelok upon the tongue.

"No, I'm... No, I didn't see. That soldier killed my friend." The girl was sobbing now, her whole body shaking.

"Who sent you? Orben? Are you from the north?" The soldier was threatening in his manner and advanced his horse a pace or two, cutting down the distance between himself and the girl.

"Please listen to me. One of them was dead when I first saw them. Then the other soldier murdered Anton."

"Liar! You and the boy were sent to take the life of my son. Tell me who gave the order and I will let you live. And stop the sobbing. You will not fool me with your theatrics, which is no doubt how you took my son unawares."

Lunyai did not know what to do. She could not run and leave this situation to unfold. The rider seemed bent on revenge because this girl had apparently murdered his son. But Lunyai saw only a frightened girl up there, who did not seem capable of riding a horse, let alone taking someone's life.

"Sylvanus!" the girl suddenly cried. Lunyai didn't understand what that meant but the soldier replied, a poisonous venom practically spitting out over his words.

"Yes, Sylvanus survived the assassination attempt. But you took my son from me, you little witch!"

"No. Sylvanus lied. I don't even know how to kill!" Lunyai couldn't see the truth yet but she felt sure that the soldier was mistaken.

The girl wobbled on her feet, her legs looking ready to buckle. In that moment, Lunyai made a decision. She must help this girl. Something was not right here, and she couldn't just watch the soldier carry out a reckless act in his rage. However, the Tarakan girl had no idea what she could achieve. Where she had no weapons, the soldier had a spear; he was on horse and she was on foot. What could she possibly hope to do?

"Come down and I will give you leniency if you tell me who was behind the murder." Lunyai hesitated but felt herself getting ready to run in and at least come between these two.

"By the Spirits" the girl wept. "Anton was an innkeeper's son and my father is a glass-blower. We are no assassins. Please believe me, soldier of Meridia."

"I am Lord Rencarro, the *ruler* of Meridia. And Marcus was my son."

Lunyai was puzzled. This made no sense at all. The ruler of Meridia out in the night, accusing some girl of murder? Lord Rencarro dismounted in one fluid motion and brought his spear to bear. Lunyai felt her heart freeze at the sight of the weapon in his hands.

"Now tell me, girl. Who are you?"

Lunyai could almost touch the terror that the girl's voice was drowning in.

"I am no-one. I did not kill your son. I am no-one. Please, please."

Lunyai gasped as the girl made to retreat, but then slipped and began sliding off the roof. The Tarakan girl felt her body tense, ready to leap forward and help the girl. But the soldier's spear made her think twice.

Lunyai held her breath as the girl dangled from the roof, her feet trying to find a ledge. But her body was still moving sluggishly towards the edge.

The slide suddenly became a swift drop, a fatal fall stopped only by one hand grabbing a window ledge.

Please Tlenaii.

The girl's hand let go and she fell, landing badly with a shout of pain.

Lunyai noticed the soldier had not moved at all. The Tarakan girl knew she must act. She was unarmed though and knew she could not best this soldier without a weapon.

Then she saw her chance. It was the only thing she could do.

Lunyai crept to the other side of the tiny street, keeping herself out of the man's peripheral vision, and quietly approached the now riderless horse that stood patiently behind its master. Lunyai gently put her hand on the horse's side and whispered in the Tarakan language. The horse did not startle or even take a step.

"Why did you flee to Argyllan?" A question from this Rencarro.

Lunyai placed her head against the horse's neck, stroking its mane and whispering in a soothing voice. She struggled to remain calm, willing herself to focus on the horse. If this lord caught sight of her on the far side of his mount, Lunyai would surely feel the cold of his steel.

The lord moved closer to the prostrate girl, coming to stand over her. Lunyai put her cheek to the horse's neck and whispered more words of peace. The lord was speaking again.

"You know how it feels to take a life, don't you? You know how it feels when you draw out the blood of another. The knowledge that you have sent some poor soul to the Void."

Lunyai gripped the horn and silently pulled herself up, easing into the saddle. The man kept talking but rage was building in his voice. Lunyai sat astride the horse and carefully took the reins in her hands.

"It really is quite something to kill a man. You take away all he strived for, all he was at that moment and all he would ever have been. You steal his very *essence*." Lunyai felt a moment of crushing silence. And then it was broken.

"Murderer!"

Time slowed for Lunyai, as if she were singing the Tarakalo when half asleep. The man had turned his spear and now had it raised, ready to plunge it into the girl.

Lunyai jerked hard on the reins, pulling them towards her. The mare snorted and reared on his hind legs, front legs flailing. The lord spun around and received a horse's hoof in his chest. He cried and fell back, the spear clattering to the ground.

Lunyai urged the horse forwards and stretched out her left hand to the girl.

"Quick!" she whispered urgently.

Wide-eyed the girl struggled to her feet and thrust out a shaking hand. Lunyai grasped it. She was strong for her age and the girl not that heavy. She pulled her up and the girl was then seated behind her, grasping her waist.

"Hold on" cried Lunyai as she saw the lord trying to stand, despite what must have been a serious injury. She wheeled the horse round and kicked the animal into motion.

Lunyai picked up a bit of speed to get some distance between themselves and the fallen lord, but was aware how a galloping horse would wake the city. She slowed to a trot and heard someone shouting, with all likelihood the lord.

Lunyai guided the horse down another street and then spoke hurriedly to the girl. "We must leave the horse and hide. That lord will have guards searching soon. Can you walk?"

The girl's head pushed against Lunyai's back and did not reply.

"Can you walk?" she repeated, more urgently.

"I.., yes, yes, I can walk."

Lunyai slid off the horse, careful not to pull this girl down with her. Then she raised her arms to help the redhead down. She groaned when her feet touched the ground. Lunyai remembered she had fallen from the roof. Lunyai put an arm round her waist to take the weight off the injured leg.

"Listen to me. I am Lunyai. What is your name?"

"Emiren" came back the answer, barely audible to Lunyai's ears. "That man was going to —"

Lunyai interrupted. "Emiren, we can talk later. Now we have to hide."

She stroked the horse, whispered words of sorrow for having used the mare in such a way and slapped his rear-quarters. The horse trotted off.

Lunyai turned to Emiren. "Are you with me?" she hissed sternly. Before waiting for a reply, the Tarakan hooked the girl's arm around her own shoulder and gave it a pull.

The girl jerked and spoke in a slightly stronger voice.

"I am with you."

"Good. Let us find somewhere to hide" said Lunyai and she began walking, bearing the weight of Emiren.

A clamour rose in the distance; men shouting and running footsteps. Advancing agonisingly slowly, they turned down a side-alley, Lunyai searching desperately for somewhere to hide. She wasn't sure what to do after that though. The Tarakan girl suddenly realised that trying to get back to the Cromlech Brotherhood and the other Tarakans was the wrong path to take. Lunyai might slip away with her people in the morning but the girl with her would surely be noticed. How could the two of them escape when Yaai rose? The gates would be heavily guarded and patrols would be walking the streets. How could they hope to leave this place?

Then she saw something that made her thank the All-Mother with all her heart. Lunyai couldn't believe her luck. She pulled Emiren along with her and begged Tlenaii to hide them this night and hoped that Yaai would shine on them at dawn.

Part Three

Ch 1

Wulfner

Wulfner woke from a restless night. There had been some kind of disturbance in the city of Argyllan last night and he had woken up several times. He opened the shutters of the room where he had stayed these past few days, and then pushed the windows open. The wooden frames squeaked as he did so, reminding him of his own creaky joints. The sky was a dull, charcoal grey but there was the pale white glow of the sun still away to the east, so the big northerner reasoned he hadn't overslept.

Wulfner breathed in the morning air and ran his hands through his copper-red hair that was now beginning to fall foul of grey strands here and there. He pondered the day ahead. He planned to leave the port of Argyllan this morning. It had been four days now since the Meridian soldiers had marched into town with rumour of war in the east and promises of protection from raiders. He had come here the following day to trade his wares, cursing his luck to have not left Lowenden earlier and been able to cross into the north before their arrival. The death of High King Sedmund seemed to have sent the realm into a merry spin.

Wulfner was nearing his fiftieth year, or around there, and he had seen much in his time in the realm of Ragnekai. The Meridians struck him as a little too eager to help a neighbour that didn't appear to be in any immediate danger. Wulfner wondered if the rumours of long-boats were just that—rumours. The Throskaur hadn't raided in a very long time and some said few of their people lived anymore, out there on the Barren Isles. Wulfner scratched his thick beard. Something else was going on here and if his many years on the road had taught him anything, it was that gut feelings such as this shouldn't be ignored, and it was time to move on.

He splashed water on his face from a basin but that did little to refresh him, the water now tepid. *A strong ale might set the world to rights,* he thought, and began to pack up his belongings. He left a copper for whoever would clean the room and ducked out through the doorway, his six-foot six frame and broad shoulders an impressive sight despite his advancing years. He rolled his shoulders, eased out the cricks and knots and headed downstairs. The innkeeper's wife was there, putting glasses on the racks. She smiled at him as he approached.

"Some trouble last night in the neighbourhood?" he asked.

"My husband said there was but I slept right through it. I could sleep through a Western Sea storm, my husband says. And I probably did when I was a child. Can't remember much though, being some years ago."

Wulfner feared he might not get away as swiftly as he'd hoped.

"My sister probably could. She remembers everything. People's names, who said what and when." She stopped and put a hand on her hip. "Can't remember much myself though. All such a long time ago, mind. Been here a—"

Wulfner coughed and stopped her seemingly endless tale by holding up a silver and asking how much he owed.

"Of course, of course, just a moment, dear." And she bustled off into a back room. Wulfner looked around the tap-room. Inns were reasonably similar wherever one went but there was something special about the drinking houses in his native land, north-west of Westhealfe. Maybe the ale. Maybe the music. More likely the people.

The return of the innkeeper's wife broke his reverie. He looked questioningly at her and she smiled again.

"Two and six, please."

Cheaper up north too grumbled Wulfner inwardly. He withdrew the coins from a pouch at his waist, put them on the counter and thanked her for her hospitality.

"There'll be a room for you whenever you pass through again" she said as he was turning to leave. The wink that accompanied the words left Wulfner in little doubt that if he ever stayed here again, there would be knocks at his door during the night. She had been a terrible flirt.

Wulfner stepped out into the street and strode round the inn to the stable. His wagon was where he had left it, but he'd known it would be. He whistled.

"Where are you, you lazy mutt?"

In answer to his less-than-polite enquiry, a huge Argollat Mastiff trotted out from behind Wulfner's cart. There was a spring in his step and something close to a smile around the dog's maw.

"What's up with you, Trob? You meet a nice lady last night while your master was asleep? You were supposed to be on guard, not gallivanting through the alleys."

Wulfner held out his right hand and Trob came up to lick it. With his left hand, the northerner pulled out a piece of dried beef from his sack and tossed it in the air between them. Trob snapped his jaws around it and wolfed it down with no more than one chew.

"You'll give yourself a stomach-ache" muttered the hound's master.

Wulfner took in the streets around him as the morning sun managed to pierce through the grey mass in the skies, sliding down the small lanes that criss-crossed the city. He sniffed the air and was certain that each morning since he had arrived, the smell had changed. Less scent of food being prepared and more stench of sweat permeating the streets. The sounds were also changing. At first, there had been a hustle and bustle with so many Meridian boots stomping around, which Wulfner reckoned created a mixed sentiment within the populace. Armed men could be reassuring but they could also be

211

intimidating.

The second day he was here, various city sounds had returned as people had shrugged and seen the soldiers as little more than customers or nuisances depending on the trade. This morning, though, there seemed a tension in the air.

As if to confirm this perception, Wulfner heard shouts from a few blocks down. He couldn't make out what was being yelled but it sounded like something definitely had happened in the night. Wulfner hoped there hadn't been some sort of violent resistance to this newly arrived military force. More likely the city guard had gotten into a drunken brawl with the Meridians, each side eager to show some swagger. But the latter were trained soldiers, whereas the Argyllan lads were a presence more than an actual fighting force.

Wulfner gave his trader's cart a cursory glance and decided nothing had been stolen. He knew that would be the case. There had been noises in the night but nothing from Trob. If the muscular mastiff had barked, Wulfner would have been down to the cart in less time than a man downs an ale after a hard day's work. And Trob would have scared off any would-be thieves anyway.

The hulking northerner entered the stable and peered into the gloominess for the stable-boy. The young lad wasn't there but there was a Meridian soldier looking around. Wulfner nodded a good morning and pointed to his horse, indicating his intention. The soldier barely noticed him, seemingly looking for something other than horses in the stable. Wulfner shrugged and pulled out a few barley sugars for his horse, Azal.

"C'mon, girl, time to move to new pastures, methinks."

Azal snickered and allowed Wulfner to lead her back to his cart. Trob was patiently waiting. The mastiff seemed more interested than usual in all the goods Wulfner had in his cart. As he attached the harness to Azal, he frowned at Trob.

"Five years I've been running along these roads trading and you pay no attention whatsoever to my wares. Now you seem to think there is something nice in amongst all that stuff for you.

I reckon you did get lucky last night. Well, if you want that luck to continue, we had best move on. Something isn't right this morning."

Wulfner's suspicions were further heightened when four Meridian soldiers hurried up the road, their boots scraping the cobbles as their chain-mail shirts rustled with a metallic clink. They glanced at Wulfner but moved quickly by.

"Obviously not looking for an ugly northern brute like myself" he murmured to himself.

Wulfner turned at the sound of voices in the stable. The stable-boy had arrived accompanied by the innkeeper, and now both were conversing with the soldier who had been poking around. They seemed to be counting the horses. The innkeeper caught sight of Wulfner and pointed at him. The soldier looked over but immediately looked away, asking questions of the now anxious stable-boy.

Wulfner went back to making ready for his departure. When Azal was firmly secured to the cart, he led her by the bridle and headed towards the north gate, which would lead him to the bridge over the River Freo and into the north-west. Trob trotted alongside his master, his shaggy fur looking in need of some trimming.

Wulfner ran a hand through his own straggly hair, catching a few knots as he did so. He yawned and began thinking about the Journeyman's Inn on the other side of the river, a place where he could relax and enjoy some of their excellent ale. The innkeeper, Yarcus, had a home-brew that was well known throughout the entire north-west and beyond. A pale ale that had a pinch of spice, a tang of fruit and a crisp finish. It went exceedingly well with one of Yarcus' wife's game pies.

Wulfner looked down at Trob, who was padding alongside, tongue lolling out his mouth, this morning's enthusiasm seemingly coursing through his muscular body. Wulfner grinned, happy to be heading back to his roots.

As they made their way through the streets, Wulfner saw shops were opening up and the city's folk were starting their day as normal. But some doors and shutters remained closed and there was definitely less of the usual city clamour that accompanied the rising of the sun. Soldiers were on the move, rather than stationed at key points and on the city walls as they had been immediately after their arrival.

Wulfner considered for a moment that the city was under threat of imminent attack but dismissed that notion. Practically all forces would be manning the outer defences, not searching for what Wulfner presumed was a thief or ruffian. His size had two advantages in this kind of situation. Firstly, he was unlikely to be mistaken for most people in Argyllan, who tended to be thought of as very tall at six foot. And secondly, few soldiers would bother him just to show they were doing their job. Wulfner kept making his way onwards as the city's human cogs began turning.

The tall northerner saw the city gate at the end of the road, unsurprisingly manned by quite a few Meridian soldiers. Wulfner tried not to look suspicious or in any hurry. He didn't want them to think he was running, just going about his business. To add to this desired perception, he craned his neck up at the Shrine of Rawlin, a place of worship for those who kept faith with the old Gods. It was an impressive structure in terms of the masonry. Stone had been chiselled and smoothed into shapes of nature. The doorway was like the entrance to a grove, trees leaning to form an arch. As he passed by the lane leading to the entrance, he heard chanting from within. Wulfner wondered with some bitterness if the Gods were listening to them.

One soldier at the gate, presumably the officer in charge, held up a hand to stop Wulfner. "Morning to you, sir."

Politeness pleased Wulfner. He returned the greeting and commented, "Some kind of drunken brawl last night, captain? Lost out on some beauty sleep!" Wulfner grinned.

The officer sighed. "No. Inebriated idiots would have made for an easier task this morning. Our lord was attacked last night. We believe the assailants are still in the city. Two of them.

214

Couple of young girls, if you can believe it."

Wulfner raised an eye-brow. This was a strange happening. Wulfner knew Lord Rencarro was no pampered noble who sat on velvet cushions all day, wine dribbling from his chin. Rencarro was quite a soldier, if the accounts Wulfner had heard were correct. Bested by two young girls? That was odd indeed.

"No mistake, that isn't easy to believe" Wulfner replied, "but I don't doubt you are telling it as it happened. They caught him unawares?" Wulfner wondered if the Meridian ruler had been in his cups when he was perhaps mugged by street urchins.

The officer frowned. "Not clear on the details but one of the girls seems to have a power over animals. She leapt on his horse and the stupid mare kicked its own master in the chest. The lord is alive but suffered a few broken ribs, so I hear."

Wulfner had heard some crazy tales in the taverns of Ragnekai but this was a new one for him. A noble lord being knocked down by his own horse, ridden by some girl who controls beasts. One to tell Yarcus at the inn, mused Wulfner.

Might get an ale on the house for it.

"Well, I'm sure he'll make a swift recovery. Lord Rencarro has fierce blood running in his veins so the folk in this region say. I'll be heading north now, if you'll give me leave to depart Argyllan."

Wulfner hoped he wasn't going to miss lunchtime at The Journeyman.

The officer looked him up and down and chuckled.

"Of course! You don't fit the description of those two waifs. Does he lads?!" he said turning to the other soldiers. They laughed at their captain's joke and Wulfner joined in politely, eager to be on the other side of the Freo.

As he began to move on again, the officer cocked his head and looked at Wulfner's cart.

"What are you trading, sir?"

Wulfner groaned silently. Yarcus' wife's pies might all be gone by the time he arrived.

"Mostly salt, Argollan apples, wine up from the southern

vineyards, the odd trinket from places farther off. Nothing dangerous or unholy, I assure you" he told the officer, doing his best to look innocent.

Wulfner turned to look at his cart and saw Trob sniffing around near the back and then pawing at the canvas that covered the wares. Wulfner had no idea what was up with the silly mutt this morning. What possible reason could he have for being so frisky and interested in trading goods?

Then something clicked in Wulfner's mind as the officer spoke again.

"Mind if I take a quick look?"

"In the cart?"

He racked his brain for some way to stop the officer looking under the canvas. Wulfner had a strange feeling that there was something besides his wares under there. He was putting his faith in his hound's sense of good and bad here, and if Trob was acting up for some other reason, he would give the mutt a good cuff. Wulfner knew he was about to jeopardise any future trading in this city.

Wulfner moved away from his cart and leaned in closer to the officer, his voice lowered.

"Hmm, here's the thing. Whilst I don't have anything illegal in there according to the law up in the Veste region, I do have some items that are not exactly above board here in Argyllan, which is why I am eager to be on my way."

Wulfner winked at the man and hoped he would show an old fellow some kindness.

The soldier looked puzzled. "What kind of items?"

Wulfner silently cursed. This officer was perhaps too clean-cut to make this easy.

"You ever heard of Lorth Weed?"

The officer looked around as if the answer was written on a nearby wall.

"That the plant that people boil and then drink to dull pain?"

Wulfner mentally counted himself lucky that this officer knew a thing or two about herb-lore.

216

"That's the one!" he said excitedly. "Now it does ease suffering when boiled but does something a bit different when smoked." Wulfner grinned, hoping the soldier would understand.

The officer's face took on an almost disapproving expression. *What are you, my mother?!*

"Folks in Westhealfe do enjoy a pipe in the evenings. To let their thoughts drift, so to speak" Wulfner whispered with a wry smile. The captain's brow furrowed further.

By the Winds, show a bit of empathy to an old trader!

The officer chuckled and Wulfner relaxed.

"You've just solved a little mystery I had back home. I wondered why my cousin was growing Lorth Weed, despite the fact he is as much a physician as you and I. Said it made good tea. Bloody liar! I'll give him an earful when I get back." He shook his head. "He always was the black sheep in the family."

Wulfner pulled at his beard. "Well, far be it from me to see a business opportunity here but how long you lads going to be here in Argyllan?"

The smile faded from the officer's face and Wulfner was worried he might have inadvertently shut the door he thought was opening to him.

"Can't say for sure" the officer replied. "Could be a while. There was a rumour we'd be here on a more or less permanent basis." He shrugged.

Wulfner saw the door was still open.

"Well, if you are still here when I'm back through, and open to earning a bit of silver, I'd appreciate it. Nothing dangerous or nefarious, you have my word. A lack of inspection on my wares though could be a nice little earner for us both."

The officer looked over his shoulder at the other soldiers. Then turned back to Wulfner and winked.

"Well, safe travels, sir." he said loudly. "Let the big man through, lads. He's yearning for a bit of northern ale to wet his whistle."

"That I am!" laughed Wulfner. "The Journeyman's Inn will be my first call. Pies and ale that you won't forget. Unless you have too much of the ale!"

The soldiers laughed and Wulfner started pulling Azal through the gate. "Give my regards to your cousin, captain!" he called as he waved farewell to the Meridians. And then moved on up the road to the bridge, trying not to look as relieved and surprised as he felt.

There were more soldiers at the bridge but they waved him on, scanning the river and the banks this side. *Looking for Lord Rencarro's assailants,* Wulfner thought.

He carried on up the road for about a mile, until he was well out of sight of any Meridian soldier and then drew Azal off the road. They headed down a muddied track that twisted away to the west, then entered a small area of trees and brush and stopped.

"You want to get out of my cart now?" he said, looking at the canvas covering his wares. Nothing happened.

"Two of you in there? Can't see how you could fit any more than two in there." He gave the wheel of the cart a kick and raised his voice. "Come on, game's over now."

The canvas shifted. It startled Wulfner despite the fact he was sure there was at least one person hiding in the cart.

"Please don't hurt us" came a weak voice and a hand emerged from beneath the canvas, trying to pull it back.

Wulfner took hold of the edge and threw back the cover in one motion. What was below was a new sight for him, despite many years roaming the realm. A girl with chestnut skin, black upon black hair, wearing clothes that looked to be made of animal skin was emerging from a small space in the cart where she had been squeezed in with another girl. This one had pale skin, fiery red hair, and was wearing a long green coat, looking either sick or exhausted.

"Well, this is a bit different" he murmured.

"Please" said the dark-haired girl. "Please help us. We are in trouble."

"I can see that" said the big northerner, "and you'll need to tell me what the story is here, but first I think you both need a bit of nourishment."

He helped them out of the cart, the pale-skinned girl letting out a small cry of pain as her feet touched the ground. She gingerly lowered herself to sit on the ground and began rubbing her right ankle. Wulfner passed them his water-skin and leaned against his cart.

"Slowly now."

The two girls took sips in turns, again the pale one needing help. She seemed in an absolute state.

Trob lay down and put his head in the dark-haired girl's lap. Wulfner started in amazement. "So you did meet a lady last night" he commented. The girl smiled and ruffled his ears, whispering something to the mastiff.

"I am Lunyai" she said, "I am Tarakan."

Wulfner nodded.

"This is Emiren. I don't know anything else."

The pale-skinned girl looked up. Her eyes were blood-shot and it was obvious she had been crying.

"My name is…" she croaked. "My name is Emiren" she said after taking another sip of water and finding her voice. "I am from the village Fallowden. Are we going that way?"

Wulfner frowned. "I'm sorry, young one. We are on the other side of the River Freo now."

The two girls looked at each other in horror. Then the red-head started sobbing softly.

The Tarakan girl hugged her and turned to Wulfner. "But I thought you were from the south. I saw you at the gate when we arrived. And your dog is an Argollat Mastiff. We hid in your wagon to avoid the soldiers last night. I was going to ask you to take us south with you when you left but we could hear you were leaving this morning, so stayed quiet. I thought…" Her voice trailed off.

Wulfner shook his head, feeling sympathy for how the Winds could blow in a merry dance and trick people into hearing what they wanted to believe.

"I was coming from the south, returning to the north. I'm sorry ladies but we left by the north gate of Argyllan. My name is Wulfner and I am heading home as it were."

The girl whose name began with an L hung her head. She did not cry but Wulfner felt desperately sorry for these two. He tried to put the pieces of the puzzle together in his mind. He had guessed at the gate that the two supposed assailants of Lord Rencarro were hiding in his cart. A girl who could control beasts had struck Wulfner as a fanciful tale but it did explain why Trob was acting the way he was. And two girls taking down a trained soldier had seemed to be an *official* version of events. What had actually happened though, Wulfner couldn't fathom. But he wasn't sure now was the right time to ask questions.

He retrieved a couple of apples from his cart, noting that they hadn't already eaten his wares. That told him something. It suddenly occurred to him that they had made space for themselves in the cart. Something was missing. Wulfner winced as he realised it was two barrels of wine. He assumed the innkeeper would find it somewhere near the stable. He shook his head as he wondered what the wife would perceive the wine to be. A gift no doubt.

Best not lodge there again anytime soon.

Wulfner passed the apples to the girls and watched them nibble away. He scanned around and couldn't see or hear anything so reckoned they were safe to sit here a while and consider what to do next.

What have I got caught up in?

He was not the reckless adventurer he had been some twenty to thirty years ago and whilst he was always ready to help someone in need, he worried this little situation here might not stay so little.

"I can see there is a lot here that I don't understand but can also see you're in a spot of bother so..." he paused and gestured to his hound and mare, "with my friends Trob and Azal here, I will help."

The gratitude in their eyes as they looked up was reward in itself.

"Thank you" whispered the girl from Fallowden.

The other smiled at him.

"We'll have time for questions and the like later but first we must make some kind of plan. You both need to get south but I can tell you that we were lucky getting out the gate and across the bridge back there."

"We heard someone ask to look in the cart" said the Tarakan. "We thought we would be found at any moment but Yaai the Sun smiled upon you, I believe."

Wulfner shifted his feet and scratched his beard. He had not been comfortable with talk of deities for a very long time. His had failed him long ago and the only higher powers he believed in anymore were the Winds. They still blew.

He continued. "So we are going to have to look at the long way round. I'm talking about the sea here."

He gauged their reaction and whilst there was no panic there, he could see neither of them were enamoured about taking a boat. The easier way would be to take a barge heading south from the Icefinger River to the Freo and get off somewhere before the Freo joined the Unn. But that wouldn't really get them past the Meridian presence. The more difficult, but unobstructed way, was to go by the open sea.

One possibility was to find a vessel that would take them to Argyllan but that would be even more reckless than the first option. *No,* thought Wulfner. They would have to go all the way round the White Sisters, the cliffs that lined the west coast past Argyllan, and farther still till they could land some place where they could reach the Tarakan Plains. Wulfner had to admit to himself that he had no idea just how far south one had to go to find such a place. The White Sisters were sheer and stretched a fair way.

"First things first though. We need to get somewhere safe, find a place where you two can take a bath and get some hot broth down your throats." He smiled encouragingly.

"Will we go to the Journeyman's Inn?" asked the Tarakan girl. "We heard you talking about it. Is it as good as you say?"

"It is indeed and while I would love to go there and share tales with Yarcus, the innkeep, I think we'd best avoid it." He grinned. "One reason why I made a fuss about it was just in case they send anyone after us. Unlikely, I know, especially as this is Veste territory now and they believe I am alone. But I have been around long enough to know that once people eliminate all other possibilities, they will pursue the last one open to them, no matter how bizarre it seems. Someone may follow us, and if they do, hopefully they'll only find good pies and ale."

Wulfner held out his strong hands and they each took one. He pulled them to their feet with ease and studied them quickly. The girl from Fallowden had obviously injured her ankle but the Tarakan girl seemed unhurt in any way.

"I'm thinking you can walk, erm, Lula was it?"

She corrected him.

"Right. Lunyai can walk. Emily?"

"Emiren."

"Right, right. Blame my advancing years. Emiren, you might be better in the cart for a bit longer but stretch your legs out. Both of you must be cramped."

They set off again, continuing down the track Wulfner had set them on. The weather was kind to them, the clouds had thinned and there was a cool breeze. Under other circumstances this would have been a pleasant hike. Wulfner kept snatching glances at the two girls and was satisfied both were calmer, although the Emiren girl had a haunted look to her eyes.

They walked on in relative silence for a good couple of miles. Trob trotted along beside Lunyai, seemingly very taken with the Tarakan girl. *Traitor* thought Wulfner but smiled at the pair. The girl clearly had a way with animals. It looked like there'd been some truth in the officer's tale after all.

After a time and some distance covered, Emiren called out,

her voice stronger than before.

"Where are we heading?"

"I'm making for a better road than this one, one with a few less bumps." He tried to put some cheer in his voice. "And hoping we can reach a place where I have good friends. People who will help us."

"Westhealfe?" asked Lunyai, which Wulfner guessed was the only place she knew north of the River Freo.

"No, lass, Westhealfe is farther east. And it was where I told those guards I'd be going so another place to steer clear of." He winked at Emiren and received a smile, the first he'd seen on her face. There was hope yet.

He turned to Lunyai and had to laugh at Trob frolicking like a fool as he ran around her as she walked.

"You seem to have charmed my mutt, Lunyai."

He was pleased with himself for remembering her name this time.

"My mother would agree with you…forgive me but I have forgotten your name."

"Wulfner. It's Wulfner. At your service!"

Emiren spoke from where she sat in the cart. "Thank you, Wulfner. You and Lunyai have saved my life." She looked set to burst into tears again but took a deep breath and composed herself. Wulfner sensed she would tell her story so he came to a halt.

"Shall we rest a while and tell our stories?"

The two young ladies exchanged glances and then both nodded. Wulfner unharnessed Azal from the cart and let her wander to a grassy knoll nearby. With Lunyai supporting Emiren, the three of them followed and sat down near Azal. Trob scampered up and flopped down by Lunyai.

Wulfner's eyes widened as they told him how they'd come to end up stowing away in his cart. The Winds had blown him onto a very strange path today.

Emiren had witnessed her friend murdered by a Meridian officer called Sylvanus. The fiery-haired girl said his name as if it was foul water on her tongue. This Sylvanus had then pursued her, told his men that she had been the assassin and to kill her. Emiren had fled to Argyllan to find her uncle, deeming a return to her village too dangerous. Wulfner wondered at how this young girl could have survived nights in Argol Forest and avoided capture.

He was even more amazed at how Emiren had navigated Argyllan across the roof-tops. He would have laughed if it hadn't been for the flat tone with which she spoke of it.

Lunyai picked up the tale, quickly explaining she had been returning from a pilgrimage to the Sacred Mount, was taking a walk under the moon, and had come across Emiren and Lord Rencarro. Wulfner's jaw dropped when she described her mounting the horse and knocking down the Meridian.

"Lunyai saved my life" whispered Emiren. "Another moment and that spear would have fallen."

Wulfner rubbed his hands and tried to think. He wanted to put this incident within the wider picture of what was happening in the realm. He raised his eyes and saw them both looking at him expectantly.

They think I can provide a few answers here.

"Well, I have heard some tales in my time but this has taken the wind from my sails. I think all three of us have been caught up in something that suggests the realm is in murky waters."

He paused.

"Emiren, I am truly sorry for your friend."

The girl nodded, muscles in her face tightening as she fought back emotion. She composed herself and spoke.

"I cannot believe what has happened. But it has. And something that eats away inside me is that Anton's family will not know what happened to him unless I can get word back. I cannot begin to think what that Sylvanus has done with Anton's bo…" She couldn't finish, anger twisting within sadness upon her face.

Lunyai touched her arm.

"We will get back and tell his family. We will bring justice to

224

Sylvanus."

Wulfner was impressed with the Tarakan girl's conviction. There was a fierce spirit burning within her. He sensed Emiren possessed something similar, but it had been tossed around on a stormy sea so much that it was bedraggled and confused.

Something in Emiren's tale came back to Wulfner.

"Emiren, you said that Rencarro accused you of murdering his son, which was presumably the body in the clearing."

The girl was silent for a while. Wulfner worried he had been wrong to make her relive this episode. But after a deep breath she spoke.

"Yes. His son was dead when I saw them, although I didn't know who the dead soldier was at first. But it could not have been Anton who slew him. He was the gentlest soul you could ever meet." Her voice cracked and she visibly struggled to keep herself from weeping.

Wulfner frowned. "Judging by what Sylvanus said to his men, it seems likely he killed Rencarro's son."

He shook his head. Wulfner was mystified.

"Why would a Meridian officer murder his own lord's son? Doesn't make sense" muttered Wulfner. "One thing is for certain though. The death of High King Sedmund has kicked off a strange chain of events."

Their little group fell into a silence then. Wulfner looked up into the sky and wondered if he would be able to get these two back to their homes.

Ch 2

Svard

T he First Ranger of the Helligan Nation looked over his shoulder at the city of Meridia, which grew smaller and smaller as he and the other Rangers headed east, returning to Gamle Hovestad. Orben had made it clear that once the city was taken, the Rangers were to head back. Rorthal was in command of the regular forces, now encamped outside the Meridian walls, and Brax and his Sentinels were within the city. The violence was over for now.

Svard clenched his teeth and said a silent farewell to Lorken, whose body had been burned yesterday with all the other soldiers who had fallen, Helligan and Meridian.

In death we are all the same. Ashes.

Then Svard turned his head back to the road ahead and kicked his horse into a canter, bringing himself to the front of the column of riders. Cuyler acknowledged his presence but said nothing. Svard had been silent aside from giving orders since Lorken's death. His men knew he had lost someone close to him and kept a respectful distance.

It had taken Rorthal's harsh words to pry Lorken's body from Svard's arms the day before, the burly Battle-Sergeant reminding Svard of his rank and duty. Svard had been ready to use his fists to respond but when he had locked eyes with Rorthal, he had seen empathy. The fight had left him and he had become the First Ranger again. The friend of Lorken, the brother of Lorken, would surface later to mourn.

Lord Rencarro's son Eligius had made the transition of authority in the city a bloodless and civilised affair. Svard had a grudging respect for this intelligent young man. Eligius was not a warrior but he had clearly seen the battle was lost. Svard considered that this wasn't due to any cowardice but from an ability to rapidly see the reality of a situation. The man was astute and perceptive. Svard was slightly worried the man was too clever and was already planning on how to liberate Meridia. But if he tried, he'd be unlikely to succeed with Brax and Rorthal still there.

Without saying a word, Svard increased the pace of his mount and his fellow Rangers followed his lead. With all of them on horseback, and no infantry or siege weapons, the journey back to Gamle Hovestad would take less than two days. Svard almost wished they were on foot. Part of him didn't want to go back. He knew Orben would send them on another mission, this time likely to be north of the Mimir River, but he could face that. What made his chest hurt was the thought of bringing word to Jenna and the children.

The Rangers passed through what had been Meridian lands, now theoretically under Helligan rule. There were thirty-six Rangers making the return journey. The squad of Tarben, the man who had fallen from a cut line, had stayed in Meridia. Tarben had broken a leg in the fall and could not move. As was ever the case with an injured comrade, his squad had stayed with him. The Rangers never left one of their number behind.

The countryside here was one of rolling hills and scattered homesteads. The geography had allowed the Helligan force to remain undetected for a significant length of time when they had advanced upon Meridia. When they had crossed the River Unn, Svard and his Rangers had gone on ahead to stop word spreading too far of the Helligan army approaching Meridia. It had been relatively simple work as most of the folk had just scuttled indoors.

As they had closed in on the city, word had reached them that Lord Rencarro had gone west with the majority of Meridia's strength. Svard had known this would be the case so hadn't been surprised. The majority of the intelligence he had been given for this entire mission had been frighteningly accurate, and he was now starting to look at the past few days with the benefit of hindsight.

Svard could understand Orben had his agents within Meridia who were known only to the Helligan ruler. Brax, Rorthal and Svard had never met a Helligan spy and it was clear Orben wanted it kept this way. But what struck Svard as strange was Orben hadn't simply *found out* that Rencarro had ridden west; Orben had known the Meridian Lord *was going to* ride west before it happened. How had the Helligan ruler lured Rencarro away to the west and thus left his city under-manned? That was a feat beyond the skills of spies and scouts.

And then there was the revelation from Eligius that his brother had been assassinated. Had that been on Orben's command? It seemed another *coincidence* too well-timed for it to have been a random killing, and it was unlikely that anyone in Bregustol would have ordered the murder of Rencarro's son. Yet Svard believed Orben wouldn't dirty his hands with this kind of act either. To the best of the First Ranger's knowledge, there had never been a clandestine killing authorised by Orben. He had always deemed his lord too proud of the Helligan fighting prowess to resort to daggers in the shadows.

Svard saw a homestead ahead and two children playing outside. When the sound of their horses' hooves reached those inside the building, a man and woman rushed out and hurried the children within. Svard pitied them to be in a state of such fear. He wanted to tell them that life would go on much as before for them. It was those who held the power who suffered with a change of rule. And the soldiers who perished.

A memory came back to Svard of the last time he had a drink with Lorken. His friend had listened and laughed as he had recounted a few tales of a recent expedition. As usual Lorken had told Svard there was nothing of interest in his own life to entertain the Ranger. Svard had shaken his head and told him he wanted to hear everything that Darl, Torg and Eira had been doing.

"Knowing they are well and growing up to be fine Helligans like their parents, that is what gives me the strength to do what I do. When I am shivering with cold, soaked through to the bone, hungry and tired, as my men and I trudge through the depths of Bresden Forest, pursuing outlaws, I picture the faces of your family. They warm me, Lorken."

His words had clearly moved Lorken and even brought a lump to his own throat. They had laughed and started ripping into each other with humour, the emotion difficult to deal with. And of course, they had done what they always did in such a moment, which was to buy more ale.

And now Lorken was seated in the First Warrior's Hall, quaffing the finest ale ever created, sharing songs and tales with all the others who had fallen.

It wasn't your time to go, brother.

Svard gritted his teeth, thinking about how the cavalry was supposed to be far away with Rencarro. But they had come and slain Lorken and many other Helligans. The riders had died for this small victory, almost as if it were a feat of rage and fury, not an act that was meant to swing the battle. From a tactical point of view, the charge didn't make much sense. Svard was starting to feel there were a few things here that didn't add up. A great deal was going on behind closed doors.

He recalled how Orben's sister, the Lady Ulla, had seemed concerned or maybe disagreed with the plan to occupy Meridia. The strategy of playing the longer game had seemed to Svard a sound one, taking control of the south and not charging north. Orben had mentioned it was possible there could be an internal conflict north of the River Mimir, with General Torbal's native region breaking away from the capital.

Is that a possibility or does Orben know it will happen, just as he knew Rencarro would be away?

Svard suddenly felt swamped by the dense forest of shadow and rumour that his mind had wandered into. A woodland drenched in secrets; paths that were overgrown but still there; trees bent with age but still fiercely alive. The feeling that someone or something was ahead in the gloom, watching and waiting. Svard shook his head to clear it.

Cuyler moved closer to him and offered his First Ranger a water-skin, saying nothing. Svard accepted it and took a swig. He almost choked with the instant realization it wasn't water but wine. Svard cast a sideways glance at his captain, who shrugged.

"Wanted a taste of Meridia before we headed off."

Svard nodded and took a second drink, this time letting the wine run freely into his waiting throat. It served to remove the murkiness muddling his thinking. He handed the skin back and said a word of thanks.

The First Ranger tried to inwardly recount all he knew or had learnt. He made a few assumptions that he found distasteful but he felt the pieces fit together.

Ulla had poisoned Sedmund, he proposed to himself. He didn't like the notion but it did seem Orben was prepared for the High King's death. Ulla rode back to Gamle Hovestad soon afterwards and then Orben initiated the next stage of his design, mustering soldiers and giving the order to march.

Orben must have had some help from within Meridia.

Svard accepted this to be the case. Orben and this traitor had planned together, and the latter had seen to it that Rencarro rode west with his own plan after hearing of Sedmund's passing. This meant the traitor had to be someone of high standing within Meridia.

Eligius?!

It seemed slightly insane at first but it made sense. Eligius was extremely clever and then there was the fact he knew a lot about the Helligan nation, was even fluent in the language. Svard found himself nodding quietly. This was starting to form a complete picture, albeit a dark and twisted one.

Eligius was the resentful younger brother and had entered into an unholy alliance with Orben. Rencarro's older son would have been the natural heir but had been murdered. A tingle went through Svard as he began to see how it had all transpired.

That little bastard.

Orben must have promised Eligius the rule of Meridia, as a vassal to the Helligan nation. And in return Eligius would facilitate the city's fall to Helligan forces. The older brother's demise must've been part of this terrible pact. Svard wondered how Rencarro would be removed. The Meridian Lord was still alive and it seemed likely Eligius would need his father gone too for the people of Meridia to accept the younger son as their ruler.

Svard found himself marvelling at Eligius' cunning while feeling an equal measure of disgust that someone could be so utterly despicable in their pursuit of power. The First Ranger was beginning to taste something foul regarding many of the players here, his own lord and the Lady Ulla included.

And then his anger rose, and he growled low in his throat as he considered how all this treachery had led to Lorken's death. Svard knew many would die in the coming months but until now he had seen it as a righteous campaign to restore the Helligan nation to its rightful place in the realm of Ragnekai. Now this struggle had taken on a sickly hue with Svard's ruminations. A determination rose within him to find out the truth. He spurred his mount to a gallop and pulled ahead of his fellow Rangers.

Ch 3

Rencarro

7th Day of Maia, Twelve Days After Sedmund's Death

Two Days After Meridia Fell

Rencarro tried to sit up but pain lanced through his chest. He gasped and let his body sink back onto the bed. His physician had bound up his chest tightly, diagnosing three broken ribs but judged there to be no internal damage. He had given Rencarro some foul-tasting broth to consume and the pain had dulled somewhat.

The Lord of Meridia closed his eyes and tried to breathe deeply. The Widow seemed to be punishing him relentlessly and with great malice. Marcus murdered, the assassin turning up in Argyllan, then he himself struck down by his own horse, ridden by some strange girl. A Tarakan pilgrimage party was missing one of their number it had been reported and it was possible this was the girl. It seemed likely when one considered Tarakans were renowned for their ability with horses.

Widow, are you playing with me? Is this some cruel game and you are cackling like a crazed witch?

His horse, Amacum, had been found wandering the streets in the south of the city yesterday morning, seemingly unaware of having injured his master. Rencarro winced at the memory. He had been lucky the beast had not struck him full on but had dealt him more a glancing blow. It had still been enough to render him unable to pursue the two waifs.

Who are they? How did she make Amacum attack me?

Rencarro flexed his fingers and toes, trying to get his blood circulating. He turned his head gently from side to side, then tried to take deeper breaths. It hurt but he gritted his teeth and embraced the pain.

The fight left him though after a few moments and he let his body go loose. He lay back and wondered how he could lead his men effectively here with such an injury, on top of the mental anguish of losing his eldest son. He was in no condition to command if the rumours his own Velox Riders had spread became reality and the Throskaur actually did attack. He would have laughed at the farcical nature of their situation had it not been so serious. Here he lay, useless and in grief.

He had given his orders to Tacet yesterday, his words slurring from the heavy dosage of whatever was in the broth, but his commands crystal clear. *Find those two girls and bring the red-head back to me.* Tacet had bowed his head and left without a word. Rencarro did not have to tell Tacet anything else. The Velox Rider would use whatever method necessary to find the assassin and her accomplice. Rencarro wanted to catch them not just so he could deliver justice for the murder of his son but also to understand who this girl was. She hadn't seemed to be a killer by any stretch of the imagination. Rencarro was impressed by how convincing her act had been and had almost believed her story. But not quite. There *was* something strange about it though and Rencarro owed it to his late wife Shansu to learn exactly how and why their son had died.

Then he had sent another Velox Rider, Umbran, to relate to Sylvanus what had befallen him two nights ago and to confirm that Sylvanus was in command now of all the Meridian soldiers near Lowenden as a result of Marcus' death.

Rencarro was about to let sleep take him when he heard hurried footsteps coming closer. Then the door burst open without a knock and Sylvanus stood there, breathless and sweating.

The Lord of Meridia felt his world contract and the Void open up before him. Only something terrible could have brought Sylvanus to Argyllan, away from the troops under his command. Rencarro held his eyes and there was a moment when neither spoke, the silence like a heavy weight upon his injured chest.

"Rencarro" began his Second. No title uttered, just his name. Rencarro was sure grave tidings were upon Sylvanus' tongue.

"Rencarro" repeated Sylvanus, "Meridia has fallen."

His chest tightened, his breath coming in short-sharp stabs. The room seemed to be twisting and folding in around them. Rencarro struggled to regain a footing in the real world.

Sylvanus sank to his knees by his lord's bed, laying a hand on his fore-arm. His face was dirty and his eyes were blood-shot.

"Helliga. They marched west, not north. Forgive me, my plan has brought us to ruin." Sylvanus hung his head.

Rencarro's mind reeled. His city had fallen to the Helligan nation. Orben had set out on exactly the same path as Rencarro: the long game. Clearly Orben meant to rule the south and head north another day, perhaps waiting for Bregustol to become victim to civil unrest. And Rencarro had practically invited him in, leaving only Eligius and the Custodia city guard.

Eligius!

"Is Eligius alive?" he whispered.

Sylvanus raised his head. "We don't know. They did not sack the city so there is hope Eligius lives. A Helligan prisoner now, no doubt."

Sylvanus' jaw tightened. He continued relaying the bitter news.

"They came well prepared. It seems they were not aware, at least initially, that we had gone west ourselves. May the Widow take Orben's treacherous heart."

Rencarro was suddenly filled with an overwhelming anguish. He had nothing. Marcus was dead. His city was occupied and Eligius was possibly alive but a prisoner of the Helligan nation.

I lost. I rolled the dice and I have lost already. The game had only just begun.

Perhaps Sylvanus could see the despair clearly etched into his lord's face. His hand gently tightened on Rencarro's arm.

"We will fight back. We have our men with us and can maybe persuade the people here to join us against this foreign invasion."

Rencarro was hit by the absurdity of his Second's words when held up against the truth of what they had come here to do. The Meridians had only just arrived, promising their protection, but planning on annexation. And then they hadn't been there to protect their own city. They were victims of their own making.

Rencarro turned his head slowly and looked into Sylvanus' eyes. It was clear his Second did not really believe they could fight back. Not immediately anyway.

Sylvanus stood and went to retrieve a stool from the other side of the room. He brought it back and sat, elbows resting upon knees, his shoulders sagging.

"Atticus told me you were attacked. What happened?"

Rencarro sighed and began to relate the events of the night before last.

"The assassin was here?!" blurted Sylvanus.

"Yes. Why she came here I cannot fathom. If she were one of Orben's, why did she not head south and take the long way back to Helliga?"

Sylvanus looked uneasy. He gazed at the floor.

"Maybe she was attempting to find a boat to take her far away. Maybe she is a native of this region and was merely paid by Orben."

Sylvanus' suggestions were valid but Rencarro couldn't shake the feeling that it didn't add up.

"She seemed a petrified girl when I confronted her."

Sylvanus straightened his posture, hands on thighs, tension in his arms.

"She was no such thing when she cut me." Sylvanus spoke with venom in his voice. Rencarro turned his head back and stared at the colourless ceiling, devoid of any decoration save a spider's web in one corner.

"My lord. How do we proceed?"

Rencarro said nothing. He had no idea what to do now. He needed to first accept this hideous reality which had been visited upon him. Then consider the lives of his men who had come with him to Argyllan. He would not lead them in a rash bid for revenge. He wondered how they would react to the news that their home had fallen and the possibility that loved ones were dead.

"I need time to think. Brief Atticus and Julius, then have them come here at the midday bell. We will consider our options. Orben has won the opening act of this tragedy. We must ensure that we do not lose the second act to blind rage."

Rencarro turned his head again and saw Sylvanus slowly nod. "It will be done" said his Second, his voice devoid of the ambition that had been there before they had embarked upon this ill-fated path.

As he turned to leave, Rencarro called his name.

"Sylvanus. We will endure and we will secure victory."

Something returned to the soldier's face. Hope perhaps.

"And Sylvanus. Find the quartermaster Camran and ask him to come here with some of that rum. He'll understand."

Sylvanus nodded and left the room, leaving Rencarro alone. People would often say that terrible situations felt like bad dreams. Rencarro felt nothing dream-like about this. Perhaps he was too pragmatic, too aware of the world around him.

They had misjudged and made a grave error. Hoping to secure the entire west of Ragnekai, they had only succeeded in losing their home to Helligan expansion.

Rencarro considered the possibility that his men would demand they return and retake Meridia. Marcus would have argued for such a move. How many soldiers and civilians would die though? Rencarro was well aware the Helligan people were more war-like in their culture than the other factions in Ragnekai. Taking back a walled city from them would exact a heavy toll in life, and success was far from guaranteed.

Fatigue, mental and physical, came over him. Marcus. Meridia. Eligius. Rencarro let the tears come. He saw his dead wife, Shansu, in his mind's eye. He saw such sadness in her.

Shansu. I yearned for greatness. I have found only failure and loss.

Eventually the tears dried upon his cheeks and he felt a strange calmness descend upon him. He lay still and soon his eye-lids became heavy.

Damned herbal medicines…

When he awoke he was surprised to find Camran sitting there reading a book. The quartermaster looked up.

"I would tell you to rest easy but that would make little sense in this cruel world we have woken up to this day," lamented Camran. He reached to the floor and picked up the rum. He offered a sad smile.

"Your Second told me to bring this. Not sure if your physician would approve but anyway…"

Rencarro raised himself to a sitting position, the wall behind him providing sturdy support. His chest ached but the pain had subsided somewhat.

Camran picked up the same glasses they had used the other day, square in shape and quite impressive to the layman's eye and possibly the eye of a glass-blower too.

Something shifted within Rencarro's memory as he watched the amber liquid slide from the bottle's neck into the glasses.

"Who did you say made these glasses?" he asked.

"My brother" replied Camran, and raised his glass. "Let there be no more ill news today" he said, and continued speaking but Rencarro's mind was elsewhere. He stared at the glass.

"So your brother is a glass-blower?"

Camran looked at him quizzically, perhaps wondering how the Meridian lord could be interested in such a thing at this time, on a day of yet more chilling winds from the east.

"Yes. His work is quite well known round these parts."

"Where does he live?" Rencarro continued the questioning.

The quartermaster was taken aback. "Down in Fallowden. Why do you ask?"

"I recall you said he has a child."

Camran frowned and nodded. "Yes. A daughter. Perhaps eighteen summers. My Lord, you have lost me here."

"This daughter. Her hair. What colour is it?"

"Why in the name of the Spirits would you want to know that?"

"Please just answer the question" Rencarro said firmly.

Camran shook his head in bewilderment.

"It is red. She is a red-head like—"

"Like her mother" interrupted Rencarro. "Like her mother."

Camran gulped his rum and poured another into his glass. Rencarro was still yet to touch his. The quartermaster took a sip, wiped his mouth and studied Rencarro as one might an elderly relative who was losing their grip on reality. He took another sip.

"Your niece was here in Argyllan, Camran."

The quartermaster jerked forward and almost choked on the rum. He coughed a few times to clear his throat and looked at Rencarro in disbelief.

"My lord, I think you are either addled by whatever your physician gave you or you are suffering from shock. My niece is in Fallowden. Or more likely climbing trees in Argol."

Rencarro knew he was right then. A red-haired girl with a father who was a glass-blower, from Fallowden and quite familiar with the forest. Rencarro fixed Camran's gaze and spoke with a clear voice.

"I am not muddled, Camran. Your niece was here, I almost killed her and she escaped with another girl." His jaw tightened. "And I now do not believe she was the assassin."

Camran was silent. His mouth was slightly open, his eyes wide and Rencarro noticed the hand holding the glass was trembling.

"Emiren" he said quietly. He stood up and started to pace the room. "This is madness. How is my niece caught up in the murder of your son? Surely there must be some mistake."

Rencarro was reliving the encounter with the girl in his mind, and trying to understand where the mistake or lie lay. He felt a growing sense of unease as the likeliest explanation reared its ugly head.

Camran stopped pacing and ran his hands through his hair, which wasn't tied back today but falling loose to his shoulders.

"Something is amiss. Your son was a trained soldier. Emiren helps in the village hospice. How could she have cut down Marcus?"

"She was no such thing when she cut me."

And there it was. According to the original account of his son's murder, delivered by a Velox Rider, it had been the girl who had felled Marcus, and the boy who had struggled with Sylvanus.

"She was no such thing when she cut me."

Rencarro hadn't noticed the slip earlier when Sylvanus had spoken, his thinking not as sharp due to the herbal medicines. Sylvanus had lied. And the truly damning question was why had he lied? There could be only one terrible answer to this.

Sylvanus had murdered Marcus.

"Rencarro!" Camran's hands were on his shoulders, restraining him. He realised his body was shaking. A rage boiled within him and he wanted to tear out the throat of his Second.

"Shall I call for your physician?" spluttered Camran, his face a mask of panic.

Breathe. Calm. Release.

Rencarro repeated the words in his head and tried to bring the anger under control.

"No. No, there is no need."

Camran released his shoulders and sat back on the stool.

"Camran" began Rencarro slowly, thoughts forming as he spoke, "something foul has occurred and I must ask for your aid."

"Of course," the Argyllan replied, "though I am lost at sea as to what is going on here."

"Drink your rum and pour us both another." The two men knocked back their drinks and Camran let the amber nectar slide once more into the glasses. He held the bottle vertical above his own glass to empty out the last drop. "Shall I fetch another?" he asked, though appeared to think it a foolish question.

"Later perhaps."

Rencarro closed his eyes and gathered his thoughts.

"Camran, I believe that my Second, Sylvanus, is the one who murdered my son. Your niece and whoever she was with were witness to this or saw something."

"Spirits above and beyond!" whispered Camran.

"Sylvanus created the narrative that your niece was an assassin and thus she was pursued. She made her way to Argyllan, avoiding detection, perhaps reasoning a return to her village was too risky."

The pieces were starting to come together. As he spoke another fact slotted into place.

"I even asked her that night why she came here. Because you are here, of course. She came to seek refuge with you. But by some bizarre twist of fate I happened to be out that night, restless after Marcus' death and spotted her. It seems your Spirits were smiling upon her though as the Tarakan girl stopped me from thrusting my spear into her heart."

"Emiren" breathed Camran, his relief palpable that his niece had come so close to death but had escaped. The quartermaster looked up.

"Where is she now?"

Rencarro shook his head.

"I do not know but I have someone out looking for them. He will find them and bring them back here. I assure you he will not harm your niece in any serious fashion, though I regret he may not treat them gently." Rencarro was relieved he had not ordered Tacet to execute the girls, although he had said that only Camran's niece be brought back to him.

Rencarro felt his mind focusing and the inner-strength that had helped him rule Meridia for so many years was returning. Perhaps anger concentrates our purpose better than loss and grief, he thought. There was now something rotten to deal with under his very nose.

Sylvanus. How could you? And why?

Camran took a deep breath, bringing Rencarro's attention back to the moment. The quartermaster stood now with hands on hips, frowning.

"Well, it would be a relief to see Emiren safe and sound. It is possible she is still in the city, no?" offered Camran hopefully.

Rencarro hadn't considered this, having presumed they would flee the city walls that very night. It was quite plausible. His soldiers had not searched every corner of the city, far from it judging by the reports he had received as he had lain in this bed. With a bit of luck, Tacet would find them in hiding somewhere. That would be a small victory here.

"We must hope that is the case." Rencarro paused and looked at Camran, wondering how much he should pull this man into this bubbling cauldron of deceit. "I hope I can rectify some of this mess that surrounds us."

Camran shook his head, an expression of resignation on his face.

"Things beyond your control have conspired against us all."

He sat down again but immediately jumped up startled as there was a knock at the door.

"Enter" called Rencarro, feeling strength returning, coming from a deep well within.

The door opened and a Velox Rider stood there. Rencarro saw it was Umbran, a very capable man for reconnaissance.

"My lord" said the Velox Rider, his voice quiet and controlled.

Rencarro gestured for him to speak. Umbran's eyes moved to Camran, perhaps deciding on whether this information was for his lord's ears only. Rencarro nodded to show he could proceed.

"I have seen General Sylvanus is here in the city so have not ridden out myself. I bring word that one Velox Rider has departed the city, acting on information gained and headed north across the Freo into the Veste region."

Rencarro thought he could hear the Widow laughing at him again. One thing that he could have made right had now moved beyond his grasp. He would have to rely on Tacet to carry out his orders.

Why did they cross into the Veste region though? And how did they elude the guards?

The Lord of Meridia resigned himself to the likelihood this riddle would not be solved today. Now he must focus on a more immediate problem. He addressed Umbran.

"General Sylvanus will be here at the midday bell with Julius and Atticus. I want you and one other Velox to be here before that time. Tell nobody except your fellow Velox that you will do this."

There was no hesitation from Umbran. He bowed his head and left the room, closing the door smartly behind him.

Camran let out a breath. "This is beyond me, Rencarro. But I will help if I can. What would you have me do?"

Rencarro looked at the quartermaster who had become something of a friend in a short time. Strange paths were certainly being laid out before them.

"I appreciate your words, Camran. And will need your help. I don't want you here though when I arrest Sylvanus. He may become violent, like a cornered animal. I know not to under-estimate him, so for your safety, be about your duties at the midday bell."

Rencarro held up a finger.

"But I would ask you to return here later this afternoon. I will send for you."

"Of course," replied the quartermaster.

Rencarro spoke again, his voice quivering as he tried to master his anger.

"Camran, my most trusted aide and companion appears to have betrayed me and murdered my son. And your niece has become caught up in this. Help me unravel this tangled web."

Camran nodded grimly and it was if a fire had been lit within the quartermaster as well. Rencarro hoped this was so.

"I hope you show this Sylvanus true justice."

"I will do, have no doubt about that. First, I would have him

242

admit his guilt though. And I must know why he betrayed his lord in such a heinous manner."

Rencarro looked ahead then, his teeth clenching, fists forming.

"And then I will kill him myself."

Ch 4

Lunyai

7th Day of Maia, Twelve Days After Sedmund's Death

Two Days After Meridia Fell

The sky was a brilliant blue and Yaai was shining down on them as they walked, filling Lunyai with a hope that she would soon return to the Tarakan Plains, Emiren would be back in Fallowden and Wulfner would be free to get back to his trading. The Tarakan girl had to admit though that she would be sad to part ways from these two, and Trob and Azal.

Wulfner had led them along paths on which his wagon could travel but they certainly weren't well used. He had told them most people journeyed by the Vesten Causeway these days, being a well maintained and more direct road to the city of Westhealfe and then onto the east. The little company had passed only two other carts yesterday and seen a handful of homesteads, some far in the distance, a couple close enough to wave at men, women and children working in the fields. It had been very peaceful and Lunyai felt she could have forgotten her worries had they not been so serious.

Lunyai had called upon Tlenaii the previous night when they camped under His milky white glow, almost showing His full form. She had begged Him to give her the strength to help Emiren, this girl who had been caught up in a storm of hate and lost her friend. And to have seen it happen. She would bear that pain for the rest of her days, no matter how much it dulled.

Lunyai had watched the other girl sleep last night. Emiren had slept but her slumber had been a mixture of deep murmuring breaths, more ragged ones and sometimes even gasps where her body would shudder but her eyes remained shut. A troubled sleep for certain.

This morning though Emiren had seemed more spirited. She had woken before the other two and started a fire, even getting Wulfner's pots out and boiling water.

Perhaps she has dispelled some of the darkness that plagues her heart.

They had drunk the tea that Emiren had prepared, using some leaves she had gathered. Lunyai had never tasted such a tea before. It was slightly bitter but seemed to expel any weariness from her body. Wulfner had produced some black sausage from his cart and another apple for each of them. The day had started well, Lunyai thought.

"Ah, finally a better road" commented Wulfner as they came over a rise and saw a clearly defined road, rather than the path they had been on, which had been mostly flattened grass and weeds. Emiren had noticed the bumps more, being in the cart for much of the time. She did put her weight on her ankle though when they stopped for a rest and Lunyai felt it was healing gradually.

The new road was one of packed mud and dirt, and reasonably straight as opposed to the meandering, winding paths they had trodden till now. It was wide enough for a cart either way and Azal certainly seemed eager to get on it, throwing his head and whinnying. Wulfner spoke, his voice somewhat cheerful.

"This is the Westwind Road. If we follow it north, we will come to a coastal town called Ceapung, where I have friends. There are boats there for sure. Whether we can find one to take us down the coast to the Tarakan Plains and that inlet you spoke of, Lunyai, I can't be sure. It's a good, long way but we may be lucky."

The big man smiled and Lunyai believed she could see Yaai's radiance shine from him. This was a good man. She trusted in him and felt certain they would return safely.

With Trob bounding on ahead, they took to the road and found it kinder to their legs than the path before. Wulfner's wagon rolled smoothly along and Lunyai felt like she could extend her stride here and keep a good pace. She shook her flow of hair, black as a night when Tlenaii hid, then gathered it and fed it through a ring fashioned from deer bone. She breathed deeply of the morning air, turned to Emiren in the cart and smiled.

"How do you feel, Emiren?" She knew the simple answer was obvious but hoped Emiren would search for something more optimistic.

"I feel blessed by the Spirits that I am with you and Wulfner" Emiren replied warmly to Lunyai's relief.

Azal snickered.

"And Azal and Trob" laughed the girl.

Lunyai grinned and reached out to rest a hand on Emiren's shoulder as they pressed on.

"I am glad to hear this. Your Spirits are with you, I believe. And with Yaai burning brightly from this beautiful sky, I feel it will be a good day."

Lunyai squeezed the other girl's shoulder, then released her hand, raised both arms to the sky, and closed her eyes as she turned her face to Yaai.

"Never look directly at Yaai. She will blind you with Her beauty."

Lunyai remembered her mother's words well.

She opened her eyes and turned to Wulfner.

"Do you have a god, Wulfner? Do you feel we are favoured today?" enquired Lunyai good-naturedly.

The Tarakan girl saw a shadow pass over his face and he opened his mouth to answer but then hesitated. Lunyai realised she may have touched an old wound.

"Forgive me, I have perhaps assumed too much."

Wulfner shook his head and smiled sadly.

"I used to believe there were higher powers out there in the realm. I have travelled far and wide, and everywhere I have been, people believe in gods. The names are different but I felt the gods were actually the same ones."

"Now you believe there are different gods?" asked Emiren.

Lunyai knew she had misunderstood his meaning.

Wulfner sighed.

"No. Now I am not sure there are any gods at all." His voice was sad. And Lunyai felt a sadness herself that was mixed with confusion. She wanted to talk more about Tlenaii, Yaai and the All-Mother, showing Wulfner there were higher powers. But she hesitated. Words were lost to the wind if uttered at the wrong time. She hoped she could restore his faith in the higher power of nature, the strength of the All-Mother and Her children.

"What happened?"

Emiren's question was direct and it surprised Lunyai. Not only because it was asking Wulfner to reveal something perhaps painful, but also because she had been so focused on how she could bring him back to his faith that she hadn't even considered what the reason might be.

Wulfner let out a long breath and Lunyai was worried Emiren had angered him.

"I think I will tell you, despite the fact we have known each other only one sunrise."

He pulled his beard and massaged his forehead, which Lunyai took to signify this was painful to remember.

"I had a wife and daughter many years ago."

So few words but they spoke of so much pain. It was obvious his wife and daughter no longer walked in the realm and had returned to the All-Mother. Wulfner continued.

"They were so beautiful and gentle. It was as if the Four Keepers of the Seasons blessed them every time the Winds brought change. My dear Rowena's hair seemed golden in the summer, but then tinged with shades of ruby when the trees started to turn. My little Sunniva's skin was pale as the Icefinger River in winter, yet seemed to blossom when the warmth returned. And their eyes…"

Tears were slowly spilling out of Wulfner's eyes, tracing invisible lines down his cheeks until they were lost in his beard, its copper now glistening in a handful of places.

"Their eyes could calm any storm that raged within me. Rowena's were much like yours, Emiren, a deep green that seemed to be emeralds nestled in a quiet forest. And Sunniva had eyes blue as this sky we walk under today."

"Like her father's" said Lunyai softly.

Wulfner choked on emotion and squeezed his eyes shut, shaking his head. They had all stopped now. Trob was nudging his master's legs, a mournful little whine coming from him as he perhaps shared his master's grief.

Lunyai made no eye-contact with Emiren but they moved as one to lay hands upon the big northerner's back. No words were said for a time.

Finally Wulfner inhaled sharply, wiped his eyes roughly and ran a hand through his hair.

"You've got an old man crying, you young trouble-makers" he joked. "I'm supposed to be helping you both, not sharing my sadness."

"Sadness shared is friendship gained" said Lunyai, remembering another of her mother's sayings.

Emiren nodded, wiping her own tears away.

Wulfner suddenly laughed.

"What a sight we must make! A big brute of a northerner sobbing away, being helped by two young ladies who are from the other side of Ragnekai."

Both Lunyai and Emiren smiled. The young Tarakan woman silently said a prayer to Yaai, asking her that She give Lunyai the strength and guidance she needed to help not just Emiren, but to take away some of the sadness that lay within Wulfner.

They began walking again, commenting about the weather and pointing out things of interest to each other. It seemed they each had knowledge to share. Emiren seemed to know every single tree and plant they passed, Wulfner explained the geography and how the culture changed as they went farther north, and Lunyai for her part told them about the many animals that roamed the Tarakan Plains and the Izachu Wildlands. The pain of remembering for Wulfner seemed to have eased. Lunyai was glad. He hadn't told them how his wife and daughter died, but Lunyai was not sure she wanted to know. She didn't think she was ready to share that sadness yet.

Ch 5

Torbal

7th Day of Maia, Twelve Days After Sedmund's Death

Two Days After Meridia Fell

I still can't understand it, brother of mine. Falling into bed with that Helligan lady? Never took you for a man easily beguiled."

Cyneburg, Torbal's sister and wife of the First Lord of Westhealfe, had not let up in her admonishing since she had been told of the relationship. Torbal had considered keeping it a secret but with the realm in a state of uncertainty, it seemed a more sensible choice to be open with his sister and her husband. He had asked that they keep it between them, though. Torbal felt his niece Lucetta in particular would be disappointed in him.

"I wouldn't say I was easily beguiled but I concede it complicates matters" he said quietly. They were standing upon a balcony of Saxnot Keep that gave a view so very much more appealing than any on offer from the High King's Palace in Bregustol.

"An understatement, if ever there was one" cried Cyneburg in her none too soft voice and turned to look out over Westhealfe.

She crossed her arms across her chest, pinning down two of her five braids of ashen hair. The stance added to her already formidable presence. Cyneburg stood almost as tall as Torbal and was built like an elk. Torbal had probably benefited from his elder sister's might when they were children, having had to learn how to fight back from an early age. Torbal had of course not seen much merit in the rough and tumble at the time.

"Two fools tangling the reins of power in Bregustol and the

man who should be ruling is miles away, lovelorn for a lady who is on the other side of the realm!"

Torbal sighed. He would rather be fighting a Helligan Sentinel than having this conversation with his sister. If it could be called a conversation. Most of the hot air was coming from Cyneburg's mouth.

Torbal was about to grumble in defence of his feelings for Ulla when Lucetta came bounding up a set of stairs to the side of where they stood. Torbal saw in her face something that said this day wasn't going to get any better.

"Mother, Uncle, please come to Father's solar."

"What does your father want now?" asked Cyneburg in an exasperated tone.

"Meridia has fallen."

Not much could silence Torbal's sister, but this piece of news did. Cyneburg turned to her brother, eyes wide but then quickly narrowing. Her arms unfolded and fell to her sides, hands curling into fists.

"What have those damned Winds blown forth this day?" Cyneburg cried.

"I do believe we shall learn more if we go to Kenric's solar, sister" said Torbal, trying hard to keep his own surprise from his voice. And his exasperation with his sister's relentless judgment.

Cyneburg made a sound that Torbal took to be acceptance of his proposal and then marched off down the steps, leaving Lucetta and Torbal watching her go.

"I see your mother has mellowed of late" commented Torbal.

Lucetta gave him a look that said she thought he was mad, and then laughed realising he wasn't being serious.

"She does make the realm tremble at times, no doubt about that."

Lucetta put her arm through her uncle's and pulled him towards the stairs. They followed after Cyneburg but made no hurry.

"Meridia has fallen."

Torbal couldn't quite believe it.

"Yes" replied Lucetta, "It seems the Helligan nation looked west and not to the north. The realm has slid into conflict already." Her tone was sad.

Torbal wanted to say something of comfort or worth but his mind was tracing its way around the new development. The Helligan nation had seen the lack of rule in Bregustol as a chance to expand their territory without any repercussions, and perhaps avenge themselves upon Meridia for their part in Helliga's defeat all those years ago. Orben had made a surprising but actually quite cunning move.

Torbal suddenly remembered what Beornoth had told him when they arrived in Westhealfe. Rencarro had taken men west to Argyllan, which meant that Meridia would have been under-manned. A stroke of luck for Orben.

Or was it more than just luck?

The King's Shield frowned, his mind opening to various possibilities, none of them appealing. It may have been that Orben's spy network had informed him of the lack of defending troops in Meridia. Sedmund had not been dead two weeks though. Torbal thought it unlikely for Orben to have made such an impulsive move, before knowing how the situation in the north would play out. The general couldn't shake the feeling that Orben had been preparing for this for some time. Which raised the ugly prospect that Ulla was involved in the planning.

Torbal stopped dead in his tracks, startling Lucetta beside him.

"Uncle?"

Ulla, did you poison my friend?

Lucetta squeezed his arm.

"You've gone pale, Uncle. Do you know something about all this?"

"I hope not" he replied, his voice barely a whisper.

He broke away from his niece and hurried on to Kenric's solar, mentally telling himself that nothing could be certain yet. But if the rumours were in fact true and Ulla had indeed poisoned Sedmund, then it meant their relationship was all a sham. Torbal was angry with himself that this revelation hurt more than the thought she had murdered his friend.

Lucetta caught up with him but said nothing as they followed in his sister's footsteps through an archway, stones of varying shades of grey spreading out from a white keystone that was losing its brilliance. Down a spiral staircase they went, sunlight from slit windows creating immaterial lines across their path. And then through a stout oaken door which was wide-open. Kenric stood there waiting, his hands clasped behind his back. Cyneburg stood with arms crossed her chest as before, her jaw set and her brow furrowed so much it looked painful.

"Torbal" hailed Kenric.

Torbal's brother-in-law was not as tall as him or his sister. Standing next to his wife, he appeared slight in build but Torbal knew Kenric was solid muscle under the loose, purple tunic he wore. He had won the heart of Cyneburg by winning over her bicep. The story of Kenric beating Cyneburg at arm-wrestling was a well-loved story in Westhealfe. The man's dark eyes still sparkled with a certain humour just as they had done that day. Age had added grey to his long hair and beard, crinkles to his face and a regular rolling of his shoulders to ease the stiffness. But his playful spirit seemed immune to advancing years.

"It seems Orben is in no mood to grow old gracefully" Kenric remarked.

"So it would seem" replied Torbal.

"Annoying little shit."

"Ken, mind your language. Lucetta is present" scolded Cyneburg.

"She has a far more colourful tongue than I" he stated to his wife, and threw a wink at his daughter, who grinned.

Torbal would normally have enjoyed the quirkiness of this family but right now there was little to laugh about. Kenric looked at him, nodded vaguely and spoke again.

"He looks to take the south while the north is in a state of uncertainty."

Cyneburg chipped in.

"It doesn't have to be uncerta—"

"Damn it, Cyneburg, please give me some peace from your constant jabs!" cried Torbal, startling all in the room. He went on.

"I know I have complicated the situation with my relationship with Ulla, and yes, I could have stepped forward and taken the rule. But has anyone looked farther down that road to see what would follow?"

The others were silent. Lucetta's mouth was slightly open, eyes wide, obviously rather surprised to learn Torbal was romantically engaged with the Helligan ruler's sister.

"And my dear friend has just passed" said Torbal, his voice laced with sadness.

Cyneburg came over to her brother and laid a hand on his shoulder.

"Forgive me, Torb. I speak before I think. Sometimes I neglect to even think."

Torbal was taken aback by this rare show of sympathy from his sister.

"There is nothing to forgive, Cy. Kenric and I need you to slap some sense into us sometimes."

Cyneburg smiled, then turned to Lucetta.

"Don't you dare tell anyone I was nice to my little brother!"

Lucetta laughed and the tension in the room dissipated instantly.

Kenric motioned for them to come over to a table where he had a large map spread out and held down by four silver goblets.

"We can assume Orben is there to stay in Meridia but will he soon move into the Argol region?" Kenric posed the question, moving a hand across the map over Argyllan, passing over the smaller settlements and the forest itself.

"Difficult to know" said Torbal, folding his arms.

"We could muster our forces and cross the Freo, confronting him in the south-west." Kenric stroked his beard. "But I think that an unwise move."

"But why?" blurted Lucetta. "Lord Rencarro is in Argyllan with his forces. He would surely join us and we could drive the Helligans out of Meridia."

Cyneburg placed a large hand upon her daughter's head and physically turned it round and down towards the map.

"A noble course of action but one likely to end in hundreds dead, many of them common folk" she stated gently but firmly. "Look and think once more."

Torbal said nothing, patiently waiting for Lucetta to consider how such a move would play out. Kenric was also silent. The young lady stared at the map and then slowly nodded.

"If Orben learns we are coming, he may advance to meet us. If we were forced to engage the Helligan soldiers in the Argol region, the folk there would be caught in the middle. And die in great numbers."

"I fear so" said Kenric. "Argol dominates the landscape there. The small folk not in Argyllan, are all to the east of the forest dotted here and there. With the Widow's Teeth also sitting there, there isn't much room to fight. The fields they tend and homes they care for would become the battleground."

Torbal imagined it as his brother-in-law had described. It would be a tragedy if the Argol region bled in a conflict which they did not start.

Lucetta nodded, clearly accepting what her father had said.

"And taking the city of Meridia itself back from Helligan forces would be bloody" she muttered.

"And probably fail" added Kenric. "The Helligan nation knows a thing or two about defending."

Cyneburg tapped the word Argyllan on the map.

"And it isn't clear why Rencarro is here anyway. Was he hoping to expand his borders also?"

Torbal considered his sister's words. The Meridian presence in Argyllan was odd but the people there had welcomed them. Whatever Rencarro's motives, he had seriously misjudged his eastern neighbour.

Kenric sighed.

"I think we will have to accept that there is no viable course of action south of the Freo. We will of course tighten our defences in Manbung and along the banks of the Freo up to the Icefinger. Orben will have to take on whatever strength Rencarro has in that region if he seeks to occupy the entire south. I doubt he will risk that yet. The city of Meridia is a defensible position and a worthwhile prize. Orben would stretch himself thinly by going farther" finished the First Lord of Westhealfe.

Torbal agreed with Kenric's summation. His eyes roamed over the map, ending up in the north east where lay the Jagged Heights and beyond them to the east, Unvasiktok.

"Vorga."

It was Cyneburg who spoke, as if she had read his mind. His sister looked to her husband, who then turned to Torbal.

"Yes, Vorga." Torbal winced.

"Vorga?" enquired Lucetta, looking puzzled.

"Vorga. High Chief of the Unvasik tribes and a nasty piece of work if the rumours are true" explained Kenric to his daughter. The First Lord of Westhealfe placed his palms together and raised his hands to his chin, gently tapping it as he looked down over the map. Torbal waited to see if Kenric would reach the same conclusion as himself, which was often the case.

"If Vorga receives word about what is happening to the south of his lands, he may deem the time right to do a bit of plundering" said Kenric, his fingertips still tapping his chin.

"The Ruby Road" gasped Lucetta.

Cyneburg nodded.

"Yes, if Vorga learns that the capital is being run by two headless chickens who now have a mobilized Helligan nation to their south, it is highly likely he will raid."

Torbal inhaled deeply. The realm did indeed seem to be rupturing, splitting along cracks that ran deep. Worsteth and Eswic could probably deal with the Helligan threat, mainly because the tools were already in place to do so. The bridge over the Mimir River could easily be closed and the fortifications there reinforced. The captains in Bregustol were experienced men and would simply step up patrols along the river banks and request the reserves be called up in the event Orben did appear to be contemplating an invasion. Torbal felt it unlikely, though. Orben was no fool and would probably tighten his grip on Meridia before he looked north.

Vorga, on the other hand, was a completely different kind of problem, and one Torbal didn't think Worsteth or Eswic could handle. If Vorga came down from the far north and began raiding the caravans, any response would have to be carefully considered and accurately executed. Torbal could see those two throwing lives away by treating the raids as simple warfare with two sides facing across a field. They would likely send a large force north to the mines and have them sit there, waiting for the enemy to kindly show up. The enemy needed to be lured forth with bait and then swiftly annihilated. Neither Worsteth or Eswic had any experience dealing with conflict, let alone hit-and-run tactics.

Torbal stopped studying the map and looked up to his sister, niece and Kenric.

"I propose we mobilise the Bladesung Legion. I will take them east, cross the Icefinger at the ford and head towards Bregustol. Once over the river, a detachment will head north to Morak, brief them on the situation and also swell their numbers."

"And the plan is?" enquired Cyneburg.

"Be ready for anything" Torbal shrugged.

Cyneburg rolled her eyes and Kenric looked at his brother-in-law sceptically.

"That doesn't sound like much of a plan."

"It isn't. But it allows us to make a plan when we need to."

"Fair point" conceded Kenric.

Lucetta pointed at Bregustol on the map.

"Uncle, what will the chamberlain and that priest think though? If the Bladesung Legion crosses the Icefinger, will they not assume you are coming to take the capital by force?"

Torbal smiled. His niece was learning the ways of the world quickly. He noticed Cyneburg was looking at her daughter proudly.

"You are correct, my perceptive niece. Which is why we will not approach the capital itself. We will send riders ahead to inform Worsteth of the possible threat and our main host will hold just across the Icefinger."

Torbal pointed to a spot just east of the Black Stone Ford. "Here at the recently renamed Ever-Father's Garden" he said with a grimace. "Bloody Eswic. Morak's March was a perfectly suitable name."

Kenric nodded.

"A sensible foundation to a plan that is beyond our sight for the time being."

Lucetta clapped her hands.

"When do we leave, Uncle?"

"*We?*" Cyneburg gaped at her daughter in disbelief. "You are not going anywhere, Lucetta. If Vorga comes down with his Unvasik thugs, I don't want you anywhere but here."

Torbal saw his niece's crest-fallen face and sympathized with her. Lucetta was a very capable fighter and possessed leadership skills uncommon for one so young. But nobody in this room had ever fought an Unvasik tribesman before. The word was that they towered over even men from the north-west. Lucetta was extremely skilled with a blade but sometimes sheer brute force could nullify such swordsmanship.

Cyneburg looked to her husband. Torbal saw Kenric make the slightest of nods. The two had agreed without saying a word. Cyneburg turned to her brother.

"You will lead the Bladesung east and I will accompany you with the Bradlastax. I will then head to Morak" she said.

Torbal nodded.

"Agreed. Eorthe will be pleased to see you" he commented with a smile.

Kenric put his fists on the map and leaned in, surveying the realm laid out before him, then looked up.

"It is settled then. With any luck, Vorga will stay put, Orben will not crave further expansion and life will go on."

"Apart from Meridia being occupied" remarked Lucetta.

Kenric gave her a sour look.

"And the realm being leaderless" chimed in Cyneburg.

Kenric shook his head.

"I need a strong ale" he muttered.

"Where is your brother, Lucetta?" asked Torbal, suddenly remembering he hadn't seen him this day.

"He's in the north tower. You know Cherin. Always looking at the skies. Think he sleeps up there" Lucetta told him with a grin.

"You've both grown into fine adults" said Torbal, feeling his own sense of pride.

"Uncle!" blushed Lucetta.

"Adult?" humphed Cyneburg, "We'll see."

Torbal laughed.

"Right, let us have lunch and thrash out some details."

Kenric grinned.

"Eat well Torbal. You'll be back on that awful Bregustol food again soon."

Torbal groaned.

Ch 6

Rencarro

8th Day of Maia, Thirteen Days After Sedmund's Death

Three Days After Meridia Fell

Rencarro was walking and he counted that as no small matter in these days of unrelenting ill news. His Velox Rider, Umbran, had returned to him well before the midday bell yesterday with the report that Sylvanus had been seen leaving the city by the East Gate with a fresh horse. Rencarro's former Second had told the guards there he must get back to Lowenden with all haste and they had of course seen nothing amiss. The murderer and traitor had fled. Quite possibly he realised his slip of the tongue after he had left Rencarro and decided the risk of staying was too high. His departure confirmed his guilt in Rencarro's mind.

Now the leader of the fallen city of Meridia walked along a street of Argyllan with his captains Atticus and Julius. The pace was slower than usual, Rencarro wary of doing further damage to his chest. But he knew he should move, not only to help with his breathing and clearing his lungs, but also because staying in that room was driving him insane. He had to act. He had to become the leader he knew he was. And he had to decide how in the Void he could turn back the tide in this ever-lengthening tale of woe.

This story is not over yet. No. This is just the beginning and it will end with Meridia back in my hands and Sylvanus hanging by his neck. Or without a head. Whichever comes first.

Rencarro's thoughts twisted and turned in his head as he neared the City Hall. He would meet with Mayor Morel and other city officials. He knew Camran would be there too, and took comfort in the fact he had an ally who was native to the city. He reminded himself though that Camran would soon be away from Argyllan. The quartermaster had requested permission from the mayor to travel to Fallowden to bring word of Emiren to her parents. He had promised to return within two days but Rencarro knew he would miss Camran's support for even that short a period.

"Is the Velox Rider away?" Rencarro enquired to Julius.

"Yes, my lord. He has gone after the general with all speed."

"Good."

Rencarro had briefed his captains on Sylvanus' treachery, taking time to give them all the details as he knew they would find it all difficult to believe. They had accepted the truth and Rencarro had felt his foundations becoming stronger. He had then sent Umbran to track down the traitor. If Sylvanus had perceived his deeds had been uncovered, Rencarro thought it unlikely he would return to the force at Lowenden, south of here. So Umbran had ridden east with orders to find out where Sylvanus was going but not to apprehend him unless a clear opportunity arose. A rather chilling thought had come to Rencarro about where Sylvanus might be heading and if he was correct, Umbran would need to break off the pursuit. News of the Meridian cavalry charge and their subsequent demise had added weight to Rencarro's theory.

Rencarro entered the City Hall with his captains and the three of them were led to an inner chamber by a clerk. Morel greeted them warmly and offered them chairs around a square of long tables. Pitchers of water and wine sat beside cups at intervals along the surface.

Rencarro, Julius and Atticus sat on one side, Morel and three councillors to their left, the captain of the city guard and two more officers to their right, and across from Rencarro was seated Camran, alongside a lady whom Rencarro believed to be the harbour-master and a man who looked too young to be present at this table.

When they were all seated, Mayor Morel stood and spoke.

"I think I speak for us all here when I say we are deeply sorry

261

for this truly evil turn of events that has befallen Meridia and you personally, Lord Rencarro. You came here to protect us from a threat that has not appeared and in so doing, left your own city without the men needed to hold it against the Helligan nation. Whatever we can do, we will. But I fear we can offer little."

Rencarro appreciated the sentiment. He had lost all sense of guilt regarding the Meridian soldiers being there not to protect but to annex. That seemed like dust in the wind now. Their coming to Argyllan had been Sylvanus' idea and if Rencarro's suspicions were correct, this had been part of a wider strategy. The city of Meridia had been under-manned and so he assumed it had been easily taken by the Helligan forces. And then his cavalry had been lost in a futile charge. The Meridian army was hamstrung and far from its sturdy walls.

Orben planned this well. And Sylvanus helped him.

Rencarro could not fathom why Sylvanus had betrayed his own people to the Helligan nation. The notion that gold had bought his allegiance was weak, as Sylvanus had never shown the slightest interest in riches. Blackmail also seemed unlikely as Sylvanus had no family that Rencarro knew of, nothing that could force his hand.

And he murdered Marcus.

The betrayal was heinous beyond all comprehension.

Rencarro's thoughts turned to Eligius. The lord's heart ached when he pictured Shansu's tears over two sons lost to her husband. One thing to perhaps be thankful for was that Eligius had been in command of Meridia when the Helligan soldiers attacked. Rencarro's younger son would have been more likely to surrender the city than he himself would have been. Eligius was not a Glory or Death soldier and this may have been Meridia's saving grace. Rencarro prayed to the Keeper that Eligius still lived.

Rencarro mused grimly that he was in the slightly strange position of having lost his city but having most of his military strength intact.

The Widow and her games. And my former Second a major piece in her designs.

Rencarro suddenly realised that Morel had finished speaking. The mayor sat down and all eyes turned to the Lord of Meridia. They were waiting for him. He stood up and took a deep breath, small needles of pain lancing through his chest.

"My thanks, Mayor Morel. Indeed, Ragnekai seems to be basking in cruelty and treachery of late. The grief I feel for my murdered son and my fallen city is great, but I cannot let this consume me."

He looked around at the faces of the Argyllans. They all seemed to be hanging upon his words, almost needing him to give them a course of action. All except Camran. Rencarro saw in his eyes not a lost sheep but a faithful friend. The quartermaster's inner-strength would be a great boon in the struggles ahead.

"It would be foolish of me to charge back to Meridia with all our strength and attempt to retake the city. And whilst I have been told some of your noble city guard here would aid us in any endeavour to retake Meridia", he motioned to the Captain, who sat up straighter in his seat, "I cannot lead us that way. It would be wrong of me to risk Argyllan lives in what would be a particularly dangerous undertaking. And proud as I am of Meridian soldiers, I am sure my two captains here will agree with me when I say the Helligan war machine is formidable."

As he said this, Atticus and Julius nodded solemnly beside him.

Rencarro paused, gathering his thoughts so he could reach out to the people here without causing widespread panic. He coughed into his hand.

"I am loathe to voice a serious concern I have but I cannot ignore the possibility that I might be right in some rather dire speculation."

The councillors, City Guard and others present shifted in their seats, looking nervously at their comrades. Rencarro lamented that this city was not just *physically* unprepared for any kind of attack, be it from raiders, Westhealfe or the east, but also woefully unready *mentally*.

"You know the Helligan nation has taken my city, but you may not be aware that the force that took it was large. Also, I have reason to believe Orben knew we would not be there."

In his peripheral vision, he saw Atticus and Julius react to this, turning quickly to look at him.

"Perhaps one could say the numbers were too many for Orben's ambitions to stop at Meridia."

He let the words sink in, knowing what was unsaid here would terrify most of them. Once again, Camran alone seemed unperturbed by it. Rencarro wondered at this. He was fairly sure Camran had never seen combat so the notion of Helligan warriors coming this way should frighten him. The man had a pragmatic sensibility to him but he seemed a little too calm. Rencarro dismissed any suspicion and continued, acknowledging to himself he was thinking and planning on the fly here.

"I propose that we fortify the city of Argyllan."

There was a collective gasp from the city's representatives, followed by whisperings and mutterings. Rencarro held up his hands for quiet and they obliged.

"We are dealing with many unknowns here, my friends. It may be that Orben merely wished to eliminate any potential threat from his western border before he launches a full-scale assault on the capital. It may be that Orben wishes to spread his forces throughout the whole Meridian region, with the view to making it part of the Helligan nation in more than just name. We simply cannot know."

He could see how their perception of their situation was easily swayed by his words. He mentioned the possibility of the Helligan nation expanding farther westwards and they practically cowered in fear. Then he reminded them that it was all speculation and they seemed to now be breathing sighs of relief.

"But it is better to be safe than sorry, wouldn't you agree? So,

264

as I said, let us fortify the city, strengthen the walls and build some worthy defences. I will not fail Argyllan as I have Meridia." His voice rose in volume with the last statement and it seemed as if he had lit something within the Argyllans.

Morel stood up abruptly, his chair falling over behind him.

"We are with you, Lord Rencarro."

The captain of the city guard stood also, though did so in a more controlled manner.

"My men are yours to command."

Others began to stand with similar sentiments that showed these folks had some courage and a bit of grit in them after all.

Camran was last to stand. He stood slowly and looked at Rencarro, their eyes locking. A smile grew on his face. It was at that moment that Rencarro realised why the quartermaster had seemed unfazed by the threats they might face.

He has faith in me.

The Lord of Meridia could see it in his new friend's eyes. This man trusted him to lead them all against any coming storm and he seemed to be confident they would overcome whatever the winds threw at them. With Sylvanus' betrayal so fresh on his mind, Camran was bringing him hope, simply by the quartermaster's own belief in a man he hardly knew. Rencarro silently wished the quartermaster a safe journey to Fallowden and a swift return. He didn't envy Camran having to tell his brother that his daughter was missing in the north and bringing the news to an innkeeper that his son was dead.

Ch 7

Svard

Svard's legs felt like they were encased in iron as he trudged towards Lorken's home. Each step was agonisingly heavy and part of him just wanted to turn around and leave the city of Gamle Hovestad. But he owed it to Lorken. Owed it to his family to bring the terrible news himself. Lorken was dead and nothing could change that. Death was the one happening in the world that you could not fix nor search for a better path to take you away from it. It was final, like a door that only swung one way and slammed tightly shut after each new arrival into the darkness beyond.

The First Ranger knew he should be reporting to his lord but he had to do this first. Orben would have to wait this time. Svard had lost a brother because of his lord's ambitions. He had lost men and women under his command before, sword-brothers and shield-maidens. But each and every one of the Rangers knew death was just around each corner or hiding behind one of the trees in the forests of the realm. Every soldier he had lost had died in the course of being a Ranger. Lorken was a carpenter who had died because Orben needed the numbers to hold the south and still have enough soldiers to defend the Helligan nation should those in Bregustol decide to strike.

Svard saw their home just up ahead and felt his innards churning. He hadn't eaten this morning and was glad, for at that moment he retched. A dribble of bile spattered onto the cobbled road. A passing citizen stared but quickly hurried on when Svard returned the look with an icy glare.

He stood up and took a deep breath, trying to at least bring himself to a state from which he could offer some comfort to Jenna and the boys, and little Eira.

Damn you Dark Raven! Did you choose Lorken out of sheer spite?

He knew this was ridiculous. If it hadn't been Lorken, it would have been another lady's husband or some poor fellow's shield-maiden wife, or someone's child. Over eighty people had died in what should have been a swift and relatively bloodless battle for their side. The unexpected arrival of the cavalry had taken many lives, soldiers skewered in agony on the end of a lance or swiftly crushed under one and a half thousand pounds of horse.

They were supposed to be too far away to interfere.

Svard continued his sluggish pace, as the carpentry shed at the side of the house came into view. The crunch of wood being chopped and the grunts of exertions from Darl and Torg made Svard clench his fists. He fought to hold back tears. He stopped again and hung his head, courage failing him and misery overwhelming the Helligan First Ranger.

When finally he raised his head, she was there. Jenna was standing with the front door open. Her smile disappeared the instant she saw Svard's face. She knew. Her sob was worse than a spear to the chest, tearing at Svard's heart.

She collapsed to her knees and he ran to her, skidding down and grabbing her. Svard pulled her close, hugging her tightly.

"I'm sorry, Jenna, I'm so sorry. I thought I could… Lorken… I'm so sorry."

The chopping of wood had stopped, the boys obviously hearing their mother's anguish. Darl and Torg appeared from round the side and they too immediately understood what it meant.

"No!" Torg cried out. "No, no. Father…"

Svard watched over Jenna's shoulder as Darl grabbed his brother and hugged him fiercely. Then he noticed a small hand touch Jenna's back. He pulled back to see Eira standing quietly behind her mother. She looked at Svard, holding his gaze. There was no anger in her eyes, only a deep well of sadness. The little one rested her head on her mother's back and stroked her hair.

The five of them stayed like that for how long Svard couldn't tell. Torg's wailing eventually subsided and Jenna's sobs turned to ragged breaths. She gently pushed Svard back and stood, taking Eira's hand as she did so. Lorken's widow moved over to her sons and the four of them hugged together in a circle, their tears silent drops in an ocean of sorrow.

Svard stood back and looked upon the goodness in Gamle Hovestad that he hadn't been able to protect. The loss of even one life suddenly seemed a terrible price to pay for the glory of the Helligan nation. And what would follow this but more death and grief?

He turned to leave, thinking his presence was not needed but in truth he knew that he didn't have the courage for this. He could face five men with sharp steel and snarl defiance, but seeing Lorken's family broken was too much to bear. He took a step but then Jenna called his name.

"Svard, don't leave."

The First Ranger turned back and saw a family without a husband and father. He fought to control the anguish he himself felt and hesitantly moved towards them again. Jenna motioned for them all to go into the house.

Entering the house triggered memories and recognition of what it all meant. Lorken's coat hanging on a peg, five chairs at the table, Lorken's mug upon a shelf and his glyph etched into the mantelpiece above the hearth.

Jenna stumbled but was caught by her two sons, who guided her to a chair. She sat there, eyes staring ahead. Torg took a seat beside her and Darl fetched a pitcher of water and a cup for his mother. Lorken's oldest son motioned to Svard to sit as well and then went to retrieve more cups. Eira hid under the table.

Jenna looked at Svard, her eyes blinking to clear her vision. She opened her mouth to say something but then just let out a breath. Torg gently pushed a cup of water in front of her.

"Mother, drink."

Jenna lifted the cup to her mouth but Svard wasn't sure if anything actually passed her lips. Before him was the stark reality of losing a loved one. It wasn't just the loss of that person. It was the cruel destruction of the love that existed between that person and those around him or her. Death broke circles of harmony, leaving flailing strands that might never connect again.

Darl spoke.

"How did my father die, Svard?"

Svard had been ready for this question, mentally preparing an answer that he hoped would give them some sense of peace. But now the moment had come, Svard realised it was all dust in the wind. Nothing he said could make a difference. He held Darl's eyes and bit his upper lip, trying desperately to say something that would honour his fallen friend, the boy's father.

"I was not there. I wa —" he began.

"Why weren't you there for him?" blurted Torg.

"Torg" whispered Jenna. She placed a hand over her son's fist and gently lowered it to the table.

Svard sighed, slowly letting out his own tension.

"I am sorry Torg. I wish by the First Warrior's shield that I had been there but the Rangers had a different role to play in the battle. I was on the other side of the city when the Meridian cavalry arri —"

"Cavalry?" interrupted Darl. "Far was killed by cavalry?"

Svard winced inwardly. He hadn't wanted to reveal the details of Lorken's death so soon.

"Yes, cavalry."

Jenna sobbed and Torg let his head fall to the table, arms wrapping round his head as he wept. Darl turned his back but Svard could see his body shaking with grief. Svard felt something touch his leg and he looked under the table to see Eira. She was looking up at him and there was something unsettling in her eyes. It was as if she had already accepted her father's death.

Maybe she is too young to understand all this.

Even as he thought this though, he knew that wasn't true. Her little hand squeezed his knee and he felt as though she were reassuring him. The very notion of that seemed wild at best but Svard saw something in her eyes that was far beyond her years.

Jenna's voice brought his attention back to the three of them above the table.

"Darl, Torg, take Eira outside. Give me some time to speak with Svard, please."

"Course, Mother" responded Darl. "Come on you" he said in a croaking voice, and beckoned to the young girl under the table. His younger brother stood, placed a hand on his mother's shoulder. "We'll be outside then, Mother."

The two lads walked out, Eira in the middle, holding a hand each. Svard ached to see these three wonderful children with futures stretching out that Lorken would not see. He returned his gaze to Jenna to see she was looking at him. He marvelled at the inner-strength she possessed to be able to even want to speak to him now.

"He loved you like a brother."

Svard choked on tears when he heard these words. He too had lost family. Lorken hadn't been of his blood but he had been his brother in every other respect. Lorken had been the heart of Helliga and Svard had been the one who protected it. But when swords were drawn, he had failed. And now the beating heart of Svard's Helliga was gone.

"And I loved him" he whispered. Anger rose within him. "I will avenge his death, Jenna. I will —"

She cut him off. "Against who, Svard?" Her voice was harsh but not biting. "Who will you kill to avenge him? Then will that person's brother kill you in vengeance? Revenge is a cycle in which the Dark Raven revels. You are the First Ranger. Heed the words of the First Warrior. *"My shield is before me, my sword held back."* It is not the other way round, Svard. Another death will not bring Lorken back."

Svard knew she was right and felt foolish for uttering oaths born from rage and impotence.

Jenna sighed, running her fingers through her hair.

"Would that Orben had reflected on the First Warrior's words before he set out on this course of action" she lamented.

Svard had no response. There was no good answer to the question of why Orben had drawn the first blood. The Helligan nation was at peace and enjoyed prosperity. Was creating a larger nation worth the lives of a thousand or even one Helligan man or woman?

"I'm sorry, Jenna" he whispered, the only words he could say.

*

Svard made his way to Orben's keep, having left Jenna and the children to their grief. He felt so worthless. As the First Ranger of the Helligan nation he led his men and knew little of failure. Yet he was powerless to help Lorken's family, lacking even helpful words of comfort.

He walked past The First Hammer inn. The innkeeper was outside watering flowers hanging in baskets beneath the windows. The man noticed Svard and held up a hand in greeting.

"First Ranger" he said, using Svard's formal title, his voice solemn, perhaps sensing all was not well.

"Gervas." Svard took a deep breath. "Lorken will not come back."

The innkeeper placed a hand against the wall of his establishment, his legs suddenly wobbly. He opened his mouth to speak but no words came. He shook his head.

"I have brought the news to Jenna" said Svard in a hollow tone.

The innkeeper found his voice.

"I am truly sorry. Lorken was your brother and a true son of Gamle Hovestad. The First Warrior will welcome him into his Hall with the other brave men and women who fell. When you are settled, come by and let us remember them and raise a cup to their names."

The words were thoughtful and appropriate. Svard realised Gervas had probably said them more than once in his life-time as an innkeeper listening to the tales of soldiers.

"I will do that, Gervas. And we will remember. It may be some time though as I fear our lord will send me abroad again. When I return."

"When you return." Gervas nodded and waved.

Svard hurried on.

He reckoned he was more than acceptably late when he finally knocked on the door of Orben's solar.

"Enter."

His lord's voice rang out clearly through the wood but there didn't seem to be anger there, which surprised Svard, who'd expected something more like fury. Svard pushed open the door and entered.

"Forgive my lateness, my lord. The battle for Meridia took more from me than I was prepared to give."

Orben looked up from the map-table and locked eyes with his First Ranger. No, there was no anger in his face but neither was there any sympathy. Just a ruler with a hundred matters swirling through his mind.

"Sit" he said in a flat tone.

Svard looked for a chair and found Kailen approaching him with a chair in hand. She too met Svard's gaze and there was something entirely different within her hazel eyes. Deep pity. As she passed him the chair, her fingers brushed his in what he took as a sign that she understood.

"Congratulations on a well-executed mission, First Ranger" said the Helligan ruler, his hands pressing down upon the wooden representation of the realm.

"Kailen, some wine for Svard, if you please."

Svard watched her as she obliged, then turned back to his lord. He told himself he needed to be the ready-to-obey First Ranger here, not Lorken's friend. But he was also determined to dig deeper to find out more. He mentally noted that Ulla was not present.

"Your information regarding Rencarro's son was accurate, which made our task fairly straight-forward, my lord."

Orben nodded, his lips pursed. Svard probed.

"Rencarro's son, Eligius, seemed to take the fall of his own city in his stride, quickly bringing an order to the transition of power."

"The boy is intellectual to the point of seeing everything in practical terms, or so I have heard. An administrator, not a warrior." There was no unusual reaction.

Svard saw an opening.

"Not a warrior like his brother, Marcus."

Svard concentrated so as to see the reaction to his next words.

"An assassin's blade was no way for Marcus to die."

Orben regained himself quickly and feigned surprise, but Svard had seen a momentary hint of a smile on Orben's lips.

He knew.

"Marcus is dead?" Orben said innocently.

"So it seems, my lord."

"Well, one less Meridian to worry about" said the Helligan ruler dismissively. Orben pointed to the capital Bregustol on his table.

"First Ranger, I want you to take a small group, perhaps four of your best men, cross the river to the opposite bank and make your way round the foot of the Sacred Mount. When you are at a suitable position, cross back and into the north-east. Make your crossings at night. I want nobody to see any boats coming from Helliga travelling round the Warrior's Ring."

He paused and looked up at Svard.

The First Ranger nodded, mentally deciding on which Rangers he would take.

"Your mission will be to infiltrate Bregustol. Choose whatever disguise you see fit. Traders, labourers, mummers, it matters not."

Svard blinked and involuntarily cocked his head to one side.

Spying and disguises had rarely been a task for the Rangers. Orben seemed to read his mind.

"I know this is a rather unusual mission for the Rangers but a crucial one if we are to recapture Nortrone and restore the rightful rule to the realm."

Svard's curiosity had got the better of him and he lost focus with regards to learning more about why Meridia had fallen so easily. He waited for Orben to say more, sipping on the wine Kailen had passed him moments before.

"I need you to bring Brother Eswic back here to Gamle Hovestad."

Svard choked on his wine. He coughed to clear his throat. Orben continued, ignoring the First Ranger's surprise.

"I know that Torbal is now in Westhealfe so Eswic and the chamberlain are currently sharing the rule in Bregustol. Eswic is quite the zealot and has dreams of a holy crusade no doubt. The chamberlain Worsteth is a more practical man so removing Eswic will open up possibilities."

Svard's mind reeled with his lord's words. Orben knew a great deal and had planned on an ambitious scale. The First Ranger couldn't help but marvel at the audacity of it all but was less than happy about their mission being one of abduction.

"Svard."

The use of his name shook him out of his thoughts.

"Sedmund's death was the end of Rihtgellen superiority in the realm. The pendulum swings and now we will see a return to days of old, a return to Helligan dominance. No more will Bregustol take from the realm more than it gives. No longer will the Ever-Father stretch his fingers, dirtying our lands and corrupting history."

Svard felt himself swayed by Orben's words. The notion of a realm ruled by Helliga and the end of the Ever-Father's influence were things he would gladly welcome. He nodded slowly and locked eyes with his lord.

"Good" said Orben, a gleam in his eyes. "That is all. Make your preparations today and cross the Mimir tomorrow night."

The words startled Svard. But his mission had been given and he knew what he had to do. He slowly rose from the chair, handed the half-empty glass of wine to Kailen and bowed his head to his Lord. Then he hesitated, questions about Meridia racing back to him.

"Something on your mind, First Ranger?" asked Orben, although his tone suggested he expected the answer to be in the negative.

"My lord—" began Svard.

"Lord Orben" interrupted Kailen, "let me bring the First Ranger up to date on all other matters relevant to the coming mission. By your leave."

She stood almost between Svard and Orben, with one hand behind her back making a cutting motion at the Ranger.

"That would be appreciated, Kailen" responded Orben with a measure of gruffness in his voice.

Kailen turned and ushered Svard to the door. Svard bowed his head again but Orben had his eyes down, once again studying his map.

Kailen opened the door, the two of them left the room, and then she closed it, leaving the two of them outside in the corridor.

"Come with me" she said quietly and started walking before Svard had a chance to respond.

Svard felt a weariness but followed Kailen. She clearly knew something and Svard also sensed she was ill at ease with Orben's plans.

I owe it to Lorken to find out more.

Ch 8

Emiren

8th Day of Maia, Thirteen Days After Sedmund's Death

Three Days After Meridia Fell

The friendly nature of Ceapung put Emiren at ease. Wulfner had brought them to the port-town, telling them they could find help here and rest after their two nights on the open road. Emiren couldn't dispel all the terrible images of that day in Argol from her mind but she felt able to keep them from overwhelming her.

Lunyai had saved her life that night in Argyllan and looked after her with such care since, and Wulfner had begun an unintended journey without a thought for his own concerns and obligations. After the cold-blooded nature of Anton's death and Lord Rencarro close to killing her with his spear, Emiren had given up that the world was a good place, as she had always used to believe. But these two had restored her faith and more importantly, given her hope that she would make it back to Fallowden and that Sylvanus would face justice.

Wulfner led Azal by the bridle and the cart trundled through the main street of Ceapung. Emiren and Lunyai followed behind, Trob loping alongside them, his tongue lolling out his mouth. Emiren's ankle was getting better but still felt tender. She had been in the cart so long though that she wanted to stretch her legs as they entered Ceapung.

Even though the seasons were giving way to summer, they had come a good distance north and the winds were cool like spring, reminding Emiren of Fallowden.

The shops and houses here were of a different nature to those south of the Freo. Thatched rooves sat upon wooden walls and Emiren could only see a few buildings that had walls of wattle and daub. Many of the houses seemed longer and most only had one storey. The smell here was so different than that in Fallowden. Her home village smelt like the trees of Argol in many ways, the woody aroma lingering in the air, complimented by a heavy scent of damp leaves or a crisp air depending on the weather. Here in Ceapung, Emiren found there to be an earthy smell hanging in the air. She commented on this to Lunyai.

The Tarakan girl shrugged.

"It smells very different to my home also. Perhaps the aroma that seems to be forever coming back to me is the scent of the evening meal being cooked over the fire." Lunyai closed her eyes and inhaled deeply. "They are not roasting Mehdi hare here. Of that I can be sure."

Emiren gasped as she realised why the smell was so different. From many of these low homes came a fog-like smoke, easing its way out of chimney stacks and seemingly in no hurry to float away upon the breeze. They were burning peat here, not wood. The smell spoke to Emiren of cold winter nights.

Lunyai breathed in deeply again when Emiren pointed this out. The Tarakan girl laughed.

"I would like to try food cooked over such a fire. The taste must be something special."

Emiren smiled. The Tarakan girl possessed a strength of spirit and a curiosity towards the realm. Emiren felt the two of them had very different beliefs but very similar yearnings.

"I am glad to see you smile" said Lunyai.

"What? Oh. Maybe I don't feel like I'm in the middle of a never-ending nightmare anymore." Emiren looked into Lunyai's deep brown eyes. "Thanks to you and Wulfner."

Lunyai put an arm round Emiren's shoulder and drew her close.

"We will get home. And once we have made things right in our own lives, you must come to the Tarakan Plains. I will teach you to ride a horse and you will gallop across the lands with me. And we will laugh at the wind!"

Lunyai seemed so alive talking about her home that Emiren could not help but be taken by thoughts of riding a horse across grass that she knew to be a shade of green so different to her beloved Argol.

"I would like that very much."

Wulfner's wagon came to a halt and the two of them almost walked into the back of it. He turned and called back to them.

"Just a bit farther now and we can rest our—"

"Wulfner!?" came a shout from their left.

Emiren and Lunyai turned, and both their eyes widened. The man who had called out was clearly older than Wulfner but what amazed the girl from Fallowden was this man was *bigger* than their travelling companion. Wulfner was well over six-foot-tall Emiren reckoned, but this man had to be near seven foot. A giant in Emiren's eyes.

The behemoth of a man strode over, a huge grin splitting a weather-worn face. Grey hair fell to his shoulders in unruly straggles, his beard behaving in much the same way. He wore a simple brown tunic over trousers bound with leather straps. The tunic was sleeveless, revealing thick, muscular arms inked with forms that looked like letters or glyphs. Emiren thought some seemed familiar.

"Balther!" cried Wulfner and soon both men were hugging like long-lost brothers, in an embrace that Emiren believed would have crushed either her or Lunyai.

"Didn't expect you back here till the autumn!" roared Wulfner's friend. Emiren wondered if he always talked at such a high volume or if it was just the excitement of seeing Wulfner again.

"Ha! The Winds have blown in a strange way for me of late, Balther" replied Wulfner. He turned to the two young women and Emiren shifted her weight from one foot to the other nervously as the giant's gaze took them in. He looked puzzled.

"What have we here? You two ladies look far too young to be travelling with an old rogue like Wulfner here. And I'd also wager you're too wise!" He laughed and Emiren let herself smile.

Wulfner chuckled. "There is a tale that will take some telling but let's just say for now that we had some bother with some Meridians."

Balther frowned. "Meridians? Seems the realm is stumbling after the death of Sedmund. Word is that Torbal is back in Westhealfe. Not sure if that is good or bad news."

Wulfner inhaled sharply and shook his head. There was a short silence that was broken by Balther slapping Wulfner on the back.

"I guess you were on your way to Cuthbert's. Let me walk with you. But first introduce me to your two friends here."

Trob jumped up at Balther, the Argollan mastiff looking like a puppy next to the towering form of Wulfner's friend.

"I know you already, Trob! Down now! Remember your manners."

Lunyai walked forward and introduced herself. Emiren saw that the Tarakan girl trusted Trob's judgment and felt this man posed no danger to them. Emiren felt no threat but some of her inner-strength had been lost that day in Argol.

"Thought you might be from the Plains, lass" Balther said kindly. "I roamed the Plains for a spell when I was younger, which was an age ago. Still remember the way the wind coursed over the grass, making it seem alive and urging a man to keep going."

Emiren saw Lunyai's eyes widen and her smile stretch almost ear-to-ear as this man from the north waxed lyrical about the Tarakan girl's homeland. Emiren found herself wanting to ask if he rode a horse when he trekked across the Plains, as she couldn't conceive of a steed big enough to carry him.

"And you are not from the Tarakan Plains, I take it?"

She realised he was looking at her, a gentle questioning expression smoothing out some of the lines on his aged face.

"Emiren. I come from Fallowden, a village on the edge of Argol Forest. It is good to meet a friend of Wulfner. He has helped us so much already."

Balther nodded as if taking in all he had heard. "Fallowden huh? Don't suppose Banseth has learnt how to use those sticks yet?"

Emiren was shocked, her jaw dropping. "You know Banseth?" she asked in disbelief.

Wulfner chuckled. "My cousin Balther here has seen a lot of Ragnekai. We say here in Ceapung that he knows at least one person in every major settlement and knows at least three ales from every region."

"Only three?" said Balther in mock surprise. "Reckon I'd better get on the road again." They all laughed.

Balther then spread his arms in a gesture that said welcome.

"Come, let us get your weary legs rested." He winked. "And my dry throat wetted."

The small group continued on their way to wherever this Cuthbert's was. Emiren wasn't sure if it was the name of the place or the owner. She quietly thanked the Spirits that they seemed to be with good people here, something that became clearer as they walked along and people hailed Wulfner, many expressing the same surprise as Balther that he had returned this side of summer.

Emiren felt a strange kind of contentment. One that was fair to look upon but hid beneath it a terrible sadness. She was safe here and happy in this moment but she carried an open wound. Anton was gone and she was far from her parents. It hurt to think of how worried they must be. A stab of sorrow tinged with guilt hit her as she recognised the harsh reality facing Nicolas and Cale. Her parents would hopefully see their daughter again but Anton's family might never know where he was buried. She couldn't stop the tears slowly seeping from her eyes and then sliding swiftly down her cheeks.

Emiren felt Lunyai's hand take her own, squeezing it gently. Nothing was said but perhaps there were no words for this. The gesture was enough to give Emiren the strength to keep on walking and not fall to her knees.

Wulfner and Balther were leading Azal and the cart. Trob

was nipping at Balther's heels but Emiren wasn't sure the huge man even noticed. He was laughing and talking raucously with his cousin.

As they wound their way through the town, the smell of peat burning became mingled with the unmistakable scent of the sea. It made for an interesting combination filling Emiren's nostrils but one that was pleasant and tugged lightly at the anguish swirling within, calming the maelstrom of emotion.

After another couple of hundred yards they arrived at their destination. Cuthbert's Cave was an inn a stone's throw from where the harbour seemed to begin. Emiren looked at the sign hanging above the door. A bearded man was painted onto the wood, in what looked to be a wet robe, a weary look on his face. Two otters were at his feet.

Balther addressed them all.

"Now get yourselves into Cuthbert's and order some ale and hot food. I'll get Azal settled in the stables round the back and then join you. Be sure to order my drink too. Wulfner knows what I'll have."

Lunyai raised a hand. "Let me help you, Balther. Azal has taken a different road to that intended, walked many miles because of us. I would make sure she is warm and content."

Balther shared a look with Wulfner, who shrugged and grinned. "She probably knows more about horses than this whole town, Balther."

"That I find quite easy to believe. Come, young one. Teach me some Tarakan words that will soothe this mare." Balther gestured for Lunyai to lead the way, indicating the direction of the stables. They headed off with Trob in tow.

Wulfner rubbed his hands together. "Come then, Emiren. Let's make sure there is something on the table for when they finish."

Emiren followed him into the inn, noticing how his hair brushed the horizontal of the door-frame. Balther would have to duck to enter.

The inn was not crowded but there was a lively atmosphere

within. Large windows let in generous amount of sunshine, lighting up the near-side of the tavern. Not all the tables were taken. Some looked to be groaning under the weight of the many elbows resting upon them. As the laughter was accompanied by pounding on these tables, Emiren hoped they were made of a sturdy wood.

Farther into the inn were lanterns, burning with oil, Emiren presumed. The flickering flames illuminated the faces standing near the counter, smiles abounding and not a hint of any unsavoury character to be found.

Are we too far from the troubles of the realm here? Or will they spread from Meridia?

Wulfner's name being shouted out brought her attention back to the inn.

"Back already, you old scoundrel? Who's this? A niece?"

The speaker was standing behind the counter and clearly the innkeeper, judging by his apron and rosy cheeks. He was a similar shape to Anton's father Nicolas, of a medium height and there was evidence of quaffing too much as he worked, his ample stomach visible under the apron. Dark hair flecked with grey circled his head but had disappeared from the top.

"Helping out a *friend's* niece actually, Sig." Wulfner looked around at the inn. "Ah but it is good to be back in Ceapung. Business healthy?"

The innkeeper, Sig, slapped his belly and laughed.

"Business is good, health on the other hand... Bah, I still rise in the morning and take a shi –" Sig stopped mid-sentence, his cheeks turning a deeper shade.

He cleared his throat. "What can I be getting you and your friend then, Wulfner?"

"One flagon of Mariner for myself and then a second for Balther who's out back stabling Azal. Two halves of Otter's Luck, one for Emiren and one for another lass who is out helping Balther. And four bowls of whatever delight Gayna has cooked up in the pot today." Wulfner placed two silvers on the counter, telling Sig they'd be here a while and to let him know when the silvers had been used up.

"Emiren" said Wulfner, "go and sit yourself over there. I'll be along with the drinks."

Emiren nodded and made her way to a decent-sized table. Other patrons smiled at her as she passed, uttered a greeting or two, then turned back to their companions. It was friendly but not intrusive here, Emiren thought.

She sat down on one of the solid chairs and instantly realised the chairs here were noticeably larger than back home. She looked around and could see that, even though most were sitting, the folk up in this area were taller than around Argol. Maybe it was the northern sea air, she mused.

Wulfner remained at the counter, one elbow resting upon it, the other lifting a mug to his lips. The other drinks were there also but Wulfner seemed deep in conversation with Sig. Emiren was content to let him take his time. She was safe here and could do with a few moments by herself to think.

A fiddle suddenly sprang to life, its bearer standing at a table of what looked like seafarers. The men clapped as the fiddler played what was clearly some well-known shanty. One of the sailors stood and started singing, his voice surprisingly clear and resonant. Emiren sat back and joined in the clapping.

This garnered the singer's attention and he winked at her, moving a few steps closer to her table as he sang.

"Come ye all, now hark to me.
I swear my song'll charm thee."

Emiren noticed Wulfner watching them but could see he wasn't worried, smiling and enjoying the performance himself, so she felt at ease. The singer opened his arms wide.

"I've just sailed the Western Sea,
Do ya not have a smile for me?"

Emiren obliged with a warm smile. The singer clapped and

twirled to face his mates, bowing to them as if he had just won a small victory. He turned back to Emiren, who found herself shaking her head and laughing quietly.

"I have silver and gold in store
Hidden on a far off shore.
Blow me a kiss, fair maiden you,
And I'll show ye much more."

Emiren laughed out loud despite herself, even though she wasn't sure if this was a light-hearted song about maritime courting or a bawdier piece that would end Spirits knew where. She found herself enjoying the show though so blew him a kiss.

The sailor and his friends cheered and the fiddler increased the tempo of his playing a fraction. The singer took another step closer.

"Ah but woe is mine, it blew away
The winds are strong this day.
Do ya not think you can share another,
One that on my lips will stay?"

Emiren tried not to giggle, shook her head and was about to beckon Wulfner over when another voice burst out from near the inn's entrance, feminine in its pitch but hale in its delivery.

"Ah, but look at you, bedraggled lad
You've made that beauty there so sad.
Go back to your ship and pray a while
That the waves don't treat ya bad."

The fiddler stopped playing, his face a picture of utter disbelief as he looked to the new singer. Emiren turned and saw Lunyai standing there, one hand on her hip, the other arm raised and a finger pointing at the sailor. She had a wicked grin on her face.

The inn exploded as one into a storm of laughter, clapping and thumping upon tables. Emiren stared at Lunyai, wondering how her new friend knew this song.

Lunyai cocked her head as if goading the sailor into some kind of response. The sailor turned to the fiddler and motioned frantically for him to start up the tune again. The fiddler obliged and the sailor placed a hand upon his heart and pretended to stumble.

"Now who is this, wretched sea thing?
Who has come to steal the ring
That I was going to give to ye this day
And then forever I will sing."

The inn was enthralled by this performance now, definitely something they did not see every day. Lunyai clapped her hands, did a twirl, and stepped towards the sailor, stamping her foot in time with the music.

"You promise wealth untold
Yet you've never seen gold
Be gone now, back to your cups
I will shield this maiden from the cold."

The sailor stood up straight and shook a fist in Lunyai's direction, his smile a mix of humour and mock outrage.

"Are ye a siren from the deep?
To make a poor sailor weep
Back to the waves you must go
This lady's heart I shall keep."

Lunyai sidled up to Emiren on her chair and to the red-haired girl's surprise, sat on her lap. The inn clapped and cheered. Lunyai raised a hand into the air.

"A sailor boy cannot conquer me.
My spirit unchained and free
But this firey-haired beauty here now
She has bedevilled me, can't ya see?"

Lunyai then held Emiren's face in her hands and kissed her on the lips. It was a full kiss and lasted perhaps three moments of silence as the inn just stared at the two young ladies.

Lunyai broke off the kiss, jumped up, twirled once more and bowed to the sailor who had been singing. Emiren felt confused; she was giddy with a feeling she couldn't understand.

The cacophony of noise that followed was truly deafening. The sailor and his friends roared with laughter, pounding their table so much so that two mugs fell to the floor, one shattering into shards of clay.

Wulfner was slapping his thigh with one hand, wiping tears from his eyes with the other, as he tried to catch his breath between guffaws.

Balther was standing just inside the doorway, shaking his head and pointing, but almost doubling over with laughter.

Lunyai held out one hand to Emiren and one to the sailor. Emiren stood up and took it, and the sailor also accepted the gesture. The three of them bowed which resulted in another eruption of applause and table-thumping.

The sailor produced a purse from his belt and took out five silvers. He slapped them on the counter and shouted to be heard above the din, which subsided as folk saw the shine of money being put down.

"I haven't laughed so much since my wife ran off" he cried.

More mirth answered but this time the inn didn't shake.

"Ales all round if you will, Sig. Reckon the good people here must have dry throats after all that racket."

This was greeted with grateful cheers.

The sailor kissed Lunyai's hand while bowing and returned to his fellows. Emiren and Lunyai sat at their table and were joined by Balther and Wulfner, who carried four mugs in his huge hands. Emiren noticed his was a fresh one so concluded he must have drained his first cup during the song.

"Well, that was a fresh gust of wind that just blew through here and no mistake!" chuckled Balther.

Lunyai looked almost embarrassed, her cheeks a bit flushed.

"How do you know that old shanty, Lunyai?" asked Wulfner.

"My tribe was out near the coastal cliffs two years ago. A ship had to make land midway on their voyage because of an almighty storm on the Western Sea.

"They came to land in one of the coves. It is actually the one I hope we can reach. We led the sailors up to the Plains, welcomed them to our tribe and shared our food. The storm lasted a whole half of Tlenaii's cycle so they spent many an evening fire with us. I learned a few of their songs. That one was my favourite."

The two northern men looked almost as surprised as Emiren felt. Her heart thumped within her chest, the giddiness falling away to be replaced by a sense of excitement.

Wulfner raised his mug. "Let's raise our cups to this wily singer and her fair maiden." The four of them knocked their mugs together and then drank.

The beer went down very easily for Emiren. It had a strong flavour of apples. Emiren determined that the apples farther north were not as sweet as those in Argol.

Lunyai turned to Emiren. "I'm sorry I just kissed you like that. I was caught up in the moment." She grinned sheepishly.

Emiren shook her head and smiled. She wanted to say something but the words wouldn't come. She wanted to tell Lunyai that in that moment when she had kissed her, the world had been reduced to just the two of them. The Tarakan girl's lips upon hers had instantly banished the bitter sadness within, and Emiren had felt as if she were floating down a river with no care as to where she was heading.

Her thoughts were interrupted by the arrival of a young lad carrying steaming bowls of stew to their table. Sig followed him and laid down a pie that gave off the most wonderful aroma.

"Compliments of Gayna and myself. Never seen or heard anything like that. You certainly made my customers happy!"

They all expressed their thanks and set about their food with a barely restrained ferocity, such was their appetite. As the food began to fill their bellies, they slowed their pace, sipped their ales and began talking about their homes. The mood was too good to break with any talk of the terrible events of late and for this Emiren was grateful.

Under the table she felt Lunyai's hand take hers. She didn't move her hand away but let the warmth of her friend's touch reassure her. They sat there like that, one hand holding an ale, the other gently holding each other. Emiren felt she could face tomorrow now, her courage rising, but was content to let this day stretch out for now.

Ch 9

Tacet

L ord Rencarro's Velox Rider was certain he was on the right trail now. Tacet had been forced to ride hard to make up the time lost going to the Journeyman's Inn, but he believed that to have been his only mistake so far.

Before leaving Argyllan on his assignment, he had questioned the city guards who had been manning the gates since his lord's attack. The east gate had yielded no results, which was unsurprising, since this gate and the road leading from it ran straight past the Meridian camp. Nobody had left that way the morning after the incident.

Tacet had gone to the north gate next, hoping this would bear fruit, for if the two girls had indeed taken a boat from the harbour, it would be that much harder to track them. At first Tacet had thought he was out of luck as the only person who had passed had been a big northern trader with a dog. But he had been thorough in his enquiries, pressing the captain of the guards to relate all that had been said. The captain had been hesitant to say too much, but the man had eventually relented. Velox Riders could be intimidating with only their eyes visible.

The northerner had not wanted the guards to look into his wagon, saying he was carrying Lorth Weed. Tacet knew the medicinal properties of Lorth Weed and the more relaxing nature of it when smoked. But he also knew that it was extremely difficult to find and the chances of a trader having enough to sell were remote.

So Tacet had reasoned there was something else the man had hidden among his wares. Two fugitives seemed quite possible.

Tacet had turned his back on the captain, who had been midway through an apology, and walked away. Tacet had then met with another Velox Rider, telling him to have all gates carefully watched, and all carts inspected thoroughly. From there, he had saddled his horse and left Argyllan, charging through the north gate and across the bridge that led into the Veste region, the Journeyman's Inn his destination.

When away from prying eyes, Tacet had changed his clothes, removed his facial coverings and taken on the guise of a minstrel, the same one he had used in Fallowden to spread rumour of impending war and a realm in peril. Tacet was a very talented musician. In fact, this was his trade when he was first approached by Rencarro all those years ago. The Meridian lord had complimented him on his skills and asked him if he had ever considered branching out into other trades.

Tacet had arrived at the Journeyman's Inn within the day. With a fancy bit of fiddling, he had impressed the innkeeper and gained his trust, then begun to ask questions about a big northerner who had offered him work in Westhealfe. Tacet had explained that he had missed their morning rendezvous due to too much ale the previous night and was thus now chasing after the trader in the hope the offer of work still stood. The fabricated story had come easily to Tacet thanks to years of practice. The innkeeper's wife had visibly blushed when he had told her his northern acquaintance had highly recommended the pies in this establishment, which had been a useful nugget of information unwittingly passed on by the captain at the Argyllan gate.

"It must be Wulfner, Yarcus" she had said to her husband, "He does have a liking for my pies. Sometimes has two all by himself!"

"Wulfner, yes, that was the fellow's name" Tacet had said, slapping his thigh. "He spoke of good coin to be made in Westhealfe so I am eager to catch up with him. Was he here at today's lunch hour?"

The innkeeper had said they hadn't seen this Wulfner for

quite a while, a month or more maybe. Tacet had realised in that moment that the northerner had been cunning, throwing him a shiny silver as he headed off in a different direction.

Tacet had kept up the act with little effort, feigning disappointment, and continued his enquiries.

"Wulfner is a native of Westhealfe, I take it. Well known in the city, perhaps?"

"No, not Westhealfe," the wife had said. "He hails from Ceapung, on the coast."

And that was all that Tacet had needed.

Tacet had thanked them, told them he would carry on up to Westhealfe in search of work anyway, then excused himself by saying he had to see to his horse—but promised he would be back for one of those *wonderful* pies before he departed. He had left the inn and immediately struck out west, cursing the time lost but tipping his hat mentally to this Wulfner for his guile.

Now Tacet was closing in on the northerner and the two girls. He had rested his horse and himself during the night, reckoning his quarry would not move on from this coastal town, and knowing a wrong step in the night could effectively hobble his mount. As the sky began to lose its dark bluish hue and a glimmer of sun appeared in the east, he rose and set off again, galloping up the road towards Ceapung.

Tacet felt he owed Lord Rencarro a great deal. That day Rencarro had offered him another path in life, it had perhaps saved the young Tacet from an early grave. Tacet used to spend practically every copper he earned on drink and women, and sometimes took coin from the husbands of women whose hearts he had won with his music. One such husband had offered a reward to some of the more unsavoury characters in Meridia to track down a minstrel who had taken advantage of his wife. Tacet had wanted to inform the cuckolded man that the woman, at twice his age, had taken advantage of *him* but it was likely that would have fallen on deaf ears.

Tacet had been playing his fiddle in a quiet corner of Rencarro's gardens, trying to calm his fearful mind. Rencarro had been out for a stroll and had heard the music. Fearing punishment for trespassing Tacet had blurted out the nature of his predicament to the Meridian lord. Rencarro had smiled and made the offer. That day Tacet had turned onto a new road.

This was why he wanted to catch this assassin. Not only had her accomplice murdered Rencarro's son, Lord Marcus, but now some new wretch had injured his lord. Tacet was determined to bring them to justice. He wondered if the northerner was in league with them or some mercenary. He was an obstacle but Tacet would do what was necessary to carry out his mission successfully.

The Velox Rider came upon the tell-tale signs of a settlement ahead. Smoke spires drifting skywards, carried to the west by a cool sea wind, and the general clamour of a town reduced to a low buzzing noise at this distance. The morning breeze carried the faint smells of peat fires, roasting meat, fish being hung out to dry and the unmistakable scent of the sea.

He cantered up the dirt road leading into Ceapung, his horse tired but gaining a sprightliness as it perhaps sensed rest and water ahead. Tacet stroked its mane and felt an anticipation within himself, knowing his prey was close. He knew this might not be as straightforward as he had hoped. Ceapung was this Wulfner's home so Tacet was on enemy territory so to speak, and far from any allies. Taking the two girls away would have to be done with great stealth. Perhaps a reconnaissance by day and then swift action when darkness fell. Tacet wasn't overly concerned though. He had succeeded in more precarious missions before so was confident he would be back in Argyllan with his lord before too long.

Tacet slowed his mount and plodded into the town, falling in behind a cart carrying large slabs of peat. The Velox Rider nodded at townsfolk in the streets, his minstrel persona taking over. He saw a drinking house ahead and decided this was as good a place as any to start. He guided his horse to the inn, dismounted and tied the animal next to another mare and entered the building.

Tacet was soon back on his steed. He had used the same ploy as he had at the Journeyman's Inn. This Wulfner was well known in these parts, as Tacet had suspected, and learning where he probably was had been effortless: an inn called Cuthbert's Cave was just by the harbour. Tacet kicked his ride into motion.

He had to be careful now as it was possible word might reach Wulfner's ears that a minstrel was looking for him, and Tacet knew this could be all that was needed to make his prey bolt and hide in the wilderness somewhere.

Tacet mulled over his options as he carried on up the cobbled street. He needed an opportunity to get the three of them away from Ceapung. If he only had to deal with Wulfner, he believed he could get the girls back to Argyllan. If not both, then just the red-head.

But how do I lure them away from this place?

Tacet said a silent prayer to the Widow, asking her to spin a thread that would aid him.

Ch 10

Wulfner

9th Day of Maia, Fourteen Days After Sedmund's Death

Four Days After Meridia Fell

Trob, you be a good lad now. Don't go giving Balther here any grief!" said Wulfner, as he mussed his hound's fur.

"He'll be fine so stop your fussing, cousin" laughed Balther. "And Azal will be well looked after too. It's you and these two young ladies I'm worried about. Taking a boat south down the coast might be quicker and help you to steer clear of the Meridians, but the Western Sea is not the most docile of beasts."

Balther's tone was serious and Wulfner did wonder if his plan was the wisest route home for Emiren and Lunyai. Balther was right that the open water posed a greater challenge than the open road but Wulfner just couldn't see how they could get past all those soldiers in and around Argyllan if they journeyed on foot.

"We'll keep near the coastline and hope the north wind keeps up" Wulfner assured his friend.

The north wind did help many a vessel speed its way down to Argyllan so Wulfner reckoned they would make good time. He was more concerned with ensuring they avoid the Bay of Vestevel and navigating down to this cove of which Lunyai had spoken. He conceded to himself he was putting a fair bit of faith in the Tarakan girl's grasp of geography, which had not been tested at sea.

Balther clapped his cousin on the back and then turned to the two fugitives.

"You're in good hands with Wulfner here. I'm sure both of you will make it back to your homes and Wulfner will be back up here for midsummer. Make sure you two come back one day also. The realm will probably right itself soon enough" he finished cheerily.

Wulfner could see Lunyai and Emiren were lifted by Balther's words, but he knew his friend didn't believe this optimistic outlook. Balther was older than Wulfner and both could see that Ragnekai was sinking into something of a quagmire.

"We will return" said Lunyai and hugged Balther. The Tarakan girl was tiny in comparison to the hulking northerner. Emiren also embraced Balther and leaned up to kiss him on the cheek. Balther blushed.

"You make an old walrus like me feel young again! May the Winds guide you home!" he cried.

Wulfner grinned, nodded to Balther and turned away, not wanting to make the parting too difficult on Trob. Or himself. The three of them walked off, Trob's mournful whine painful to hear. They headed down to the jetty where their boat was waiting. It was a small cog, measuring no more than twelve feet in length. It had belonged to a friend of Balther's, a fisherman who was now too old to sail himself. The boat had just been sitting in the harbour so Wulfner had bought it off him for a very reasonable price. Emiren had apologised profusely for Wulfner needing to spend his hard-earned money on them but he had laughed it all off, saying they could help him one day with his trading. Wulfner knew this was unlikely to ever happen but Emiren seemed to be satisfied with it.

It was mid-morning when they began to load their few possessions into the boat, Wulfner passing things one by one to Lunyai who had climbed down into the vessel already. Wulfner had bought food and water for the journey, Balther had provided them with furs to ward off the unforgiving chill out at sea, and a large square of tanned leather had been acquired to keep these few belongings dry in case of rain. Wulfner desperately hoped though that the recent good weather would continue and stay with them all the way down the coast. He had also picked up his war-hammer, which had been concealed in a secret compartment of his cart. He moved to pass it to Lunyai but she gasped at the size of it.

"Emiren, please help me with this giant's weapon!" cried Lunyai. "I fear I'll drop it and send our boat to the sea bed. By Yaai's brightness, how do you wield such a heavy thing, Wulfner?"

"All in the swing!" said Wulfner laughing.

"I hope we will have no need of it" said Lunyai solemnly.

"As do I, lass" responded Wulfner warily.

The big northerner glanced back to where they had said good-bye to Balther and Trob. His eyes weren't as good as they had been in years past, but it looked like Balther was talking to someone dressed in garish colours. A wandering jester perhaps, thought Wulfner. He shrugged and turned back to the business of launching the boat.

"Hop in then!" he said cheerfully to Emiren.

The Fallowden girl joined her Tarakan friend in the boat and Wulfner unwound the mooring rope. He then hurried to get in himself, sliding somewhat clumsily off the jetty and landing in the boat not so gracefully. The small vessel swayed and rocked. The scared expressions on Lunyai and Emiren's faces quickly fell away and turned to laughs.

"Not a very auspicious start to our little voyage" said Wulfner, settling himself at the oars.

He looked back to cast a final farewell to Balther and saw the jester running down towards the jetty.

Are you coming to show us your juggling?!

Emiren noticed him staring and looked over her own shoulder.

"Who is that? A friend of yours?" she asked.

Wulfner frowned.

"I don't think so. Seems quite interested in us though."

Lunyai also turned back to see this man.

"He wears very colourful clothes."

"A colourful character perhaps" muttered Wulfner.

"Wait!"

The jester was calling out to them.

"Wait, I beg you!"

The man ran up, panting but wearing a cheerful smile upon his face. He was a handsome man, long black hair tied loosely behind the head and pale green eyes.

"Thank the Spirits! You are a kind man to wait upon a stranger."

Wulfner threw him the mooring rope, which he deftly caught. But then simply held in his hand.

"Better tie us up if you wish to speak, else we'll be shouting out over the waves, friend" said Wulfner.

The man looked at the rope as if it were a complicated piece of engineering. Then he laughed and clumsily put the rope over the cleat. When he had done this, he stood back, hands on hips and looked very satisfied.

Odd fellow thought Wulfner.

"Well, we're not going to drift now so how about introducing yourself?"

The man was still looking at the mooring rope and cleat, almost marvelling at it. He visibly jumped and broke from his reverie.

"Forgive my manners" he said in an almost theatrical voice. "I am Rowan the Rhymer! The most famed minstrel in the entire realm."

He looked down at them in the boat and winked.

"Well, one can dream, wouldn't you agree?"

Lunyai and Emiren smiled at this lively character with his warm colours and wit. Wulfner still wanted to know why he had stopped them.

"Are you here to sing a song to send us safely out upon the waves?" Wulfner enquired.

The man chuckled.

"Would that I could be so noble and generous. But I fear I am in need of *your* noble spirit and northern generosity. You see, I am somewhat adrift. I was with a troupe, moving from town to village, from village to city, entertaining the good folk with our

297

theatre and music. Alas…"

Rowan the Rhymer looked embarrassed. Wulfner waited.

"I spent too long with a fair maiden and my former friends abandoned me at an inn to the east of here. I am rather far from home. That kindly giant of a gentleman back there told me you were heading south…"

Wulfner could see where this was going.

"And you were hoping to join us?"

Rowan slapped his thigh and laughed.

"Indeed that is the truth! I am extra weight, but I can be another pair of hands at the oars if the winds do not favour us. And I can sing, which may make the journey pass by more quickly."

Wulfner didn't trust this minstrel but that was mainly down to his many years on the roads creating a certain cynicism within him. He wished Trob were here to sniff this fellow and offer up his canine judgment. Wulfner looked at the two young ladies in his charge and could see they too were unsure of him.

Rowan smiled and raised his eyebrows.

"I have some silver if that will help me secure passage on this sturdy vessel…"

Wulfner sighed.

"It's not about the money, friend. We won't be stopping in Argyllan but going much farther south."

Rowan looked disappointed but would not be deterred.

"South is good. If we encounter another vessel near Argyllan, perhaps I can jump ship so to speak. If not, then I will go wherever you take me and roll the dice of fortune once again." He paused. "Where *are* you going?"

"I'm hoping to get these two girls back to their homes. First stop will be the Tarakan Plains" replied Wulfner.

Rowan's eyes widened.

"A long way indeed." The minstrel snapped his fingers. "The way ahead is clear. You need my help as much as I need yours."

To Wulfner's surprise, Rowan then burst into song. It was a ballad about strangers becoming friends, one Wulfner had heard before. But he had never heard such a fine voice in all his life. As fresh as a spring wind yet steeped with the soulful beauty of autumn leaves. Rowan the Rhymer certainly could sing. Wulfner glanced at Emiren and Lunyai and could see they were entranced by this minstrel. The Tarakan girl clapped.

"Let Rowan join us, Wulfner" she pleaded.

Emiren nodded.

Wulfner held up his hands and laughed. Rowan stopped singing.

"Alright, Sir Rhymer, it seems you have sung your way onto our little boat here. Are you ready to leave now?"

Rowan showed them his fiddle case and a small sack of belongings.

"I travel lightly." He smiled at them and Wulfner started to relax. Perhaps the Winds were blowing kindly for a change. He motioned for Rowan to untie the mooring rope. Rowan did this and stood there with the rope in hand as their boat begin to rock gently away from the jetty.

"You might want to jump in" said Wulfner with a grin.

Rowan's expression changed to one of panic. He threw the rope to Wulfner and then took a step back. He hesitated and Wulfner was worried he would end up getting wet before their journey had properly begun.

"Rowan, hurry!" cried Emiren.

He took two strides and launched himself into the air, landing practically in Wulfner's lap, gripping the northerner's arms as he struggled to right himself. The boat rocked and swayed but no water came in. Wulfner gently pushed Rowan back, wondering if this man would be a help or hindrance on their voyage.

"My apologies" said Rowan sheepishly. "I assure you that you can count on me to help guide this vessel and ferry these two fair maidens to sanctuary."

Emiren and Lunyai were giggling uncontrollably. Wulfner forced a smile. He turned his attention to getting their ship ready for the open sea.

"Right, let's get the sail up now and take advantage of this nice northern wind coming down."

Wulfner was no mariner but neither was he a novice at sea. He raised the sail without knocking any of the passengers off the boat and counted that as a success. Whilst doing so, he kept half an eye on Rowan.

Sanctuary.

Wulfner considered it to be a strange choice of word. He hadn't mentioned anything about the girls being in danger; only that they were on their way home. And when Rowan had fallen into his lap, Wulfner couldn't escape the feeling the minstrel had been taking in the measure of him, assessing his strength.

Am I getting too suspicious in my old age?

A gust caught the sail and it billowed out. Emiren let out a laugh as the boat lurched slightly, the cold wind taking a hold of the small vessel. Wulfner figured they'd need those furs sooner rather than later. He mentally noted Rowan clearly had no cold-weather clothing of his own.

Lunyai and Emiren moved aside as he went to the tiller.

"Mind your heads with this" he cautioned, touching the boom, "It can knock you out into the depths if you aren't careful."

As one, both girls slouched down into the boat, their eyes fearfully watching the sail and its parts as if it were a wild beast. Wulfner shot a glance at Rowan and could see his eyes were not on the boom but looking back to the jetty, now fifty yards away.

Wulfner took a deep breath. The sea air filled his lungs and stirred memories of his childhood. He watched as Emiren hung her arms over the side and scooped up some water. To his surprise, she put it to her lips. And instantly pulled a face. Wulfner was about to ask her if she had ever been anywhere near the sea when she spoke.

"I knew it was salty but had never tasted it. My father promised me we would taste the sea together one day."

Wulfner smiled.

"Well, he might be a bit upset you didn't wait for him" he

joked.

"My curiosity got the better of me." She grinned. "Da will understand."

The girl from Fallowden went quiet and looked out to the wider sea. Wulfner imagined a hundred thoughts going through her head, ranging from seeing her parents again to returning to a village that had lost a son. He noticed Rowan was still looking back to the jetty, now almost a hundred yards away. It was as if the minstrel was gauging the distance.

"Where do you hail from Rowan?" he asked in as light a tone as possible.

"Hm? Why, I hail from the fair town of Lowenden. But have travelled far and wide in Ragnekai, bringing my voice to kind folk. And one or two most generous ladies." He winked at Wulfner and then adopted a look of shame as he turned to Emiren and Lunyai. "Forgive me, sweet ones. A man gets lonely on the road!" The girls laughed.

Wulfner continued to tend to the sail.

"Emiren, what was the name of the fellow with the sticks Balther knew?"

Emiren looked up. "Banseth. I cannot believe Balth—"

"Banseth still manning the gates at Lowenden, Rowan?" Wulfner asked, cutting Emiren off. He turned his head to look at the minstrel.

"I fear I do not know if the good man still guards Lowenden. It has been over a year since last I was in my fair town" Rowan replied, inhaling deeply. "This sea air is bracing indeed."

Wulfner could see Emiren frowning at him. The northerner continued to probe.

"The wind is picking up. Just like the strange winds blowing through the realm right now. Can't believe Lord Rencarro's son was murdered by a fellow Meridian."

Rowan's face lost its mask for an instant. He assumed the façade again almost immediately but it was enough to confirm Wulfner's suspicions.

"Look at those clouds!" he cried.

All three turned to look out to sea. Wulfner held the boom and swung his leg, aiming a kick at Rowan's chest. The minstrel's reflexes astonished Wulfner.

Quick as lightning Rowan lurched back, grabbed Wulfner's boot as it came driving forward, and then pushed it skywards. Wulfner lost balance and fell over backwards, crashing into the bow area of the boat.

The northerner pulled himself up and onto one knee. Before him, Rowan crouched with a knife in one hand, the other grabbing Lunyai's hair. The Tarakan girl yelped.

"Easy now, big man. Don't want to hurt this one."

Rowan's voice had completely changed.

Wulfner carefully raised himself, one hand up, palm facing Rowan. Or whatever his name really was. Wulfner assessed the situation. He was in the bow, Rowan mid-ship with a knife to Lunyai's throat and Emiren crouching back in the stern. The boom began to come to port so Wulfner slowly raised a hand to steady it, keeping Rowan visible.

"Meridian?"

"Of course. And I will be taking the red-head back to Lord Rencarro so that she may answer for her crimes." Rowan the Rhymer was gone and in his place was a Meridian agent, who Wulfner reckoned was no stranger to killing. Emiren was crumbling behind the Meridian, the terror returning and the nightmare begun once again.

"You have it wrong, *Rowan*. There is more going on here than you have been told."

"Silence!" he cried, pushing the blade into the skin of Lunyai's neck. She gasped as a small dribble of blood slid down from the knife's point.

Wulfner furiously fought the urge to launch himself at the man. He knew Lunyai would pay with her life if he did.

"I need you to get out" said Rowan calmly to Wulfner.

"I don't think so" replied Wulfner firmly.

"I only need the red-head."

Lunyai cried out in pain as Rowan ran the blade gently down

her neck, a deadly quill writing in red ink.

"Alright!" cried Wulfner. "Stop, damn you. I will get out."

He slowly raised himself to a standing position. He was powerless to help. He would have to comply with Rowan's demand or Lunyai would die. But if he did so, the two girls would suffer unknown fates. He had to act.

There was a splash from the stern.

All three turned. Emiren had hauled herself out the craft and into the water.

Rowan cursed and his grip loosened. Lunyai rammed her head back into his face, her skull connecting with his nose. He cried out in pain. Lunyai scrambled away and tumbled out of the boat herself.

Wulfner stooped to grab his hammer, planning to brain this wretch and then save the girls. But his adversary was quick. Rowan now stood facing him, his face twisted in rage, the blood from his nose smeared across his mouth. The knife was still in his right hand. Wulfner saw a thin of pole of sorts slide from Rowan's sleeve into his left hand. The man crouched into a stance and glared at the northerner.

Wulfner could hear Lunyai calling to Emiren. He prayed they could both swim.

"You've lost!" called Wulfner over the rising wind.

"Not yet" he cried back and launched himself at Wulfner, slashing with his blade.

Wulfner parried the knife with the pommel of his hammer but could not stop Rowan's other weapon snapping into his left temple. He reeled, feeling as if a slinger had found his target. Yet the knowledge that Emiren and Lunyai would die if he lost this fight burned inside him and he took the pain through gritted teeth.

Wulfner managed a short jab with his hammer, the head connecting with Rowan's mid-riff. The northerner had not been able to put much power into the strike but the weight of the hammer compensated for it. The Meridian agent grunted and fell back towards the stern. He was back on his feet in a breath.

But Wulfner now had some space to swing and took his chance. He hefted the hammer and took aim. Rowan's reflexes saved him again, the iron passing inches from his face as he jumped backwards. Wulfner couldn't stop the momentum and the hammer crashed into the mast. There was an explosion of splinters. The wind seemed to delight in this misfortune and blew all the more strongly. The shattered mast and a billowing sail combined to rupture both timber and canvas. The sail tore through the middle and half of it flew out over the waves. The mast's upper half toppled sideways and slid off the side of the boat, dragging an oar with it.

The destruction caused both men to pause. Wulfner held his hammer across his chest and tried to steady himself in the rocking vessel. Rowan's eyes furtively looked around, darting from Wulfner to the sea on the port side, then to Wulfner again and then to the starboard waves, and back to the northerner once more.

There was a mutual understanding that both of them were in danger of losing not just the two girls but also their own lives. Wulfner saw a chance to maybe reason with this man.

"You've been given orders but they were given without knowing the truth. A Meridian officer murdered Marcus. It wasn't that red-head. She's no murderer. Can't you see? She just jumped into the sea to save the Tarakan, damn it!" Wulfner's voice was desperate; desperate to be heard over the gusting wind and desperate to be believed.

Rowan was hesitating. Maybe Wulfner's words had lit the fire of doubt within him. Wulfner couldn't see Emiren or Lunyai but prayed they were swimming back to shore. It was maybe a hundred yards.

Rowan suddenly took a step and leapt into the sea. Wulfner cursed. If Rowan caught up with them, they were his and he might even kill Lunyai to make his task easier. There was only one thing Wulfner could do. He set his hammer down and jumped over the side after the Meridian.

The water's ice-cold touch hit him and he gasped. He

searched around and saw Rowan swimming back to land. He couldn't see Emiren or Lunyai but was determined not to let Rowan catch them wherever they were. He started pulling powerful strokes. The sea was getting more boisterous though and his water-logged clothes began to pull at him with their weight.

Too old. I could swim a mile in freezing cold water twenty years ago.

Then he heard shouts from behind him. He turned in the water and couldn't believe his eyes. Emiren was back in the boat and calling to him as she helped Lunyai climb back in.

Thank you! Somebody answered my prayer.

Emiren was beckoning for him to swim over and get back in. Treading water, Wulfner turned and saw that Rowan had heard the shouting. He was now swimming back this way.

Bastard never gives up.

Wulfner turned back to Emiren and Lunyai and shouted with all his voice.

"Go! Get away! Go! I will find you. Go!"

Wulfner didn't wait for any response. He turned back and saw Rowan trying to swim round him.

No, my friend. I'll drag you down to the bottom with me before I let you anywhere near them again.

Wulfner screamed an oath and swam to cut Rowan off. The Meridian saw what he was doing and picked up his pace. Wulfner knew this was it. He had to reach that rat and nothing else mattered. He began to pray to Gods he had abandoned years ago.

I stopped believing because of what happened to Rowena and Sunniva. Give me this last drop of strength now and I swear I will come to the Everglade and worship You all for eternity.

Wulfner was closing the gap. He heard Rowan shouting obscenities.

"You will die old man! Your day is done."

Wulfner ignored him. But his clothes were like chainmail upon his body, dragging him down. His limbs ached and his lungs were on fire. He started to doubt he would overcome the waves and reach Rowan. He tried to take a deep breath but only took in a mouthful of sea water. Spluttering, he tried to clear his wind pipes.

No. Please don't let me fail now. One last thing.

Wulfner heard shouting and what sounded like barking, but his senses were blurring. He felt himself going down and the fight suddenly left his body. It was too much. The sea was a powerful beast and not something to be conquered alone. Wulfner's head dropped below the waves and the world became dark. A strange calm descended upon him. Knowing he could do no more meant he didn't have to fight any longer. Wulfner let himself slip into the murky blue depths.

Forgive me, Emiren, Lunyai, forgive me.

Epilogue

The Grey Sister saw that Brother Eswic could barely contain his excitement. The grin splitting his face told the small lady that he yearned hungrily for the Sceptre of Gastgiefu that supposedly lay beyond. She assumed possession of it would bring him some greater standing in the eyes of his faithful. Her grey hood hid her tiny smile from his greedy sight.

"Hurry!" he spluttered as she led him down the dark passageway. "To think it was here all along under the Holy Sepulchre, right under my very nose. Sedmund hid this well, even from Worsteth and his many spies. Hurry now, little sister."

The Grey Sister stiffened as she felt Eswic's hand on her posterior. "You will be rewarded, my dear."

She swallowed her revulsion and quickened her pace.

"Ho ho!" he said in a harsh voice, "Remember your place, grey one."

They came to a blank wall and Brother Eswic began to vent his anger. But he stopped mid-tirade as she reached into an alcove to the left and turned the cog inside six times to the left, then six times to the right. She pushed against the wall and was impressed with how smoothly it swung inwards. Her hands could feel that the wall was not made of stone as it appeared but a painted wood. A door basically.

"Ever-Father, what is this?" whispered Eswic when the *wall* was fully open and a way ahead was clear despite the gloom. The Grey Sister removed a torch from a sconce and moved inside, not waiting to see if he would follow. She knew he would. Men were so easily led when their desires were aroused. This sceptre was to Eswic what a beautiful siren was to a weary sailor; irresistible and full of promise.

She slowed as they reached an iron door, half as tall again as

Eswic and a man's height across. She lit two torches that hung to either side of this portal. There were three locks and a long, solid bolt that was slid across. She moved forward, withdrew the keys she had taken from the three secret compartments in Sedmund's chamber the night he died and put the first key in the correct lock.

"What is this, woman?" Eswic demanded. "How is it you have keys to anywhere within the Holy Sepulchre? Are you a thief?"

She ignored him, although it amused her to hear his indignation. Part of her desired to stretch this episode out and torment the fool some more, but time was against her.

The Grey Sister had been pleased with how quickly the poison had worked on Sedmund. Her order, her *true* order, had given her the vial of Moon's Milk one night when the White One was dark in the sky. It had been as undetectable as they had promised. Sedmund had succumbed quickly but not so much so that it was immediately suspicious. The Grey Sister had enjoyed the irony of Ulla then being suspected of committing the crime after the High King had died.

"Where did you get those keys?" blurted Eswic, unable to contain himself. "Give them to me!"

The holy man did not wait for any answer to his question but snatched the keys. He fumbled them in the locks, his fat fingers trembling. He finally got the right key in the last lock and the click was louder than the first two. Eswic then grabbed the handle on the long bolt and pulled. It moved but was heavy, and Eswic was not possessed of great physical strength. Not wanting to help him in the slightest, the Grey Sister watched him huff and sweat as he gradually slid it out of its holds.

Eswic jumped back as the bolt fell to the floor, making a terrific crash in the silence of this underground tunnel. He looked back down the tunnel in what the Grey Sister took to be fear. Again, she felt herself considering the irony of Eswic being more afraid of what lay *behind* them.

A creek turned Eswic's head in an instant and his eyes were

fixed upon the door. The holy man gaped uncomprehendingly as the door gradually swung open, the creek becoming more like a wraith's moan. A musty odour seeped forth. The holy man gagged and covered his nose with his sleeve.

"What foulness is this?" hissed Eswic.

"Deliverance" answered the Grey Sister.

Eswic stood looking at her with confusion in his eyes. "What do you mean?"

She said no more but instead walked through the open doorway, her torch illuminating an empty room, save for a table at its centre. Upon the table was a chest. She threw her torch to the stone floor, ignoring Eswic who had now entered the room.

"How dare you presume to look upon the Sceptre before me! I am... What is this? It can't be in that chest. The Sceptre is supposed to be as tall as a man." He was standing just behind her now. "Is it broken?"

The Grey Sister held her arms aloft.

"Eirik Duthka, eirik gealak, Seolta Ard-Rigut!"

The Grey Sister's voice rose in volume.

"Have you gone mad, woman? What..." Eswic stopped speaking but his mouth remained open as she pulled back her grey hood and revealed to him the swirling patterns inked onto her shaven head.

"Ever-Father! Who are you?"

The Grey Sister had had enough of this fool. Before he could retreat, she had withdrawn the long knife concealed in her robe, grabbed his wrist with her free hand and twisted his arm. He gasped as she slipped the long, needle-like knife into his arm-pit and pushed the blade deep within.

A savage gasp erupted from his mouth as his eyes held a look of utter disbelief. She stepped away, pulling back the weapon. As it slid out from the holy man's body, an ever-widening patch of darkness spread out upon his pure white robe. The Grey Sister, or Sister of the Moon, felt no pity as the hypocritical holy fool stumbled back, hit a wall, and then crumpled into a heap, breath ragged and slowing.

She turned back to the chest and lifted the lid. There was no lock. Inside were not the broken pieces of a sceptre. The Sister of the Moon had no idea where that relic was, nor did she care. Her eyes widened as she looked upon a leather-bound book, ancient symbols written on the cover. Symbols she could read but knew few others in the realm of Marrh could in this age. Next to the book, resting in a leather cradle was a glass jar. Inside the jar was a dark powder. She produced a canvas sack from beneath her robes and carefully put them both in. She then concealed the bag back underneath her garb and left the chamber, not sparing even a glance at Eswic. She had known exactly where to insert the blade and knew how long a person lived after such a wound. He was dead.

The Sister of the Moon retraced her steps back through the false wall and shut it carefully behind her. She wanted the corpse to be discovered but not yet.

She exited the Holy Sepulchre into the streets of Bregustol. She gazed up at the night sky, seeing The White One in all its glory.

"*Athair*" she whispered and then walked on through the sleeping city.

She felt the shapes of the book and jar against her body as she contemplated the future. Ragnekai would fall as Marrh rose once more. Within these pages was written the means by which her people could take back what was theirs. For many long years they had remained hidden and unseen. Now they would come forth. The sworn words of her order: *Be unseen but be ready to serve when called upon.*

The story continues in…

Ragnekai Under The Moon

Book Two of The Old Wounds Trilogy

An Urami World Novel

Due to be released winter 2018
(updates available on www.buckmasterbooks.com)

Note on language

Please forgive me if I have mangled any real languages! I took words of various existing languages to hopefully give the reader a feel for each culture and to also ground the history of this fantasy world in reality. I hope some readers will pick up on the playfulness regarding some of the characters' names.

Note of thanks

Thank you for taking a chance on this debut novel. I sincerely hope you enjoyed it and are intrigued to know where the story goes from here. As I write this note, it is almost December 2017. Christmas is always a busy season for us as I try to recreate the Christmases I loved as a child for my family and friends here. So, I think I am unlikely to start writing the second book in the Old Wounds trilogy, tentatively entitled "Ragnekai Under The Moon", until January 2018. I have the chapters planned out and a stack of notes already prepared so hope progress will be swifter than it was with "Ragnekai Winds". Thank you for reading my first novel and I very much hope you will want to read the next!

www.buckmasterbooks.com

Acknowledgements

There are so many people who have helped me to publish my first book. I am so grateful to you all and hope you all feel the finished work is a success!

Thank you to Stephanie Diaz. Not only did she do a wonderful job of proof-reading Ragnekai Winds but was also a great teacher, generously sharing her knowledge of grammar, writing and structure. (www.stephaniediazbooks.com)

Thank you to Karin Wittig for a beautiful front cover. If Ragnekai Winds does catch a few eyes, it will be down to her artistic skill and vision. (karinwittig.com)

Thank you to Robert Altbauer for his excellent map. If readers can mentally navigate the realm of Ragnekai, it will be thanks to the clarity of his work. (www.fantasy-map.net)

Thank you to my friend Katie Lorford for her fantastic advice on marketing. (www.beautyandtheboutique.com)

A huge thank you to my friend of thirty years, Sarah Crabb. I can't imagine how much time you spent reading through each chapter and then typing up such helpful feedback.

And thank you for each and every boost you gave me with your enthusiasm and kind words.

Thank you to my brother Nick for all his support, techy and otherwise.

A word of thanks to my uncle Andrew, who keeps my mind working.

A massive thank you to Dad for making this dream possible. I told Mum it would be a log cabin in Norway. Turned out to be Japan.

And last but not least, thank you to my wife and partner in life, Eriko. You believed in me when I didn't. And you worked while I wrote. Arigatou ne.

And to Haruki & Tomoki: Daddy wrote a book!

Made in the USA
Columbia, SC
04 June 2018